Nicole Jordan is the *New York Times* bestselling author of seventeen historical romances including, the Regency-set *To Pleasure a Lady*, *To Bed a Beauty*, *To Seduce a Bride*, *To Romance a Charming Rogue*, *To Tame a Dangerous Lord* and *To Desire a Wicked Duke*, as well as the medieval romance, *The Warrior*.

She recently moved with her real-life hero to the Rocky Mountains of Utah. You can e-mail her via her website at www.NicoleJordanAuthor.com.

D1470815

THE
LOVER

THE
LOVER

NICOLE JORDAN

1 3 5 7 9 10 8 6 4 2

First published in the United States in 1997 by
Ballantine Books, an imprint of
The Random House Publishing Group
A Division of Random House, Inc., New York

Published in the UK in 2012 by *Rouge*, an imprint of Ebury Publishing
A Random House Group Company

The Random House Group Limited Reg. No. 954009

Addresses for companies within the Random House Group can
be found at www.randomhouse.co.uk

A CIP catalogue record for this book is available from the British Library

The Random House Group Limited supports The Forest Stewardship
Council (FSC®), the leading international forest certification organisation.
Our books carrying the FSC label are printed on FSC® certified paper.
FSC is the only forest certification scheme endorsed by the
leading environmental organisations, including Greenpeace.
Our paper procurement policy can be found at:
www.randomhouse.co.uk/environment

Printed and bound in Great Britain by Clays Ltd, St Ives PLC

ISBN 9780091950309

To buy books by your favourite authors and register for offers visit
www.randomhouse.co.uk
www.rougeromance.co.uk

The pleasure in love is in loving. We are happier in the passion we feel than in that we arouse.
FRANCOIS, DUC DE LA ROCHEFOUCAULD

Prologue

Edinburgh, Scotland
September 1739

She never intended to eavesdrop. Never meant to intrude on a celebrated libertine enacting a practiced seduction. Yet neither did she anticipate being captivated by a dark, caressing voice as sleekly velvet as the night.

Her restless mood ebbing, Sabrina Duncan stood beyond a hedge of topiary yews, an unwilling interloper upon Niall McLaren's amorous pursuits. She'd escaped her cousin's betrothal ball for the refuge of the moonlit terrace gardens only moments before the Highlander unexpectedly appeared for an apparent rendezvous with his latest conquest, the noble wife of an English colonel.

Hidden from view, her presence further disguised by the muted strains of a minuet issuing from the ballroom above, Sabrina scarcely dared breathe. She should have made herself known at once, but she hadn't wished to cause embarrassment. And then she'd found herself held captive by that enchanting voice as it beguiled its way into her senses.

"Well met, my bonny Belle. . . ."

Sweet heaven, how could he infuse so much warmth into a simple murmur? It was like being stroked. No woman alive could remain unmoved by those low, honeyed tones: lilting, warm, devastatingly sensual. Full of the heather and mist of the Highlands. Doubtless it was a prime reason for the man's remarkable success with the fairer sex.

1

"They say he can draw a woman's soul from her body," her cousin Frances had confided with great relish. "And that no female's virtue is safe."

Sabrina could well understand the Highlander's appeal. She recalled being stunned earlier when Niall McLaren strode into the crowded ballroom, eliciting excited feminine whispers and dreamy sighs. Powerful, virile, sinfully handsome, he cut a bold figure in full Scottish garb.

He wore the McLaren plaid draped over his coat of black satin, while his belted kilt bared strong, muscular legs above tartan silk stockings. The rapier at his side seemed a natural extension of his person—and a stark contrast to the touch of lace at his throat and wrists. With his ebony hair and sun-bronzed features, he stood out among the crowd of painted, bewigged aristocrats like a Highland mountain against tame lowland hills.

Sabrina knew him by reputation only. The youngest son of a fierce Highland chieftain, Niall McLaren was a thief of female hearts, infamous for his sexual exploits. "The Darling of Edinburgh," the ladies were wont to call him. Yet he'd cut a wide swath through the female populations of France and England as well.

Now, having returned from his travels abroad, he was engaged in another sensual chase—that of seducing a married lady. Most of the company at the ball tonight had seemed more titillated than shocked.

"Everyone is wagering on the outcome of his pursuit, whether or not Lady Chivington will surrender," Sabrina had heard her cousin remark.

She knew how *she* would wager. Hearing that enchanting voice, she couldn't suppress a dismaying ache of longing, an inexplicable yearning for impossible dreams. What would it be like to be pursued by Europe's most infamous rogue? To have him gaze at her with such single-minded devotion, to be the recipient of the formidable charm she'd seen him lavish on his chosen partners earlier in the ballroom. . . .

Clutching her fan, Sabrina chided herself. What was

wrong with her? She rarely lamented her circumstances or felt such melancholy as she did tonight. The bitterness she'd known when her chief suitor had fallen in love with her beautiful cousin had mellowed to regret by now. She was content with her life; she was needed, appreciated, loved by her family. She found pleasure in being a dutiful stepdaughter. She *enjoyed* quietly spending her evenings with her stepfather and his account books for company.

If there were times, like now, when she felt moments of restlessness, if sometimes she was bedeviled by romantic yearnings and the depressing suspicion that life was passing her by, well then, she was usually practical enough to quash them.

Except for tonight. Her pragmatism couldn't quell the sense of envy that pierced her now, or repress the yearning that stirred deep within the secret recesses of her heart. Or stop her fascination with the man whose reputation was a byword for wickedness. Was this how rakes enticed females into carnal love?

"Come and sit beside me," he exhorted in a murmur, his voice a warm handstroke on her heart. Sabrina almost wished he were speaking to her.

She could picture the moonlit scene on the other side of the yew hedge: the handsome Highlander lounging on a stone bench, while Lady Chivington kept her distance—to tease and torment him.

She recalled the Englishwoman's stylish elegance, her voluptuous figure resplendent in a wide, panniered ball gown of blue silk brocade, her towering, powdered hairdo adorned with pearls and ribbons. Her voice, however, currently held a note of waspishness that didn't match her beauty.

"I am not certain I *wish* to sit beside you, sir," Lady Chivington observed, pouting. "I think perhaps you deserve a punishment for your neglect of me this afternoon. You did not come to me as you promised."

"Surely you will forgive me, my sweet. As I mentioned, I was unavoidably detained."

A faint scoffing sound issued from the lady's lips. "By a tavern wench, no doubt. Or another gentlewoman."

"Never, *ma cherie*," he replied, his voice holding a uniquely seductive rasp in his apparent attempt to win her from her sulks. "How could I contemplate another lass when the hope remains you might favor me with your attention?"

"You never even replied to my note."

"Yet I am here now, am I not? And if we are at all alike, Belle, you've found that anticipation only heightens the pleasure."

In the resulting silence, Sabrina could imagine the lady unfurling her ivory fan and plying it vigorously.

"Do you make it a habit, sir, of ignoring a lady's request to call?"

"Only when the lady in question has a jealous husband . . . a colonel in the English army, at that. I do cherish my skin."

"Pooh! I doubt you fear my husband in the least. Besides, Richard cares little if I engage in dalliance."

"He is a fool, then, to neglect such a beautiful wife."

The compliment seemed to mollify her only slightly. "Perhaps you should seek out another lady who will dance to your tune."

"Do you wish me to withdraw, then, Arabella?" The question held skepticism and a lazy amusement.

"I suppose not," she replied petulantly. "I was facing an evening of unutterable boredom."

"I shall endeavor to relieve it, if you will permit me."

"If you can, then I expect I can contrive to forgive you."

"I am gratified." His reply was edged with a smile. "Finding a new object of worship would require too much effort."

"*Do* you worship me, sir?" It was a flirtatious, coy remark.

"Indeed, I do, Belle. Behold me enraptured."

"Hah! You are little better than a knave, sir. A disreputable Scot preying on womenfolk."

"Surely not *preying*."

"We English consider the Highlanders barbarians," Lady Chivington remarked.

"Which I suspect is part of our appeal," he returned smoothly. "Confess, you occasionally tire of fops in velvet and lace, with soft hands and powdered wigs."

She laughed in an apparent capitulation. "*Occasionally*. But you, sir, could well be a savage. In England you would be considered half naked if you arrived at a ball with your lower limbs exposed."

"Ah, but I wore my kilt for a reason."

"And what is that?"

"The better to pleasure you, my dear."

"Wicked man," she murmured in a husky, intimate tone. "Is it true a Scotsman wears nought under his kilt but bare skin?"

"You are welcome to discover the answer to that for yourself."

"A rogue to the very bone," she breathed. " 'Tis scandalous, what you are thinking."

"Is it, Belle? Can you claim you are not entertaining similar thoughts?" His languid voice dropped to a husky resonance. "Does your heart not beat faster with anticipation at the thought of having a wild heathen inside you?"

Behind the hedge, Sabrina caught her breath at his implication, a flush warming her cheeks. She nearly missed Lady Chivington's playful reply.

". . . claim you are the greatest lover in Europe. By all accounts you've made countesses swoon in Paris and brought baronesses to their knees in Venice."

His laughter held a casual charm. "Modesty prevents me from replying to such an observation."

"But 'tis true, poets have composed ballads about the amorous adventures of the dashing Highlander, Niall McLaren."

"An exaggeration, I assure you."

"Is it an exaggeration that you are endowed like a stallion?"

"Why do you not come here and find out?"

Lady Chivington hesitated. "Here? In the garden?"

"I can think of no more interesting way to enliven a ball, can you?"

"What if someone should find us together?"

"Danger is the greatest aphrodisiac, I've always thought. Come here, sweeting," he murmured in a low, throaty command. "I will take care not to dishevel your coiffure if you will contrive to contain your moans."

Hearing the lady's skirts sweeping the gravel path, Sabrina felt a measure of panic. It was bad enough to eavesdrop on a gentleman whispering heated love words to his newest inamorata, but his seduction apparently intended to go much further. She took a careful step backward.

"That is far better," he murmured in satisfaction as Sabrina retreated deeper into the shadows. "Here, allow me to assist you, pet."

The pause that followed his offer was filled with the whisper of silk.

"How lovely your nipples are this way . . . hot, peaked, eager for my kisses."

Sabrina felt a shameful tingling in her own breasts as she envisioned his gently roving hands moving languidly over her own skin.

"Oh . . ." the lady breathed, the word ending in a lush, purring resonance. "Niall . . ."

"Patience, sweet . . ."

Sabrina took another cautious step backward. She dared not remain any longer. Yet it would be impossible to pass the lovers without being detected. She would have to move deeper into the garden, make a wide circle—

The snap echoed like a pistol shot. Sabrina winced as the delicate ivory sticks of her fan splintered in her hand. An instant later she bit back a gasp as the menacing form of a kilted Highlander loomed before her, moonlight flashing off his drawn rapier.

His unpowdered raven hair was drawn back from a broad forehead and secured at the nape with a ribbon, emphasizing high, hard cheekbones and a lean, square jaw. Beneath slashing ebony brows his blue eyes were narrowed at her threateningly.

Alarm kept Sabrina rooted where she stood, but even had she tried to flee, Niall McLaren would have prevented her. His strong fingers clasped her wrist in a velvet manacle, thwarting her movement.

"What do you here, mistress?" he demanded sharply, his voice holding little hint of the magic that had recently held her spellbound.

In spite of her own tall stature, he towered over her. Moonlight played over his features in stark accents, making his anger all too apparent.

"Who is there?" Lady Chivington demanded shrilly as she rounded the yew hedge, still plucking at the disheveled neckline of her gown. She stopped short when she spied Sabrina. "You! How dare you intrude this way?"

"You know this lass?"

The lady's aristocratic English nose lifted. "She is the heiress to the Cameron fortune. Can you not detect the smell of the shop about her?"

Sabrina stiffened. This was not the first time she'd been accused of being tainted by trade, since her stepfather was a wealthy merchant, yet it stung more coming from this haughty Englishwoman with her aristocratic assumptions of superiority. Class distinctions mattered far less in Scotland, Sabrina thought defiantly. And the Scots saw nothing shameful in making money.

"I would hardly term myself the intruder, my lady," Sabrina retorted coolly. "This is my aunt's house, after all. And my cousin's betrothal ball."

"You deny you were spying on me, you nosy little snoop?"

"Of course I deny it!"

"Arabella," Niall McLaren interjected, "perhaps we misjudge the situation."

"I pray so, or I am ruined! Her aunt is the greatest gossip alive! If this girl should tattle, I will never live down the scandal."

"I assure you, Lady Chivington, I am not in the habit of bearing tales."

"Hah! I doubt any relative of your aunt knows how to keep her tongue between her teeth. Indeed, I wouldn't put it past that woman to orchestrate a deliberate attempt to discredit me."

"Arabella," Niall said calmly. "You are overwrought."

She turned on him with a fierce stare. "Are you in league with her, too, sir? Did you lure me out here to dishonor me?"

The Highlander's striking features grew cool in the moonlight. "My Lady Chivington, perhaps you need a moment alone to compose yourself before returning to the ball."

Her fierce look faded. "Niall, I . . . I never meant to accuse you of complicity. I spoke rashly, in the heat of the moment."

"I know, my dear. Which is all the more reason to allow our tempers to cool."

"Will you call on me on the morrow?"

His hesitation spoke volumes. "I think perhaps it wiser to delay any further meeting between us for a time."

With a smoldering glance at them both, Lady Chivington spun on her slippered heel and swept away in a flurry of hooped skirts. In the resulting silence, Sabrina found herself alone in the darkened garden with the notorious Niall McLaren.

When she hazarded a glance up at him, she nearly flinched at his stony gaze.

"Kindly unhand me, sir," she said unsteadily.

To her relief, he released her wrist, but his tone held more than a hint of annoyance. "With pleasure."

"You need not fear," she began nervously, rubbing her

bruised wrist, "that I will divulge a word of this, to my aunt or anyone else. This incident would reflect almost as poorly on me as you. I shan't tell anyone what you were up to."

His anger remained unplacated. "Do you make it a habit of eavesdropping on your aunt's guests?"

Sabrina felt her cheeks flush. She *was* guilty of eavesdropping, yet it had been wholly unintentional. Defensively she lifted her chin. "I am sorry to have spoiled your seduction."

"So am I," Niall responded without the least sign of embarrassment or shame. "Your timing was wretched."

"Perhaps, but I believe I arrived here first."

"You might have made your presence known."

"You might have chosen a more appropriate place for a liaison!"

"In my experience, a moonlit garden *is* generally considered appropriate for a liaison." She could hear amusement warring with irritation in his lilting voice, though the emotion was not reflected in his piercing gaze.

"Yes, well . . ." Her chin rose another inch. "If you wish I shall send out another lady to take Lady Chivington's place. There are certain to be scores of females eager to supplant her in your good graces."

A muscle in his jaw flexed as he appeared to bite back a smile. "Hundreds, possibly, but none so willing as she."

Sabrina stiffened at his teasing reply. "I pray you will accept my apology, sir," she murmured. "Now, if you will excuse me . . ."

She started to brush past him, but Niall McLaren held up a hand. "One moment, Mistress . . . Cameron, is it?"

She hesitated reluctantly. "Duncan. Sabrina Duncan. Cameron is my stepfather's name."

"Well, Mistress Duncan," he said as he sheathed his rapier. "I suggest we allow the lady to return to the ball first. It will better serve to shield her reputation."

"I'm surprised you are concerned with protecting any lady's reputation," Sabrina remarked archly.

He eyed her sharply, his penetrating gaze fixing on her in

the darkness. In the moonlight his blue eyes were the color of midnight.

Sabrina found herself catching a deep breath. He was handsome as the devil, tempting as sin, yet his starkly masculine beauty was not the sole reason a woman's heart beat erratically with curiosity and fascination when this man was near. He had a quality about him that was intently compelling, dangerous.

"I collect you know me?" he asked finally.

"By reputation, merely. Who has not heard of the infamous Niall McLaren?"

His sensual mouth curled at one corner. "I believe I detect a note of censure, Mistress Duncan."

"It is hardly my place to judge you, sir."

"But you disapprove of me even so."

She did disapprove of him, an attitude she strongly suspected amused him. Prudish, Sabrina was sure he would define it. "In most circles it is considered scandalous to pursue an affair with a married lady."

"Apparently we move in different circles," he responded dryly. "I don't suppose you would credit it if I told you the lady was pursuing *me*?"

She could well believe that might be the case. The brazen Highlander would be idolized for his startling physical beauty alone. Yet there was an air about him that was utterly irresistible to women. To her as well, Sabrina acknowledged reluctantly.

"I don't remember you putting up any resistance," she said, mimicking his dry tone.

"But then 'twould hardly have been the act of a gentleman to disappoint the lady."

She *was* amusing him, Sabrina realized. Even in the darkness she could see his arresting eyes were lit with a mocking sparkle.

"I assure you, mistress, this would not be the first time a lass has lured me into a secluded garden."

She bit back a smile at the thought of this bold rogue hiding from over amorous females. "It must be a great trial, being hounded by languishing ladies eager to be seduced."

His grin was unwilling—and devastating. "You might be surprised by the tribulations I must endure to uphold my reputation."

Sabrina shook her head. She should know better than to enter into a duel of words with an expert in verbal swordplay. Indeed, she should leave at once. Simply being alone with this man could compromise her.

Yet before she could respond, the Highlander spoke. "If you were not spying, what brought you out here to the garden when a ball is in progress?"

Sabrina suddenly looked down at her clasped hands. She had no intention of divulging the true reason she'd fled the ballroom: to escape the painful sight of her former suitor dancing with his betrothed—her own cousin. "Is it a crime to partake of fresh air, sir?"

"Not that I'm aware. I do not recall seeing you earlier this evening, mistress."

There was a simple reason for that, Sabrina reflected. Niall McLaren simply hadn't noticed her. Such a man would scarcely give her a second glance, a wren among a flock of peacocks. She was still in half mourning for her mother, so she had worn her plain gray bombazine gown, much to her aunt's dismay. Now she wished she had swathed herself in armor of silk and lace, for it might have helped disguise her lack of beauty.

"Doubtless," Sabrina forced herself to reply, "it was because I sat with the spinsters and chaperons while you held court with your legion of admirers."

"You are unmarried, are you?"

Sabrina found herself fighting a swift surge of wanton rebellion. At one-and-twenty, she was past the common age for marriage and considered almost on the shelf. "I am, sir."

"I own surprise that an heiress would lack for suitors."

She averted her gaze from his measuring scrutiny. He could not know how deeply his casual remark wounded her. She'd *had* a suitor. She and Oliver had met during her mother's illness and developed an understanding after her death: they would marry only after an appropriate period of mourning. But then Oliver had caught one glimpse of her cousin Frances and tumbled head over heels. When he pleaded with Sabrina to release him from his pledge, she had agreed. What else could she do? And indeed, her pride had suffered most. If her heart had also shriveled a little, if his defection had killed something elusive inside her, well she didn't delude herself that she was the only female who had ever been jilted.

"My mother was ill for some months before passing away," Sabrina answered defensively, "so I had little time for suitors. I have not yet wholly put off mourning."

To her dismay, his gaze raked over her, coolly appraising. Sabrina tensed. Tall and angular, she lacked the soft pretti-ness that characterized the other women in her family. Her mother had been a celebrated beauty, as was her Aunt Helen and her cousin Frances.

Moreover, she was not in her best looks this evening, Sa-brina knew. She wore face paint, which washed any color from her complexion and rendered her features pasty and indistinct. And the hairstyle she'd adopted at her aunt's insistence covered her most attractive attribute, her rich brown hair. It was dressed and powdered and artfully arranged in intricate puffs and rolls, yet she felt awkward and pretentious in it.

"Duncan . . ." he mused, not taking his eyes from her. "I call numerous Duncans friend. Would I know your kin?"

"No doubt you are acquainted with my grandfather, laird of Clan Duncan. I understand you hail from the same region of the Highlands."

"Your grandfather is Angus Duncan?" One black eye-brow rose. "Aye, I know him well. We are near neighbors, in fact. Angus once saved my father's life in a feud with the Buchanans, a debt I am not likely to forget. But I do not re-call him ever speaking of a granddaughter."

"Oh, Grandfather Duncan would doubtless prefer to disregard my existence. I was not the right gender, you see. A granddaughter was useless to him, since I could not carry on the clan name. And he never really approved of my mother, either."

"Ah, yes . . . I recall your father married against Angus's wishes during a visit to Edinburgh."

"For which he was never wholly forgiven. Papa was expected to marry a Highlander to uphold our clan honor. A lowland Scotswoman was not good enough."

"Ranald died in his prime, did he not?"

"Yes, a tragic mishap—a fall from his horse."

A grim frown claimed Niall's features. " 'Twas no mere mishap. It transpired during a raid by the bloody Buchanans, if memory serves."

"So I understand. I have little recollection of him, or the Highlands, though I've heard tales. I left when I was quite young. After Papa's death, my mother returned with me to her family here in Edinburgh, and remarried some years later. My stepfather is a merchant who trades successfully in wool and fine cloth."

"You must return to the Highlands someday, mistress," he commented in a tone of polite boredom.

"I doubt that will be possible," she replied, a bit vexed by his apparent dismissal of her. "My stepfather has need of me. He holds little faith in clerks, and with his failing eyesight, he relies on me to check his accounts each evening."

"Brains in a woman. How fascinating."

His languid tone held a hint of teasing and made her stiffen.

"I have found it just as unusual to discover brains in a man," Sabrina retorted.

His half smile was indulgent. "Reviewing accounts is a rather odd occupation for a lass, you must admit."

"Perhaps," she said a little too sharply. "But I have a head for figures—and I'll not apologize for it."

"Apparently you also have a temper that is easily provoked," Niall said, sounding amused.

That wasn't quite the case, Sabrina reflected. Normally she was remarkably even-tempered. Yet tonight she was feeling defiant, reckless, rash. Definitely not herself. This man seemed to bring out the worst in her.

"My temper is usually considered quite serene."

"I confess surprise. For a wallflower you lack a decided meekness."

"For a hedonist, you possess an amazing degree of frankness. I expected more subtlety."

His slow smile was wickedly disarming. "Is that what you think me? A hedonist?"

"Hedonist, pleasure-seeker, libertine . . . Rumor paints you in rather unflattering terms."

He laughed with careless amusement. "Rumor claims that I regularly engage in perversions and bacchanalian orgies as well, but not every tale you hear is true."

"I'm not aware of any specific perversions. Merely that you seduce every woman you meet."

"Now *that* is a bald untruth. I only seduce the ones who interest me, I assure you." He paused, gazing down at her, a speculative gleam in his deep blue eyes. "I wager I could seduce you, little mouse."

Sabrina caught her breath. She could not possibly interest a man such as he. He was merely amusing himself at her expense. "I sincerely doubt it. I have a great regard for my virtue."

"How tiresome."

She wanted to laugh, but she forced it back.

Lazily he adjusted the froth of lace at his cuff. "'Tis just as well, I warrant. Despite my vaunted reputation, I have yet to be accused of deflowering prudish maidens."

Strangely Sabrina felt disappointed. "I own relief to know I am safe."

"Did I say 'safe'?"

He took a step closer. "It seems a pity to waste such a braw evening." His tone was casual, but all her senses went on full alert. "I think I could truthfully promise you would enjoy my attentions, mistress." His sudden smile, part wolfish, was wholly enticing.

Sabrina took a step backward, feeling very much the vulnerable lamb. He was far taller than she, broad of shoulder and powerfully muscled, and when he turned the full force of his charm on her, she felt overwhelmed. He was remarkably good at this game of seduction, but that was all it was to him, a game. He knew very well his power over women. Over *her*. Sabrina felt a mutinous flash of stubbornness course through her. "You'll not have any effect on me, I promise you."

"No?"

How did he manage to invest so much sensual promise, such beguiling tenderness, in a single word? In a glance? There was something warm and exciting in his eyes. Dangerous.

Suddenly the night seemed alive with sound and sensation. Sabrina was overwhelmingly conscious of how alone they were, of how hazardous this situation had become. What idiocy was she indulging in, remaining out here with such a man? She lacked the experience needed to bandy words with a celebrated rake. His earlier banter with Lady Chivington had obviously been a sophisticated game between carnal equals, but she was no match for him in that regard.

Evidently she'd taken leave of her senses—or been bewitched by the moonlight and this legendary rogue.

"I should go . . ." she said rather too breathlessly.

"No . . . stay." He reached up to touch her cheek, a featherlight caress.

"This . . . isn't wise," she murmured, startled by the delicate sensation.

"And do you always do what is wise, sweeting?"

"Y-Yes . . . always . . ."

"Surely you cannot fear me."

Sabrina bit her lip. What she feared was the temptation he offered. The timbre of his voice had changed; it was low, muted, as liquid silver as moonlight. She couldn't stop the warmth that suffused her body at that enchanting voice.

She watched, spellbound, as his sensual lashes lowered lazily to shadow even more sensual eyes. "It would be the work of a moment to kindle your passion, sweet mouse."

Sabrina felt herself tremble to realize she'd become the target of his seduction. He was close enough for her to share his fluid warmth, to detect his scent, a faint natural fragrance that was disturbingly male. It made her feel disturbingly feminine and fragile.

He moved even closer, his voice a seductive murmur, hot and deep and full of temptation as he said, "Would you like me to make your skin burn, sweeting? Would you like to flame at my touch?"

Her lips parted in a wordless protest, but no sound came out. She couldn't have spoken had her life been at stake. Nor could she move when, with gentle boldness, his palm cradled her face.

Sabrina closed her eyes, trying to resist the hypnotic stroke of his thumb on her cheekbone. His fingertips fluttered across her skin . . . downward over her lips, his touch lingering and provocative.

"Look at me, cherie."

Helplessly she obeyed to find him scrutinizing her.

She had the wild idea he meant to kiss her. His head was bending, his beautiful mouth descending toward hers. With a mixture of desire and excited apprehension, she waited tensely.

When his breath fanned warm against her lips, Sabrina gave a shiver of pleasure. Her own breath seemed suspended, even as it mingled with his.

Then his mouth brushed hers tantalizingly, and the primitive sensations that rippled through her were like nothing she'd ever felt before. The sensual assault of his lips made her feel wanton, helpless, weak.

Her cousin was right, Sabrina thought, dazed. Niall McLaren knew how to draw a woman's soul from her body.

When he lifted his head, a fierce and unexpected pang of disappointment shook her. She raised trembling fingers to her lips.

Her bewilderment must have shown in her eyes, for his smile held amusement. "Have you never been kissed before, sweet mouse?"

Not like that, she wanted to cry.

His palm cupping her cheek, he lowered his head once more, while his voice dropped to a rough, seductive whisper. "Shall I show you what you have been missing?"

Reason urged her to resist, to make him stop, yet she didn't want to resist. She wanted to know what it was to feel desired, to be the object of this legendary man's passionate attention.

Her silence was all the invitation he needed. His lips covered hers, seducing her with heart-stopping tenderness.

His kiss was a slow, intimate knowing of her mouth. His lips stroked hers, playing, conducting an exercise in sensual pleasure, his passion leashed for the sake of her sensibilities.

Sabrina felt lost in a thick, dreamy pleasure as he filled her with his tongue in a sensual invasion. Need broke over her, warm, rich, loosing a tide of longing. The slow glide of his rough-soft tongue was sleek, wet, intoxicating beyond anything she'd ever known, arousing a hot flush of desire and excitement within her.

Helplessly, her hands rose to his shoulders, clinging to him for support, while his mouth and tongue tantalized and coaxed in a slow erotic dance that probed and explored and expertly enticed.

Her limbs grew warm and honeyed, her body liquid and weak. She was only dimly aware when McLaren shifted his stance slightly. His pliant fingers moved to caress her shoulders with practiced sensuality, drawing her even closer against him, gently accommodating her body to his, making her feel an ache that began imperceptibly in her breasts and gradually spread downward to gather between her thighs.

A whimper escaped her lips as she felt the bold press of his body, his maleness. She couldn't fight the sweet tempest he was arousing in her, didn't want to fight . . .

He was caressing her again, stroking the column of her throat with his long fingers, making her intensely aware of her bare skin above the square neckline of her bodice. Then his hand slid lower, to brush her breast. A sweet blinding hunger flooded her.

Suddenly alarmed by the fierce sensation streaking through her, Sabrina gave a soft cry and abruptly pulled free of his embrace.

Her breath coming in soft pants, she stared at him in shock.

The Highlander returned her stare, his gaze hooded.

When he finally spoke, his laughter was muted, softly triumphant. "I think we can safely say you enjoyed that, mouse."

Sabrina felt all color drain from her face. He was entirely correct; she hadn't wanted his embrace to end. For a few brief moments, he had made her feel special, cherished, sought after. Yet his mockery was like a douse of cold water. Absurdly she felt spurned, when she should be grateful he had ended his seduction before it went too far.

She understood his intent now in kissing her, though. He had meant to prove his power over her, perhaps in punishment for interrupting his liaison with his latest paramour.

It was impossible to recover her dazed senses so abruptly, but Sabrina summoned every shred of dignity she possessed as she stepped back on shaken limbs.

She took a deep, steadying breath and forced a feeble laugh. "I suppose I should thank you for your instruction, sir. After all, one isn't honored every day with such noted attention from a renowned rake. But in truth"—she lifted her chin defiantly—"I found your kiss rather overrated."

A frown of irritation swept his handsome features. Yet before he could reply, a sudden commotion from beyond the yew hedge made him turn his head abruptly.

Sabrina gave a start. What if she should be discovered here with him, like this?

"Niall?" a man's voice called out in a harsh brogue. "Niall, are ye here, lad?"

"John?" the Highlander replied sharply.

From the direction of the terrace came the sound of booted feet running down the stone steps.

When Niall McLaren strode swiftly around the hedge, Sabrina followed, a vague sense of alarm raising the hair on the backs of her arms.

"What brings you here, John? What's amiss?"

"I've come to fetch ye, lad. Ye're needed at home. I fear . . . I have terrible tidings. 'Tis yer da."

A powerful hulk of a man came to a halt before Niall. He wore the McLaren plaid, Sabrina noted, and looked savagely out of place in the moonlit garden, dressed in Highland battle gear, complete with claymore and leather-covered targe, the round shield carried by fighting men.

"Lad, I fear yer father has met with treachery," John rasped, his voice rough with emotion and fatigue. "Caught in an ambush. 'Tis suspected the hand of the bloody Buchanans at work. Hugh is not expected to live through the night. He calls for you, lad. Yer the last of his sons now."

"The last?" The word was a hoarse whisper.

"Aye, there's worse. Jamie was killed."

"Merciful God, not Jamie . . ." McLaren staggered, his hand rising to his temple, and Sabrina caught a glimpse of his expression. Stunned disbelief and savage pain warred in his eyes.

Instinctively she reached out to support him, her hand grasping his arm. Reflexively he clutched her wrist with a force violent enough to crush it, yet his devastation hurt her more than his grip. He had been the youngest of three sons, she recalled, but now he was the last.

Sudden tears blurred Sabrina's gaze. She had lost her mother last year, but after such a long illness, she'd had time to prepare herself for the loss. She could only imagine the anguish of losing a father and a brother in one fell stroke. She wanted to reach out to Niall, to hold him to her breast and comfort him. Powerful feelings for a man who until a few moments ago had been a stranger. Yet she was dimly conscious of the throng of ball guests gathering on the terrace.

John paid them no mind, nor did he even seem to notice her.

"Yer to be the new laird, Niall," the brawny Highlander said gravely. "Ye must come home."

"Yes . . . home . . . at once . . ."

Bestirring herself from her own numbness, Sabrina interrupted quietly. "You will want your horse, sir. Shall I direct you to the stables the back way and thus avoid the crowd?"

He blinked as if dazed and focused his gaze on her face. "Aye . . . the stables . . ."

"I will make your excuses to my aunt," she murmured, her tone gentle, compassionate.

She took his hand to lead him deeper into the garden, yet she evidently had underestimated his resiliency. His jaw clenching, he shook off her clasp suddenly and drew himself up to his full, imposing height.

The long-fingered hand that had so recently caressed her with such erotic strokes closed on the hilt of the rapier, while his handsome features hardened with cold fury, leaving no sign of the sensual lover who had played such havoc with her senses only a short while ago.

This man was a stranger. A man of purpose, of danger. The son of a fierce chieftain, with the blood of countless generations of savage Highland warriors running in his veins.

Sabrina shivered involuntarily. Niall McLaren had no need of her direction or her support. Instead she felt a brief flash of pity for his enemies, who would soon know his wrath.

"Aye." His harsh voice was unrecognizable as he agreed softly. "Make my excuses, mistress. I've a matter of grave import to settle in the Highlands."

Chapter
One

The Scottish Highlands
April 1740

His teeth clenched as the frenzied, panting woman beneath him wound her legs tighter around his hips, drawing him deeper into her voluptuous, writhing body. Her naked breasts strained lush and wanton against his palms as with an expert rhythm, Niall McLaren satisfied his former mistress's ravenous need.

They hadn't managed to attain the bedchamber upstairs. Eve had not permitted it. Instead he had taken her standing in the drawing room, not pausing to remove his leather breeches or her silk dressing gown. Pressing her back to lie on the whist table, he had plunged deep between her welcoming thighs, not surprised to find her wet and pulsing for him.

She was flame-hot with desire, begging him in erratic whimpers for the intense pleasure only he could give her. And in his present mood, Niall was more than willing to comply. He had called at her elegant manor house directly after his meeting with Angus Duncan. And just now he wanted nothing more than to lose himself in the dark grip of passion.

He succeeded momentarily with their primitive, restless coupling. His blood surging thick and hot, Niall covered her fully with his body, thrusting into her sleek, heated passage with a driving motion of his hips. His lips smothered her wild moans as his fingers closed tauntingly around the hard-peaked nipples of her lush breasts.

Another tremor shook her and Eve cried out with ardent hunger. Yet only when he felt her first convulsions ripple around his shaft did he allow himself his own gratifying release. Urgently Niall surged into her, propelling her over the edge to an explosive, cresting pleasure.

His own climax followed swift and fierce, his powerfully muscled body contracting with stabbing pleasure as Eve quaked and sobbed beneath him.

Even when it was over, she clung to him with feverish strength, still impaled on his receding erection, gasping as the aftershocks of his violent release abated.

"Welcome back, my bonny rutting stallion," she exhaled at last, the breathless, throaty sound loud in the hushed quiet of the room. "I had almost forgotten what a ferocious lover you can be."

Perhaps, Niall thought unamused, because he rarely displayed such violence in his lovemaking. Just now he'd employed little of the finesse he was renowned for, although the sated woman sprawled beneath him seemed well pleased by his savagery.

The candles on the carved mahogany sideboard flickered, sending shadows dancing over her beautiful features. Eve lay gazing up at him contentedly, her pale skin glowing from exertion and arousal, her smile languorous.

Niall murmured a muted oath. He had gratified her lust and his own, yet it hadn't managed to cool his temper. His frustration hadn't diminished with the appeasement of his body, nor had he found the oblivion he'd sought in her arms. His dilemma still hadn't changed.

He must shortly wed a bride not of his own choosing.

Disentangling himself from Eve's silken limbs, Niall pulled down her skirts to cover her naked thighs and fastened his breeches. Then turning, he made for the crystal decanter on the mahogany side table and poured himself a tumbler full of malt whisky.

Declining his silent offer of a drink with a shake of her head, Eve lay back on the table, stretched her arms lazily above her, and gave a replete sigh.

"To what do I owe the honor of this call, my lord? I vow I haven't been ravished so well since . . . since your last visit. It has been months since you've shared my bed, Niall. Indeed, I've scarcely even laid eyes on you since you became laird."

"Clan duties have occupied far more of my time than I envisioned," Niall prevaricated.

"I have missed you sorely."

"And I you, sweeting," he murmured, his mind elsewhere.

"Niall, will you not tell me what is troubling you?"

"How do you ken something troubles me?"

Her smile was indulgent. "That black scowl you're wearing is proof enough, even had I not felt it in your embrace. And I don't remember ever seeing you quite so distracted. Tell me about it, and perhaps I can help."

"I rather doubt you can." His mouth curled cynically. "Tomorrow I ride to fetch my bride."

"*Bride?*" The word was a gasp. "You are to *marry*?"

"The idea is not mine, I assure you."

"Then what . . . ?"

"Angus Duncan has demanded that I wed his granddaughter to fulfill a debt my father owed him."

"What debt could possibly require such a high price as payment?"

"Angus once saved his life. My father promised him any boon he asked."

"Oh." Falling silent for a moment, Eve raised herself to a sitting position on the table, before saying regretfully, "Then you have no choice. I had thought . . . hoped . . . we . . ."

He knew what she had hoped. As a wealthy widow and one of his nearest neighbors, Eve Graham had contemplated a match between them for years. And she might have been an acceptable choice, had she cared ought for clan affairs. But new ball gowns and elegant soirees were her chief interests. And she had already run through the greater portion of her late husband's fortune. Eve was not the bride for him, Niall knew.

Nor was Mistress Sabrina Duncan.

Niall muttered another oath. Angus's demand this afternoon had left him feeling cornered, trapped. It was not a pleasant sentiment.

"Why has this matter come to a head now?" Eve asked. "Because Angus is dying?"

"Just so. He fears Clan Duncan will be leaderless at his death, at the mercy of any rival clan, most particularly the Buchanans. Angus wants a strong laird to insure his kinsmen's protection after he's gone and has chosen me for the task."

Niall took a long swallow of whisky, welcoming its sweet burn as he recalled Angus's weakened voice imploring him.

Ye're a warrior born and bred, lad, despite yer randy ways, and I need a good mon to lead my clan after I'm gone. The Duncans will follow you willingly into battle, 'tis all I care about. As for the rest, yer eight and twenty, lad. 'Tis time you settled down to raise a family. You'll find wedlock no' so burdensome as ye fear.

Niall grimaced. It was not wedlock he objected to. He was the McLaren now, chief of a mighty Highland tribe, and as such, he would eventually need heirs to succeed him. Yet he preferred to choose his bride himself.

He had never expected to become laird of his clan. In truth, he would give his own life to have his father and brother back, hale and hardy. It was Jamie who should have succeeded to the lairdship. Jamie who had been groomed to fight and breed strong sons to carry on the line. Or Thomas. Hugh McLaren's middle son had perished in a storm at sea two years before while crossing the Channel to France.

Niall had accepted the chieftain's reins with grave reluctance and a fierce determination to prove himself worthy of the momentous responsibility. Over the past seven months he'd managed to demonstrate an able leadership, avenging his kinsmen's murders in a swift raid on the Buchanans. He'd sent two of the culprits to perdition and the rest scurrying from the country.

The fighting did not distress him overmuch. Blood feuds were a way of life in the Highlands, where clan wars lasted for generations. And he'd been schooled for battle nearly from the cradle. As for the burdens of the lairdship, he'd discovered an unexpected talent for the role. In truth, he'd found immense satisfaction in working for the good of his clan.

It was being forced to wed that stuck in his throat. To the Duncan lass, no less.

And yet he was bound by duty and honor to satisfy his father's debt to Angus Duncan.

"Who is the lucky bride, if I may ask?"

A vein hammered at his temple. "Sabrina Duncan is her name. She stands to inherit a sizable fortune one day from her stepfather, a prosperous merchant."

"That *is* a prime advantage."

Niall could not disagree. With such poor ground for farming, the Highlands boasted precious little resources to support so many mouths. Indeed, much of his time went to seeing that his clansmen were adequately fed and housed. Any wealth a bride brought his clan would be welcome. It was the bride herself he could summon little desire for.

Niall stared grimly into his whisky, remembering quite clearly his one meeting with Mistress Duncan the night she'd interrupted his pleasure at her aunt's ball. Plain, prim, sharp-tongued. A thoroughly nondescript figure of a girl, one he would not normally look at twice. Except perhaps for the intelligence in her dark eyes, her features fell far short of beauty.

Certainly not the sort of lass to appeal to a man of his discriminating tastes and strong appetites.

God's blood, a prudish, disapproving virgin was the last

woman he wanted in his bed. Mistress Duncan was too tame, too proper and dispassionate for him. Too vexing.

He was passionately fond of women in general, long addicted to the charms of lushly endowed beauties. He preferred women like Eve Graham, who were startlingly attractive and who could match him in passion.

In truth, his requirements for a bride were not so exorbitant. He could forswear beauty in a wife if necessary. And perhaps even passion. He was willing to make most any sacrifice for the sake of his clan. Since becoming laird, he had searched for a bride who would make a worthy mistress of Clan McLaren. He needed a lass who would give him strong sons to carry on after him. One who would put the welfare of the clan above her own interests.

His own mother had been such a woman. Judith McLaren's husband and sons had fairly worshiped her. He could not see mousy Sabrina Duncan filling her shoes. Mistress Duncan knew nothing of the Highlands or the needs of his clan.

Nor could he picture her as his lover. They would not suit in any respect, not if the virginal inexperience he'd tasted in her kiss was any indication.

He had kissed her because . . . why? For the challenge, perhaps. He'd been irritated with her from the first. And she seemed unimpressed by his face and form, completely immune to masculine charm. Her obvious skittishness over his advances had brought out the primitive male urge to chase fleeing prey.

Most assuredly, he would never have seriously considered indulging his desire.

But before he could put it to the test, he'd received the terrible news about his father and brother. He still winced to recall the savage blow. And even now he could not think of Sabrina Duncan without recalling that terrible time of pain and grief.

"Well," Eve murmured, interrupting his grim thoughts. " 'Twill be unfortunate if you must enter into an arranged marriage, but not catastrophic. An unwanted bride cannot expect you to remain faithful to the marriage bed. You can still enjoy your former pursuits, can you not?"

Aye, Niall thought silently, resentment and frustration flaring anew. He would do his duty. He would endure a cold-blooded marriage for the sake of his clan. But he had no intention of changing his way of life to satisfy his bride's prudish notions of conduct. If Mistress Duncan could not accept him on those terms, then she was free to find another husband.

When Niall made no reply, Eve eased herself from the table and sauntered over to stand before him. "You will still be welcome in my bed any time, my lord," she breathed coyly, her hands reaching up to part the bodice of her dressing gown, baring the voluptuous curves of her breasts for his sensual appreciation. "Will you stay the night, Niall?"

His mouth twisted without humor. "I doubt I will make pleasant company. My disposition is not the sweetest at the moment."

"Then I shall contrive to soothe your dark mood." Her fingers trailed lazily down his chest to unfasten the buttons of his leather breeches, slipping inside the folds to find heated skin. "You consoled me most generously when my husband died. 'Tis only fitting I console you."

For a moment he stood contemplating her, wondering if he could summon the desire she expected; inexplicably his vaunted appetite had deserted him.

"Please . . . Niall . . . I want you again." Her eyes were heated with passion, imploring, as she traced the pulsing length of his swelling manhood.

With a mental sigh, Niall set his glass on the table and solicitously turned to her. Reining in his frustration, he softly murmured a lie. "And I want you as well, pet."

He forced a smile to his lips as he cupped her lush breasts in a practiced arousal. When he bent to take one distended nipple into his mouth, Eve moaned sharply and closed her fingers around his stiffening erection.

Niall's body responded automatically to the sensual intimacy, but his mind remained distant and apart from his pleasure, his caresses habitual, his thoughts still on his dilemma.

In all honor he could not refuse to acknowledge the obligation to Angus Duncan. He had no choice but to agree to the marriage.

But Mistress Duncan would discover that all her vast wealth could not buy her a tame lackey for a husband. He would not give up his pleasures for her sake.

And she would find little enjoyment in being his bride.

" 'Tis not so far to the tavern, mistress," Geordie Duncan claimed cheerfully. "Then ye can rest awee and drink a dram."

Sabrina gave the brawny Highlander a grateful smile. For one unaccustomed to riding, seven hours on horseback buffeted by a chill, blustery wind had sorely tested her endurance. And they'd only just now reached the Scottish Highlands. It would require two hours more through difficult terrain to gain Banesk, the seat of Clan Duncan, where her grandfather Angus lay gravely ill.

She and her two Duncan escorts had followed the wretched roads north and east from Edinburgh across lowland country, but as they emerged from a pine forest, the sight of the uplands in the distance made Sabrina sharply draw rein.

The spectacular vista stole her breath away. She had been but a child of four when she'd left the place of her birth, and had forgotten the rugged beauty—the rolling glens and misty lochs and wild moors, interspersed with magnificent craggy hills that changed hues with the seasons. Just now the green-gray slopes were splashed buttery yellow with spring gorse and Scotch broom; in summer they would be dusted violet with wild bell-heather, and in autumn, russet with dried bracken.

" 'Tis so beautiful," she murmured almost reverently.

"Aye," Geordie agreed. " 'Tis a braw land, for cert."

Sabrina shook her head, wondering how her mother could have failed to appreciate such splendor. Yet gentle Grace Murray had hailed from civilized Edinburgh before wedding the only son of Laird Duncan. She'd never felt easy during her half dozen years in the Highlands, with their harsh way of life and brutal blood feuds. And she'd been intimidated by Angus Duncan. Angus had made no objection when, after her husband's death, Grace had returned to Edinburgh with her young daughter.

Sabrina had no particular love for her grandfather, a man she scarcely even remembered, but neither did she bear him any ill will for ignoring her. She was pragmatic enough to understand his bitterness that she was not male. Only the most powerful clans ruled Scotland, and without sons to carry on as laird, Clan Duncan would not survive.

They forded a swift-flowing burn, and Sabrina had to call out to her dog to prevent him from stopping to trout-fish. Part mastiff, Rab nearly rivaled a Highland pony in size, and possessed ten times the appetite.

Rab seemed to be enjoying himself immeasurably as he bounded beside her mount. He had sniffed out a rabbit for breakfast, but she was hard pressed to keep him from pursuing the herds of shaggy cattle and flocks of grazing sheep they passed.

He, too, was unaccustomed to such glorious freedom. This rough countryside was a far cry from the narrow wynds and hidden closes of Edinburgh, where timber-framed houses stood packed so tightly they blocked out the sky. Here at the edge of the Highlands, whitewashed cottages roofed with thatch gave way to stone crofts covered with peat, where farmers eked out meager crops of barley and oats from the poor soil.

"Half a league to Callander," Liam pointed out solemnly. " 'Tis a village of considerable size, the last ye'll find in these parts."

The two Duncan kinsmen whom her grandfather had sent to escort her were her distant cousins. Liam, dark and silent, claimed to have been a close friend of her late father's. Geordie, red-haired and garrulous, was much closer to her own age and, Sabrina had discovered, a fountain of knowledge regarding her clan's history. Both men considered it vital that she learn even the most insignificant details, since she was Angus Duncan's sole direct descendant, his only grandchild by his only son.

Since leaving Edinburgh early that morning, Geordie had kept her entertained with his constant prater, regaling her with vivid tales of feuds and battles and risings, when clan swords ran with blood and vengeance meant more than daily bread.

"There's no' so long a memory as a Highlander's, nor greater loyalty," Geordie had boasted but an hour ago.

A savage feud raged even now, according to her kinsmen. Angus Duncan was a proud Scottish chieftain, but not powerful enough to protect his clan from the Buchanans, who had been their enemies for generations. Reportedly, the situation fretted him greatly; she'd listened to little else for the past seven hours.

She'd been surprised at Angus's acknowledgment of her after so little contact over the years. Once, several years ago, he'd written to ask her to return to the Highlands for a visit, but she couldn't possibly have left her ailing mother then. And the offer had never been renewed. Their last correspondence was when he'd sent condolences upon the death of her mother.

She remembered Angus Duncan as a gruff, blustery figure who was always shouting, yet she was saddened to be summoned to his death bed. She had no notion what he wished of her, except perhaps a desire to see his closest kin one last time. But as her grandfather's sole surviving heir, she felt obligated to pay her final respects.

In truth, she had been eager to come, even though it meant leaving her stepfather to fend for himself with the household and his bustling trade. The visit afforded her an opportunity to avoid a particularly persistent suitor who was more interested in her dowry than her person. And if she were entirely honest with herself, she would admit relief in escaping the proximity of her former suitor and the constant reminder of her loss. Her cousin Frances had made a radiant bride, her happiness with Oliver apparent. Sabrina could not help but experience a twinge of envy whenever they met.

But all that was behind her, Sabrina vowed, her spirits lifting as they neared the large village of Callander. She was here now, and she felt an inexplicable attachment for her father's homeland. The Highlands held a powerful enchantment for her . . . the promise of excitement and adventure and romance, so different from her own tame existence. She felt drawn by this magnificent land, as if it were in her very blood.

The tavern where they paused to rest was a two-story, rambling hostelry with a thatched roof and mullioned windows. Her muscles aching, Sabrina gingerly allowed Liam to aid her to dismount in the yard.

"I trow the McLaren is here," Geordie observed, nodding at a band of horses tethered to one side.

Sabrina felt her heart skip a beat, knowing he referred to Niall McLaren, now the Earl of Strathearn and laird of his clan. To her dismay, she'd thought of him much too often since that moonlit night so many months ago when he'd kissed her in her aunt's garden. Despite her dislike of him and his bold arrogance, he'd invaded her dreams far more intimately than was proper. When she'd agreed to come to her grandfather's side, she couldn't help but wonder if she would see the dashing Highlander during her visit. Now it seemed as if she might before she even arrived.

Willing herself to calm, she called to Rab and followed Liam stiffly inside, while Geordie saw to the horses.

She spied Niall McLaren at once. Across the smoke-hazed taproom, a half dozen men sat gathered at one long oaken table, quaffing mugs of foaming ale. She felt her pulse quicken in response—yet, fortunately, he seemed to take no notice of her arrival.

"We'll take a wee bite, mistress," Liam informed Sabrina.

When she had settled on a bench at an adjacent table, she pointed to the floor beside her. "Rab, lie."

The great hound flopped down obediently, his chin on his paws, his brown eyes gazing adoringly up at her.

Liam ordered their dinner from the harried innkeeper, while Sabrina found her gaze drawn to the McLaren. He sat in profile to her, but she was still afforded a view of the startling physical beauty that made women's hearts scamper and men's grow green with envy.

Niall McLaren was unforgettable under any circumstances, but she had good reason to recall him.

Remembering their one confrontation, Sabrina felt her cheeks flood with color, yet she couldn't drag her gaze away. He was dressed much less formally than their last encounter, his broad-shouldered frame garbed in a full-sleeved saffron shirt unlaced at the neck; his powerful legs clad in black jackboots and trews—close-fitting knit trousers made of tartan cloth.

At his waist he wore a belted sword, and over one shoulder he'd flung the McLaren plaid of vivid green crisscrossed with squares of sky blue and thin lines of red and yellow. His unpowdered raven hair, which was clubbed at the nape, gleamed with blue-black highlights as he turned his head toward her—

Sabrina gave a start as his bold gaze collided with hers.

Unnervingly, she realized he was watching her, his eyebrows meeting in a thick black line over incredibly blue eyes.

He seemed unsurprised to find her here—or perhaps he simply had no remembrance of her. She wore no hair pomade this time, or any of the elaborate puffs and rolls that had adorned her coiffure the evening of her cousin's betrothal ball. And doubtless kissing strange females in moonlit gardens was so common an occurrence for him that he thought nothing of it.

Absurdly the thought disappointed Sabrina. *She* would never forget his brazen arrogance the night he had breathed life and excitement into her dull existence, never forget the sensual feel of that hard body flush against hers, the taste of his lips. . . .

Forcing herself to release her bated breath, Sabrina chided herself roundly. She was no swooning maiden, to be swept off her feet by a handsome face and form, or to be unsettled by his odd scrutiny. The McLaren was regarding her intently from under dark lashes, his expression almost grim. She couldn't explain the glitter in his sapphire eyes, but it seemed somehow menacing . . . a menace unaccountably directed at her.

Just then, a rosy-lipped serving maid entered the taproom and commenced doling out ale to her male patrons at the McLarens' table.

"Cora, lass, I've missed ye," one Highlander exclaimed. "Have ye missed me?"

" 'Tisn't likely, Colm McLaren," she retorted with a laugh. When he patted her derriere, she hauled back and slugged his beefy arm with her fist with an admonition to stop. She finished pouring and set down the pitcher, yet rather than leave, she remained hovering over Niall McLaren.

"It isna fair, Cora," the first complained, "ye saving yer charms for the laird."

"Aye," another Highlander chimed in, "I dinna ken why ye'd let yer head be turned by a bonny face."

Cora gave a saucy sway of her hips. "For sure my head wouldna turn at the likes of ye, ye great lout."

Guffaws of laughter followed, making Sabrina grateful when the innkeeper delivered her dinner.

Trying to disregard the revelry at the other table, she applied herself to the thick barley soup and black bread, yet she was palpably aware of Niall McLaren's presence, of the smoldering vitality that emanated from him even across the room.

She was able to discern his murmur from among the din

as he spoke to the serving wench. His lilting brogue was more pronounced than Sabrina recalled, but it had the same effect on her; the rippling burr echoed through her like the memory of his caress.

It disturbed her that merely the sound of his voice could affect her so—and disturbed her even more that he shared an obvious intimacy with the tavern wench.

Cora was laughing down at him, openly flaunting her ample charms. She appeared to be challenging him to join her abovestairs.

At first Niall appeared disinclined to accept her invitation, but when her flirtations progressed to rubbing her full breasts against his arm, he acquiesced. Reaching out casually, he drew Cora onto his lap and, amid much ribald male laughter, kissed her full on the mouth.

Sabrina went rigid as the lass fairly melted in his arms.

With a lazy, heart-stopping grin then, Niall tucked a silver coin in her bodice and set the wench on her feet. "Go, sweeting, we'll talk later."

For a moment Cora stood straightening her disheveled apron, glancing down at him with a flustered, yearning look that Sabrina recognized as desire.

She winced at the familiar emotion.

She had no notion why that shared look should disturb her so. She knew very well Niall McLaren's sexual appetites were legendary. He was every inch the rakehell who stole female hearts for sport. It shouldn't surprise her that he would avail himself of what was offered so willingly.

Suddenly, though, his gaze returned with relentless precision to *her*. It seemed almost as if he were gauging her reaction to his dalliance.

To Sabrina's utter dismay, then, Niall rose and casually strode toward her. She felt her heart flutter wildly as she watched his long, powerful legs come ever closer. He gave the impression of effortless grace, of power and strength held lightly under control.

She was grateful when her dog Rab rose to his feet and stood at attention.

Niall paid the huge mastiff no mind. Pausing before her, one hand on the hilt of his sword, he swept her a deep bow. "Welcome to the Highlands, Mistress Duncan," he said in a lilting Scottish voice that somehow mocked her.

Against her will, Sabrina lifted her gaze to meet his stunning blue one. Managing to swallow the dryness in her throat, she replied, "I confess surprise that you even recognize me, my lord."

"Your grandfather mentioned that you would be arriving today. And I know your kinsmen." He nodded to Liam in greeting, then raised one dark eyebrow. "She does not know?"

The elder Highlander shook his head. "Angus wished to broach the matter himself."

"Know what?" Sabrina asked, puzzled.

Niall's penetrating blue eyes returned to her. "Your grandfather will apprise you soon enough."

Frowning uncertainly, she queried, "You have seen my grandfather? Is he very ill?"

"I fear so. He asked that I act as your escort for the last leg of your journey."

"Oh . . ." The thought of having to endure this man's company for the next two hours was distinctly unnerving. "That is not really necessary, is it? Liam and Geordie are accompanying me."

"The Highlands can prove dangerous to the unwary, mistress."

His tone seemed hard, almost as if he were issuing her a warning. Sabrina fell silent, not knowing quite how to react. Finally she said quietly, "I hope we meet under happier circumstances than the last?"

She could see the challenge in his eyes swiftly banked, to be replaced by a fleeting look of sadness. She was struck, not for the first time, by the suspicion that there was far more to Niall McLaren than met the eye. He apparently held more complex feelings than the usual libertine. She had seen his pain at his kinsmen's deaths, and knew he must have cared deeply for his family.

"I suppose you could call them happier," he replied with cryptic dryness. He glanced around the taproom. "Have you no tire-woman attending you?"

"I did not like to impose on any of the women in our household. They are unaccustomed to traveling such a distance or being away from home for any length of time."

"Still, you should have female companionship."

"I am not entirely without companionship. In addition to my kinsmen, I have Rab for protection. Rab," she said lightly, "guard."

Bristling, the giant dog bared his teeth up at the man—but only for an instant. When the McLaren offered his hand for the animal to sniff, Rab whined once, uncertainly, and then licked the laird's fingers hungrily.

Sabrina winced in dismay. Her canine guardian did not appear fierce enough to frighten a rabbit.

Niall must have had the same thought, for his beautiful mouth curled at one corner.

"He is usually more cautious with strangers," Sabrina said defensively.

"I trust so."

Sabrina froze when he propped one booted foot on the bench beside her. Reaching down, he gently fingered a tendril of her hair as it fell across her cheek.

"I wondered what the true color was."

The intimate gesture startled her, as did his intent scrutiny. She felt her breath cease. If he intended to intimidate her, he was succeeding. That careless, indiscreet charm was so potent it was almost a visible force—reaching out to her, enveloping her. For an instant the others faded away. It was as if she and Niall McLaren were the only two people in the room.

"You should never hide your hair beneath powder, mistress. It is more fetching without it."

She found herself glad that as a general rule Scotswomen didn't cover or powder their hair, and sorry that the hood of her traveling cloak had disheveled the careful arrangement of her rich brown tresses she had made that morning.

When Niall McLaren continued studying her, she felt a dissatisfaction with her looks such as she hadn't felt in years. But then Sabrina shook herself. She could hold her own with this rake. The blood of Scottish kings ran in her veins. She was a chieftain's granddaughter, even if she had lived away from the Highlands for much of her life.

With cool aplomb, she lifted her chin. "I shall take your opinion under advisement the next time I dress for a ball."

"And you should loosen that severe knot, as well," he murmured. "The style is not right for you."

"Are you such an expert on ladies' coiffures, then?"

"Say rather, I am a connoisseur." He grinned casually. "I've always considered a lass's hair much bonnier flowing free, spread over my pillow."

Sabrina felt her breath catch at his outrageous remark. Pretending a sophistication she didn't feel, though, she said pointedly, "Perhaps you should return to your companions, my lord. They doubtless are missing you."

The McLaren's dark blue eyes widened fractionally in mock dismay. "I believe I have just received my dismissal. How lowering."

Ignoring his dry commentary, Sabrina glanced at Liam. "Should we not be on our way?"

"Aye, if ye've rested enough."

"Are you certain then," Niall asked, "that you won't accept my escort?"

"I thank you, but no," Sabrina assured him. "I should not like to take you away from your pleasures." Glancing at the other table where Cora had been, she added archly, "You seem well occupied in ruining the local wenches."

His eyes gleamed in appreciation. "More disapproval, mistress?"

"How you choose to spend your leisure is no affair of mine."

"Indeed. But that has yet to prevent you from voicing your opinion of me."

"I believe I have confined my remarks to common knowledge. Your exploits are adequately documented."

"Aye, I'm a reprobate of the first order. You would do well to remember it."

"You have given me scant reason to forget it," she retorted tartly. "Both times we have met, you've been indulging your libertine propensities."

When his lips tilted in arrogant amusement, Sabrina wondered if he had any notion just how devastating that half smile was. But of course he did. He looked as though he could read every thought that passed through her head.

Yet it was difficult to dislike him. His mind was uncommonly sharp, and his boldness appealing, even if it often caught her off guard—as it did now when he reached out to take her fingers and bow over her hand. The facile charm was automatic, effortless, yet it disturbed her all the same.

"I shall take my leave, then."

She wanted desperately to withdraw her hand from the sensual invasion of his, but he wouldn't release her. As he raised her fingers to his lips, Sabrina silently cursed him. It was unfair, how this man's mere touch left her breathless and set her heart to pounding. Indeed, it was criminal that this dangerous rogue should be left free to unleash his compelling sexuality on helpless females.

He seemed aware of his potent affect on her, too, for his eyes were wickedness itself as he pressed a delicate kiss on the sensitive skin at her wrist.

The careless caress sent wanton images flooding through her mind, images of her surrendering to his seduction in a moonlit garden. The appalling realization struck her that she wanted to surrender again . . .

In almost a daze, she heard his low, musical voice saying, "As you please, mistress. But we will follow close on your heels," he added for Liam's benefit, "should you require aid. Never let it be said that a McLaren shirks his duty."

Sabrina was infinitely grateful when he at last released her trembling hand—and rather startled when his striking features suddenly turned cool.

"There's danger in the Highlands," he repeated. "You would do better to return home to Edinburgh where you belong."

Sabrina glanced up at him sharply. The menace she had sensed in him before was back, as was the hint of smoldering anger she'd glimpsed in his eyes when she'd first arrived at the tavern. She wasn't imagining that the air was filled with a new kind of tension as Niall McLaren stepped back a pace.

"We shall doubtless meet again," he murmured grimly, making Sabrina certain he was not looking forward to the occasion.

Chapter
Two

"*Wed?*" Sabrina gasped, feeling the air flee her lungs. "You wish me to wed the McLaren?"

She stared at her grandfather as he reclined weakly against the pillows.

"Aye, lass," the old Highlander rasped. "You're the last hope of Clan Duncan. Your union with our McLaren allies will secure the future of our clan."

Dazed, she shook her head. So *this* was the meaning of her grandfather's urgent summons. She had scarcely arrived at his bedside when Angus launched baldly into his proposal, with no thought to sparing any sensibilities she might have.

"I'm dying of a weak heart, lass, and I must settle my affairs before I go. 'Tis left to you to save our clan."

The fierce Highland chieftain she remembered from her childhood didn't look as ill as she'd feared, Sabrina thought distractedly. The natural ruddiness of his age-lined cheeks shone through his pallor. And while he seemed to suffer a shortness of breath, his constitution appeared nowhere near as frail as she expected.

"I . . . don't understand," she said finally.

"What dinna ye understand? Yer kin need ye, Sabrina."

"No . . . you've made that clear. But Niall McLaren . . . he cannot possibly have agreed to the marriage."

"Aye, that he has."

Still stunned, she raised a hand to her temple. "But why? Why would he wish to wed *me*?"

"Ye're an heiress, are ye not?"

Of course, Sabrina thought with a twinge of bitterness. Her dowry was her chief attraction for any suitor.

But that did not explain why Niall McLaren would choose *her* over any other genteel woman of fortune. With his title and his devastating appeal and his legendary powers of seduction, he could doubtless have any bride he wished. He had not even seemed pleased to see her this afternoon—

A flush of embarrassment besieged Sabrina as she remembered her brief encounter with Niall McLaren several hours ago at the tavern. He *must* have known about her grandfather's plan all along. Was that why he'd scrutinized her with such smoldering—almost hostile—intensity? And why he had tried to warn her away from the Highlands?

Because he was not eager for the marriage?

"There must be any number of heiresses he could choose from," she protested.

"None that would suit so well. Our lands march together, and we share the same enemies. He's laird of a powerful Scots clan, willing to fight our foes to the death."

Sabrina glanced around the darkened bedchamber, lit by a single candle. She vaguely remembered Angus's medieval manor house from her childhood. This room clearly belonged to a fighting man. More weapons than tapestries graced the stone walls, and the chamber boasted few comforts other than the massive four-poster bed and a huge hearth. It should have struck her as cold and gloomy, yet inexplicably she found it intriguing. This had been the Duncan Clan's family seat for over a hundred years.

"Still," she murmured, "that doesn't seem reason enough for the McLaren to agree."

"I tell you lass, he's willing. 'Tis not so far-fetched that he should look favorably on the union. The marriage will bind our two clans together."

Perhaps it wasn't beyond the *realm* of possibility that Niall McLaren should be willing to wed her, Sabrina conceded. Political marriages between clan allies were entirely common, after all—indeed, the rule rather than the exception.

"Can ye not see how vital it is that ye wed him?" Angus demanded, the question an urgent plea. "When I'm gone, the bloody Buchanans will ravage Clan Duncan if the laird is no' strong enough to prevent it."

Sabrina nodded unwillingly. She understood very well what her grandfather wanted of her. He wanted her to marry a laird powerful enough to protect her clansmen from their enemies.

But his choice of husband for her . . . The very notion of wedding Niall McLaren dismayed her. A rogue and a libertine. He would as soon break her heart as look at her.

No, the thought was preposterous. They were supremely ill-suited for marriage. In truth, they had rubbed each other wrong from the first.

"Is there no one else who can act as your successor?" she asked unhappily.

"Liam would be next in line. He's a good mon, but no' so good as the McLaren. Liam himself kens it."

"But . . . surely there must be someone else who can take over—"

"Nay, there's no one. Do ye no' ken I would hae acted were there another choice?"

"But Grandfather—"

Suddenly a violent cough shook Angus's wiry frame, and he spent a long moment wheezing into his fist.

Alarmed, Sabrina took a step closer, reaching out a hand to help him.

Impatiently he waved her away and lay back panting. "Is there nothing I can do to comfort you, Grandfather?"

"Aye . . . ye can ease my mind by agreeing to wed the McLaren."

He must have seen her misgivings in her expression, for he took another rasping breath and continued with relentless fervor. "Niall McLaren is a valiant leader of men, a warrior born and bred, like his da. He's strong enough to hold this clan together and lead it against the bloody Buchanans. He kens how to fight. And he has good cause to hate the Buchanans. His da perished at their hand, cursing their name. Just as yer own da did."

Sabrina gazed down at her grandfather, understanding his immense hatred for the Clan Buchanan. Angus held them to blame for the death of his only child. Sabrina's father had been thrown from his horse while pursuing the Buchanans after they'd raided Duncan cattle, and Angus considered them mortal enemies.

Indeed, the feud between their clans had existed for over a hundred years.

There was no government to speak of in the Highlands, other than the relic of a medieval feudal system. The lairds ruled their clans loosely, at the volition of their followers. Highlanders looked to their chiefs for protection, even for food, but they would only support a leader they respected— which ordinarily meant a man. The mantle of clan leadership passed through sons and brothers and rarely came to rest with women.

When Angus was gone, Sabrina knew, she would nominally be head of her clan, but she was in no position to lead them against the Buchanans. She had neither the skills nor the experience.

And the threat to a clan's survival came not only from enemies without. Unless Angus chose a strong successor, his death could cause conflict within their clan, prompting a bloody battle over who next would be laird.

Sabrina shook her head in dismay. A union with Clan McLaren alone wouldn't bring peace to the warring clans, yet by wedding their chieftain, she could at least provide the means to protect her kinsmen once Angus passed away.

She rubbed her throbbing temple. "I should have been born male," she murmured absently.

"Aye, that would have served. 'Twould have been far better had yer own da not died so young. Ye've the look of my dear son about ye, Sabrina." Angus searched her face, his rheumy eyes blurring. "I ken ye'll do what's right."

Sabrina felt her throat tighten with emotion. His methods of persuasion were unfair—using the memory of her late father against her, as well as his own deteriorating condition and her strong sense of duty. It wasn't fair, either, of Angus to ask so much of her. He had washed his hands of her all this time, yet now he expected her to become the Clan Duncan's savior.

She could refuse his plea. Her inheritance gave her independence enough to chart her own future. Her stepfather was the only person whose blessing she needed.

Yet fair or not, Angus was depending on her. It left her feeling trapped, cornered, helpless to deal with an impossible dilemma.

"Is it so great a sacrifice I'm asking ye to make?" he said as if he could read her thoughts. "There's gain in it for ye, as well."

"Is there?" she couldn't help retorting.

"Aye, 'tis true. Ye belong in the Highlands, lass, as I told yer mother before she took you away. As I told ye yerself lang syne."

Sabrina shut her eyes for an instant, remembering Angus's letter to her years ago, when her mother lay dying. He had implored her to return home, but only now did she regret being unable to. Not until this day, when she'd spied the rugged grandeur of her homeland, had she realized how truly she belonged here. The Highlands were in her blood; she couldn't escape it.

But was wedding the McLaren the only option?

"Surely there is another clan we can ally ourselves with. Another laird who would not be averse to an arranged marriage."

"Nay," Angus replied abruptly, putting that line of argument to rest. "None within two days' ride. None who are in need of a bride. None I would trust to deal fittingly with the

Buchanans. And none who have such strong ties of kinship to the Duncans."

His penetrating gaze searched her face. "Ye canna be afraid, can ye, Sabrina? Ye have pluck, lass. Even as a wee bairn ye dinna fear me."

No, as a child she had not been frightened by his gruffness or overly awed by his power. In truth, she'd felt an affinity for the crusty laird that she felt even now. But being unafraid was not the same as being *willing*.

"Then there's family," Angus added. "A lass should have a husband . . . bairns of her own."

That was indeed a prime benefit of marriage. She wanted children. She wanted a husband . . . a loving relationship like her parents had known. A permanent commitment that only death could sever.

Yet she had few illusions on that score. She was unlikely ever to marry for love. She'd had several suitors in recent months, but she was realistic enough to know they sought her primarily for her inheritance. As an heiress she would always be the target of fortune hunters. Oliver had been different, she was certain—but then he'd fallen in love with her cousin.

"And the lad is no' so poor to look at."

Sabrina wanted to laugh at that understatement. Niall McLaren was endowed with a physical beauty that startled at first glance. Utterly masculine, dangerously sensual—and quite out of her league.

She was well aware of her own merits. Her breeding and education alone made her a worthy candidate for a laird's wife. But in truth her personal attributes were modest. She was practical, dutiful, resourceful . . . *Desirable* in no way described her. Niall himself had called her a mouse.

Sabrina wrinkled her nose in remembrance. Yet she'd always known gentlemen favored beautiful women, with softer, rounder shapes than she possessed. Oliver had, certainly. Her dark hair—and perhaps her darker eyes—were her only claims to beauty.

Niall McLaren's discriminating instinct for ravishing females was legendary. She felt decidedly drab and plain in
comparison to all the lovely women he'd surely known.

"Is there another mon ye wish to wed, then?" her grandfather demanded.

"No . . ." Her choices of husband at the moment were
slim. "There is no one else."

"Aweel, then, it should pose no problem. So what is yer
answer, lass?"

Her answer?

Sabrina shook her head dazedly. She couldn't possibly
give Angus a response just yet. At the moment she was too
weary and stunned to make any rational judgments.

"Grandfather . . . I must have time to think . . . I cannot
make such a momentous decision without giving it careful
consideration."

"Well, take yer time, lass—but I should like to hold the
ceremony before the week is out, before the Buchanans take
it into their dim heads to gain advantage from my illness.
Now, lass . . . I must rest. Will ye leave me for a time?"

"Yes . . . of course, Grandfather," Sabrina said courteously.

"Send Liam to me when ye see him . . ."

Angus sank deeper into the pillows, his eyes already
closed in exhaustion. The discussion had taken a toll on his
fading health, Sabrina noted with regret.

Quietly she let herself from the chamber and nearly stumbled over Rab, who had been waiting anxiously for her. Absently she stroked the dog's huge head, before turning to
descend the stone stairs to the great hall below. Her footsteps lagged while her mind whirled.

Wife.

She was being offered the chance to become Niall
McLaren's wife.

A pulse of excitement throbbed within Sabrina before she
could repress it. What would it be like to be the wife of a
man like that? To share his home and his bed? To bear his
children? To feel his touch, his passion each night . . .

No, it was absurd to feel such anticipation. She didn't have even the least *liking* for him. Yet she couldn't deny that he had invaded her dreams far too often. There was something about Niall McLaren that compelled fascination.

He was a man as dangerous and beguiling as the Highlands itself. A boldly sensuous lover whose name women whispered like a prayer.

And as dismaying as it was for her to admit, his kiss had done something to her that night in the garden. Changed her in some indefinable way. He'd stirred a fiery, restless need in her, arousing a fierce yearning deep inside a secret part of her.

Before that night she had been satisfied with her life. She was virtual mistress of her stepfather's household, running his affairs and supervising his account books. And she enjoyed a measure of independence unusual for an unmarried woman.

She'd convinced herself she needed nothing more from life. She might still be a romantic, but she'd learned to repress any reckless longings. She might have suffered a painful betrayal by a feckless suitor, but she'd hidden her hurt well. She was too pragmatic to pine over lost wishes and broken dreams.

At least she had been until Niall McLaren.

Fiercely Sabrina shook her head. She was mad to be remembering their moonlit encounter with anything other than distaste. His kiss had meant nothing to him but vengeance, an exercise in frustrated carnal desire.

And yet . . . since that night she was no longer so content to watch from the sidelines, experiencing the unsatisfying life of the perpetual onlooker. She didn't *want* to be left on the shelf, resigned to dull evenings with her stepfather's account books.

She was not born for so little.

All of her life she had been quiet and responsible, but in recent months there'd been moments when she'd felt longing well up inside her, gathering like a fountain ready to erupt. She felt desperate to live, to have adventures, to feel passion. She wanted to experience life to the fullest. To decide her own role, influence her own fate. She wanted to make a difference in the world.

As now. Her clan *needed* her.

Now she must make a choice.

Was she willing to put obligation and duty before all else? Could she endure a marriage of convenience with a profligate rogue in order to protect her clan from the bloody feuds that ravaged the Highlands? She was half Highlander by blood. And the bonds of family and duty were strong, the call of danger and excitement even stronger . . .

She was halfway down the stairway when she became aware of an unnatural quiet in the hall. Sabrina glanced down to find a sea of faces gazing up at her solemnly. In the crowd, she recognized Liam and Geordie, but the rest were unfamiliar to her. Apparently, though, the men of Clan Duncan had gathered in the hall and were waiting to speak to her.

Liam had been chosen spokesman, it seemed, for he stepped forward as she reached the last stair.

"Mistress Duncan, if we might beg a word with you?"

"Yes?" she replied politely.

"We wish you to know that . . . should you wed the McLaren, we'll follow him, every last man of us. You have our oath on that."

It was a public pledge, she realized. Liam was abdicating his position as her grandfather's successor and accepting the McLaren as chief. He was putting the good of the clan above personal power or gain.

Could she do any less?

Sabrina glanced around her at her kinsmen. Their grave, hopeful faces tore at her heart. She couldn't turn her back on these people, even if it meant sacrificing her own happiness. She was needed here.

Sabrina forced her lips into a semblance of a smile. "I shall think on it carefully, I promise you."

Yet there was little choice left to her. When she'd come home, she had never expected to be caught up in the fiery passions of a proud people. But her fate had been decided for her even before she stepped foot in the Highlands, Sabrina realized.

She knew she would consent to her grandfather's marriage plans. She would protect her clan the only way she knew how.

Even if it meant enduring a loveless marriage to the infamous Niall McLaren.

Chapter Three

Sabrina passed a restless night, assaulted by wicked, treacherous dreams of the McLaren. Dawn found her tossing in her bed, grappling with the tormenting question of whether to wed him as her grandfather asked.

Their union would not be the ideal, based on love and esteem and shared goals. Doubtless Niall held her in as much dislike as she did him.

Their mutual antagonism did not bode well for happiness in marriage. But then was happiness truly a necessary requirement? Sabrina demanded honestly of herself. She would be no worse off than most women. If she could not have love, she could gain fulfillment in doing her duty, in working for the good of her clan. It would be a marriage of convenience, nothing more.

Faith, it was not as if she had more estimable suitors pressing for her hand. And while she and Niall McLaren had started off on the wrong foot, perhaps something positive could be salvaged of their relationship.

By the time she rose to dress, Sabrina had reluctantly reached a decision: to fulfill her grandfather's dying wish and provide Clan Duncan with a protector. She would wed the McLaren.

She informed her grandfather of her resolve directly after breakfast, before she could change her mind. From his sickbed, Angus rejoiced at the news, calling for Liam to break out a barrel of his finest malt whisky. Dozens of Duncan kinsmen crammed into his bedchamber, where with trembling hands, Angus raised a toast to his granddaughter, who would be the saving of Clan Duncan.

Then dismissing any misgivings Sabrina might still have, he sent word to the McLaren of the wedding to come, putting the date of the ceremony for a week hence, and issued invitations to neighboring clans to attend the festivities.

Sabrina was pleased when her grandfather's health seemed to improve measurably at the prospect of Clan Duncan's deliverance, but dismayed that events were moving so quickly.

It was two days more, however, before she managed to speak to the prospective bridegroom—and then she was forced to go to him, since she received only a terse response to her note requesting that he call to discuss arrangements for the ceremony. He was, he regretted to inform her, too busy at the moment to answer her summons.

It vexed her that the McLaren could not make the time to meet with her. She desired to speak to him privately, the man to whom she would soon give herself in marriage, whose life and bed she would share, whose children she would bear.

"Doubtless he is occupied with clan matters," Angus said in his defense.

Or engaged in his usual licentious pursuits, Sabrina thought tartly.

The weather had turned stormy, with gusting rain lashing at the manor and enveloping the interior in a chill, gray gloom. Unhappily, the delay gave Sabrina too much leisure to regret her decision. Her grandfather attributed her qualms to bridal nerves, but when she remained determined to speak to her future husband, Angus sent her kinsman to accompany her.

"Take Geordie with you, lass," he ordered. "It isna safe for womenfolk to go traipsing about the countryside with the Buchanans lurking about."

With an armed Geordie riding escort and Rab bounding along beside her mount, Sabrina struck out for the McLaren's home, Creagturic.

Her spirits rebounded as she rode through the rugged hills. The rain had ceased, and on this bright, blustery spring morning, the early mists had burned away, leaving an emerald vision of untamed grandeur.

Sabrina felt her breath catch with enchantment. Whatever doubts she had about her marriage to the McLaren, she was glad she had returned home to this splendid country. The Highlands were seeping into her soul, calling to her; she felt the lure deep in her blood.

And as she drew rein and sat gazing up at the imposing stone castle that would soon be her new home, her heart hammered with delight and trepidation.

Set against a range of sweeping hills, surrounded by forested glens of alder and birch, the ancient family seat of the McLarens stood overlooking the clear blue waters of a tranquil loch. Despite its stark beauty, it was a formidable stronghold, obviously the domain of a warring clan.

" 'Twas built by Malcolm the Bold, Niall's great-great-grandda," Geordie volunteered. "Besieged twice, but never been taken."

They rode across a stone bridge to enter the walled bailey, although the portcullis, a relic of feudal days, was no longer in use. The yard was immense, boasting a dozen timber out-buildings including a stable and smithy. After dismounting and securing her mount's reins to a ring, Sabrina ordered her canine escort to remain at the foot of the sweeping stone stairway, and climbed with Geordie to the great oaken entrance door.

The interior of the castle, at least, appeared to have been gentled by a civilized hand, Sabrina reflected admiringly as they were shown inside. The stone walls of the great hall had been brightened with whitewash and adorned with fine tapestries in addition to weapons, while the massive oak furniture gleamed with beeswax.

The elderly housekeeper eyed Sabrina curiously. " 'Tis pleased I am to make your acquaintance, Mistress Duncan,"

Mrs. Paterson asserted, "but I fear the laird isna home presently."

"Do you anticipate his return any time soon? I have been attempting for several days to speak to him."

"Aweel, he's been gone the night, but told me to expect him this morn."

Sabrina pressed her lips together dryly, well able to imagine what had kept the laird out all night. "Perhaps you would be so kind as to allow us to await him?"

"Aye, of course. Come with me, if you please."

With Geordie, Sabrina followed the housekeeper upstairs, past the minstrels' gallery overlooking the great hall, to a handsome drawing room. The walls were decorated with rich wainscoting and flocked damask wallpaper, and an exquisite pianoforte of inlaid rosewood stood in the far corner opposite the hearth.

"That fine instrument belonged to Mistress McLaren," the housekeeper said, correctly interpreting Sabrina's expression of pleasure. "A saintly woman, if there ever was."

"Would that be the McLaren's mother?"

"Aye, indeed. She passed on to her Maker some three years ago, a fierce blow to us all. If you will make yourself at home, mistress, I shall bring you a wee drop of refreshment."

"Thank you, but that isn't necessary."

"But the laird may be long in coming."

"I am prepared to wait all day if need be," Sabrina said darkly. When the housekeeper had gone, she settled herself on a brocade settee while Geordie walked the floor restlessly, more comfortable out-of-doors than in the refined environs of a drawing room. It took some prodding to persuade him to tell her of the McLaren family, but Sabrina managed to learn a good deal about Niall's late parents and brothers.

It was perhaps an hour later when they heard the clatter of horses' hooves beyond the drawing room window. Geordie stopped his pacing to gaze down at the courtyard.

" 'Tis the McLaren and John."

"John?" Sabrina asked, rising to join him at the window.

"Aye, Niall's cousin . . . and a great friend to his da."

There were two horsemen below, Sabrina saw. One was Niall; the other the brawny Highlander who'd come to fetch him at her aunt's ball in Edinburgh so many months ago with the terrible news of the laird's ambush by the Buchanans. The two men had halted before the stable.

Below her, Rab jumped up, ears alert. Abandoning his post by the stair, the great animal bounded across the yard to greet the new arrivals.

It irked Sabrina to see Rab dancing in circles, emitting excited barks of welcome. The McLaren laird had been a total stranger to him until a few days ago.

To her further dismay, she saw Niall stiffen and glance up at the window where she stood. Apparently he had recognized her dog and took no pleasure in her presence.

His expression grim, he murmured something to his companion, who also looked up.

Sabrina stepped back from the window. "Geordie," she said curtly, trying to keep hold of her patience. "When the McLaren arrives, would you be so kind as to step outside the room for a moment? What I have to say to him is better said in private."

"How splendid," Niall muttered sardonically. "A visit from my betrothed. A fitting end to a delightful morning."

"Do ye require my help dismounting, lad?" John asked.

Shaking his head, Niall swung down from his mount and winced at the sharp ache in his ribs. Guardedly he bent to scratch the fawning dog behind his ears. "I'll see to the horses, John. I'd be obliged if you would go and discover what Mistress Duncan wants."

"I've nae doubt she wishes to see you."

"Perhaps, but I'm in no humor to play the ardent suitor."

As a result of the recent torrential rains, a nearby dam had washed out last night, flooding tenants' crofts and destroying newly planted fields. Niall had spent the night helping to divert the burn and shore up the dam, but he hadn't been quick enough to elude a log that had slipped its chains and barreled into him. In addition to nearly drowning in the burn, he'd suffered bruised ribs and a gash in his right hip.

The wound was not life-threatening, but painful enough to cause discomfort. And now, besides lacking sleep and being soaked to the bone, he had to face his betrothed who had come to call.

"I'd deem it a favor if you would make my excuses and send her on her way."

At least John did not argue. "I'll do my best, lad. I'll send Jean to you. That wound must be tended."

A chambermaid in the laird's employ, Jean sometimes assisted the local midwife in difficult deliveries and knew about patching wounds.

"Very well. And find me some dry clothing, if you please. I'll await Jean in the herbal."

Niall turned the horses over to a stable groom and entered the outbuilding that had once been part of the castle garrison and now served as an infirmary. Bundles of herbs hung from the rafters while jars of unguents and potions lined the wooden shelves.

His plaid was the only garment that hadn't been drenched, and when he'd tossed that aside, he had to clench his teeth against the chill air.

With care he removed his damp shirt and boots, then gingerly shed his trews, wincing at the gash on his hip as he peeled away the tartan cloth. Then wrapping his plaid around his bare body, Niall settled himself on the cot to await Jean and wearily closed his eyes.

He had resigned himself to marriage with Mistress Sabrina Duncan, but at this moment, he was more than gratified to escape an audience with her.

"Ye're the lass from Edinburgh," John pronounced when Geordie had made the introductions.

"Yes," Sabrina replied, unoffended by his fierce scrutiny of her, knowing it was because she would likely become the mistress of Clan McLaren. He doubtless felt a proprietary interest in any decision regarding the laird's bride and felt the need to pass judgment on her.

A hulking Highland warrior with the same wavy black hair as many others of his clan, including the laird, John towered over her and outweighed her by some eight stone. But while Sabrina might have been a trifle intimidated by his brawn and his dark scowl, she dared not show it, not if she hoped to win his respect.

Almost defiantly, she lifted her chin and returned his gaze steadily. "Well, do I meet with your approval, sir?"

His intense expression relaxed, and to her surprise and relief, he grinned. "Aye, I ken ye'll do. Ye've the look of Angus about ye. And ye've his spirit as well, I trow."

"Thank you," Sabrina said, taking his reply to be a high compliment. "I should like to speak to the McLaren, if I may."

Averting his gaze uncomfortably, John equivocated. "I fear the laird is indisposed at present."

"Indisposed? But I saw him below just a short while ago . . ."

She glanced briefly out the window, just in time to see a young woman garbed in a white apron slip inside the same outbuilding Niall had entered.

Her jaw hardening for an instant, Sabrina forced herself to take a calming breath to control her vexation. It was not only that her betrothed chose to conduct his amorous affairs directly under her nose; she could make no demands on him before they were even wed. It was his gall in leaving her to cool her heels while he did it!

"Forgive me, John McLaren," she said with a dryness bordering on the acerbic. "I seem to have chosen an inappropriate time to call. Pray tell the laird when next you see him that I am most anxious to discuss the particulars of the wedding arrangements with him."

It took every ounce of restraint Sabrina possessed to calmly take her leave from the Highlander and make her way down to the yard outside.

Asking a bewildered Geordie to wait for her then—and ordering a disappointed Rab to stay—Sabrina left her guardians to march across the yard to the building where Niall and the young woman had disappeared.

It came as no surprise to hear the sound of feminine laughter issuing from within or, when she rapped lightly, to hear a rich and familiar voice bid entrance.

Sabrina had scarcely taken a step inside, however, when she halted abruptly at the brazen sight that greeted her. Upon the cot, in a state of complete undress, Niall McLaren reclined with his back to the wall. The lass sitting beside him at least was gowned, but she was leaning over him so-licitously, one hand resting on his bare chest.

Niall looked up, a look of annoyance hardening his stubble-shadowed jaw.

"F-Forgive me," Sabrina stammered. "I did not real-ize . . . I never . . ."

He sighed in resignation. "Now that you've intruded, you may as well stay." He gave the serving lass a pat on her well-curved hip. "That will be all, Jean," he murmured, his voice a husky drawl. "We will resume this later."

With a glance at Sabrina, the young woman rose and made a curtsy. "As ye wish, milord."

"Oh, and Jean, bring refreshment for Mistress Duncan, if you please."

Too flustered to countermand the request, Sabrina merely stepped aside. Jean brushed past her, leaving her alone with her host.

He was a breathtaking man, she thought distractedly as her eyes adjusted to the muted light. Freed of its queue, his hair fell in silken disarray, emphasizing the corded width of his shoulders. His broad, bronzed chest was lightly furred with ebony down that whorled lower in a sensual motif, narrowing over his flat, hard stomach . . . Sabrina's gaze faltered momentarily.

He was not totally naked, she realized with relief. A tartan plaid lay strategically draped across his narrow hips. Below the cloth stretched long, powerful bare legs built of well-honed muscle and dusted with hair. Sinewed and hard, he gave an unmistakable impression of raw strength.

The shock of it, the absolute beauty of him, was a jolt to her senses.

"Did no one ever tell you it is impolite to stare, mistress?"

Sabrina's cheeks heated with bright color, and it was all she could do to stand her ground instead of turning tail. Niall McLaren's near nakedness was distinctly unnerving—and the libertine knew it full well, to judge by the dancing light in his blue eyes.

"How may I be of service, mistress?" he queried, his gaze amused and knowing.

"I came to . . . pay you a visit," she replied unevenly, trying to marshal her scattered wits.

"So I see."

"Did you not receive my message asking you to call?"

"I regret I was engaged and was unable to spare the time."

"So I see," Sabrina echoed tartly, glancing pointedly at his disheveled state.

Niall shrugged his bare shoulders as he casually tugged up the plaid to cover his worst bruising. "You do have the most annoying habit of showing up when you are least wanted, mistress."

She met his bold gaze impatiently. "I had no intention of interrupting your pleasures. But I hoped you might spare five minutes of your precious time."

"I can manage five minutes," Niall observed with a wicked slant to his lips. "I am entirely at your service, mistress. You command my undivided attention."

Oh, but he was bold, Sabrina thought with grudging

admiration. The villain was laughing at her. She could see the devilment in his eyes.

He appeared even more treacherously handsome than she recalled. His raven hair tumbled around his face, accenting the ruggedly sculpted planes and angles and the dazzling blue eyes framed by thick black lashes. Her woman's heart beat faster just looking at him. She found herself staring at that beautifully shaped, sensually curved mouth and the burning smile that twisted into a mocking curve.

She almost turned and walked away. But she had vowed to face this situation head-on. She refused to continue suffering the state of uncertainty she'd endured for the past three days. She wanted matters settled between them. "I wonder if you would deign to consider putting on some clothing."

"Why? Do you dislike the sight of a naked man?"

Sabrina opened her mouth to reply and then snapped it shut. That was not a question a lady answered.

"Or perhaps you are merely faint of heart," the rogue had the audacity to add.

"I am *not* faint-hearted—"

"Then why do you remain standing in the doorway?"

A scarlet blush rose high and bright in her cheeks. Stiffly Sabrina stepped into the room, but she was careful to leave the door ajar.

She froze suddenly when, with a languid movement of his body, Niall stretched his powerful arms overhead, making the muscles in his bare chest and torso ripple and flex.

He grimaced slightly, then laughed at her apprehensive expression, showing white flashing teeth. "Welcome to my den of iniquity, Mistress Duncan."

The infuriating gleam made her scowl—but at least it helped her regain some of her composure. "I don't particularly find this a subject for levity, my lord!"

"That is quite apparent."

"I suppose it *is* in keeping with your dissipated reputation, receiving a lady in a complete state of undress."

"Ah . . . now resumes your continued assault on my character."

"In the unelevated circles in which I was raised, taking advantage of serving maids *is* considered indicative of a lack of character."

Niall shook his head in feigned hurt. "Why are you always so swift to accuse me of taking advantage of the gentler sex?"

"Perhaps because in every instance we've met, you've been engaged in luring females to their ruin."

"I am loath to correct a lady, but the females I lure are *never* unwilling."

"I doubt that would prove an impediment for you, in any case," Sabrina remarked archly.

"I fancy it wouldn't," he agreed with a tantalizing spice in his voice.

"No." Her tone was grudging. "You are obviously graced with an unreasonable measure of persuasiveness."

"To say nothing of my charm and wit."

Sabrina shut her eyes for a moment in a silent appeal to heaven. He was the most incredibly arrogant man she had ever met. She devoutly wished she could take him down a peg. "I hardly consider it a virtue to have broken scores of female hearts!"

"Ah, lass, never would I purposely wound the fairer sex."

"Not purposely. I suppose you cannot help it, considering what you are."

"And what is that?"

"A . . . a womanizer. A . . ."

"Hedonist," he supplied lazily. "Ah, yes, I well recall your opinion of me."

"Do you deny it?"

He cocked his head, considering her. "No, indeed. My infamous repute is well deserved. I am a man of great lusts."

She didn't need him to tell her that he was sexually promiscuous. Doubtless he had bedded more women than she even *knew*. She wondered if he ever slept alone. "That is supremely evident!" Her gaze swept his nearly nude body with a hint of disdain. "Most polite society would consider it the height of depravity to be carrying on so in the middle of the day."

Niall's amusement faded while his expression turned cool. "Firstly, it is not midday. It is scarcely ten of the clock, a perfectly appropriate time to be 'carrying on so,' as you so delicately put it. Secondly, I believe this is my domain, where I may conduct myself as I please. And thirdly, Mistress Duncan . . ." His gaze bored into her. "What right do you have to censure me?"

Sabrina drew herself up. "I claim none. Indeed, it is nothing to me if you choose to while away your time in idle pursuits. But there is more to life than chasing skirts."

"Oh? And what, pray tell, is there?"

"Duty and honor, for instance. Family. Sacrifice."

His blue eyes turned hard and challenging. "I have been willing to sacrifice for duty and clan loyalty. I assumed the lairdship of my clan, for which I held neither expectation nor avocation. And," Niall added in a velvet-honed voice of steel, "I have agreed to consider your proposal of marriage."

Sabrina raised her eyebrows. "*My* proposal?"

"Is that not why you sought an audience with me this morn?"

Her mouth dropped open. "Wedding you was not *my* idea, I assure you!"

"Nor was it mine." Niall favored her with a wintry smile. " 'Tis solely your grandfather's wish."

"But I . . ." She frowned in confusion. "Angus spoke as if the decision was settled. He told me that you concurred."

"I concur that Angus needs the connection between our clans, that is all."

Dropping her gaze, Sabrina stared down at the floor, her heart squeezing with a strange pain. Niall McLaren didn't wish to marry her. She should have known.

"I have no desire to be forced upon any man," Sabrina replied stiffly. "Certainly not *you*. I was only willing to consider marriage to you for the good of my kinsmen. For some reason, my grandfather believes that you offer the best chance to ensure our clan's survival."

"I know what Angus believes. But if I might indulge in some plain speaking?"

"Let us be frank, by all means," she agreed acerbically.

"You would do far better to find yourself another husband."

Sabrina glanced up at him, her half smile scornful. "And just why is that?"

"Because you and I are ill-suited."

That she could agree with wholeheartedly; it was no more than she had concluded herself.

When she did not dispute him, Niall's tone softened a degree. "You don't wish to marry a philanderer, Mistress Duncan, I assure you. I would make you a deplorable husband. I cherish the lasses too much to give up my freedom and settle down with a wife. I wouldn't be faithful to any woman. It isn't in me."

No, Sabrina thought somberly. She couldn't expect such a man to be faithful to her. He was a man of passion without promises. He wouldn't want her love, or any other tender feelings. But then she didn't want his love, either. She only wanted him to protect her clan.

"You need not fear on that score. I'd not deprive you of your pleasures. Ours would be a marriage of convenience, nothing more. However, I . . ." She took a deep breath, uncomfortable discussing such private issues in so intimate a manner. "I . . . would like children eventually. And I should think you would as well. A man in your position needs heirs."

Niall was a long time in answering. "I expect I could comply in that regard."

"I have little doubt," she observed, her tone wry. "I imagine Scotland and France are littered with your by-blows."

"Then you imagine wrongly. I have two children to my knowledge, and both are well provided for."

"Then that should prove no problem, should it?"

"I think perhaps you underestimate the difficulties you will face as my bride. We Highlanders are a rough and tumble lot, and our existence a hard one, particularly in winter. I warn you, you should have no expectations of a life of luxury."

Sabrina stiffened at his implication. He made her sound so frail and useless. "I expect nothing of the sort. I may have lived in Edinburgh for much of my life, but I am unaccustomed to a life of ease. I should think the dowry I bring would compensate you for any inconvenience, in any case. However"—she started to turn away—"if you refuse the marriage, then there is no further point in discussion."

"Did I say I refuse?" A muscle worked in Niall's jaw as resentment flared in him. He could not honorably reject the betrothal, not with the debt his father owed her grandfather. He could not, would not, shirk his obligations. On the other hand . . . he would not object if Mistress Duncan chose to call off the betrothal herself.

He crossed his arms over his bare chest. "I am prepared to be convinced."

She hesitated. "Convinced? What . . . do you mean?"

"Perhaps I wish to be courted."

"You wish me to *court* you?" His audacity knew no bounds! "If you expect me to flirt and banter idiotically and fawn over you merely for your amusement," she snapped, "your wits have gone begging."

"Please yourself, mouse. 'Tis you who needs a husband."

His words slashed at her pride. "*I* do not need a husband! My clan needs a laird—there is a world of difference. I desire a union between us even less than you do, I assure you."

"Then call off the betrothal."

"Call it off?" Her brow furrowed as she stared at him. A long moment later, Sabrina shook her head. "I have no intention of abandoning my clan and disappointing my grandfather. My kinsmen have pledged to follow you, and I'll not gainsay their choice. As disagreeable as I would find marriage to you, I am prepared to make the best of it. If you are so set against it, sir, *you* may have the honor of withdrawing."

She saw Niall's jaw harden briefly. But then he smiled— slowly, wickedly, and not at all pleasantly. "As I said, I can be convinced to accept your suit. But you will have to persuade me."

He *was* taunting her, she realized with renewed fury.

"Am I to understand," she enunciated, her ire ringing in the tartness of her voice, "that I must extol my worth, like a prize heifer at a cattle fair? I must *audition* for the position of your bride?"

"I am suggesting that there are certain virtues I require in a wife and the mistress of my clan."

And *she* didn't possess them, Sabrina was certain he was saying. She could assess her attributes well enough. Physically she was no match for a man whose lovemaking prowess with the most beautiful women of Europe was legend, whose exploits in the glittering ballrooms and bedrooms of the aristocracy were unrivaled.

"I make no claim to beauty—or fashion, either, for that matter."

Niall shrugged his powerful shoulders. "Beauty is not so vital an attribute in a lass."

She eyed him doubtfully, not crediting that a man of his notorious tastes would settle for plainness. "Then what is?"

His gaze made an unhurried journey from the tips of her toes to the slight swell of her breasts, hidden by her drab traveling cloak. "Suitability, for one. How can we be certain we are compatible unless we put it to the test?"

"What do you mean? Put *what* to the test?"

"You are inexperienced in matters carnal. You've never lain with a man."

His blunt words sparked a flush of embarrassment within her. "How . . . can you be so certain?"

"That you're a virgin?"

Again her cheeks flamed. "Y-Yes."

"Any number of telltale signs. The innocence I tasted in your kiss some months ago. Your shock when I stroked your breast. The pulse that flutters at your throat just now. The blush that stains your cheeks . . . To an experienced connoisseur like myself, you are a mere babe."

"I was under the opinion that gentlemen preferred innocence in their brides."

"Many do, perhaps. But I like my lasses eager and willing, hungering with desire for me. Tell me, sweet mouse, does your pulse quicken at the thought of my bedding you? Do you feel a honeyed warmth between your thighs when you imagine yourself naked in my arms?"

Sabrina clamped her lips together as she tried to think of a suitable rejoinder, more unsettled by his talk about her body than she would ever divulge. He was making this as difficult as possible for her.

"It pains me to depress your inflated opinion of yourself, sir, but I do *not* waste time imagining myself in your arms, naked or otherwise," she lied. "You flatter yourself if you think I want you."

"Which is precisely my point, mouse. I wonder if you are even capable of being aroused. If I am to take a bed-partner for life, I prefer to know what I am getting. I have no desire to be saddled with a block of ice for a wife. I want a woman of passion—"

A soft tap sounded on the door, interrupting whatever response Sabrina might have made. When Niall bid entrance, Jean appeared, bearing a tray laden with wine and shortbread biscuits.

He favored the girl with an approving smile, an expression so sensual that it set a sharp little pain twisting in the vicinity of Sabrina's heart. "Thank you, lass. Set it down there on the table, if you please. Mistress Duncan will do the honors, I trust."

Stifling a giggle, Jean cast a sly glance at Sabrina. "Aye, milord. As ye wish."

She deposited her burden on the table adjacent to the hearth, curtsied, and walked out.

"Shall we drink a glass together, mouse?" Niall asked when the chambermaid at last had gone.

Sabrina drew a deep breath, reining in her frustration. "By all means. Perhaps it will serve to dampen your lechery a bit."

As she poured the wine into two pewter goblets, Niall carefully studied Sabrina's expression, trying to judge the effect his baiting was having on her. He had managed to fluster her, he was certain. In her eyes he'd caught the slightest glimmer of hurt, the smallest hint of vulnerability. Yet she had drawn blood herself with her sharp tongue.

It stung, knowing she held him in such low regard. Upon finding Jean inspecting his wound, Mistress Duncan had instantly assumed the worst. She thought him debauched and decadent, but despite his infamous past, he had never seduced one of his own servants, and was not about to start.

He'd been unable to persuade her, though, that he would make her a lamentable husband. And that she would make him a deplorable bride. A skittish virgin was no match for a man of his lusty passions. One embrace and he would doubtless frighten her out of her wits—

A hard smile touched Niall's lips. Perhaps he should demonstrate to her just what sort of bargain she would be getting if she chose to wed him.

"Will you bring me my cup, mistress?" Niall asked, his voice as soft as a purring cat padding across satin.

Sabrina cast him a wary glance as he lounged on the cot, the McLaren plaid an alluring foil for his blatant masculinity. Under no circumstances did she intend to approach that bed.

"Then I shall come to you," he said when she hesitated.

With lazy grace, he swung his long, sinewed legs to the floor. Sabrina's heart gave a violent jolt as she realized his intent.

His blue gaze held her startled one as he rose, a slight

smile hovering at his lips. For an instant the tartan cloth covering his loins slipped, giving her an alarming glimpse of a bare, corded flank. Casually then, Niall caught up the plaid and wound it around his waist, then flung one end over his shoulder. It served as an adequate loincloth but left most of his muscular thighs exposed.

Sabrina drew a sharp breath as he walked slowly toward her. He seemed oblivious to his nakedness, while she experienced an acute awareness of it, of him. He moved with a graceful freedom that was spellbinding, his muscled form like some pagan god . . . powerfully built, totally enchanting.

Faced with such masculine beauty, she found herself rooted where she stood. He seemed huge, all rippling bronze muscle and springy black hair. Her nerves were alive and acutely tuned to him, her senses assailed by his nearness.

She shivered as he took his goblet from her trembling fingers and raised it in the air. "May I propose a toast, mistress? To our experiment."

"Exp-periment?"

"In lovemaking."

"I w-won't make love to you."

"Ah, but you must, my sweet. As I said, I have a very lusty nature, and I intend to make quite certain it is reciprocated in my bride."

Sabrina felt her breath catch in her throat as she watched Niall take a long draught of wine. His implied threat sent excitement and an intoxicating sense of peril scurrying across the tips of every nerve ending in her body.

"You . . . would ravish me?" she asked, her breath the merest whisper.

"I haven't ravished anyone," he replied softly, "lately."

No, Sabrina thought dazedly, he would never have to resort to force when he could legitimately seduce any woman into willing compliance.

"But in this instance"—his voice dropped even lower . . . soft . . . husky—"I could make an exception. I mean to see if we are compatible, mouse."

"I . . . I will not sacrifice my innocence simply to satisfy your curiosity."

"There are ways of exploring your sensuality that don't entail relinquishing your virginity."

Curse that enchanting voice of his, she thought wretchedly. It was marked by a delicately sexual rasp that flooded her raw nerves in a warm bath of sensation.

She stood frozen as Niall took her wine cup and set it with his on the table. "Before we conclude any agreement, we need to establish if we would suit physically. To make certain you'll be a douce wife and not find the demands of the marriage bed too distasteful."

Her lips parted but no sound came out.

"You're not afraid of me, are you, sweeting?"

Afraid? Whyever should she fear a rogue of legendary charm and passion with whom no woman was safe? Sabrina swallowed. She was indeed alarmed by the overwhelming maleness of him, by his dark beauty and power, yet she refused to allow herself to be intimidated. "I am *not* afraid, sir."

She raised her eyes to meet his fearlessly. He liked that.

The air between them crackled with challenge as their eyes clashed wordlessly.

Silently Niall reached a hand toward her. "I think we should take off your cloak, mistress."

The rhythm of her heart changing perceptively, she took a hasty step backward. "N-No."

"Faintheart," he murmured. "This is hardly the way to persuade me, fleeing at the first test."

For a long moment Sabrina stared at him. He was goading her, she knew. Deliberately daring her to rise to his challenge.

Swallowing hard, she forced herself to gather her courage. "Very well . . . What must I do?"

"Perhaps you should start by kissing me."

"You want me to *kiss* you?"

"For a start. Come closer."

His smile was taunting as she hesitated. "If you quail at a

simple kiss, mouse, you are unlikely to enjoy my attentions once we are wed."

His infuriating air of supremacy roused her ire and made her determined to thwart him; to prove she wasn't the meek creature he thought her. It was not as if he posed any real danger, Sabrina reminded herself. Rab was within call. And Geordie would rescue her if need be.

Reluctantly she did as she was bid, her eyes riveted on Niall's handsome face. She had forgotten how tall he was. His nearness forced her to arch her neck to accommodate his height.

"Closer still."

She took another step, halting barely a hand's breadth away. She could feel his body heat envelop her, could smell his musky male scent, a faint, natural fragrance that was disturbingly arousing. His chest seemed very bare, and she had to control the urge to reach up and touch his skin. Her fingers tingled with warmth, her palms ached to explore that smooth, bronzed expanse.

"Now wet your lips, pet."

She wanted to refuse, yet his gaze held her captive to his will. His eyes were vividly blue and deep enough to drown in, and what she saw in their heated depths alarmed and excited her at the same time.

Obediently she moistened her lips with her tongue. "Like . . . this?"

He was watching her lazily, the curve of his lowered lashes like ebony silk. "Precisely like that. Now . . . hold me."

"I . . . I am not sure how."

"Permit me to show you."

His fingers encircling both her wrists, he drew her off balance and forced her hands to his bare chest. Sabrina knew a deliciously feminine sense of frailty, of helplessness against his strength, as she leaned into him.

"Can you not do better than that?" he prodded softly. "Use your imagination, sweeting. Put your arms around my neck."

Stung by his criticism, she found new courage. Trembling, wary, she raised her hands to Niall's naked shoulders, feeling the hard resilience in his powerful body, the intoxicating warmth radiating from his bare chest. This was the last place she wished to be, pressed against his solid, aroused form, and yet it felt so . . . right. She could feel the reckless hunger begin to stir within her, slow and insidious.

"That is better." The caress of his voice was so enticing that she could almost taste its honey in her throat. "Tell me what you feel."

How could she possibly confess the effect he had on her? The sweet tightening of her nipples. The pulse of pleasure shafting deep in her loins. The brazen heat uncoiling within her . . . Sabrina was dismayed, even horrified, by the depth of her response to him. Longing welled up in her, and she found herself struggling against the burning desire to press herself more tightly against him, to feel his entire sinewed length.

"I feel n-nothing," she lied.

With a smoldering look from those sapphire eyes, Niall reached up to touch her mouth with a forefinger. Gently he brushed her lower lip, gliding the tip slowly along the wet surface. "Then why do you shiver when I do this?"

His caress roamed lower, along the delicate underside of her jaw . . . Before Sabrina could protest, he had unfastened the clasp of her cloak and was moving downward along her throat . . . stroking the slender column with those strong, calloused fingers . . . until all she could think about was what they felt like on her skin.

"Why does your breath catch when I touch you here, sweeting?" His thumb massaged the soft, vulnerable hollow of her throat, the only skin exposed above the high neckline of her bodice.

Not waiting for an answer, he slowly bent his head. His mouth hovered over hers, his breath warming her lips.

A heated rush of feeling assaulted Sabrina. The enormous

power of his body engulfed her, aroused and tantalized and lured. He was sexuality incarnate. Shameless. Compelling.

She could feel his rock-hard thighs pressing against hers, feel the rigid muscle at his groin . . . It was impossible not to notice how enlarged he was. The awareness sent her pulse running wild.

Sabrina closed her eyes, whispering a sigh of mingled despair and need.

Niall heard the soft sound and hesitated, feeling the fluttering pulsebeat under the fine skin of her throat. He was a master at gauging a woman's minute degrees of arousal, and this lass was aroused. He knew he could seduce her and bring her to the point where she begged for him to take her. He could make her hunger to do his bidding. And yet he didn't *want* to arouse her desire, or his own. His purpose for embracing her had been exactly the opposite.

Vainly he tried to ignore the heat surging in his loins as he tightened his hold. Almost angrily then, he bent his head and covered her mouth with his own, using far more force than necessary. He kissed her deeply, his mouth ravaging with blatant intent, his tongue thrusting boldly, powerfully.

It was an act of instinct that made her raise her arms and twine her fingers in his hair, yet Niall hadn't counted on his own response. His senses jolted alarmingly at the taste of her, while heat coursed through him, pooling thickly in his groin. He knew a raw need—and felt the same need in Sabrina.

The lush honesty of her response stunned him. She was returning his kiss hungrily, measure for measure, with an innocent passion that startled him.

Desire knifed through him, sharp and insistent. He wanted to be lodged deep within her, wanted to feel her softness spread and filled by his man's heat.

Cursing himself, Niall abruptly broke off his kiss, leaving her mouth wet and wanting.

Panting for breath, dazed by the power of his sensuality, Sabrina unwillingly opened her eyes and found herself clutching the waving thickness of his silky, blue-black hair. Her breasts felt heavy and throbbed for his touch, while the heat pulsing between her legs shocked her.

She hadn't expected this wild hunger in herself. Nor had he, she realized. The expression on Niall's beautifully sculpted features looked grim as, with one powerful arm behind her back, he held her against his chest, the bold evidence of his desire pressing against her.

Sabrina flinched, feeling the hard outline of his manhood through his plaid and her layers of skirts.

Seeing her reaction, Niall at last remembered his original intent. With a dark flicker of a smile, he pressed closer, grinding himself into her slowly, sensuously, until every fiber in her body screamed with life, until heat leapt between them, scorching and primal.

Her breath abated, then, as he caught her hand and deliberately drew it beneath his plaid, against his bare flesh.

"Touch me," he ordered huskily, forcing her palm against the rigid blade of his aroused manhood, making her feel his naked maleness.

She was startled by the enormous pulsing size of him, solid and hot and so very large.

"*Now* are you afraid, mistress?" he whispered. "Does it frighten you, the thought of having my flesh deep inside you?"

The bald question jolted her out of her daze. He was deliberately trying to shock her, she knew.

Sabrina shook her head, trying to clear it as she stared up at him. Curse the rogue and his sophisticated sexual games! And curse herself for letting him maneuver her like a spineless puppet. She was no better than all the other foolish lasses who swooned over him.

Faith, but she had to do better than this.

"I did not come here, sir," she whispered finally as she struggled to pull her fingers from his grasp, "for a lesson in male anatomy."

While he stared down at her, Sabrina reached for the table, fumbling for her goblet. With the other, she pulled the plaid a scant few inches away from his body.

Taking a deep breath, she dumped the entire contents of the wine cup against his skin, drenching his bare loins.

Her unexpected act dredged a sharp gasp of pain from Niall, followed by a vivid oath. "By the bloody *de'il*!"

Yet it did have the desired effect of making him release her. Abruptly.

Stunned disbelief warred with fury in his expression as his hands curled into fists.

Warily, Sabrina took several defensive steps backward. "Perhaps that will cool your ardor, my lord," she murmured dryly. "I am through performing for you like a dancing bear at a fair. You must judge for yourself if my response to your kiss was adequate. On that evidence alone you must make up your mind regarding our marriage. Now, I believe this interview is concluded."

Setting the goblet down on the table with a thud, she gathered her skirts, then swept across the room and out the door, as regal as any queen, leaving Niall to stare after her, thunderstruck.

If not for the pain of having his arousal so abruptly chilled and his bruised ribs wrenched, he would have laughed. Mistress Duncan had won that round, he would give her that.

He shook his head in amazement as wine trickled down his bare legs to soak the floor.

He had only intended to kiss her; never more than that. He'd attempted to frighten her away with a display of passion, yet it hadn't worked in the least. She hadn't taken fright. Instead, she had tested his self-control severely. He was still heavily aroused, still felt her sweet fire. Even now, the stirring image of her dark eyes, warm and liquid with wanting, made him burn with need.

Niall cursed again as he unwound his plaid and began to

dry his loins of the sticky-sweet wine, yet an unwilling grin tugged at his mouth as he recalled her bold stunt.

He was dealing with a woman of intelligence, of no little mettle. Sabrina Duncan wouldn't cry craven at the first show of adversity. Thus far she had held her own in every encounter, parrying his thrusts with a cool wit and a rapier-sharp tongue. She was unique in his experience, and remarkably invigorating.

He prized cleverness in a lass. And in truth, she greatly underestimated her own appeal, believing she had no claim to beauty. Her comeliness was not readily apparent at first glance, Niall reflected, remembering the elusive sweetness of her skin. There was a quiet, fine-boned quality to her features, which the drab-colored garments she wore did nothing to compliment. And somewhere obscured beneath the high-necked bodice and confining stays, there was a sweet-breasted figure he longed to explore.

She was fresh and lovely, all wanton innocence—and far more of a temptation than he wished. He'd been startled to discover the spark of passion hidden beneath that mousy exterior.

Perhaps in his resentment at being forced into marriage, he had indeed misjudged her. She had a spirit he could admire, Niall conceded, recalling the defiant tilt of her chin. For a moment the mouse had transformed into a tiger, a change that was incredibly appealing. And the fire in her dark, lustrous eyes when she was angered . . . Some man would find it irresistible. He did himself. She tugged at something in him that he preferred not to acknowledge.

To a man of his jaded appetites, Sabrina Duncan was a novelty—a lass who could resist his advances. Amazingly enough, he was beginning to tire of the female sex. Beautiful women were his vocation, yet their attractions, even the hot, potent body of his lush former mistress, Eve Graham, had begun to pale. For months now he'd been experiencing a vague feeling of discontent, of restlessness, with his relationships. He eased his carnal needs in soft lips and smothered lie-words of love—fleeting words spoken for the pleasure of the moment and forgotten just as easily—and wished for something more. All women were beginning to feel unsatisfyingly identical beneath him.

Except Sabrina Duncan.

Still . . . it did not follow that he wished to wed her. He would much prefer to find some other means of protecting her clan and satisfying Angus Duncan's need for a leader, without having a bride forced upon him. Yet it was too much to hope that Mistress Duncan would voluntarily withdraw from the proposed alliance.

Wincing at the soreness in his ribs, Niall strode across the room to the window and glanced through the leaded panes to the yard where she stood. Her giant hound fawned at her feet, while Geordie Duncan prepared to help her mount her horse.

Aye, she had won this time, Niall mused. But this was merely the opening volley. If he had to wed her, it would be on his own terms. He would not be ruled by his bride.

Yet this, he had to confess, was one battle he would enjoy. Strangely, Niall found himself anticipating the challenge with relish.

A cool smile touched his lips. "We shall see who wins the next skirmish, lovely witch."

Chapter
Four

Sabrina returned home from her disastrous interview with the McLaren, feeling rash and resentful. However, she said little about the encounter to her grandfather when she visited his sickbed that evening. She couldn't dash Angus's hopes for a union between their two clans, especially when she herself was uncertain just what had happened.

Niall McLaren hadn't refused to wed her exactly, but neither was he overly eager to have her as his bride. Or lover, for that matter. She much doubted she could satisfy his requirements for physical compatibility. He was a master at passion, while she was an utter novice.

Sabrina winced, recalling Niall's fierce countenance after she'd cooled his sensual assault with a strategically targeted drenching. He would not forgive her easily for that offense. And it was, most assuredly, no way to inspire his desire.

Her impetuous action had been instinctive, spurred on by his infuriating air of supremacy and her own sense of powerlessness. Yet maddeningly, his arrogant assumption that she would fall swooning at his feet had been no mere boast. Her defenses had shattered the moment his lips touched hers.

It dismayed her profoundly to recognize her weakness for the brazen rogue. She'd thought she was strong enough to resist him, but she wasn't proof against his devastating appeal. His boldness, his sensuality, his compelling vitality, were all more than someone of her limited experience could handle.

To make matters worse, Sabrina received a long letter

from her stepfather, questioning the suddenness of her betrothal. He had received an invitation to the wedding, and
was more concerned for her happiness than the fate of her
kinsmen.

In truth, Sabrina wondered if she ought not call off the
match. Torn between wounded pride and a desire to help
her clan, she was no longer certain she could summon the
fortitude to carry out her grandfather's wishes.

She had thought Niall could be no worse a husband than
her other suitors, but at least *they* wanted to wed her, for
her dowry if nothing else. And as the McLaren's bride, she
would have to endure the indignity of knowing he might be
bedding any wench in the country.

To her dismay, she had dreamed of him that first night—
of Niall kissing her, his warm lips touching, teasing, tasting
hers, driving her slightly mad with yearning—and awoke
feeling hot and vexed and restless. Now she resigned herself
to a long wait before hearing from him again, believing it
might be several days, so it came as an unpleasant surprise
when she saw him that very afternoon.

When she rode into the yard after touring the estate with
Liam, a stable lad mentioned that the McLaren had arrived
at Banesk and had asked for her. Upon learning that he was
last seen disappearing into the barn, Sabrina made her way
there, with Rab trotting at her heels. The stone outbuildings
of the estate clustered behind the manor house in haphaz-
ard fashion. In the distance beyond lay a verdant meadow
dotted by gorse and broom, where shaggy cattle grazed.

As she entered the low-roofed barn, Rab pricked his ears
forward, but it was a moment before Sabrina caught the
slight rustling noise that had attracted the dog's notice.

At first glance the barn appeared to be empty, but as she
moved deeper into the dimly lit interior, she heard the sound
of feminine laughter, followed by an unmistakable masculine murmur. Instantly recognizing the enchanting timbre of
that voice, Sabrina came to an abrupt halt.

At the far end of the aisle, Niall lay sprawled elegantly on his back in the straw, his hands behind his head, while a voluptuous, ginger-haired woman lay laughing beside him.

Sabrina froze as she realized she had come upon her betrothed engaged in another liaison—this time with a dairymaid in her grandfather's employ.

"Indeed, I shall miss you, sweeting," Niall asserted seriously.

The woman laughed again. "Fah, do ye take me for a gomeril? You havena looked at me in years."

"And yet I carry your memory close to my heart, Betsy-love."

She struck his shoulder a playful blow. "Begone with ye, now, ye silver-tongued de'il. I must get back to work."

He pressed a hand to his chest as he turned his head to gaze at her. "How you wound me, to dismiss me so heartlessly. And to desert me for such a man . . ."

"Hah! Did ye think I would pine after ye? Ye're no' the only fish in the sea, ma fine fellow."

His soft laughter was a husky caress. "I am happy for you, in truth, sweeting. Think you Dughall would object if I were to kiss the bride?"

"I ken he would . . . but I wouldna."

Niall tossed away the straw he'd been chewing on and rolled toward her. Slipping one arm around her shoulder, he brushed back a flaming curl from her flushed face and gazed deeply into her eyes.

"For old lang syne," he murmured before bending his head tenderly.

Sabrina felt her heart wrench. She wanted to leave quietly, but just then Rab whined in confusion, calling attention to her presence.

Abruptly Niall lifted his head and looked directly at her.

Seeing his jaw clench, Sabrina took a stumbling step backward. It should not have surprised her so to discover him kissing yet another of his paramours. She'd known from the first he was a rake of the first order. But unreasonably she felt betrayed. For him to conduct his amorous flirtations under her very nose, in her grandfather's own home, where anyone could stumble across him, including herself, where her kinsmen could witness her humiliation—

Hurt coursed through Sabrina, yet anger kept her voice from trembling as she remarked coolly, "I understood you desired to speak to me, my lord."

Betsy jumped and abruptly scrambled away from the laird, staring in dismay at Sabrina.

"I shall await you outside, sir," Sabrina added with a supreme effort at calm. "Perhaps you might deign to join me when you are quite finished."

Rigidly she forced herself to turn and walk away. Her ire sustained her as she crossed the cobblestone yard, yet she was trembling when she came to a halt by a towering rowan tree.

She was scarcely aware that Rab had followed, even when he pressed his cold nose into her palm, offering silent comfort. A sheen of tears blurred her vision as she stared blindly at the emerald countryside spread before her.

Niall's dalliance this time wounded her more than she would have thought possible. She hadn't expected this heaviness in her chest, this hurt that seemed suspiciously like heartache. Faith, she shouldn't be so distressed by his public display of indifference. She'd been rejected before and survived, by a man who had won her heart with his honor and gentleness. Niall McLaren had little honor where women were concerned, and she most *certainly* did not love him.

Sabrina clenched her jaw, telling herself she would not cry. She would not dwell on the fiercely tender look on the McLaren's face when he'd kissed that . . . that dairy wench, or the intimacy they'd shared. She refused to yearn after a man who cared so little for her.

Several moments passed before Niall emerged from the barn to join her, which fortuitously gave Sabrina time to compose herself. She favored him with a disdainful glance. He wore his hair carelessly tied back in a queue, and a thigh-length leather waistcoat covered his full-sleeved linen shirt and tartan trews.

The air between them trembled with raw tension as their gazes clashed. He would never know, she vowed, what it cost her to maintain a semblance of dignity.

"I regret you witnessed that incident," Niall offered mildly.

The lacerated emotions inside Sabrina curled and twisted, yet she masked them with a wry smile. "Pray don't play me for a fool, sir, by pretending you have any regard for my sensibilities. I imagine your only regret is that I interrupted your pleasure at an inopportune moment."

Niall frowned. Despite appearances, he had not been engaged in a seduction or even a heated flirtation. His embrace of Betsy was all perfectly innocent—a kiss of friendship and celebration, nothing more.

He'd known the dairymaid forever. A widow some half dozen years his senior, Betsy had lost her husband to a rising against the English when Niall was a mere lad still wet behind the ears. To his delight and gratification, she'd assumed his carnal education, teaching him about passion and how to please a woman. Now she was to wed a distant cousin, a good man who would ease her burdens and support her ailing mother. Niall would always remember Betsy with particular fondness. He'd sought her out, merely to while away the time awaiting Sabrina Duncan's return—

But he would not make excuses for his conduct.

He raised a slashing eyebrow. "What is this, mouse? A retreat into moral outrage?"

His mockery cut deep, yet she refused to let him goad her. "Morality has nothing to do with it."

Niall surveyed her levelly. "Then pray explain your disapproval. I seem to recall your claiming to desire only a marriage of convenience. That you would not object to my diversions. This is how you display your tolerance, mistress, acting the wronged innocent at the first occasion?

As memory serves, I warned you I would not be faithful to any marriage vows—and we have yet even to be formally betrothed."

Sabrina bit her lip hard, knowing she had little right to complain. Niall had been entirely honest with her from the first. He wanted to be free to seek his pleasures outside the marriage bed—and desired a meek wife who was too spineless to interfere with his licentiousness. Well, she was not feeling particularly meek at the moment!

"Indeed you did. Yet it is not your dalliance that I object to. It is the public manner of it. In a stable . . . in my grandfather's own home, no less. Your taste is execrable."

Their gazes collided and held. Her scorn relieved Niall to a degree. He much preferred her anger to the stricken, wounded look he'd surprised from her moments ago when she'd discovered him embracing the dairymaid.

Inexplicably wanting to soothe the distress he had caused her, he adopted a conciliatory tone. "My meeting with the lass was purely by chance, Mistress Duncan. In truth, I came here to discuss with you the marriage arrangements we failed to settle yesterday. I did not seek Betsy out with any intent to insult you—"

"Spare me your explanations. It matters not to me." Sabrina took a deep breath. Enough was enough; she would no longer play his games. It was not in Niall McLaren's nature to be constant, but she was not prepared to suffer his infidelities for the rest of her days. If he wanted out of the betrothal, she would gladly release him.

"I have given our union a great deal of thought," she said resolutely, "and I have come to agree with your view."

"How so?"

"You were entirely correct when you said we would not suit."

Niall raised an eyebrow, waiting.

"Your sentiments are perfectly clear. You have no desire to wed me." She lifted her chin with evident pride. "Well, you may rest easy, my lord. You needn't fear I will force your hand. There will be no marriage between us."

"No?" He looked skeptical. "Yesterday you were set on going forward with the betrothal."

"Yesterday my wits were addled, obviously. Today I am taking myself out of consideration for the position." She smiled mockingly. "Do not look so dismayed, my lord. There are countless other women who are better qualified to be your bride. And doubtless there are dozens who would be delighted to wed you . . . who are captivated by your charm, your wit, your legendary lovemaking skills . . . But those attributes hold little appeal for me."

Niall frowned thoughtfully at her pretense of indifference. "Are you certain, mistress, you are not speaking out of jealousy?"

Jealousy! Sabrina's eyes flashed. "I wish you would disabuse yourself of the notion that I am enamored of you! My only concern is for my clan."

Niall watched the angry color flush her cheeks and was torn between remorse and admiration. He should not have taunted her so, yet Sabrina Duncan enraged was fascinating, the picture of defiant pride.

She lifted her chin regally. "I'm certain you are an excellent laird, but I would go daft if I had to endure wedlock with you—" Realizing she was nearly ranting, Sabrina forced herself to take a calming breath. "You are not what I seek in a husband. I would as lief marry a chimney sweep— or a Buchanan. Indeed, perhaps I should consider such a course. Allying myself with the Buchanans would solve the dilemma my grandfather finds himself in."

Niall's brows shot together. "You cannot be serious. The bloody Buchanans are murdering devils."

Seeing his sudden scowl, Sabrina smiled coolly. "Perhaps so. But whatever path I choose, it is no longer any concern of yours."

"In point of fact, it *is* my concern, mistress. Our clans are still allied, even if not by marriage. The future of Clan Duncan is vital to me, particularly since the issue of succession is not yet settled."

"Ah, yes, the succession . . ." She wanted to curse. It always came back to that. "Faith, I should have been a man," Sabrina muttered under her breath.

Niall studied her for a moment, the tautness easing from the set of his jaw, while a faint light of humor entered his eyes. "And what would you do if you were a man, mistress?"

"I would solve this predicament without being weighted by the chains of my gender." She squared her shoulders as she faced him fully. "Regardless of our rift, my grandfather is depending upon me to ensure the protection of our clan. And I don't intend to let him down, even if I have to lead Clan Duncan myself."

"Lead your clan? Is that not overly ambitious?"

"Women are capable of assuming the reins of lairdship," she replied stiffly.

"Some are, aye, in some circumstances. But you have no experience, and Buchanan is a crafty bastard who understands only force."

Sabrina bit her tongue to repress a retort, knowing she was speaking recklessly, out of sheer frustration. If Liam Duncan didn't consider himself worthy to lead their clan, she certainly wasn't. "Even so, you need no longer worry about it."

Niall hesitated. "I would be willing to search for another potential suitor for you."

His condescension rankled. "I can find my own husband, thank you," Sabrina snapped, losing her hard-won calm. "Pray believe me when I say you may consider yourself free of any obligation to me or my clan. Rab, come!"

She spun on her heel to return to the house, but the mastiff didn't obey. He merely looked at her and whimpered, his brown eyes confused and questioning.

Feeling betrayed by her dog as well as the libertine who'd

stolen his affections, Sabrina flung over her shoulder, "Very well, you may *both* go to the devil for all I care!"

Niall felt himself frowning as he watched her incensed retreat, experiencing a curious regret. Once again the mouse had suddenly transformed into a tiger—a change that was remarkably appealing to his male nature. She was proud and stubborn and spirited as any Highland lass. He had not expected to be so intrigued by her, or to feel such a primal attraction.

Nor had he expected to win so easily. Without quite meaning to, he had managed to induce Sabrina Duncan to reconsider marriage to him. She was hurt and humiliated enough to free him from the betrothal.

So why then did he feel as if he had won a hollow victory . . . and lost something of inestimable value in the winning?

Angus took the news badly. That evening when Sabrina told him she had called off the betrothal, the aging Laird Duncan had a spasm that threatened to finish him for good.

In a wheezing breath, he demanded a whisky, and when at last he caught his breath, launched into a lengthy recital of all the reasons Sabrina could not withdraw now, chief of which was the threat the Buchanans posed with Clan Duncan virtually leaderless. Moreover, the wedding invitations had already been issued, and it was too late to recall them.

As for Niall McLaren's debauchery, Angus excused it as youthful excess.

"Aye, he's a lusty rake in truth, but 'tis certain he's sowing his wild oats before settling down."

"He must be anticipating a bountiful crop then," Sabrina retorted with a bitterness she could not hide.

"I'll have a talk with the lad—"

"No!" The incident this afternoon had been humiliating enough. It would be even more so, having her grandfather plead with Niall to take her back. "He doesn't wish to wed me, I tell you, any more than I wish to wed him."

She would not let Angus change her mind, Sabrina vowed. By the time her grandfather had renewed his pleas, however, she was suffering fresh doubts. Had she acted too impulsively, breaking off the betrothal? She knew full well that she had responded from wounded pride. She had put personal sentiment before the welfare of her clan, forsaking them in their time of dire need. She had let them down, when she'd wanted very much to prove herself worthy of her clan name.

When at last she emerged from her grandfather's bedchamber, Sabrina was despondent and near tears, yet her jaw remained clenched. Her emotions were too raw to think clearly just now, but she had to contrive some other way to protect Clan Duncan than marriage to the McLaren.

By the time supper was served below in the dining hall, anger and hurt had given way to a grim determination to find an answer to her dilemma. After the meal of barley bannocks and hotch-potch—a thick, delicious mutton and vegetable soup—Sabrina drew her cousin aside in order to question him.

"Geordie, what do you know of the Buchanans?"

"They're our blood enemies," he said simply.

"Yes . . . but why?"

His brow furrowed. "Why? Aweel, the feud began lang syne. The Buchanans stole a bride from Clan Duncan, but she couldna bear the mon and put a dirk in his ribs when he tried to claim her. A blow from his fist killed her before he expired. The Duncans and Buchanans have been foes ever since."

"What can you tell me about their present laird? Owen, I believe is his name."

"Owen is a canny de'il, for cert."

"I understand he is a widower?"

"Aye."

"And his sons? He has four sons, does he not?"

"Aye, all wed, but for the youngest. A lad of some five-

and-twenty years." Geordie frowned at her. "Why, what are ye thinking, mistress?"

Sabrina gave a casual shrug. She didn't dare tell him the idea that was forming in her head. "I just wondered how it all began. Has my grandfather ever considered trying to end the feud? Has he ever discussed the issue with Owen Buchanan, perhaps?"

Geordie's brow furrowed more deeply. "Last year . . . I thought there might be a truce. Owen wanted peace—but that was before the McLaren was murdered in a cowardly attack."

"Niall's father? Was Owen Buchanan responsible?"

" 'Twas his kin that did the foul deed, but it doesna matter. Owen is laird, and as such is answerable for the acts of his clan."

That conversation gave her a great deal to think about. Thus when Geordie proposed a game of chess, Sabrina pleaded fatigue and retired to her bedchamber.

Yet as she began the tedious process of undressing for bed, removing her stomacher and bodice and overskirt, her thoughts involuntarily shifted from the fate of her clan to Niall McLaren and her brief, fruitless betrothal to him.

What a daft gomeril she'd been! For a few fleeting moments, she'd let herself foolishly hope that Niall might come to accept her as his wife. That their political union might blossom into something deeper, a true marriage. Faith, she'd made a narrow escape. She didn't *want* him as husband and lover—any more than he wanted her. She wasn't willing to endure the humiliation and heartache which wedding that profligate rogue would entail.

Catching a glimpse of herself in the pier-glass that hung on one wall, Sabrina faltered. She had stripped off her petticoat and stockings and stood clad only in her shift, but she scarcely recognized the fierce-eyed lass staring back at her. At the moment she looked every inch a Highlander, prepared to do battle with anyone who threatened her or her kin.

Hesitantly she drew down the neckline of her shift. The skin of her bosom was red and ribbed where the stiffened bodice had pressed, but as she let her shift fall to the floor and studied herself critically, she had to admit that her physical attributes were not unattractive. Her breasts were pale and high, the rosy jutting nipples hard and tight. The curves of her waist and hips were modest, with a dark bush of curling hair between her slender thighs . . .

Too modest. Too slender. Her charms were nothing compared to the voluptuous females Niall McLaren favored.

Sabrina frowned at her image. How could she ever have been naive enough to think a man like that would be satisfied to wed her? He would want someone beautiful and desirable and wickedly sophisticated, like he himself was. Or a wench who was lushly endowed like that dairymaid this afternoon . . .

Muttering an oath, Sabrina stepped out of her shift and roughly drew on her nightdress. She was glad she would not be wedding Niall McLaren. She was certain she despised that libertine.

Shivering in the chill then, she snuffed the candle and slipped beneath the bedcovers, burying her face in the pillow. She could not allow herself to seek slumber, though.

She had some critical decisions to make.

She could not abandon her clan, certainly. During her tour of Banesk with Liam this afternoon, she'd been appalled by the wretched conditions many of her kinsmen endured. The widows and fatherless children who'd lost their menfolk to feuds and risings lived in crofter's huts no better than hovels . . . damp, smoke-filled, with peat roofs that leaked at a hint of rain. She could not leave them to the mercy of the bloody Buchanans.

Niall was right on one score, though. She could not easily lead her kinsmen. It wasn't that a woman was incapable of being clan chief; some were. But she herself was far too inexperienced. Even if her kinsmen could be persuaded to follow her, it would take years for her to gain even a tenth of the skill a warrior needed in battle. And by then the bloody Buchanans would have destroyed her clan.

She couldn't offer to wed one of the Buchanans, either, as she'd threatened this afternoon. Her grandfather would never stand for it. Nor would Niall, she suspected, not with his fierce hatred of their clan.

But surely the barbarous Buchanans could be reasoned with.

Shifting restlessly, Sabrina rolled onto her back and stared at the darkened canopy above her bed. On the morrow she would seek an interview with the laird, Owen Buchanan, and negotiate with him if possible.

If she could contrive to ensure the safety of her clan, then she might be able to forget the arrogant, indiscriminating Niall McLaren and the hurt he had caused her with his humiliating philandering.

Chapter
Five

Her first task the following morning was to overcome Geordie's objections. Even when Sabrina explained her intentions, the brawny Highlander was reluctant to escort her into the heart of Buchanan territory so that she might negotiate with their laird.

"Are ye daft, mistress? The Buchanan is our blood foe!"

"I know. But he does not have to remain so, does he? Feuds can be ended. You told me yourself you hoped there might be a truce last year, but that it fell through when the McLaren was killed."

"Aye," the Highlander muttered. "But Angus would have ma head if I allowed ye to go."

"You will not wish to tell him then."

"But I canna go against the laird's command!"

"Geordie," Sabrina said patiently, "I dare not seek Grandfather's counsel first, or he would prevent me from going. And this is too important to disregard. Don't you see, I *must* do this?"

In his frustration, Geordie's face turned as red as his hair. "'Tis too dangerous."

"Not if you accompany me. And it is worth the risk. The Buchanan would not harm a woman, would he? Please, Geordie," Sabrina pleaded when she saw him hesitate. "Will you not help me?" She sighed at his stubborn refusal. "Very well, I will go on my own if I must."

Geordie gave in. "Aweel, I dinna like this one bit," he complained, "but 'tis better I go w' ye."

Sabrina understood his misgivings. Yet their clans had been warring for a hundred years, and no one had yet managed to arrange a peace with the Buchanans, perhaps because no one had truly made the effort. She was determined to try at least, to see if she could strike a bargain with their laird.

With Rab and Geordie as escorts, she rode south and west for a time, through wild, rough country that boasted verdant glens and rocky peaks. The sunshine of the previous day had vanished, and a chill gray mist swirled around them, muffling the ring of their horse's hooves.

Geordie sat astride his mount cautiously, with his fist clutching the hilt of his claymore, his expression so grim that Sabrina found herself jumping at imagined shadows. It comforted her to remember the dirk she'd tucked inside the waistband of her skirt.

Owen Buchanan was reportedly a vicious ogre, but she'd attributed much of his brutal repute to exaggeration. Now she wondered if perhaps she hadn't paid enough heed to the possible danger of her mission.

She had just emerged single file behind Geordie from a stand of pines when a rough voice shouted, "Hold there!"

Sabrina froze as a band of horsemen garbed in tartan plaids and trews suddenly swarmed from the forest to surround them, brandishing broadswords and claymores. Her two protectors reacted more bravely. Geordie yanked his heavy blade from its scabbard, prepared to battle her attackers to the death, while Rab bared his teeth, a fierce growl reverberating from his throat, the hair on his back standing on end.

"We come in peace!" Sabrina managed to utter past the dryness of her throat.

A swarthy, black-bearded Highlander broke from the crowd and urged his mount closer. "Peace, is it? And who might ye be, lass?"

"I am Sabrina Duncan, granddaughter of Angus, laird of Clan Duncan."

His dark eyes narrowed. "Aye, I ken ye have the look of a Duncan about ye. I'd heard ye'd come to succor Angus's last days."

Sabrina studied him in turn, concluding that he was old enough to be her father. From the description Geordie had given her, she suspected she might be confronting the Buchanan himself. "I have heard much about you as well, sir. Have I the honor of addressing Owen Buchanan?"

"Ye might at that."

She forced a smile. "And do you always greet strangers with such a threatening display of force?"

"If they be Duncans, I do."

"Faith, and I had heard so much about the famed hospitality of the Highlands. Surely the tales could not be so wrong. I can scarcely credit such a reception, particularly since I came here with the express intent of speaking with you." Sabrina glanced pointedly at the menacing broadsword one of his cohorts held aloft. "I assure you, sir," she added lightly, "if you put aside your weapons, I shall not harm you."

The laird's eyes widened fractionally, but then he gave a rough chuckle of appreciation and waved to his clansmen to lower their blades. Keeping a wary eye on Geordie, Owen made her a gallant bow from horseback. "Forgive ma men, mistress. 'Tis devoted to me, they are."

"I am certain it is well deserved. I've heard countless tales of your exploits."

She heard Geordie make a sound deep in his throat like a snort, but ignored it. "If we might have a moment in private, sir, I have a proposal to put forth for your consideration."

The laird's gaze narrowed in suspicion, but he must have deemed her harmless, for he nodded. When Sabrina made to dismount, Owen swung down from his horse and assisted her, giving her hope that she was not dealing with an unreasonable man.

"Shall we walk?" she asked with a winning smile. When she turned to stroll along the path, away from the others, Owen Buchanan had little choice but to accompany her. She was grateful, though, when Rab trailed cautiously at her heels.

"Now what is this business you wish to speak to me about?" Owen demanded as if growing impatient.

"The relationship of our two clans," Sabrina answered quietly. "The difficulties have preyed heavily on my mind."

"Ye are but a lass. What do ye ken of clan affairs?"

"Merely what I have been told. But it seems foolish to continue fighting among ourselves. I had hoped"—she took a deep breath—"there might be a way to put an end to generations of bloodshed."

Sabrina was not surprised when the Buchanan's gaze narrowed in distrust. "Did Angus send ye to treat w' me?"

"No. In truth, he has no idea I am here."

" 'Twas my understanding you were to wed the McLaren."

"True. But I've come to realize that he . . ." She hesitated as if choosing a delicate explanation. "Niall McLaren will not make the most ideal husband."

"Too randy for yer taste, is he?" Owen chuckled. "Aye, I can see how a proud lass wouldna favor her mon tupping the maids."

A flush rose to her cheeks. "I would prefer not to share my marriage bed with half the female population of Scotland, yes. In any case, the sole purpose of our union was to ally our clans against the Buchanans. But if I could be assured we were in no danger of attack from your clan . . . if we could count you as an ally . . . it would spare me the necessity of marrying the McLaren."

Owen raised a brawny hand to stroke his beard. "Whyever should I wish to befriend Clan Duncan? We've been foes for as long as memory serves."

"Because it will be far more profitable for you." Sabrina paused and turned to face the laird directly, her expression earnest. "Perhaps you have heard that I am an heiress? I would be willing to pay handsomely to ensure the safety of my clan. A feu-duty, if you will. In exchange for your word to end the war between us."

"Ye're offering to pay for peace?"

"Precisely. With payments to be made quarterly or yearly, as you choose." In feudal times, it was in fact common for weaker clans to pay a protection fee to more powerful ones. In reviewing the account books of clan activities from years past, Sabrina had seen evidence of such expenses.

"Hmmm. What sum did ye have in mind, mistress?"

She frowned, as if giving the question careful consideration. Yet having learned a trick or two from her stepfather, who was as shrewd a businessman as they come, she offered much less than she was actually willing to pay. "I thought fifty head of cattle quarterly would be adequate compensation."

She was startled when Owen suddenly reached out to grasp her elbow. The fine hairs on her nape stood up as he brought his face close to hers, his expression menacing.

"If ye're such an heiress, mistress, it stands to reason yer kin would be willing to pay for yer freedom. I trow ye'd fetch a bonny ransom."

Sabrina swallowed hard, realizing he was threatening to take her hostage, and reached for her dirk.

"Or mayhap I might wed you meself," Owen mused darkly, "since ma own wife is lang gone. Or give ye to one of my sons."

She could feel her heart pounding against her breast as his grip tightened painfully. It was not unheard of for an enterprising laird to capture a bride and forge a clan alliance by force.

"If I wished to wed," she managed to say with a serenity she was far from feeling, "I would have offered myself as part of the bargain. But I much prefer the single state."

"Do ye now? And what's to stop me from taking ye prisoner and holding ye to ransom?"

"You could try, certainly . . . if you wished to escalate the feud between our clans. But my capture might prove difficult. I will not go with you willingly. And I am hardly without protection. My dog would come to my rescue, you see."

She glanced down at Rab, who had bared his teeth again and was growling fiercely. "He will aim for the throat, sir, and you will be dead before your men can react."

The laird eyed the dog narrowly.

"You might also," she advised sweetly, "wish to consider the dirk I hold pressed against your ribs." She increased the pressure slightly on the blade she had slipped beneath his armpit. "Even if I could not strike a mortal blow, you might find it difficult to explain how a mere lass wounded such a brave Highland warrior with such ease."

Owen Buchanan stared at her a long moment, so intently Sabrina could see a vein throb in his temple.

Then abruptly his dark eyes lit with laughter. When he threw back his dark head to give a loud guffaw of delight, his men stared to see what had amused their laird so.

"Angus would be proud of you, lass," Owen declared as he clapped her on the back as he would a man, a buffet which nearly sent her sprawling.

Instantly Rab lunged forward, and it was all Sabrina could do to stop him from assaulting the laird. With effort she pulled the dog away and spoke to him soothingly, then called out reassuringly to Geordie, who had uttered an oath and raised his claymore, despite the peril.

Owen was still chuckling. "Aye, ye're kin to Angus Duncan, 'tis plain to see. Put away yer dirk, Mistress Duncan. If we're to ally ourselves with you, it calls for a dram. Ye're a gallant lass, to come here, but I warn ye, I'll no' take so wee a sum as ye proposed. A hundred head of cattle quarterly, 'tis my price, and not a hair less."

Sabrina let out a slow breath of relief. She would have willingly paid double that price to secure her clan's safety.

"You drive a hard bargain, my lord," she replied meekly.

"Ye did *what*?" her grandfather exclaimed when she confessed her actions that same afternoon.

"I struck a bargain with Owen Buchanan," Sabrina repeated placatingly.

"The de'il, you say! Over my dead body!" Angus threw off the covers and struggled to rise from his sickbed, his nightshirt hiking up over bare legs still brawny with muscle.

"Grandfather, you mustn't get up!"

"Dinna tell me what to do, girl! Ye've ruined all my plans."

"Perhaps so, but this might prove a better solution—"

"Hah! 'Tis little ye know, ye interfering gomeril."

She winced to hear herself termed a fool, but she couldn't let it bother her just now. Angus's complexion had turned alarmingly scarlet, Sabrina noted with dismay. Calling for his manservant to come quickly, she grasped her grandfather's shoulders in an attempt to restrain him. It required all her strength to press him back upon the pillows.

"I *had* to act, Grandfather, don't you see? Since I ended any possibility of a betrothal to the McLaren, I felt obliged to see if I could protect our clan some other way."

"Well, giving away our herds is not the way of it!"

"Why not?" She met his fierce gaze with a gentle query in her own. "You were willing to sacrifice *me* in the name of clan security, but you hold your cattle in higher esteem?"

Angus's answer was a muffled curse as he wheezed into his fist. "I dinna see it as a sacrifice. Ye were to wed the McLaren. 'Tis all I asked of you."

"You needn't worry that my agreement with Owen Buchanan will impoverish you. I intend to pay every penny out of my dowry." When Angus refused to respond, she added quietly, "I should think you would be glad to end the feud."

The fight seemed to go out of him, and he shut his eyes. "We'll ne'er see the end if it, lass. The bloody Buchanans canna be trusted, ye'll ken." Weakly, Angus lay back on the pillows, refusing even to look at his granddaughter.

"Grandfather, are you all right?" she asked, troubled.

"Nay . . . I'm a dying man, and ye've plunged a dirk through ma heart. 'Tis a sad trial, to be betrayed by one's own kin."

Sabrina bit her lip hard, distressed that he should have

put such a dark construction on her actions. She had managed to bring sanity and hope to a conflict that had been rife with bloodshed for decades, yet he could not forgive her betrayal.

"Go away, lass," Angus said wearily. "Go away and let me die in peace."

Sabrina was toying listlessly with her oat porridge the following morning, when Niall McLaren was shown into the chamber which doubled as a parlor and breakfast room.

He was garbed casually in tartan trews, but a broadsword gleamed from the scabbard at his waist, and his ruggedly beautiful features were as grim as she'd ever seen them.

"What in hellfire is this I hear about you arranging a truce with the bloody Buchanans?" he demanded without ceremony.

Abruptly Sabrina rose to her feet so she would be less at a disadvantage with the towering Highlander. Facing Niall McLaren again, she experienced a sharp resurgence of the hurt she'd felt at their last encounter.

"And a good morn to you, as well, my lord," she remarked, infusing her tone with wry mockery.

"Blast it, answer me! What mischief have you been up to?"

Sabrina winced at the scathing tone so much like her grandfather's. She hadn't expected praise for helping her clan's cause, but neither had she envisioned such universal condemnation.

"I would hardly call it mischief to try and forge a peace between warring factions," she retorted stiffly.

A muscle flexed in his jaw, and she could see the effort he was making at control. "You're dealing with a devil you know nothing about, meddling in affairs beyond your ken."

"I know enough to seize an opportunity when I see it. No one else here has tried to make peace among the clans. I merely offered the Buchanan a simple business proposition."

"The Highlands are a far cry from your stepfather's mercantile trade in Edinburgh. If you think otherwise, mayhap you should hie yourself back there soonest. You're daft if you expect a Buchanan to honor his word."

"Perhaps, but *you're* daft if you expect me to turn tail and run back to Edinburgh when my clan needs me."

Niall drew a deep breath. " 'Tis naive to think you can change the patterns of a lifetime, mistress."

"I only wished to help," she replied stubbornly.

The harshness of his handsome features seemed to relent a degree. "A generous, unselfish gesture—but misguided. Might is the only deterrence the Buchanans understand."

"I think you're mistaken. Owen Buchanan seemed to understand the value of coin well enough when I offered it to him."

"Owen would as soon slit a Duncan's throat as look at one."

Just then Rab rose from the floor and padded over to the man, pressing his cold nose into Niall's hand, whining softly as he begged for a caress.

Traitor, Sabrina thought resentfully as the Highlander absently stroked the dog's huge head. She pressed her lips together, frowning at the animal. "I own myself astonished at his fondness for you. Rab generally is more discriminating in his choice of allies."

A hard smile touched Niall's lips. "Pray don't change the subject. We were discussing your foolish interference."

Abruptly her chin rose. She'd lost their last battle of wills. She'd not lose this one. "*You* were discussing my interference, sir. I was attempting to explain why I felt compelled to intervene. As for slitting my throat, that was far from the case. The Buchanan even spoke of the advantages of my becoming his bride."

Niall went rigid. "The bloody bastard's old enough to be your father."

"But he has need of a wife," Sabrina replied sweetly, refusing to set his mind at ease. "I understand he lost his some years past. And he has a son of marriageable age. I confess I considered marrying into their clan."

"The devil you will!"

"Why not? What do *you* care whom I marry?"

What, indeed? Niall asked himself silently. He couldn't bear the thought of her marrying a Buchanan, yet his opposition stemmed from more than just his blind hatred of the clan that had caused him so much grief. More, even, than the obligation he felt toward Sabrina after managing to escape a forced marriage to her.

"You've made it abundantly clear that you have no desire to wed me," Sabrina continued through gritted teeth. "Thus you have no right to object if I decide to look for another husband, especially if it would benefit my clan."

"I told you I would find you another suitor."

"I don't *want* any suitor of your choosing!"

"Well, you'll have to settle for someone other than the Buchanan butchers. A Sassenach would be better."

His savage tone told her clearly that he shared the Scots' disdain for Englishmen. Sabrina raised herself to her full height, fire flashing in her dark eyes. "I'll not allow you to dictate to me."

"And I'll not let you make so daft a misstep."

"You can't stop me!"

Closing the distance between them, Niall reached for her, driven by the fierce urge to shake her. His long fingers closed over her delicate shoulders in a grip that was almost painful. "I can, mistress. And I assure you, I will."

His uncharacteristic violence startled Sabrina. She froze, her heart racing. His angry face was so close she could feel his breath against her lips. She flushed at the erotic image that suddenly invaded her mind: of Niall kissing her hotly, of Niall holding her tightly and stroking her skin, her breast . . .

Their eyes locked in defiance—a long, sensually charged spell, reverberating with tension and attraction.

"Kindly unhand me, sir," she said, seething with fury and

something more disturbingly elemental. She refused to call it desire. She did not want this man, or his kisses.

Rather than releasing her, though, his fingers only tightened on her soft flesh. "When I'm done with you."

"I never expected so boorish an assault from a gentleman noted for his finesse," she observed tauntingly.

Niall cursed, vividly aware of the primal urges she kindled in him. He could not remember being so angry with a wench, or so aroused, either. 'Twas daft, the effect this prickly, sharp-tongued lass had on him, how she made him want her. His grip tightened—

They were both startled to realize they were no longer alone. Angus slowly limped into the room, leaning heavily on a cane.

Her cheeks flaming, Sabrina twisted from Niall's embrace and drew away hastily. "Grandfather, you should not be out of bed!"

The elderly laird waved away her concern and addressed Niall. " 'Tis glad I am to see you, lad. There's trouble afoot, and I'm in no fit state to deal w' it."

"I received your summons, Angus," Niall said. "I was on my way to your chambers when I paused to speak to your granddaughter. I gather the trouble concerns the Buchanans?"

"Aye, they stole two hundred prime head of Duncan cattle last eve."

"That's impossible," Sabrina breathed. "We had a bargain."

" 'Tis no' impossible," her grandfather snapped. "The bloody Buchanans are cattle thieves of the worst sort, and canna be trusted to abide by any pact."

She shook her head, finding it difficult to credit that Owen Buchanan had reneged on their agreement so swiftly after giving his word of honor, or that he would pass up the chance for a generous quarterly income. But then . . . her knowledge of clan affairs was limited. And the habits of a lifetime died hard. Had Owen seen her as a gullible fool?

Did feuding with her clan hold more allure than the rewards of peace?

She raised a hand to her brow. "Perhaps . . . his kinsmen never heard of the truce."

Angus gave her a fierce look from beneath bushy white brows. " 'Twas the Buchanan himself who led the raid."

"How do you know?"

"How? Because he was seen, that's how!"

"But . . . *why?*" she asked in bewilderment.

" 'Tis clear enough for a bairn to fathom. With ma illness, Clan Duncan makes easy prey. Owen has the advantage and is pressing it." Angus glared at her accusingly. "This is what comes of yer refusal to wed, lass. Were ye betrothed to the McLaren, Owen would no' dared have struck. And then ye made matters worse by seeking him out."

"I . . . don't understand . . ."

Niall answered that query—grimly. "You showed a fatal weakness by offering to bargain with him."

Perhaps they were right, Sabrina thought with dismay. Perhaps she had drastically misjudged Owen Buchanan. Perhaps her interference *had* compounded the difficulties her clan faced, when she had only been trying to help.

"I . . . I am sorry, Grandfather," she said lamely, even as anger at the Buchanan's betrayal surged through her. She had bargained with the laird in good faith, but he had deceived her, had played her for a fool, seeing her eagerness to bargain as vulnerability.

" 'Tis all right, lass," Angus replied with unexpected forbearance. "Ye could no' have kenned the treachery of the bloody Buchanans. But Niall will handle matters from here out. Will ye not, lad?"

"Aye, I will indeed," he replied darkly.

Angus pressed a hand to his heart. "I fear 'twas too muckle excitement for me. I'd best return to bed."

Still dazed by the grave turn of events, Sabrina stepped forward. "Allow me to assist you, Grandfather."

"Nae, lass. Ye've assisted me enough as is." He waved her away and shuffled from the chamber, leaving a chastened Sabrina to stare after him dispiritedly.

In the resultant silence, she turned to gaze at Niall McLaren. He had not moved, but there was a quiet lethalness about him that was palpable. He no longer resembled the sensual rogue who could charm the very soul from a lass; there was no sign of the practiced cavalier.

Instead, he was every inch the Highland warrior. Dangerous, deadly, full of purpose. A ruthless stranger whose violence was barely leashed.

"What will you do?" she asked quietly.

Niall gave her a long glance. "Deal with the matter, as I promised," he said as he turned to leave.

Sabrina followed him. "What are you planning?" she demanded as he strode through the great hall toward the front entrance.

"To retrieve your grandfather's stolen cattle."

"I want to go with you."

He halted abruptly. "A cattle raid is no place for a green lass."

"But this is my clan's battle, not yours."

A muscle flexed savagely in his jaw as Niall gazed down at her. "You are *wrong*, lass. I've made it my battle. The butcher Buchanans will get what they deserve."

His menacing tone frightened her. "Do you mean to recover our cattle, or to seek revenge?"

"Aye, revenge has a measure to do with it. If I can do them an ill turn, I will, with great pleasure."

Sabrina shook her head apprehensively. She didn't want blood on her conscience. She felt guilty enough as it was, for rekindling the feud.

Imploringly she placed a hand on Niall's sleeve. "Please," she entreated. "I want to make amends. Take me with you."

"You heard your grandfather. You've caused trouble enough."

It stung to be dismissed as a nuisance, although he had

ample justification. But Sabrina refused to concede. If Niall allowed her to accompany him, she might possibly redeem herself by helping recover the lost herd. More crucially, she could try to restrain his vengeance. "Causing trouble was far from my intention."

"You know nothing about lifting cattle," he replied tersely.

"No, but you could teach me."

"If I were daft enough—which I'm not."

"But I want to *help*."

Niall stared down at her with reluctant admiration. She was gazing at him so earnestly that he felt an unexpected tenderness.

His harsh expression softened. Essaying a smile, he reached up to tuck a stray tendril behind Sabrina's ear. " 'Tis too dangerous, lass. You could be hurt. Leave the cattle reiving to more experienced hands."

Chapter
Six

Under cover of misty darkness, Sabrina urged her sturdy Highland pony along the hazardous trail beside Geordie's mount, the swirling fog muffling the animal's hoofbeats.

Niall would be vexed to discover she was acting counter to his wishes. Yet she could not possibly have endured the suspense, waiting tamely at home, fretting while he led her Duncan clansmen on a retaliatory raid against the enemy Buchanans. The tension would have driven her mad. Particularly since she was to blame. She felt responsible for the recent assault on her clan, and desperately wanted to make amends.

Her grandfather at least understood her compunction. When she had applied to Angus, he'd granted her permission to accompany the reivers, so long as she didn't get in anyone's way. In truth, he seemed gratified by her concern. Cattle raiding was a rudiment of every Highlander's education, but more critically, Angus wished her to see how urgently Clan Duncan needed a leader to unite them against the Buchanans.

Niall was right about her participation, Sabrina knew. Her inexperience would likely prove more hindrance than help to her kinsmen. But she would do nothing more than observe.

The talk at supper had been all about the impending raid. Geordie, who lived above the mews at Banesk, was to accompany Liam and several other Duncans to join the McLaren at midnight at the edge of Buchanan land. A dozen men only would carry out the raid, the better to maintain stealth.

With a casualness she didn't feel, Sabrina questioned Geordie about the plan.

"We'll ride against bloody Owen Buchanan himself," her cousin divulged with relish, "and claim our cattle under his very nose."

Geordie's enthusiasm for the task was evident. A moonlit cattle raid was a Highlander's favorite sport, but vengeance against the Buchanan added a prime enticement.

Sabrina couldn't share the pleasure of wreaking havoc upon a rival, even one who had deceived and betrayed her. In truth, the recent turn of events dismayed her. To many Scots clans, a feud was more game than war, but she feared the conflict with the Buchanans would never end till the Highlands ran with blood.

Her apprehension increased as the hour drew near. After supper she busied herself finding the proper attire. Then, dressed as a lad, she went down to the stables in advance to await Geordie's coming.

Now she rode beside him, nerves raw, heart thudding.

The darkness held an uncanny chill. The night was shrouded in veils of gray mist, the midnight sky lit only by a thin sliver of moon. Shivering, Sabrina drew her borrowed Duncan plaid more tightly about her and wished she'd dared bring Rab along. She had left the dejected animal behind, knowing she couldn't control him if events got out of hand.

When they heard the quiet murmur of voices up ahead, Geordie drew his horse to a halt, and Sabrina followed suit.

"Ye'll stay here, out o' sight," Geordie whispered. "Niall willna be glad to see ye."

"Yes, certainly."

He rode on, while Sabrina slipped quietly to the ground. Inching forward, she found a place to observe, taking care to remain hidden by thick-growing bushes of gorse and bracken.

The small band of Highland raiders was armed to the teeth.

In addition to the Duncans, she recognized John McLaren, Niall's second in command, and his cousin Colm. And of course Niall himself. When a shaft of moonlight touched his features, Sabrina felt her heart give a feminine jolt. She suspected she would never grow accustomed to his rugged masculine beauty.

From their muted conversation, she deduced that Colm had already scouted out Buchanan land.

" 'Twill be easy pickings," the Highlander asserted.

"Perhaps too easy," Niall replied. "I find their laxness hard to credit. Their cattle should be better guarded. Owen kens we'll strike back and soon."

"It could be a ruse to trap us," Liam Duncan offered.

"Indeed." Despite his grim tone, Niall grinned, his teeth a white glimmer in so much dark and shadow. "Yet trap or no, we'll show the bloody Buchanans the folly of plundering Duncan herds."

Sabrina shivered at the note of satisfaction in his voice, suspecting that at that moment at least, his love of danger almost rivaled his love of women.

The Highlanders spoke for a few moments more, refining their plans and strategies in case of discovery, and then turned to their horses. Seeing Geordie wave furtively to her, Sabrina waited till they had ridden off before remounting and following at a careful distance. In the swirling mist, she was required to give her full attention to the treacherous terrain. The rocky land dipped and twisted between craggy hills and ink-black forests, but she knew they were headed for the massive stronghold that was Owen Buchanan's lair.

She judged it nearly an hour later when she heard the quiet rasp of steel as the Highlanders drew their broadswords. Halting her mount on a rise, Sabrina glimpsed a shadowed valley below, where herds of shaggy cattle grazed.

Her kinsmen rode silently forward, but she remained where she was, taking refuge behind a copse of junipers, where she could watch the proceedings. She held her breath as the men passed a crofter's hut, her vision straining for any sign of danger among the ghostly cowsheds and haystacks. Appearances were deceptive in the obscuring fog, she knew, yet strangely there was no evidence that the Buchanan herds were guarded.

The raiders spread out and melded with the mist, their dark outlines fading from view. Sabrina felt her heart thudding as she waited in the taut silence.

They must have managed to cull out some two hundred head of cattle, for a short while later she saw a herd of softly lowing beasts moving slowly toward the north, driven by the raiders. They would not return home by the most direct route, Sabrina remembered overhearing. Niall meant to send the others back by a different path while he waited with Liam Duncan to fend off any pursuit.

When they disappeared from view, Sabrina let out a breath of relief. The raid had gone so easily, precisely according to plan.

She was about to turn her mount toward home when a shout of warning came from the distant crofter's hut. A light appeared below, winking like a star, followed by the rapid staccato of hoofbeats from various directions.

Instinctively Sabrina plunged into the bordering black forest to hide, a moment before a dark, menacing figure came flying along the path at a gallop, broadsword drawn.

She caught the wicked gleam of steel, but the rider must have missed seeing her, for he raced on. She recognized Niall more from his silhouette than any distinguishable features, and was debating whether to follow when she froze at the sound of thudding horses' hooves behind him.

An instant later a trio of mounted men burst from the tangled woodland. One carried a torch, which lit the night, while all three brandished weapons.

"After the bloody whoreson!"

"Aye, kill the bastard!"

Without pause they pounded after their quarry in hot pursuit.

Jolted to her senses, Sabrina desperately set her heels in her mount's side and put him to the gallop. Ignoring the dangers of hidden footfalls and low-hung branches, she sped along the rocky path, clutching a fistful of mane and praying.

It was several moments before the path widened enough for her to see what was happening up ahead. In the glow of torchlight, the enemy leader raised a pistol and fired. A shot rang out, and Sabrina gave a cry of alarm. Yet there were no additional reports. She hoped it was because he had spent his bullet and could not take time to reload.

Yet the Buchanans were closing in on their quarry.

To her horror, Niall sharply drew rein and wheeled his horse to face his enemies, planting himself directly in their path.

Broadsword raised, the leader gave a blood-chilling cry and charged. Sabrina heard the scraping clang of steel against steel an instant later. Her heart in her throat, she dragged her mount to a stumbling halt, gasping for breath.

She would forever remember the next moment like a hauntingly bad dream. Niall parried the first attack with ease, but hard on its heels came a second man, the vicious blow by another enraged Buchanan nearly unseating him.

Finding his sword ripped from his hand, Niall flung himself off his horse and dove for the blade. He rolled to his feet in a continuous, fluid motion, his fist clutching the hilt, but the leader gave him no time to recoup. Instead the man charged on horseback, lunging in a deadly assault.

Sabrina gave a cry of fear, an instant before Niall leaped behind the broad trunk of a birch tree, narrowly avoiding the arching downward slice of his enemy's blade.

The silence that followed pulsed with tension, while the combatants regarded one another.

The torch had been flung to the ground but remained lit, so Sabrina could clearly see the Buchanan men in the flame's glow as they dismounted. Apparently roused from their beds, they were bare-chested and barefooted, but had taken time to wrap their plaids around their waists. Half naked, their hair flowing wild, they seemed the epitome of savage warriors . . . warriors stalking their prey.

Their expressions fierce, they slowly moved forward, intent on encircling Niall, predators closing in for the kill . . .

"Niall . . ." Sabrina cried hoarsely, terrified by such uneven odds.

His head came up sharply, and he stared, as if taken aback by her presence.

Spying her along the path, Niall swore. "Sabrina, keep away!"

When he dodged a blow from one of his assailants, she made a choked sound in her throat.

"For God's sake, go!"

Sabrina pressed her hand to her mouth to keep from crying out again and distracting him, but even as she watched, the three men attacked at once.

Niall met their driving offensive with slashing steel, but even a novice could see he could not fight for long against such overwhelming might. She had to do something! He wouldn't thank her for interfering, but she couldn't leave him there to die.

Desperately Sabrina glanced about her. She was armed with a sword Geordie had given her, yet it would be useless except at close quarters, and she had little skill with the weapon, in any case.

Her terrified gaze found Niall again, engaged in a grisly dance with his assailants, his blade ringing against tempered steel. When a Buchanan broadsword cut swiftly through the air, Niall deflected the razor edge and parried with a strong blow of his own. Yet the man on his left lunged with a deft thrust, forcing Niall to stagger backward.

Not daring to think, Sabrina slid to the ground and scooped up a fist-sized boulder. Targeting the nearest Buchanan, she threw it with all her might. To her amazement, her aim was true, hitting the side of his head with a crack. He reeled and pitched sideways, landing hard on his shoulder. Rolling, he came to rest on his back, his vacant eyes staring heavenward.

As one, the two remaining Buchanans turned to eye her with fury. When the tallest took a half step toward her, Niall vented a curse and demanded his attention with a flurry of slashing strokes. The Buchanans resumed the battle, a murderous bloodlust in their eyes.

Desperately Sabrina wrenched her own sword from the saddle scabbard. She had no conscious recollection of charging into the conflict. All she could think about was helping Niall . . . getting close enough to strike the broad, naked back of the man who was hurting him.

She raised her arms for a two-handed blow, yet the Buchanan must have sensed her presence, for he spun around, his powerful arm swinging out in a clean, swift stroke.

She tried to dodge the blade but only managed to deflect the main impact. She felt a savage pain slice through her upper left arm as she stumbled. She heard a scream and knew it came from her own throat as the ground came up to meet her.

A tremendous roaring filled her ears, then a blessed silence as blackness claimed her.

Awareness returned gradually and painfully. Every part of her body throbbed. Her aching head was filled with the sweet-pungent scent of crushed bracken, her ears with Niall McLaren's golden-throated voice, savage in its fury.

He was venting a blistering flood of Gaelic curses she was better off not understanding. Sabrina hoped his rage was directed at the Buchanans and not merely her, but she feared otherwise.

Her vision hazy, she tried to focus in the light of the pitch-pine torch. The dark beauty of his face filled her gaze as he knelt beside her.

"Niall . . . ?" The words came out a muted croak, but he

seemed not to hear. He was too busy condemning her folly of putting herself in danger.

"She refused to leave me, the wee fool. I thought my heart would fail when she charged into the fray."

"Aye," Liam Duncan agreed solemnly. "She could hae been torn apart by that pack o' Highland rogues."

"But she's a brave lass, for all that," she heard Geordie claim in her defense. "She took up the battle with nary a qualm. And t'other day, she scarce flinched when the Buchanan threatened to take her for ransom."

"Owen threatened her?" Niall demanded sharply. "She never said so."

"Mayhap she dinna care to mention it. She's a proud lassie, and she doesna want us to fret o'r her. She's a Duncan through and through."

"Who would believe the lass could possess such spirit and courage?" John McLaren wondered aloud.

"Who indeed?" Niall murmured as if to himself.

Sabrina swallowed convulsively and tried again to whisper his name. He must have heard her then, for he bent closer.

"Can you speak, lass?" he queried, his voice suddenly deep and gentle.

"They didn't . . . kill you . . ."

"No, they didn't kill me—wholly to your credit." His expression had softened, holding a tenderness that made her heart skip a beat. "We sent them fleeing."

She tried to turn her head, searching for their enemies, but she saw no sign of the Buchanans. It seemed she was still in the forest where she had fallen. "They . . . got away?"

"Aye, but not unscathed," Niall replied grimly. "I wounded the one." In the golden glow of torchlight she could see his eyes: brightly blue, furious, beautiful. "Our kinsmen heard the pistol shot and came to our aid. The Buchanans fled when they arrived."

"Aye, the bloody cowards," Liam muttered.

Sabrina caught the look that passed between the men, grim with churning emotions. "Please," she murmured, "there's been enough bloodshed."

Niall laughed darkly. "Not nearly enough. They'll rue this night's work, I promise you."

She could have pointed out that the Buchanans had only been defending their holdings, but she suddenly spied the bloody cut on his right temple. "You're wounded," she said in dismay.

"Don't fash yourself. 'Tis no more than a scratch. I would that I could say the same for you, lass. Where does it hurt?"

"My . . . head . . . my arm." Both throbbed savagely.

His hands moved over her with gentle insistence. "You've a lump on your head and a nasty gash on your arm that's bleeding. It wants tending." Even as he spoke, he withdrew the kerchief from around his neck and fashioned a makeshift bandage around the bloody wound on her upper left arm.

"I'll be all right. . . ."

"Even so, we must get you home—before the Buchanans return with reinforcements."

Sabrina shivered. She did want to go home. She'd seen for herself the reality of a raid, the blood and savagery, and she wanted no more part of it. She wasn't trained to be a warrior.

Seeing her tremble, Niall brushed a loose tendril from her cheek. He couldn't explain the startling emotions he was feeling toward her just now. He wanted to shake her for frightening him so—at the same time he wanted to crush her to him and comfort her till he banished her fear and his own.

Perhaps, though, his fierce urge to protect and shelter her from harm was only natural. Her wounding had resurfaced all the old fury he'd felt at his father's murder, bringing out his most ferocious instincts. Or perhaps he merely needed to assuage his own guilt in some measure. Sabrina had doubtlessly saved his life, when she could easily have been killed. He'd watched in terror as she ran fearlessly to his side, hurtling herself at an armed brute twice her size.

More than guilt, though, more than the need to comfort and protect, he was aware of a fierce thundering in his blood, a primal reaction of male to female.

Yet now was not the time to dwell on his primitive impulses. For all her valor, Sabrina was unaccustomed to physical danger; shock had set in now, and she was shaking.

"I'll carry her home," he said to Liam and Geordie. "You'll see to the cattle?"

"Aye, that we will."

Niall gathered Sabrina in his arms and stood. He'd been wanting a reason to hold her, yet he was unprepared for the sudden shaft of desire that knifed through him at the feel of her softness. He felt his lower body harden painfully, a wild response that was irrational and totally inappropriate.

On the other hand, perhaps that too was natural. His heart was still pumping from the recent sword fight, and although the battle was over, his violence leashed, the blood was still surging thick and hot through his veins.

His lack of control vexed him, however, so that when Sabrina protested that she could walk, he reacted more harshly than he intended.

"Be still," Niall commanded. "You're in no condition even to stand. For once you'll do as you're told."

Inwardly Sabrina bristled at the unfairness of his rebuke, but she hadn't the strength to argue.

As if she weighed no more than a thistle, he lifted her in his arms and set her on his horse, then mounted behind her, settling her back against him. Her bottom nestled snugly between the hard muscles of his spread thighs, and he wrapped his plaid around her, sharing its warmth.

"Hush, now. You need rest."

Sabrina shut her eyes against the ache in her head. She felt so warm and secure in Niall's embrace, so safe and cherished . . . She felt herself being lulled by the sway of the horse . . .

The next thing she knew, Niall was lifting her into his arms, carrying her across the courtyard at Banesk. In the darkness he made his way swiftly toward the manor house.

Once inside, Sabrina roused herself from her daze. "Please . . . don't awaken Grandfather. His heart cannot bear the excitement."

"Hush, sweeting. You show concern for everyone but yourself. Where do you sleep?"

Sabrina caught her breath at the question, which only made her head pound harder. "What does it matter?"

"I'm taking you to bed." She discerned his faint grin in the moonlight that slanted through the high window. "I don't intend to ravish you, if that's your fear. I draw the line at taking advantage of wounded damsels. Your arm needs dressing."

He mounted the back stairs swiftly and quietly.

"This isn't at all proper," Sabrina protested lamely. "You should call for one of the household women."

"There's no need. I can see to it well enough. Which chamber?"

"The last on the right . . . but you cannot . . . you shouldn't be in my bedchamber. You'll cause a scandal."

"If I do, it will scarcely matter. You'll be my wife soon enough to still any gossiping tongues."

Her brows gathering in a frown, Sabrina shook her aching head to chase away the fog. Clearly she had misheard.

She knew she should object in stronger terms to his brazen intimacy and make him set her down, yet she didn't *want* Niall to release her. She wanted the strength of his arms around her, needed their promise of warmth and safety and comfort. Against all common sense, she hungered for his touch and the shameful pleasure he aroused in her.

It was folly, she knew. It was dangerous to let herself yearn for things she couldn't possibly have. Foolish to succumb to the treacherous heat of desire. Laughable to think this man would ever want her.

Silently cursing herself for her weakness, Sabrina closed her eyes with a weary sigh.

In a moment she felt herself being gently lowered to the bed. With quiet efficiency then, Niall lit a candle, flooding the chamber with a golden glow. She heard a soft rustling as he moved around the room, searching for items he would need.

The feather mattress gave way as he sat beside her. When he reached for her left arm, Sabrina winced, more from his nearness than any jar to her injury. Plague take the man, why did her heart lurch so wildly at his merest touch?

She felt a gentle probing along her arm, then a sudden shaft of pain that brought tears to her eyes.

"I regret this must be done, sweeting."

Slicing the fabric of her gown with his dirk, he peeled away the left sleeve to expose a deep gash in her upper arm. The raw flesh glistened darkly with blood in the candlelight.

Sabrina bit her lip hard to stifle a moan.

"I confess," Niall said to distract her, "at knifepoint is not my preferred way of undressing a lady."

Sabrina rallied enough to respond archly, if breathlessly. "I shall not ask you what *is*."

Her brave pretense in the face of pain made his heart wrench, yet he scrutinized her wound in silence, carefully probing. The blade had sliced through the fleshy outer part of her arm. "It could be worse," he said critically, restoring his dirk to his belt. "But it should heal cleanly. I shall return in a moment."

Sabrina sank back among the pillows. The next thing she knew Niall was sitting beside her again, a brandy decanter and glass in his hands.

"I could not find the laudanum. Here, drink," he urged, holding the glass to her lips.

She forced herself to swallow a sip of the burning liquor. "My aunt warned me . . . about gentlemen who press spirits upon unsuspecting females."

He favored her with a slow, brilliant smile. "You are the

least unsuspecting female I know, Mistress Duncan. Even had I any nefarious designs upon your person, there would be little danger in my succeeding."

There would be little chance of him having designs upon her person, either, Sabrina thought sadly.

At her wistful look, Niall paused, gazing down at her pale face. How could he find her so appealing? The circumstances were not the least conducive to dalliance. He could understand his earlier desire for her in the wake of the sword fight. Then, his blood was pumping with anger and battle-lust and that compelling aphrodisiac, danger. But it offered no explanation for his powerful feelings of attraction now.

Devil take it, he was beginning to be positively haunted by visions of bedding this lass. Mayhap the mouse was a witch! He wanted to taste her again. He wanted to join her in her virginal bed, to stretch out beside her and cover her with his body. He wanted to ease between her silken thighs and explore the hidden depths of her sensuality . . .

Damn and hellfire, he had to remember that she was injured—a wound she had sustained while protecting *him*.

His jaw clenching, he forced himself to say calmly, "I shall let you escape with your virtue intact this time. But we must take care of your injury."

He cleansed the blood from around the gash, then glanced at her regretfully. "I fear this will hurt, sweeting, but it's thought to keep wounds from putrefying." As quickly as possible, he poured a stream of the potent liquor on the wound.

Sabrina cried out in pain, her back arching in shock. She would have shot up off the bed had Niall not pressed both hands over her shoulders to hold her down.

"Easy now." Watching as she bravely struggled against the pain, he bent closer. "It's over now, lass," he whispered against her temple. He held her thus for a moment, breathing in the clean, sweet fragrance of her hair.

Panting, Sabrina lay rigidly, waiting for the savage ache

to subside. "My kinsmen," she said through gritted teeth, "may not hold me in great affection, but they would not thank you for murdering me."

He drew back a little, returning a grin that was magical. "Would they not?"

"If I should expire . . . you might have difficulty disposing of my body."

"I shall hide it in the clothes press."

A murmur of ill-advised laughter broke from her lips, which abruptly made her moan.

"Be still, tiger. Save your strength."

"Not a tiger . . ." she muttered breathlessly. "A mouse . . . you said so yourself."

"I was wrong. You gave me a rare turn, taking that blow on my behalf."

"It . . . doesn't signify."

"I think it does," Niall replied a bit grimly. She felt his fingers tenderly brushing her hair back from her damp brow. "I am rather fond of living, and I might not have survived but for your intervention."

"Anyone would have done the same."

"Any Highlander might, but a Lowland lass . . . As Geordie said, you're a brave lass. And there's little a Highlander admires more than bravery. You've made your clan proud."

Sabrina shook her head. She had wanted to make her clan proud of her, but she wasn't a saint. "I was terrified."

Niall placed a finger under her chin. "As well you should be. Which reminds me . . . I've a score to settle with you, mistress." His penetrating gaze pinned her. "What the de'il were you doing out in the hills at night, putting yourself in such danger?"

"I only thought to watch the raid," Sabrina said meekly. "I accompanied Geordie—"

"By God, I'll have his ears."

"He wasn't to blame. Grandfather gave me permission to

go . . . and I would never have interfered had the need not been dire."

Niall scowled. "I particularly told you to remain at home."

"No, you did not. You merely refused to take me with you."

"For good reason. As you witnessed, lifting cattle is dangerous business. It was reckless and foolhardy, accompanying a raid."

"Perhaps so, but"—her chin lifted—"I don't recall having to answer to you, sir."

Niall swore beneath his breath. His fingers tightened on her chin in warning.

"I thought you said you wouldn't take advantage of wounded damsels," Sabrina hastily reminded him.

He seemed to recollect himself. Releasing her, he returned his attention to her arm. "The bleeding seems to have stopped. Let us see if we can make you more comfortable."

She clenched her teeth as he wrapped a fresh bandage around her arm. His hands were long-fingered, strong, elegant, his touch gentle enough to almost take her mind off the pain.

"Now," Niall said softly when he was through. "We should remove your gown so you can attempt to sleep. Where is your nightshift?"

Sabrina exhaled sharply. "My . . . nightshift?"

"I presume that *is* what you sleep in?"

"Yes . . . but I have no intention of showing it to you."

"A certain display of modesty is pleasing in a lass, but less so in a wife. When we are wed, I shall attempt to break you of the habit."

Sabrina abruptly felt the remainder of her breath rush from her lungs. Her eyes flew wide as she stared at Niall. "I fear I misheard you."

He raised an eyebrow. "What did you not understand?"

"You said . . . 'When we are wed.' "

"So I did."

"You cannot be serious."

His eyes held hers, brilliant as sapphires. "Loath as I am to correct a lady, I am not given to jesting on matters of such import. You may consider us betrothed."

She stared at him as if he'd taken leave of his senses.

"Pray contain your delight," Niall said wryly. When she still remained mute, his black brow rose another degree. "I suppose your lack of mental acumen can be attributed to the blow to your head."

Sabrina sat up, bristling despite the aching throb of her wound. "All my faculties are in satisfactory working order, my lord, thank you!"

"Then you might try for a modicum of enthusiasm."

"Why should I be eager to wed you? *You* have no wish to wed *me*."

He shrugged his broad shoulders. "In truth, the prospect terrifies me."

"Then why on earth would you even consider it?"

"A demonstration of nobility, perhaps?"

"This is no laughing matter!"

"No . . . in truth, it is not." Sobering, his blue gaze held hers steadily. "Very well, then. I intend to wed you because of the debt owed to your grandfather. And to Owen Buchanan." At the thought of his mortal enemy, a dark emotion passed like a fuming wave across Niall's eyes. "I pay my debts," he added softly, his resolve showing in the determined line of his jaw. "And Clan Duncan needs my protection. The Buchanans' theft yesterday was proof enough of that."

Sabrina frowned, knowing he was right. With her grandfather dying, her clan was far too vulnerable. They needed to unite under a strong leader. Had Niall been laird, it was unlikely Owen would have dared strike.

"I understand," Sabrina said carefully, "that you feel an obligation to defend my clan, but there must be some way other than marriage."

"Regretfully nothing else comes to mind."

Sabrina raised a hand to her aching temple, trying desperately to think. She felt dizzy, lightheaded, as if she had drunk too much wine. "Perhaps I could lead Clan Duncan as laird. I could take my grandfather's place—"

"Now I perceive the brandy talking."

"You could teach me what I need to know," Sabrina insisted.

His thumb brushed her cheekbone. "You have the mettle, tiger, I don't doubt that. But not the training. It would take years to bring you up to snuff. Meanwhile Buchanan would carve up Clan Duncan for trout bait."

"But . . . I don't wish to marry you. And I'm certain you don't want to be saddled with a wife for the rest of your days."

For a moment, Niall hesitated. If an adequate successor for Angus could be found, then he might escape the clutches of matrimony . . . But no. For too long now he had avoided this particular responsibility.

And perhaps marriage to Sabrina would not be the hardship he'd envisioned. In truth, several of his previous objections toward her had been laid to rest in the past few days. She was not the self-effacing mouse he'd first thought her. Nor was she some feckless lass who ran at the first sign of trouble. It was possible she would even make an adequate mistress for his clan. She exhibited a passion for her beliefs that was unusual in a lass. And she cared for her kinsmen.

He'd seen her compassion firsthand. He could still recall, these many months later, Sabrina's quiet sympathy at her aunt's ball when he'd been stunned by the news of his brother's death and father's fatal wounding—how comforting and calming her manner had been. Even in his shock and grief, he'd felt her solace, felt her lending him strength . . .

Grimly, Niall raised the brandy glass to his lips and drained the remainder, before saying determinedly, "You are bespoken, and that is the end of it."

Sabrina pressed her lips together, realizing he was not

inviting debate on the subject. "That is not the end of it! It is scarcely the beginning. I shall not wed you."

"Yes, you shall." There was a note of authority in his voice, despite the dulcet tone.

Their eyes clashed . . . locked. All at once their exchange was less a dialogue than a battle of wills.

Niall regarded the young woman in the bed with unwilling admiration. She looked almost beautiful with her dark eyes flashing, her chin raised at a defiant angle. For all her meekness, Sabrina Duncan could summon the cool hauteur of a duchess—proud and strong and damned if she would give an inch.

"I can see," Niall observed dryly, "that you are cursed with the Duncan obstinacy. You rival your grandfather in that regard."

Sabrina shook her head. Her objection was not merely obstinacy. If Niall were forced to marry her, he would eventually come to despise her, and she couldn't bear that. "I hardly think you are qualified to judge me, sir."

He ran an assessing eye over her. "You were eager enough to wed me only a few days past."

"I was never *eager*. I merely agreed to comply with my grandfather's wishes."

"His wishes have not changed. And Angus had the right of it on one point. You need a husband to keep you out of mischief."

"Mischief!"

Niall grinned. It occurred to him that he was sparring with her for the sheer pleasure of watching her bristle, of seeing that fire kindle in her expressive eyes. The spitting tigress was a fascinating contrast to her usual demeanor—and to all the other females he'd known, as well. It intrigued and aroused him. *She* aroused him. She managed to conjure in him the desire to best and subdue and possess her.

Realizing he was deliberately trying to provoke her, Sabrina took a deep breath, willing herself to calm. "In light of recent events, I have changed my mind. I've decided I have no desire to marry, ever."

"Ever? Surely a lovely lass such as yourself doesn't wish to be left on the shelf."

"I am entirely resigned to spinsterhood."

"You shouldn't be. It would be a terrible waste."

"It would be a worse waste to wed you. You'd make a wretched husband."

"I agree. Why do you think I've avoided the parson's noose so long?"

"Perhaps because no woman was fool enough to have you."

His eyebrow shot up. The light dancing in his eyes mirrored the amusement playing on his lips. "I'll have you know, mistress, I'm considered quite a matrimonial prize."

"Then some other lady may claim you, with my blessing."

"Your grandfather will be devastated."

Sabrina hesitated, acknowledging that truth.

Niall shook his head ruefully. "Come now, wedding me will not be so onerous. I fancy we can contrive to rub along well enough."

"There is more to marriage than merely 'rubbing along.'"

"Indeed? Pray tell."

"There is compatibility, for one. You were entirely correct. We wouldn't suit in the least. Faith, we cannot even hold a simple discussion without arguing. We would fight all the time."

"Fortunately, I like shrewish women."

"You like *all* women," she retorted, ignoring his jibe.

"Aye, 'tis true." His self-deprecating grin held a contagious charm. "Females are my besetting sin, I admit it."

"You have a vast number of besetting sins!"

"But I also have several sterling qualities, which you are set on overlooking."

Sabrina took a steadying breath, trying to steel herself against that sinfully easy charm and the warm laughter in his eyes. He had stolen a thousand female hearts—but he would not steal hers. "Sterling or no, they cannot outweigh your undesirable traits. I've told you, I have no desire to marry a lecher."

Glancing down at his sleeve, Niall plucked at an imaginary speck of dust. "I suppose you would expect fidelity."

"What a singular notion," Sabrina replied with sarcasm.

The midnight color of his eyes held her captive. "I've told you, lass, I'm not inclined to be faithful. But I can promise you I will endeavor to be discreet."

Her hand moved to her breastbone, as if to slow the painful pulsation of her heart. She didn't want a husband who could offer her only discretion.

"I won't make the ideal husband, but I will provide protection for you and your clan."

Her clan. It always came back to that.

"You haven't even proposed," Sabrina muttered mutinously.

"How remiss of me." Niall sketched a brief bow while still sitting on the edge of the bed. "Mistress Duncan, will you condescend to do me the great honor of bestowing your hand in marriage?"

His tone, edged lightly with irony, stung her. *She* would not be the one condescending, of course. Sabrina quivered with the daunting knowledge that he was far out of her realm.

"I thank you, my lord, for your kind offer," she replied slowly, in a tone of voice appropriate for dealing with the dullest of human minds, "but I must decline."

"I shan't accept no for an answer."

"You cannot *make* me agree!"

The smile he bent on her stole her breath and raised her ire at the same time. He was too bold, too cocksure. "Would you care to put my powers of persuasion to the test?"

When she remained helplessly silent, a knowing gleam lit Niall's beautiful eyes. "I do believe I have stumbled on a valuable discovery in dealing with you, tiger. In future, when I want to bend you to my will, I shall simply seduce you into compliance."

A feeling of panic rose up in Sabrina. "But I don't *wish* to marry you, I tell you!"

"That is quite beside the matter. Now . . . regarding that nightshift. Do you require help undressing?"

"No! I do *not*! And most certainly not by a vaunted libertine."

"Careful, my pet. You are in supreme danger of being kissed."

Her heart skipped a beat. "You wouldn't dare."

His eyebrow rose. "You do have the most annoying habit of challenging me."

With a casual determination, he bent closer, making Sabrina's heart leap in alarm. She tried to pull back, but there was nowhere to run. Niall leaned over her, his mouth capturing hers as he pressed her back among the pillows.

His tongue probed the locked line of her mouth, then slipped inside, hot and hard. Sabrina's pulse lurched madly. She could feel the lithe power of his chest as he weighed her down with his embrace, could feel the tender passion of his intoxicating lips overwhelming her . . .

He kissed her for what seemed like hours, coaxing, exploring, subduing . . . He was deliberately, skillfully arousing her, seducing her till she was dizzy, melting. Her skin burned where it was crushed to his hardness, while all her senses screamed with need.

She moaned beneath the sensual onslaught. His kiss was raw torment, yet when his lips eventually withdrew from hers, she felt empty and aching.

He was cruel to taunt her so, Sabrina reflected bitterly as he drew back. The hot light in his eyes might have been flattering had she thought it directed at her, but she harbored no illusions that he desired her. She was a female body, an available receptacle for his lust, that was all. He was merely using his legendary skills to persuade her to do his bidding.

Niall cleared his throat, forcing himself to relinquish his

hold, as well as thoughts of any further indulgence tonight—
an indulgence he was beginning to crave.

His own gaze enigmatic, he surveyed Sabrina's lovely
face, flushed with anger and passion. It was all he could do
to summon a shred of gentlemanly resolve. Sabrina was
wounded, and the last thing she needed at the moment was
his amorous attentions. "You need rest, sweeting. I shall
take my leave now."

"Finally, at last," she returned too breathlessly.

He stood. "Perhaps you should tuck yourself into bed.
Can you manage it on your own? I don't trust myself to
do it."

"I don't trust you at *all*. And my answer is *still* no!"

Niall gave her a sweeping bow before turning to the door.
"We shall see, tiger." The glance he cast over his shoulder
was bright with self-assurance and amusement. "I fancy
taming you is going to be a delight."

Chapter
Seven

She was delusional. She had been dreaming, Sabrina prayed when she woke late the following morning. Niall McLaren had not invaded her bedchamber last night and summarily announced the resumption of their betrothal.

But while her head no longer ached so fiercely, her bandaged arm still throbbed wickedly, confirming the violence of the previous eve. Her pain was no dream. And she very much feared she was in her right mind.

The maidservant who attended Sabrina that morning bubbled over with cheer and good wishes. It seemed that while she slept, Niall had informed their clans of their definite intentions to wed. The ceremony would be held three days hence, precisely as planned, since the wedding invitations had never been recalled.

More frustrating, Sabrina endured a dismaying visit from Angus, who unwisely rose from his sickbed to convey his irrepressible delight. His joy made Sabrina's spirits sink further. With the ruthlessness of a warring chieftain, Niall had taken matters out of her hands. Short of fleeing back to Edinburgh and forswearing all obligation to her clan, she would be compelled to go through with the marriage.

In truth, it was the right decision, Sabrina knew. It was simply that Niall's supreme arrogance galled her.

She was further dismayed when a widowed neighbor of her grandfather came to call. When the lady swept into the morning room, Sabrina could not repress a momentary twinge of envy. Mistress Eve Graham possessed a lush figure and a pair of cool, calculating hazel eyes, which she used to assess Sabrina minutely.

The raven-haired beauty seemed surprised at what she found. But then she appeared to catch herself and affected the introductions with a musical laugh. She refused all offer of refreshment, but settled herself on the settee beside her hostess.

"How dreadful, my dear," she said, surveying Sabrina's new arm bandage. "I heard of your terrible wounding."

"It is hardly more than a scratch," Sabrina demurred politely.

"Even so, the entire countryside is talking of your bravery."

"But it really was nothing."

"You are too modest. Why, Niall declared he might have been killed, if not for your quick action."

Sabrina felt a sharp pang in the vicinity of her heart. Something in the way Mistress Graham had said his name hinted at a deeper relationship than mere friendship.

"I am delighted to make your acquaintance at last," Eve said warmly. "You cannot know how I've longed for another lady with which to share confidences. You must tell me all about yourself . . ."

They spoke for a time, with Mistress Graham asking probing questions about Sabrina's family and home in Edinburgh, while relating something of her own past.

"I remember Edinburgh with great fondness," the widow said, sighing. "The soirees, the balls, the assemblies . . . My dear husband accompanied me there frequently, so that I might have a moment's respite from the dullness of the Highlands. Here we have only country dances and primitive customs harking back to feudal times. It is fortunate for us you have come. The clans are in great need of the civilizing influence of women. I've long believed there would be far less feuding among us if our lairds had proper wives to advise them . . . Which leads me to the real purpose of my visit."

Eve hesitated, eyeing Sabrina speculatively. "I came to offer my help with the wedding arrangements, Mistress Duncan. With all due modesty, I am quite proficient at managing fetes."

Sabrina was hard-pressed to think of a polite answer. "In truth, the issue of my marriage to the McLaren is not quite settled as yet."

"How odd. Niall asked me to assist with the wedding feast and so forth."

"Did he, indeed?" she asked tartly.

Eve seemed not to notice her sharpness. "I confess, it surprises me that he would choose you as his bride . . . But perhaps I can see the appeal to a man of his stamp. He called you 'a tiger in mouse's clothing,' I believe were his words."

Sabrina felt her own surprise at the admiration in the widow's tone. A beautiful woman undoubtedly familiar with male adulation, Eve Graham would hardly consider "tiger" a flattering appellation. But she apparently believed Niall thought so.

"Niall is making a great presumption," Sabrina answered. "I have not agreed to wed him. Indeed, I withdrew from the betrothal only a few days past."

One delicate raven eyebrow rose. "Surely you jest. Sabrina—may I call you by your given name? Sabrina, how can you think to spurn him?"

"I know it is shocking of me, Mistress Graham," she murmured wryly.

"Do call me Eve. I must say this is unforeseen." The lady's mouth turned up in amusement. "How many women do you suppose have ever refused him?"

Unexpectedly Sabrina found herself liking the amiable widow. "Very few, I imagine," she admitted candidly, an answering smile in her voice.

"You must possess great fortitude. No woman can resist him. Niall McLaren can charm anything in skirts."

"If he had indeed attempted to charm me, I daresay I would have succumbed, but from the first he made it quite clear he wanted no part of me or my grandfather's plans. The bald truth is, he has no more desire to enter into an arranged marriage than I do. And I have no wish to endure a profligate for a husband."

"He *is* an irresponsible rogue, doubtless, but oh so charming. And with *such* exceptional skill . . ."

The remark was probing rather than boastful, but Sabrina flushed at the intimacy it implied. "His skill impresses me but little. I am more concerned with his character."

"Well . . . I suspect it will be difficult for you to withdraw now that Niall is set on moving forward. The clans are expecting a union."

"I know," Sabrina said rather bleakly. "And I shall not forsake them. My kinsmen must have a laird. I . . . only wish it were someone other than Niall."

"Such misgivings before marriage are not unusual, darling. But I daresay it will not be so bad, being wed to Niall. Having such a magnificent lover should be *some* consolation."

The remark, meant to be encouraging, merely made her spirits sink further. A magnificent lover would want an equally superb partner in his bed. At the very least, a bride who could hold a candle to the countless beauties he had known.

"Well," the widow said briskly, "I had best take my leave if I mean to accomplish anything today. Don't concern yourself with the wedding arrangements, my dear. You may rely on me to handle everything."

Eve rose and drew on her gloves. Before she turned to go, however, she glanced sympathetically at Sabrina. "I have only one word of advice, my dear," she said a bit sadly. "When you wed Niall, do not think to give your heart to him. He will only return it, bruised and battered."

Sabrina forced a smile. She had given her heart freely once and had it rejected. She had no intention of ever repeating that painful mistake, especially with a notorious rake like Niall McLaren. He would slice her heart to ribbons if she allowed it. "I shall heed your warning quite earnestly, I assure you."

With the Widow Graham's aid, the plans for Sabrina's marriage moved forward at lightning speed. Sabrina numbly endured the storm of activity around her as the women of Clan Duncan burst into action, readying for guests who would travel from miles away, and preparing food and drink for the wedding feast.

Her one consolation was her stepfather's arrival late the following day. When a footman came to alert her, Sabrina ran down the steps to the hall, where he was being shown in.

"Papa Charles," Sabrina exclaimed. Laughing and crying at once, she launched herself into his welcoming embrace, and remained there clinging to his lean form, drawing comfort. It was a long moment before she permitted him to draw back.

Tall and spare to the point of gauntness, Charles Cameron appeared stern and forbidding until one glimpsed the lively twinkle in his gray eyes. Presently, however, he looked exhausted from his long ride, and more than a little dismayed.

"Never tell me these are tears, lass?"

"No," Sabrina lied, wiping away the telltale moistness. "I am merely glad to see you." She hadn't realized how much she missed him, or yearned for his counsel. "You should not have come all this way."

"Pah, my only daughter is to wed, and you tell me I am not invited to witness it?"

Sabrina felt herself smile at his teasing. "Of course you are invited. But your trade cannot bear your absence."

"My clerks can handle the business for a few days."

"That is not what you claim when you wish me to review the account books."

"I did not say they could *supplant* you, lass. Their errors will doubtless drive me into penury, if you can no longer oversee them. But enough of that. Tell me what you are about. First I receive Angus Duncan's invitation to the wedding celebration, then your letter saying the betrothal was canceled. Then the missive I received yesterday from Laird McLaren said the betrothal was resumed and that you are indeed to wed tomorrow."

"Yes, Papa Charles. I fear I have gotten myself into a fix."

"Have you now?" His gentle gaze held deep concern.

Sabrina looked away. "You must be weary. Let me show you to your chamber and make you comfortable."

"All in good time. What I wish to know is, have you gone daft, or is this marriage truly what you desire?"

"I haven't gone daft. I . . . think it is for the best. Our marriage will unite our clans and provide the Duncans with a powerful ally."

"I can see Angus Duncan's fine hand at work, or I miss my guess."

"Grandfather has his heart set on the marriage, true."

"But what is your heart set on?"

"I am not really certain."

"Do you love this man, Sabrina?"

"No," she said a bit too emphatically. "How could I? I have only recently made his acquaintance." And what she *did* know of Niall was not encouraging.

"Lass, I know you," Charles warned. "You will not be happy without love."

Sabrina shook her head. She had once dreamed of finding love, but this was the sort of bargain women had been making for centuries, an arranged marriage for political advantage. Love did not enter into the reckoning.

"My happiness is not the most important concern. There are lives at stake . . . the future of an entire clan."

Her stepfather patted her hand. "Well, you've a keen head on your shoulders. And I doubt you would do anything foolish. If you mean to carry through with it, I can only support you. I've brought something for you. Your mother would wish you to have it."

He opened the valise he'd brought, and drew out a garment. Carefully unfolding it and smoothing out the creases, he held it up to the light for her inspection.

Sabrina drew a sharp breath at the lovely sight. The billowing gown was made of ice blue stiffened brocade, embossed with silver thread and pearls in a pattern that was repeated in both the petticoat and stomacher.

" 'Tis the gown your mother was wed in—twice, though not at the same time." Charles grinned. "Once to your father and once to me."

Tears filled Sabrina's eyes as reverently she held the gown to her breast. For a moment she felt as if her mother were with her again, and it gave her the courage she was sorely lacking.

"Thank you, Papa," she whispered huskily, profoundly grateful for his thoughtfulness.

Her wedding day dawned bright and clear. The rugged green hills held a breathtaking spring glow, Sabrina saw from her bedchamber window, but the sight did little to cheer her flagging spirits or ease her misgivings.

After a light meal of oatcakes and milk, an army of maids descended upon her, including the Widow Graham's dresser. Sabrina allowed herself to be bathed and perfumed and painted, but she refused to let them pomade her hair. Remembering Niall's preference for unpowdered locks, she caught her dark tresses up behind, letting them sweep over her shoulder in several long curls. When she had donned the voluminous petticoat, she was laced into the gown and stomacher.

Her looking glass told her the effect was pleasing, but her dark eyes seemed too large for her pale face.

"*Mouse,*" Sabrina said accusingly, wrinkling her nose in disgust. She wanted to look beautiful for Niall—

The realization caused a small pain deep inside her chest.

It was a fruitless endeavor, fretting over her appearance. No coiffure or gown could make her beautiful enough for a man like him.

When she was fully dressed, Angus rose from his sickbed in order to present her with a gift, a silver casket which held her grandmother's jewels. The Duncan ruby was a huge polished stone set in a filigreed pendant, and Angus insisted she wear it.

His craggy face beamed as he surveyed the effect. "'Tis a wise thing yer doing, lass."

Her stepfather arrived just then to escort her below to the waiting carriage. "Come, 'tis time for you to go."

Her heart began pounding as a surge of belated panic struck her. In a short while she would be asked to pledge vows of loyalty and service, obliged to honor Niall McLaren till the day she died.

"Faith, lass, your skin is like ice," Charles exclaimed.

"'Tis to be expected," Angus chimed in. "She's over-wrought with bridal nerves."

Overwrought indeed, Sabrina thought wryly. She felt the weight of her entire clan on her shoulders. And she had little confidence in her judgment. Was she taking the right course, or was she striking a bargain with the devil?

Angus did not accompany them to the kirk for the morning ceremony, some half league away. The wedding feast, set to begin at noon, would be held at Banesk so he could attend for a brief time. The bride and her stepfather traveled by carriage over rutted trails, where they were to meet the groom at the door of the kirk.

Niall was awaiting her, Sabrina saw as the vehicle drew to a halt. As he aided her descent, she chided the sudden drumming of her heart. It was ridiculous how anxiety and misgivings could suddenly give way to joy at merely seeing him again. Joy and *relief*. She had feared he might not bother to show up for his own wedding and leave her stranded at the church steps.

He seemed fully prepared to go through with the marriage, though. He wore full Scottish dress, his tartan kilt and short jacket accentuated by a silver-embroidered waistcoat, white silk hose, and lace cravat. A silver broach secured the McLaren plaid at his shoulder, while a black ribbon bound his ebony hair in a queue at his nape, emphasizing the rugged beauty of his face—broad forehead, finely chiseled nose, and carved cheekbones.

Sabrina had never seen such a combination of polished elegance and raw virility in a man. He was devastatingly, dangerously male, and he brought out every feminine instinct she possessed.

"You look bonny, mouse," he murmured in greeting.

Sabrina glanced sharply up at him to divine if he were mocking her, but he wore an enigmatic look that gave little clue.

"How is your arm?"

"Well enough, thank you."

"Does it pain you?"

"Nothing to signify." When she felt her stepfather press her elbow, she cleared her throat to make the introductions. "My lord McLaren, this is my stepfather, Charles Cameron."

Niall offered a polite bow. "I've had the pleasure. Mr. Cameron called last eve at Creagturic."

She eyed the older man in surprise, wondering why he had made such an endeavor after so wearying a ride.

"He came," Niall explained with a bland smile, "ostensibly to present a wedding gift . . . French brandy, Lyon silk, Brussels lace. But he vowed to break my head should I make you unhappy."

Sabrina felt herself flush with warmth, both at the absurd notion of an aging merchant challenging a Highland warrior, and the comforting thought that her stepfather would champion her even against overwhelming odds.

All the leaders of the nearby clans had gathered in the kirk, it seemed when she entered on her intended's arm. It was a major event when a Highland chieftain wed the granddaughter of another laird. She was grateful to recognize a number of familiar faces among the crowd: Geordie, Liam, the beautiful Widow Graham, Niall's cousin Colm, the gruff John McLaren.

The ceremony was simple, and over too soon. The McLaren presented her with a nuptial ring, a simple gold band, and the Presbyterian minister pronounced them man and wife before God.

Then Niall bent to kiss her.

It was only a brief brushing of lips, but it roused fresh panic within Sabrina. Her fate was cast, her decision irrevocable. She was wed to the greatest lover in Europe, and she was totally inadequate to the task. She scarcely felt the warmth of her husband's mouth as it touched hers in a fleeting caress, she was trembling so badly.

The moment they left the kirk, however, her anxiety was overshadowed by a deeper fear. Sabrina's heart lurched to see a party of armed Highlanders ride up to the church steps, with the black-bearded Owen Buchanan in the lead.

Beside her, Niall went rigid, his fingers curling around the hilt of his sword. "What do you here, Owen?" he demanded when the horsemen came to a halt.

"I ken I was invited to the weddin'."

Niall's face was set like granite. "'Twas a courtesy, no more. Meant to serve notice that Clan Duncan is no longer fair game for the butchering Buchanans."

"Butchering, ye say?" His black eyes flashed. "Two of my kinsmen lie wounded, and ye call *me* a butcher?" With a creak of saddle leather, the Buchanan shifted his fierce gaze and fixed Sabrina with a dark glare. "Nay, 'tis a bloody gomeril, I am. I should hae known better than to bargain with a mere lass and leave ma herds unguarded."

Sabrina stared back at him. She was still furious at Owen Buchanan for deceiving her and breaking their pact before it had even begun, yet she could not understand his anger.

He was the one to blame for the cattle raids and the resultant bloodshed.

"Such a guileless mien," Owen sneered. "Who do ye think to deceive, lass? I suppose now ye'll claim ye couldna control yer clan."

Niall's jaw clenched. "My wife's veracity is not in dispute, but if you care to settle the issue with swords—"

"No!" Sabrina exclaimed, vexed with them both for resorting to violence. "That will be quite enough. This should be a day of peace."

The two men eyed each other savagely. Sabrina hoped they would not start a battle on holy ground, with so many of their kin present who would undoubtedly enter the fray.

Willing herself to calm, she pressed her lips together, hoping reason could prevail. "My lord Buchanan, perhaps we may defer this discussion for a more auspicious date. You and your clansmen are welcome to join us at Banesk for the wedding celebration, if you can forswear violence for the moment and put away your swords."

Owen gave her a scathing glance. "I'll no' break bread with a thieving Duncan."

Beside her, Niall gripped the hilt of his sword and took a threatening step forward.

Still fuming, Owen turned his mount and spurred it into a canter, his kinsmen following hard on his heels.

Sabrina let out her breath in relief. All it needed was a bloodbath at the steps of the church to make her wedding day uniquely memorable.

It was a somber crowd that filed out of the kirk, despite the brilliance and ripening warmth of the sun high overhead. Niall joined Sabrina in the carriage to return to Banesk, while the other guests followed on horseback or on foot.

Her new husband said little during the short journey, but Sabrina was aware of the undercurrent of anger emanating from him.

"I cannot understand," she ventured at last, "why the

Buchanan seemed so outraged by the resumption of the feud. He seemed to blame me for the raid."

"What does it matter? There will never be peace between our clans."

"Why not?"

"Because the bloody Buchanans butchered my kin in the act of a coward."

Sabrina winced. She understood why Niall held such hatred for the Buchanans; they were responsible for the deaths of his father and brother. Yet Owen reportedly had not instigated the ambush . . .

At present, however, was not the best time for a discussion of the feud. Niall could not view the issue rationally, and in truth, she was in no state to be objective, with her wounded arm throbbing and her nerves in tatters.

When Niall fell silent, lapsing into a dark mood, Sabrina followed suit, gazing mutely out the carriage window, bracing herself against the sway and lurch of the vehicle.

She could hear the skirl of the bagpipes long before they reached the castle grounds, but the cheers of the crowd which greeted their arrival stunned her. They were shouting *her* name.

"Did I not tell you, mouse?" Niall murmured at her bewildered look, rousing himself from his grim preoccupation. "There's naught a Highlander admires more than bravery. You're a credit to your Highland blood."

The clans had gathered in the yard for the noontide wedding feast, Sabrina saw. Angus had ordered kegs of whisky and barrels of Lowland-brewed ale and French wine broken out for the guests, and it seemed the Highlanders were taking full advantage of his hospitality.

To her surprise, after Niall had aided her down, he raised their joined hands high and declared in a strong, clear voice, "I give you Lady Sabrina McLaren, Countess of Strathearn!"

A roaring cheer went up, and the guests surged forward to greet the laird's new lady.

Niall remained at her side, gravely accepting the congratulations and good wishes of his clansmen. When someone pressed a goblet of wine into his hand, he solicitously held it to Sabrina's lips. He gave all the appearance of a tender lover enamored of his bride.

The women of Clans Duncan and McLaren had outdone themselves with the wedding feast. Wooden planks laid over barrels formed tables, which had been piled high with hearty fare as well as delicacies: venison, mutton pasties, haggis, syllabub, and plum pudding. When Niall offered to fetch a plate for her, though, Sabrina declined. She was too unsettled to eat.

Angus joined them then, hobbling weakly on his cane and supported by his manservant. When he proposed a toast to his granddaughter, the crowd raised their cups to salute her.

Hardly crediting their generous welcome, Sabrina felt an ache in her throat at their acceptance. She had won over their stubborn affection with her actions the night of the raid—by fighting the Buchanans and foiling their deadly aim—as well as giving them the protection of a powerful laird by marrying an ally.

"Drink up, lass," Angus urged, pressing a cup in her hand. " 'Twill give you heart."

Sabrina swallowed a mouthful of the pure malt whisky, and wheezed as it burned a path down her throat. " 'Tis more likely to *pickle* my heart," she said, gasping.

Her grandfather gave a weak chuckle, while her clansmen roared with laughter.

"Ye'll need to do better," Geordie chided. "Such good Scotch brew is mother's milk to a Highlander."

She flushed at the ensuing jocular remarks concerning her fortitude, a color which deepened when she realized her new husband was watching her with unabashed amusement.

Before she could respond, though, the lilting strains of an ancient Highland air filled the yard.

"Ah, I believe we are expected to dance," Niall murmured, holding his hand out to her. "Will you honor me, madam wife?"

Sabrina placed a trembling hand in his and allowed him to lead her into the movements of the minuet. To her surprise, Niall gave her his complete attention, watching her solely, his blue gaze making her feel as if she were the only woman in the world. It was an act for him, Sabrina knew. A skill he had honed for his repertoire of seductions. And yet it was supremely effective—with her and others as well.

She was an object of envy among the women, she could sense it in their longing looks. She had captured Niall McLaren as husband, and half the females present would give their souls to have landed so great a prize.

All too soon the dance was over. Sabrina felt a wave of disappointment as Niall returned her to the sidelines, a sentiment which turned to dismay as Eve Graham made an appearance.

All Sabrina's doubts and insecurities came rushing back with a vengeance. She felt her heart give a painful jolt when Niall bowed over the beautiful widow's hand.

"You are as lovely as always, my dear."

Eve gave a trilling laugh, as musical as crystal bells. "Not so lovely as your bride, I see."

"Indeed," Niall said noncommittally.

Although Sabrina had no tangible proof, she sensed an undercurrent of emotion between her husband and the widow. The two of them obviously shared an intimacy of longstanding.

"I suppose," Eve observed lightly, "it would not be wise to insist on a dance."

"It would not," Niall replied with a glance at Sabrina. "I must fulfill my duty with the Dowager Lady Ross, in any case."

Sabrina was profoundly grateful to them both for forbearing to dance together, where the entire company could witness their closeness.

"Why do you not ask Seumas McNab to partner you?" her husband asked Eve. "He is recently widowed and will fawn over you properly. It will permit you an opportunity to display your charms to best advantage."

"Wretched, exasperating creature," Eve said, laughing again. "You know full well Seumas is seeking a broodmare for a wife." She turned to Sabrina. "Did I not tell you, you will have your hands full as his bride? The man is a rogue, Sabrina, not to be trusted."

She could see the corner of Niall's mouth curve sardonically. "My bride has had full warning on that score."

He gave both ladies an elaborate bow that held a hint of mockery. When he had gone in search of the dowager, Sabrina forced herself to smile. She would have preferred to avoid the widow altogether, yet her being seen conversing amicably with Eve would help still the gossips' tongues.

Eve apparently shared her reasoning, for she slipped her arm through Sabrina's.

"I meant what I said," the lady remarked kindly. "It will be difficult being wed to so practiced a cavalier."

Sabrina nodded. She feared she was in store for a vast deal of loneliness and heartache.

"But I must confess," Eve added with a wistful sigh, "I do envy you."

Sabrina saw little of her husband for a space, for he was in great demand with the female guests. After his obligatory dance with the dowager, he favored a half dozen fortunate damsels with his attentions, making them flush with pride at being chosen.

Sabrina supposed she could not blame him for his conquests. Niall McLaren was recklessly amorous and irresistible to women, his flirtation as natural and effortless as breathing.

Fortunately she was given little time to dwell on her abandonment. First she was claimed by her stepfather and then several of her clansmen in various Scotch reels that left her breathless and parched. When Geordie offered her another whisky, she accepted gladly.

It was midafternoon before Niall returned to her side. Sabrina felt her heart thrum and her nerves dance at his nearness. Why did she have this overwhelming feeling her life had begun again? She would prefer to attribute her weakness to the potent drink she'd consumed. She'd been sipping on the whisky, and although it made her lightheaded, she was glad for the courage it gave her. She could face her new husband stoically.

To her dismay, though, Niall smiled at her in apology, a devastatingly attractive expression that made her pulse race. "Forgive me for deserting you, sweeting. I could not excuse myself sooner."

Sabrina took a deep breath in an effort at calm. "Far be it from me to interfere with your pleasures," she said, striving for indifference.

"It was not as great a pleasure as you credit."

"Oh, yes, I recall. You prefer more active sport. Perhaps I should remove myself from the company so that you might proceed with seducing the ladies present."

Niall eyed her sharply, but Sabrina forged bravely ahead, although her senses seemed to be swimming. "There is no need for you to remain at my side, my lord."

"It would be wiser for me to do so, for appearances sake."

"Ah, of course," she retorted with an irrepressible hint of bitterness. "You would not wish these good people to learn of the travesty of our courtship, or realize that you were forced to wed me."

"I told you, mouse, I am resigned to our marriage."

Her spirits plummeted further. *Resigned* was not what she wished her husband to feel for her.

Before she could answer, Niall placed a finger under her chin, scrutinizing her intently. "It seems you have little head for whisky after all."

"My head is perfectly clear, thank you." Sabrina lifted

her chin regally, but spoiled the effect by raising a hand to her temple. "It is my vision which troubles me."

He chuckled, which vexed her profoundly. She was amusing him again.

"You needn't worry, sir. I am resigned as well. My expectations of our union are meager. This is to be a marriage of convenience, only. I won't require you to dance attendance on me."

She could see one jet-black eyebrow winging upward. "You seem eager to be rid of me."

"I simply wish to spell out the terms of our relationship. You made it perfectly clear that you desire your freedom. Well"—she took a deep breath—"I wish to make clear that you are free to take your lust elsewhere. I shall raise no objections."

Niall regarded her soberly, trying to judge her sincerity. His new bride seemed to be giving him permission to seek his carnal pleasures in other beds.

Her generosity relieved him, yet strangely piqued him at the same time. He wanted no fits of temper or tearful pleas to deal with in a wife, no clinging limpet who fancied herself in love and expected vows of undying devotion in return.

It should delight him to find her so agreeable; this was precisely what he wanted, was it not? Sabrina was an inexperienced virgin. He doubted she could satisfy a man of his lusty nature, or that she would even wish to try. He should be pleased that she would not complain if he were forced to fulfill his sexual needs outside the marriage bed.

"Perhaps in future," he replied, his voice liquid and smooth, "I will 'take my lusts elsewhere,' as you put it. But not this night. On the eve of a wedding, it is usual to consummate the marriage vows. Or have you forgotten?"

"No," Sabrina said in a suddenly small voice, unable to meet his eyes. "I have not. But I . . . I thought perhaps you might prefer a marriage in name only."

"I'll have no one question the validity of this union. On the morrow you will be my wife in every respect."

Sabrina felt her heart falter. She would be required to bed Niall after all. She'd thought—hoped—he might forgo the duty, given the circumstances. She was certain he had no true desire for the task. And the prospect of having Niall McLaren initiate her into the act of lovemaking daunted her. She could never measure up to his other lovers.

"Very well," Sabrina replied, summoning remarkable aplomb. "But after tonight, you have full license to take up with your paramours, if you so wish."

"I am all gratitude for your consideration," Niall said wryly.

The graceful evasion told Sabrina little, and she couldn't help stubbornly pressing the matter. She glanced pointedly at the Widow Graham to make certain he could not misunderstand her. "I would, however, appreciate a warning as to which ladies are your discarded love interests, so I might attempt to avoid embarrassment in future."

"Are you certain she is discarded?"

Sabrina caught her breath at the sudden shaft of pain that shot through her.

Seeing the hurt in her eyes before she lowered her gaze, Niall voiced a mental oath. He had baited her for a response, out of pique or in an effort to test her indifference, he wasn't sure. But his mouse with tiger's claws did not deserve to have his former mistresses flaunted in her face. She had wanted this marriage as little as he did.

He bent closer. "Come, let us cry pax, sweeting. This is no time to be quarreling."

She felt the heat of his body, the strength of the arm that he draped so casually over her shoulders. Such nearness alarmed her, as did his attempt to charm her. "I don't *wish* to cry pax."

"You would rather fight? If so, we may do so in private. Indeed, love," he murmured as if they were alone in a bedchamber, or alone in a bed, "it might prove enjoyable."

Sabrina stiffened. "I am not your *love*."

A semi-grin, more devastating than its whole counterpart, sauntered across his mouth. " 'Tis a figure of speech, merely that."

She was not proof against such sensual charisma. It made her ache with longing.

Sabrina closed her eyes, damning herself for the wanting. Her desire for him dismayed her. It was imperative that she build up her resistance to that sinfully easy charm. She didn't want to fall for this man, only to have him betray her.

And yet . . . she was but human. She wanted desperately to know what it was like to be held in Niall's arms.

Marshaling her defenses, Sabrina gazed up at him defiantly. "If you expect me to fall at your feet like all your other adoring admirers, you are much mistaken."

Niall laughed with an easy sensuality, as if he knew very well she would succumb to him eventually. "If you continue imbibing, you will fall at my feet out of sheer inebriation." He took the glass from her hand. "Come, madam. I believe it is time to take our leave, before you're entirely foxed."

"I am not foxed! I have never been foxed in my life."

"Perhaps that is part of the trouble, mouse. It might help you to shed some of your inhibitions were you to become soused now and then. For now, however, you will accompany me home like an obedient wife."

Despite his light tone, Sabrina felt herself bristle. "I was not born to take your orders, sir. I am accustomed to being my own mistress."

"So I ken. But I have no intention of arguing. If you refuse to accompany me, I shall simply toss you over my shoulder and carry you off. As you are now the Countess of Strathearn, I presume you would prefer a more dignified exit."

"You wouldn't . . ." She bit off the word "dare."

His smile dawned slow and bright, as if he were anticipating the challenge.

Sabrina clenched her teeth, determined not to be provoked.

The wretch had a talent for drawing intense reactions from her. A single word from him managed to touch off the fighting spirit in her. But she would not give him the satisfaction.

She shivered, however, when Niall bent and pressed his lips against the sensitive flesh just behind her left ear. "The bedding will be a pleasant experience, I assure you," he whispered, the words like velvet on her skin. "I promise you a night you will long remember."

Chapter
Eight

Quite unwillingly, Sabrina took leave of her kin in the most public manner possible. The afternoon was well advanced when the guests gathered to bid the bridal couple farewell. When Niall very deliberately drew her into his arms, Sabrina gasped to find herself crushed against unyielding male strength. Before she could protest, his lips boldly captured hers for a lusty, rousing kiss.

She might have struggled if not for the way Niall's devastating expertise turned her knees to jelly.

"Go to it, lad. Give the wench a taste 'o yer blade!" a drunken Highlander called out.

"Dip into her honey pot!"

"Give her a wee bairn to do the McLarens proud!"

It was a long moment before Niall released her. Flushed and breathless and trembling with outrage, Sabrina lifted her head regally, but gave her husband a glare that promised a full accounting later.

With the crowd roaring approval, Niall lifted his bride upon his horse and swung up behind her.

"And just what was that spectacle in honor of?" Sabrina demanded the moment they were out of sight. She could still feel the warm imprint of his mouth on hers, the strength of his hard body at her back, though she told herself the fierce beating of her heart was due solely to anger and alarm.

Behind her, Niall smiled. The tartness of her tone held a

telltale quiver that suggested she was more affected by his sudden display of passion than she pretended.

"Everyone present will remark my devotion to you," he replied calmly. "If our enemies see that I have claimed you as my own, they will think twice before attacking Clan Duncan again. That *was* the prime purpose of our holy union, was it not?"

"I see nothing *holy* about it. I consented for expediencies' sake, nothing more. And there was no reason for you to drag me away from the celebration."

"Ah, but there was. The consummation, remember?"

"It could have waited."

"Perhaps, but your grandfather was eager for us to get on with it so there would be no doubt we are wed. In fact, he advised me to beget an heir directly."

Sabrina stiffened abruptly at his levity, but when she tried to draw away, Niall's arm circled her waist and hauled her back into position.

He gave a soft chuckle. "Settle down, mouse. You are as prickly as a hedgehog."

"I cannot be both animals!" she snapped.

Aye, she could, he thought ruefully. She was a lass to test the mettle of a saint, and he certainly was no saint. But he was certain he would easily conquer this infuriating, challenging wench—as soon as he could get her in his bed.

By mutual consent, they both fell silent for the remainder of the journey. A brisk Highland breeze bore the perfume of sweet-scented gorse, but Sabrina scarcely noticed. Her trepidation increased moment by moment as the false courage of the whisky ebbed. She felt like a prize of war, a helpless prisoner being carried off to her conqueror's ancient castle.

As they approached the imposing stone edifice, she felt her heart begin to pound. Only a few clansmen had been left to guard against attack, so the castle seemed nearly deserted when they rode into the courtyard. Niall dismounted without a word and reached up for her.

Reluctantly Sabrina placed her hands on the hard width

of his shoulders and felt the smooth muscles contract beneath her fingers. Her palms tingled with warmth as he grasped her waist and swung her to the ground.

To her further dismay, Niall deliberately took her hand and pulled her along behind him. The house was silent, their footsteps echoing on the stone flags. They met no one as they climbed the stairs, but Sabrina's pulse beat faster when she realized his intent.

She held back when he led her directly to his bedchamber, but he drew her gently, relentlessly inside.

"My lord . . . it is still broad daylight," Sabrina protested uneasily as he shut the door softly behind them.

"My name is Niall, sweeting. And it is late afternoon, an excellent time for a tryst." He shed his plaid and tossed it carelessly in a chair.

Nervously Sabrina glanced around her. His bedchamber seemed appropriate for the man—beautiful and decadent. A giant four-poster bed curtained with burgundy hangings dominated the room, while a thick woven carpet embellished the floor. The covers of the huge bed had been turned down invitingly, and a fire glowed in the grate, taking the chill from the air. Even so, she shivered.

"Don't be afraid, sweet mouse. I predict that by the morrow you will be sighing sweetly with delight and imploring me not to leave you."

She went rigid with indignity. "Has anyone ever mentioned what an insufferable, arrogant braggart you are?"

"I am merely being truthful." A grin that could only be called exquisitely decadent curved his beautiful mouth. "Seduction has been my avocation since adolescence. And I pride myself in a certain competence."

He was enjoying himself, the beast. Sabrina clenched her fingers, fighting the urge to march across the chamber and box his ears. "A consummation should be a solemn occasion. You view it as a mere exercise in lechery."

"I see no reason it cannot be both solemn and pleasurable. Be assured, I shall fully arouse you first so that you might enjoy it as well as I."

"You'll arouse nothing in me save my temper!"

Niall gazed at her measuringly. Her eyes were dark with wariness, but the spirit that flashed there suggested his deliberate provocation was having an effect. She was nervous at the coming union, he knew, but sparring with her brought forth the defiant vixen, which was the only lass he wanted in his bed. One who was unafraid and eager to match him in passion.

When he glimpsed her tongue as it flickered over dewy lips, his voice softened. "You've never feared me before, tiger. Don't begin now."

"I . . . I am not afraid. I simply have no desire to submit to a rutting beast."

His smile was pained. "You wound me grievously. I am hardly a beast. I am your husband." Niall hesitated, his eyes searching. "Did it not occur to you that this situation might be new to me as well? Despite your much exaggerated account of my debauchery, I have never before deflowered a maiden."

"Then how do you know if you can manage it?"

He wanted to laugh, and yet . . . The question was not as absurd as he might have thought. For all his nonchalance, he had never known such innocence, and the prospect disquieted him. He wanted her first experience with lovemaking to be pleasurable and memorable. "I shall give you nothing you don't ask for voluntarily."

The words were rich in promise, his voice a husky caress. He turned away then, to permit her to weigh his reassurances.

Taking his time, he drew the velvet drapes across the windows, shutting out the late afternoon sunlight, enveloping them in soft darkness. Then leisurely, he lit a dozen candles in a candelabra, at once transforming the chamber to an intimate haven for lovers, suffused with a quiet golden glow.

His gaze found Sabrina, where she stood riveted to the floor. Slowly he moved toward her, till he was a scant few inches away. Reaching up, he framed her face with his palms, disarming her with his tenderness.

"I want very much for your first time to be good for you . . . special and fulfilling. I shall be gentle and considerate, I swear it. I will do nothing you are not fully prepared for. Will you trust me, sweetheart?"

His voice was soft and warm, his eyes compelling. Sabrina felt her fear melting.

She nodded slowly.

"Tell me," he urged.

"I . . . will trust you."

The intimate smile he gave her made her feel as if the sun had burst from behind the clouds.

"Your hair . . . I like it this way."

The arrangement fell to one side in thick curls. Catching the ends, Niall rubbed it between his fingertips, as if savoring the feel. "Such rich color . . . texture. But I would like it better flowing free."

When Sabrina reached up to remove the pins, he gently stilled her hands. "No, allow me the pleasure."

Her heart beat unevenly as his fingers searched and found his targets. Loosening the heavy mass, he let it fall down her back. Smoothing a stray wisp back from her face, he gently tangled his fingers in the rich fullness.

"You are bonny with your hair down," he murmured as he bent to brush her mouth with his.

It was a butterfly kiss that seemed to draw her soul from her body. Sabrina stood dazed when Niall drew back and smiled.

"With your permission, I shall play lady's maid."

To her startlement then, he sank down to kneel at her feet. One by one he slipped off her shoes, caressing each ankle almost reverently. To maintain her balance, Sabrina had to grasp his shoulder with one hand, but she froze when he reached beneath her petticoats to find the garter that held up her stocking.

Her breath caught as he brushed her bare calf. A frisson

of fiery sensation sparked from his fingertips to her skin, yet he seemed too intent on his task to notice. She endured the delicate torment in silence, biting her lip until at last it was over and she stood barefoot.

Then he rose. "And now your gown, sweeting."

Sabrina's breath seemed to stop once more.

She tried to pretend indifference as he took her hand and drew her farther into the room, toward the warmth of the fire, but it took every ounce of fortitude she possessed to stand there quietly and submit to his skillful ministrations.

He first removed the stomacher, then the heavy skirt, and carefully draped them both over a chair. The embroidered petticoat-underskirt came next, and finally the beautiful bodice.

He seemed so casual about the whole process, Sabrina thought despondently. As if he had undressed countless ladies before her. It was only when he saw the bandage on her arm that he showed any emotion. His eyes darkened.

"I would that I could have spared you this," he murmured as he bent to press a light kiss on her arm, just above the bandage.

She flinched a little, but not in pain. Rather it was the sensual sensations streaking through her like fire at his tender gesture.

She went rigid when, with a forefinger, he touched the neckline of her shift. A vibrant shiver ran though her as he brushed the rising swell of her breast, feeling the ridge the tight bodice had made in her flesh.

" 'Tis criminal, how the whalebone has marked your lovely skin. Let me soothe it."

Bending, he pressed a succession of fleeting kisses on the side of her throat . . . her white shoulder . . . the swell of her breast . . . He left her hot and shivering when he drew back.

"You don't need this, do you, love?" The warm resonance of his voice bathed her with sensation.

Catching the hem of her shift, he drew the garment over her head and let it drop to the floor.

Entirely nude, Sabrina squeezed her eyes shut, fighting a flash of panic. She felt small and vulnerable, unprepossessing in the face of his masculine beauty.

"You have a lovely body."

Her gaze flickered up to meet his, disbelieving. The unexpected dark intensity in his eyes filled her with a strange excitement.

"I . . . I'm rather plain."

"You're perfect."

"I'm not like your other . . . like the Widow Graham. I expect you are disappointed."

The comparison was inevitable, Niall supposed; Sabrina *was* different from Eve Graham. Yet he had stopped thinking of her as plain long ago. And disappointment was the last thing he felt just now as he studied her slender, long-legged body. He wanted her.

Sabrina was prim and shy and stubbornly defiant. . . . And yet she was magnificent in her own quiet way . . . with flawless satin skin the color of ivory; breasts high and firm, tipped with distended, rosy nipples; legs that were long, slim, curvaceous; and a fire in her eyes that called to him.

He had known many lovely women, but this lass's appeal went beyond skin deep. There was a bold spirit within her, an unexplored passion that cried out for release. By him. He wanted very much to be the one to draw her from her imprisoning shell, to awaken her sexually.

"Every lass has her own special beauty, and yours is very appealing." He reached up to cradle her cheek. "You are Sabrina . . . Sweet, fiery Sabrina . . ."

An ache rose unbidden in her throat as she gazed at him. What was the matter with her that his words should bring hot, hidden tears to the inside of her eyelids?

He turned away then, eliciting a swift surge of disappointment in her. But a moment later, she felt the brush of silk at her back as he slipped a garment around her shoulders. He had fetched a dressing robe from the wardrobe, Sabrina realized. How grateful she was to him for putting her at ease, and yet . . . she didn't recognize this particular robe. Her clothing had been delivered that morning, but she owned nothing like this filmy crimson confection trimmed with swansdown.

Slipping it on, she fumbled with the hooks that fastened at the waist. She would have much preferred her white night smock, whose modest construction would completely cover her limbs and torso, toes to neck. This garment seemed too small, for the lapels would not close fully, displaying bare skin nearly to her waist and exposing far too much of her bosom to view. Worse, if she moved at all, her naked legs would show.

"Where did this come from? It's not mine," she said stiffly.

Niall looked up as he untied his cravat. "No. I had it made up specifically for you."

"For . . . me? Then you mistook my measurements. It does not fit properly."

"It fits precisely as I wished it to."

She glanced at him in bewilderment. "But . . . it is so . . . brazen."

"What if it is?" His smile was meltingly warm, lavishly sensual, his voice warm with intimacy. "In the privacy of our bedchamber, you may be as brazen as you like."

To her surprise, he then went to the washstand and poured a measure of water into the basin. Sabrina watched curiously as he wet and soaped one corner of a cloth, then returned to her. She gave a start when he raised the dampened cloth to her face.

He hesitated, one eyebrow cocked. "You aren't afraid of soap, are you?"

When she shook her head warily, he smiled. "Good. It is one of the rare failings of we Highlanders, I fear. We cherish too close an acquaintance with dirt."

"I am not dirty—"

"No, of course not." He began to wash her face to remove the ceruse that Eve Graham's dresser had applied so liberally that morning. "But it is a crime to bury such flawless skin under layers of paint. It smothers the natural roses in your cheeks. You are lovelier without cosmetics."

Shy and uncertain, she gazed up at him, and Niall found himself distracted from his task. Those haunting eyes of hers captivated him; the color of rich coffee, flecked with soft, sherry-colored lights.

He felt a shaft of desire that surprised him. He wanted to take her to bed right then, but he wanted more to reassure her.

"There is no need for shyness between us," he murmured, his husky voice echoing through her like the memory of a caress.

Sabrina felt herself fighting the pull of his magnetism. The need to protect herself from this man was strong. She had vowed she would not succumb to his legendary charm, yet she had no weapons to aid her in halting his sweet seduction. She wanted him, the part of her that was woman, the part that was lonely and desperate for love. And her defenses were slipping, moment by moment.

To her relief, he finished wiping and drying her face, then tapped her lightly on the nose in a gesture more friendly than loverlike. "Take heart, lass. I am only intent on bedding you, not murdering you."

She smiled faintly, as he'd meant her to do, which diminished the tension a small measure.

He stepped back then to undress. His eyes never leaving her, he drew off his jacket and then his fine linen shirt.

Sabrina caught her breath. It unnerved her, he was so very male, all corded muscles and bronzed skin. Like a lover's seeking caress, the flickering candlelight found the blue-black glints scattered in the light fur of his chest.

"No, don't look away," he commanded when she would have averted her gaze. "Watch."

His beautiful body drew her eyes once more. He had the finest pair of shoulders she'd ever seen, yet her nervousness grew as he removed the rest of his clothing, article by article. All too soon it was done and he turned to face her fully, standing with a relaxed nudity before her, the image of virile strength.

He was narrow of hip and powerful of leg, but she was faintly shocked to see his arousal, pulsing and erect, between his sinewed thighs.

His eyes met hers. Bold eyes, bright eyes. Eyes curiously measuring.

"So, sweeting . . . are you frightened by your new husband's physique?"

She shivered. All that bronzed, hair-roughened masculinity spoke of savage pleasures. "I suppose . . . all those women could not have been deceived. It must not be too painful or frightening . . . or all your conquests would have protested long ere now."

"Indeed. I am just a man, sweeting. I shan't harm you."

Just a man. Such a remarkable understatement.

"I own myself amazed at your modesty. I never would have expected it from you."

He chuckled, a low sound rich in pleasure. "Termagant," he replied, but the word was a soft caress, a satin promise.

An emotion something like despair curled around Sabrina's heart as she felt herself succumbing to his spell. Niall needed no steel or pistol to force past her defenses, only the rapier-sharp edge of his erotic charm.

She moistened her lips, which she realized was a mistake.

His gaze lowered from hers to linger on the soft curves of her mouth. "It is time, sweeting."

She could hear the sharp sound of her own breathing in the potent quiet of the beautiful room.

Their gazes locked, and something heated and intense passed between them.

He moved toward her slowly, his eyes warm with desire. Or was that merely the product of her wishful thinking? Her heart hammering, Sabrina stood waiting.

His hand lightly caressed the silk of her hair as it cascaded about her shoulders. For all his expertise, Niall found

himself taking a deep breath. He had never attempted to seduce a woman who was without some measure of experience. Sabrina was innocent of the demands a man could
make on a woman's body, and he had to go slowly.

His hand cupped her throat . . . lingered . . . then glided
downward, slipping beneath the swansdown to push the
lapels aside, baring her beauty. She had exquisite breasts,
small and round and high, tipped with rose nipples, hardened now into tight buds of desire. His fingertips made a
slow, circular motion around one distended peak, making
her gasp softly.

Desire flared through his senses at the helpless sound.

He wanted *her*. He wanted to savor the silk of her hair
and warmth of her skin. He wanted to touch her and watch
her moan, to wrap those long legs around his waist and
plunge hot and deep inside her, to draw out the passionate
woman she kept hidden. He wanted her beneath him as he
took his pleasure and gave her exquisite pleasure in return.

He kissed her fleetingly, a delicate brush of warm lips that
left her stunned and wanting.

"Come, sweetheart," he whispered. "Come."

Then he took her hand and led her to the bed.

Sabrina's heart beat erratically. After enduring so many
nights of erotic dreams and suppressed desires, she was
about to discover precisely what the poets and dreamers
glorified, but that women rarely enjoyed and often feared.

Hesitating, she glanced up at Niall. His face was so beautiful, its chiseled planes dark and absorbed. "I don't know
what to do. . . ."

He smiled. "Then I'll show you."

He stood behind her while his arms glided around her
waist, and unfastened the hooks of her dressing gown. She
felt the silk shimmer over her skin as the garment dropped
to the floor, felt his naked warmth at her back.

His teeth grazed her ear, making her shiver. "Lie on the
bed, love, facedown."

His hands gently prodded her, but she needed no urging

to climb onto the huge bed, her knees trembled so. Willingly she moved to the middle, leaving him a wide berth.

The mattress sank beneath his weight. Rigid, Sabrina waited, beset by tumultuous feelings. When she felt him lean over her, she pressed her face into the pillows.

His hand ran lightly over her arm, his touch lingering and provocative. He seemed aware of her fear, of her hot, flushed skin and acutely sensitive nerves.

"Do you know what happens between a man and woman when they make love?" he asked softly as he began lazily stroking her spine.

"I . . . think I am to sit on your . . . lap."

"That is one way, though not the most customary."

"It seems to be your position of choice the times I have interrupted you."

"True, tiger." Warm laughter spiced his voice. "But you are not ready for that just yet. The usual way is breast to breast. You lie on your back and I ease myself between your thighs. I will show you how, sweeting. And you will see it is the most sublime experience in the world."

Dry-mouthed, light-headed, Sabrina lay acquiescent. "I thought . . . only men enjoyed the . . . the act."

"Who told you that?"

"My cousin. She . . . her husband . . ."

"Your cousin is to be pitied, then. A considerate lover doesn't seek only his own release."

"Release?"

"You will see."

Sabrina's brow furrowed at the novel idea that her cousin Frances was to be pitied. Was it possible that her feckless suitor Oliver was not so considerate a lover?

"I am going to please you, Sabrina." Niall's husky murmur made her forget any thought of her past pain. He caressed her spine, his roving hand lingering, as if savoring the feel of her skin. "You are so lovely . . . I want to learn every sweet inch of you. . . ."

His hand glided lower . . . over her back . . . along the rise of her buttock . . . the slender length of her thigh . . . all the way down her leg to the curve of her ankle. Sabrina arched her back a little at the delicate warmth inundating her senses.

To her surprise, he shifted his body, bending to kiss the lower part of her calf. His lips moved in a light murmur over her skin, tracing the reverse path his palm had made. His silky black hair fell forward to brush her skin, heightening the sensation.

How expert he was, she thought dazedly. Every caress justified his reputation for finesse and more.

Her breath caught like warm liquid in her lungs when his mouth found the back of her knee. She had never before realized how incredibly sensitive that particular spot was.

His exploration continued, slow and ruthlessly thorough, rousing an exquisite languor that stole through her limbs. In some dazed corner of her mind, Sabrina realized he was winning . . . melting her resistance, destroying any will to fight.

"Niall . . ." she whispered his name in protest.

"What, sweeting?"

"I . . . I am so hot . . ."

"Not hot enough." His voice was soft, husky, stroking like mystical fingers through her. "I want you feverish . . . all wanton and trembling for me." His delicate kisses resumed, his mouth playing over her skin, all the while his hands kept up their magic.

"You don't yet know how much pleasure your body can give you, but you will . . . I intend to teach you. I will fire your blood until you moan my name and forget everything but how good it feels between us."

He was already teaching her, Sabrina thought as she shifted restlessly. Dear God, what was happening to her? How could she bear this tight ache in her breasts, this brazen heat uncoiling between her thighs, this hot, shameless need?

It was some moments before she realized his ministrations

had ceased. Slowly her eyelids fluttered open. Even more slowly she turned her face on the pillow to look at him.

He had stretched out beside her, and was gazing at her with a compelling tenderness in his eyes. "Now, 'tis your turn."

"M-Mine?"

"Aye, to arouse me. Touch me, sweet Sabrina," he murmured, his voice rich and commanding.

He remained relaxed and still, while she found the courage to obey. Tentatively she stretched out her hand to touch his shoulder, feeling the smooth shifting pattern of muscle beneath the sleek velvet of his skin. When she would have faltered, he reached up and clasped her hand, drawing her palm against his breast.

The center of his chest was covered with a triangle of silky-looking black hair, and her fingers tingled as they brushed the soft fur.

"Look at me," he demanded in the lush quiet.

Her heart skipped a beat. Even as he drew her hand lower, he rolled onto his back, letting her see all of him.

Sabrina drew a sharp breath at the raw power of his male body. His erection lay arched against his belly, reaching nearly to his navel. He was huge. The sheer masculinity disturbed her more than his size.

With gentle relentlessness, he moved her hand downward, over his abdomen, flat and ridged with muscle, till her fingers curled around his rigid member, hot steel covered with soft velvet.

" 'Tis . . . unnatural, touching you this way," she protested in a hoarse whisper.

A slow, sensual brilliant smile curved his mouth. "Ah, no, sweetheart. 'Tis natural as breathing. Do you feel what you do to me?"

"I . . . I've done nothing. . . ."

"Indeed you have. A man swells and grows hard as his desire mounts. And as you see, your attractions fascinate me."

Rolling on his side, he slid his hand between her thighs.

Ignoring her soft intake of breath, he bared her velvet to his fingers.

"A lass, on the other hand . . . grows wet and slick with her own honey." He slipped a finger into her cleft. "See . . . your body is preparing itself to receive me." His voice was tender, his golden-throated words spellbinding. "Will you receive me, sweeting?"

He waited for her response. When she nodded tentatively, he reached for her and drew Sabrina to him, pulling her into his arms so that all her pale softness was enfolded in his powerful embrace. Her pebbled, rose-tipped breasts pressed against his naked chest; her stomach pillowed the rock-hard flesh at his groin.

His member was intimidating, and yet strangely, as she gazed into his blue, blue eyes, she felt no fear, but rather an unfamiliar, quivering sense of intimacy. She lay there willingly, absorbing the hard, warm strength of him, feeling the strong beat of his heart, the burning of his flesh against hers. She *wanted* this. She wanted Niall to show her what it felt to be a woman. And she could almost believe, as she lay trembling in his arms, that the dark light she saw in his eyes reflected her desire.

He kissed her then, with the same exquisite languor he had shown before, enveloping her senses in the smell of him. He had a deliciously wicked kiss, so passionate, so thoroughly devouring that she could think of nothing but Niall and the powerful sensations he aroused in her. He pulled her dewy lower lip between his teeth, nipping the soft flesh, while his thigh rode intimately between hers.

Sabrina bit back a moan, trying to control her breathing, trying to deny the pulsing need. Yet all the while his long-fingered hands continued stroking her body, working a wicked sorcery on her.

A moment later, Niall heard her soft whimper with satisfaction. He could have resorted to even more provocative methods to arouse her, he knew. He could have called on his vast experience, employing any of his myriad carnal skills to drive her to heights of desire she'd never known, till she hungered to do his bidding. Yet she was not just another of his casual lovers. She was his wife, a lovely innocent who had a right to expect more from him. He desperately wanted her first time to be filled with pleasure. And he wanted her first climax to be with him inside her.

Deliberately he eased over her, spreading her thighs and positioning his throbbing shaft. Poised at her slick entrance, he hesitated, feeling the vulnerable, trembling feminine body beneath him. He didn't want to hurt her, but this one instance could not be helped.

His blue eyes like jewels, he whispered, "Take me in, love . . . sheathe me in your dark silk . . ."

He pressed home then, thrusting slowly, carefully inside her, feeling her flesh stretch to accommodate his size, all the while watching her flushed face. She seemed determined to bear whatever agony he had in store for her.

He knew she felt pain, for her lips parted for an instant as she grimaced. But then suddenly she clenched her teeth and arched her hips, bravely thrusting against him to split the barrier that was denying him entrance, impaling herself on his shaft.

Niall felt his heart stop. The poignancy of the gesture was shattering to him. Yet all he could do was wait till the pain subsided. When she squeezed her eyes shut, he gently kissed her lids, her brow, the curve of her cheek, murmuring sweet unintelligible words, telling her it was all right, that the hurt would go away.

Protecting her from his full weight, he lay inside her, intoxicated by a restless passion. The heavy, throbbing sensation of his flesh was a fierce ache that clawed at him. For the sake of her sensibilities, however, he kept his hunger tightly leashed.

He could feel when her tautness eased a little. She was growing accustomed to the alien intrusion.

"Better?" The question was soft, muted, and she answered in kind, a breathy little rasp.

"Yes . . . I . . . think so."

"Let me know when you feel well enough to proceed."

"There . . . is more?"

"Oh, yes, much, much more. But the worst is over, I promise you. The rest is only pleasure."

"I seem to recall you said that before."

"If I shielded you from the stark truth, it was to ease your fear."

Sabrina could feel the feather touch of his lips on her throat. She drew a deep breath. "You . . . may proceed."

"I am in no hurry, cherie," he lied. "We have the entire night together. We can take this slowly. And you are in control."

"I? But . . . I don't know what to do."

"Move your hips a little."

She moved against him experimentally. Her pulse leaped when it seated his shaft more fully within her.

"What did you feel?"

A flicker of fire, Sabrina wanted to answer, though she didn't quite know how to express it.

He saw her confusion and smiled. With infinite care, he increased the pressure of his sinewed granite thighs, fitting his body even more closely as he filled her.

"I want you," he murmured huskily.

Sabrina felt a searing sweetness at his tantalizing words. He moved *his* hips then and withdrew slowly, stroking her with his long length. Sabrina gasped.

"Did that hurt?"

"N-No." Somewhere between the first wild heartbeat and the second the pain had disappeared and excitement had taken its place.

"Do you want me to stop?"

"No." Her breathless whisper was an imperative. After a consoling pause, he thrust again, progressing slow inches at a time into her lush, heated interior.

He felt her velvet tremors clutch his manhood.

"Yes . . . that's it . . . love. Give in to it. Let me feel your pleasure."

"I cannot . . ." she whispered hoarsely, yearning for something unfathomable, just out of reach.

"Aye, you can."

Obligingly, he began moving gently inside her, pampering, coddling, arousing her with tenderness, yet holding his own passion leashed with tight restraint.

Sabrina closed her eyes as the fire between her thighs burned higher. Her head fell back and she whimpered, a trembling pleasure sound.

Deliberately he increased the sensuous rhythm. Her reserve, her shyness changed then. Sensing it, Niall bent his head to kiss her, refusing to let her retreat from passion. His tongue plundered her mouth, mimicking the thrust of the shaft between her thighs.

An agony of longing swept through Sabrina, and she clung to him, instinctively matching his rhythm. When she moaned, he continued his relentless assault, coaxing her with his hands, his mouth, his hard body.

"Yes, tremble for me, love. Moan for me."

She was so feverish beneath him, frantically shuddering near the brink. The next time he drove gently into her, she sobbed, but he would not let up. Demanding her complete surrender, he thrust again.

Stunned, she arched up, straining wildly, striving to escape the desire that was drowning her, clawing through her. He moved once more and all her senses shattered. She convulsed beneath him, twisting, crying out, clutching blindly at his shoulders, oblivious to her scratching nails and wrenching grip.

Niall felt each sharp little cut, each wracking tremor of the impassioned woman clinging to him with such feverish strength. With every stab of her budded nipples against his chest, every soft surge of her thighs, fiery sensations ripped through him. But he would not give in. His lips drinking her wild moans, he held her vibrant, pulsating body against his own.

When it was over for her, he lay rigid and still, his own savage need held barely in check. She was weeping softly, with a turbulence of emotion, and he felt his heart wrench. She needed time to absorb what had happened to her, yet it had gone too far. He could not stop the throbbing of his body or the tempestuous passion burning through his senses.

He gritted his teeth, fighting against the hot tide of his desire, but he found it impossible to hold back the rampant hunger. Calling on all his control, he shuddered convulsively, groaning at the first drenching rush of sensation, even while trying to quiet the jerking movements of his body. His eyes shut against the wild delirium, until the galvanic, peaking splendor burst through him and he pulsed into her in an explosion of white-hot need.

He held her tightly in his arms afterward, a primordial possessiveness overcoming him. Bedding Sabrina had been far more enjoyable than he'd anticipated.

He had pleased her as well; he knew it by the languorousness of her eyes when her lids slowly lifted. But he had hurt her, too. The champagne lights in the dark irises were blurred by tears.

"That was what you meant . . . by release?" Her voice was hushed and bewildered.

Her faltering question surprised him. "That is what I meant, sweeting. The French call it *la petite mort*, the little death."

"How . . . appropriate. I thought . . . for a moment I was dying."

"From pain?"

"No . . . not pain. Pleasure. Just as you promised."

A slow, brilliantly devastating smile crept across his lips. "So you liked it?"

"Yes . . . I liked it . . . No . . . more than liked."

He laughed against her mouth, the sound thick, sensual, raw. "I applaud your honesty."

"You mock me."

"No." His expression instantly sobered. "I feared I might hurt you too much for you to feel pleasure."

"Well . . . it did hurt at first . . . but afterward . . ."

"Afterward?"

"I felt . . . it was . . . I can't really explain . . ."

He thought he understood what she had felt, but he wanted to hear it from her own lips. "Try," he commanded softly.

"It . . . was like I was soaring and falling at the same moment, but that . . . you would catch me. . . ."

He drew back, his gaze capturing hers. She sensed his burning triumph and satisfaction, saw it reflected in his look.

Wordlessly, Niall pressed his lips against her temple, before carefully easing himself from her body. Sabrina winced at the twinges she felt between her thighs and the unspoken fear that he would leave her. After covering them both with a sheet and quilt, however, he held her in the curve of his arm, while his fingers toyed with a lock of her hair.

Her alarm ebbing, she lay there, breathing the warm, musky scent of his skin, savoring the novel experience she'd just undergone, her senses still in thrall to the lush mysteries of passion. She hadn't realized such a degree of sensuality even existed. Her husband had, of course. In the game of love, Niall was an expert who commanded a vast array of weapons. And he had used them to great advantage in their battle of wills. She'd been a fool to think she could escape surrender. He had won handily . . . although she would not consider herself the loser. Not tonight. Tomorrow, though, she would have to face the painful knowledge that she was not unique.

I want you, he'd told her. How many other women had he said those exact words to? In this very bed? In truth, she was not so special, though he had made her feel so. He had taken great care to make her initiation into love a tender

awakening, but it was no more than he would have done for
any other woman.

Sabrina bit her lip, trying to still the sudden stab of jealousy that curled through her. Faith, it was better that she
face the truth squarely now, better that she allow herself no
illusions. She had to crush the fantasy that she held any special place in her husband's heart or bed.

Passion was a sport to Niall, a game at which she was a
hopeless novice. It had been imprudent to confess to him
how profoundly his lovemaking had affected her. She
should have tried to pretend indifference at least.

Feeling suddenly awkward, Sabrina started to ease from
his embrace, but Niall merely tightened his hold.

"Where do you go, madam wife?" he murmured lazily.

"I thought you . . . we . . . were finished."

"We are, for the moment. But savoring the aftermath of
passion can be enjoyable." He turned his head to gaze at her
intently. "There is no point in fleeing me now, tiger. The
deed is done."

A hesitant smile curved Sabrina's lips before her natural reserve reasserted itself, and she buried her face in his
shoulder.

That shy, heartrending flicker of a smile affected Niall
strangely. As the chamber grew hushed, he lay there holding
her, attempting to understand the myriad emotions his new
bride had evoked in him.

It was some long moments later when he realized from
her soft, even breathing that Sabrina had succumbed to
nerves and exhaustion and had fallen into a deep slumber.

Sleep was not forthcoming for Niall, however. He could
not shake the unsettling feeling that he had passed a point
from which there was no return.

It was not merely because he was irrevocably wed now.
With the consummation he had fulfilled his duty regarding their marriage, and considered himself free to go his
own way.

It was Sabrina herself who troubled him.

It should have been a simple exercise for him to conquer her with pleasure. He was a master at seduction, and no woman had ever resisted him for long. In truth, the bedding had gone well. He had demanded and received her surrender, just as he'd intended. He'd made Sabrina trust him enough to lower her prickly defenses.

Disturbingly, though, he hadn't expected her passionate response, or his own. He had meant to satisfy a fleeting desire for her, but carnal craving had spiraled into something more profound. When she'd given herself to him so bravely tonight, he'd felt the same primitive, overpowering urge as when she'd defended him in battle. Protective and possessive. Needy and yearning. He had wanted her, desired her, more than was rational.

Perhaps it was her very inexperience which had engendered his response. Remarkably, Sabrina's combination of innocence and shy eagerness had made the act of lovemaking seem fresh and new to a man of his jaded passions.

He might also attribute his powerful reaction to frustrated desire; he'd refrained from indulging his needs for some time now, and he was not accustomed to abstinence.

Her defiance was a powerful aphrodisiac, as well. She was a challenge to his masculinity. A tiger in mouse's clothing.

Niall found himself biting back a smile as he stared at the velvet canopy overhead. Sabrina was not like the shallow, self-serving beauties who usually pursued him. Her naivete might amuse him, yet at the same time her spirit and courage had won his respect.

Oddly, he *liked* his new bride. He liked her innocence. He liked her soft and mellow and trusting. He liked her defiance and her tart tongue. He liked her beneath him, arching with ecstasy and sobbing his name.

She was not the cold, unresponsive woman he'd feared. She possessed a hidden fire that was tantalizing. In the throes of passion he'd glimpsed a bewitching enchantress.

No, perhaps being wed to Sabrina would not be the hardship he'd envisioned. He might be furious at Angus for forcing his hand, but his fury did not extend to his bride.

Indeed, Niall reflected, Sabrina might be getting the worst of the bargain. Perhaps he *was* the hedonist she'd termed him. He would admit to excesses in matters carnal. He was a man to whom women had always come too easily and too often. From the time he'd been breeched, the female sex had practically been at his feet. And he had responded in kind, intent on losing himself in the pleasures of the flesh, regardless of who his lovers might be, seeking nothing deeper than carnal gratification. Both he and his partners had accepted that.

He formed attachments based purely on sensual pleasure. With Eve Graham, for example. His former mistress had lasted longer than most. Their expert couplings had left him breathless, spent . . . and hollow.

Unlike with Sabrina tonight. Lovemaking with her was somehow different . . . exciting and new. He was profoundly touched by her abandon and ingenuous appreciation.

The novelty would undoubtedly wear off with time, Niall suspected—but for the moment it might be satisfying to discover what sort of bride fate had given him. To see if he could remake her into the woman he wished her to be, a desirable woman who was, if not a match for him, then at least a skillful bed partner.

Absently picking up some silken strands of Sabrina's hair, Niall let them slowly shift through his fingers.

He was wed to her now, and he would make the best of it. He would explore the hidden, sensual side of her nature to their mutual enjoyment. He would pleasure her and teach her to pleasure him in return.

It would be a challenge, no doubt, but he intended to bring out the tigress in his mouse of a bride.

Chapter
Nine

Sabrina stirred slowly awake, then sharply inhaled with awareness. A warm, nude, and very male body lay beneath hers, the sensual feel of sinewed flesh arousing against her sensitive skin.

Niall. Her husband. Her arms and legs were braided with his, her hair a wild tangle across the breadth of his chest.

Sabrina's face flushed as disorientation fled and memory came rushing back. This was her marriage bed. And this must still be her wedding night. Dawn evidently had not yet arrived. Shadows wreathed the bridal chamber, the candle flames burning low in their sockets.

Thankfully Niall was asleep. His breathing was deep and easy, his strong body relaxed—may the devil take him.

Her heart thudding, she slowly eased herself from his side. She needed time to regain her composure before she had to face him again.

She felt different, strangely so, Sabrina reflected as she lay there rigidly taking inventory. Her mouth was tender from his kisses, her nipples even more so, while the secret hollow between her thighs throbbed with a twinging ache, almost as though he were still inside her. She could feel him moving within her—

Shying away from the remembrance of what he'd done to her, she carefully slipped from the bed and drew the velvet curtains around him to give herself privacy. After stirring the fire, she hastily washed away the musky scent of their lovemaking which clung to her skin, then dressed in a day gown which had been delivered yesterday to her husband's home.

Feeling somewhat refreshed and more able to deal with the demands of her current circumstances, Sabrina realized she was famished. When she started to slip from the room in search of food, however, she discovered a tray directly outside the door. Someone had thoughtfully provided wine and a cold collation of meats and cheese and bread. Gratefully, she curled up in a chair before the fire and satisfied the worst of her hunger.

She was lost in reflection when a deeply masculine voice spoke behind her—the same voice she'd heard whispering endearments and bold persuasions in her ear last night.

" 'Tis a first, a lass leaving my bed before the night is through."

Starting, Sabrina glanced back over her shoulder at her husband of a few short hours. Niall had parted the bed-curtains and propped himself on one elbow. He looked dismayingly, sinfully beautiful, lounging there among the tumbled sheets, the covers falling to below his waist, nearly a day's growth of stubble darkening his jaw. The nakedness of that broad, bronzed, rippling chest made her mouth go dry.

"W-Would you . . . like something to eat?" she managed to ask.

"Later, sweeting. I have in mind satisfying a different appetite first."

"What . . . appetite?"

"Come here, and I will gladly show you."

Her heart twisted in her chest. Niall seemed so easy and normal, unchanged by having made love to her, while she had been devastated by his tender eroticism. With his invasion of her body, he had laid claim to some secret part of her. But then, he doubtlessly had honed that particular skill. He was a veteran of more beds than he could probably recall.

He flashed her a slow, lazy smile, more brilliant than sunshine. "Come to bed, love."

"W-Why?"

"Because I want you." His voice was pleasant, unhurried, rich in timbre. "And because I want to pleasure you."

He was in an enchanting mood, Sabrina thought, her heart sinking. It was all she could do to resist his potent sexual power, yet she had to try. She had already exposed more of her vulnerability to him than she could bear.

"Do you never think of anything else but lovemaking?" she muttered.

"Occasionally." The warm blue eyes were amused and beguiling. "The third Tuesday of each month I devote to clan affairs."

She bit back a smile, cursing the overwhelming urge to run into his arms. "You may cease your efforts to seduce me. Our marriage has been consummated, you might recall."

"True." He regarded her with lazy anticipation. "But we have barely begun your education." His voice held a uniquely seductive rasp. "You delighted me far beyond my expectations last night, but it will take time and practice for you to become proficient."

"You have enough proficiency for both of us. And I have no desire to repeat the experience."

"Did you find your initiation too painful?"

"I found it . . . disappointing," Sabrina lied. "I cannot comprehend why such fuss is made about so awkward a procedure."

His eyebrow shot up. "You render me inarticulate."

"I doubt it."

His grin was audacious and captivating, his eyes a vivid, wicked blue. "I think you must be telling a shameful falsehood. Come, admit it, mouse, you find me irresistible."

A warm laugh bubbled past her control. "I find you impossibly conceited."

Niall tilted his head at the bell-like sound of her laugh. "You are entrancing when you laugh, do you realize that?"

Her heart tumbled over itself at his remark. Doubtless he was giving her false coin, but still she felt herself succumbing to the virile charm. "I expect countless women find *you* entrancing, but I think your prowess as a lover much overrated."

"Come, now, pet, I might become insulted."

"That would be impossible!"

His smile softened. "I shall take pleasure in proving you wrong. No lass has spent a night in my bed and yet been unsatisfied."

"I am honored to be your first."

"Did you not enjoy the feel of me moving inside you, sweeting?"

Sabrina shut her eyes briefly, fighting the erotic image of their bodies joined. His sensuality was a weapon he held over her, and the wretch damn well knew it. "If you expect me to pay homage to your carnal talents, you will have a long wait."

"Just so I do not have to wait for *you*. Come, sweeting, I am not accustomed to begging for female companionship."

"Perhaps you should. You might find it beneficial."

He shook his head. "I can see you have a great deal to learn about the art of dalliance. When a man asks if you enjoyed his lovemaking, you should declare yourself enchanted."

"Had I been enchanted, I might have admitted it."

Niall was the one to laugh this time, a wry, pained chuckle. "My wounded vanity may never recover."

"I'm certain it will. You have only to seduce your next female and it will be quite whole again."

"I want no other female but you."

"Now who is telling falsehoods?" Sabrina plucked at a thread of her skirt. "I . . . am not the kind of woman who could ever please you."

His expression suddenly grew sober. "You can and shall please me in every possible way. Come here, Sabrina." When she remained frozen, he patted the mattress beside him. "I never took you for a timid lass. But perhaps our

Highland ways are too fierce for you, and you are not up to the challenge."

Vexed as he intended her to be, Sabrina rose abruptly, determined to prove him wrong. She might be unable to change her plain appearance, but she was not a mouse in spirit.

She hesitated, however, when Niall tossed aside the covers, exposing his nudity. He presented a riveting contrast to the pale linen sheets, his body an awesome line of broad chest and naked, rippling thigh, all lean-muscled strength and bronzed skin.

She wanted desperately to avert her gaze, but then she noticed the discolored flesh on his right hip—a wicked gash that in her nervousness she had missed seeing previously.

"You are hurt," she murmured in sympathy.

Niall's mouth twisted wryly. "A wound from an unfortunate mishap. But it is healing. Do not think to change the subject, mouse. Do as I bid and come to me."

A mixture of desire and excited apprehension coursed through Sabrina as she forced her feet to move.

When she was close enough, Niall reached out to capture her wrist and drew her down to sit beside him. The warmth in his blue eyes seemed very real as he lightly stroked her cheek with the back of his knuckles. "Did you truly not like kissing me last eve?"

She couldn't answer with the sudden constriction in her throat; indeed, she was finding it difficult to breathe.

"*I* very much liked kissing *you*," he murmured.

"You were . . . merely performing your duty."

"Surely you do not believe a man embraces a woman like I did you out of simple *duty*?"

"Yes . . ."

"Indeed," he said almost to himself, "a great deal to learn."

Sabrina forced herself to reply lightly. "You cannot persuade me that last night was not a disappointment to you. Doubtless you prefer ladies of experience."

Niall gave her an odd look. "Don't underestimate your-self, lass. Such spirit as yours is entrancing. It will be a for-tunate man who can unleash all the fire you've hidden from the world." He smiled softly. "And I intend to be that man."

He reached up and flicked the high neckline of her gown, making Sabrina tense. "Surely this is too constricting, sweeting. And unflattering. It doesn't do you justice."

She made a face. "You have a most annoying habit of criticizing my taste in attire."

"Because I am not fond of the stiff Presbyterian frocks you wear. The style is all wrong for you—and you don it like protective armor. A gown should flatter the wearer. The neckline should show the lovely swell of your breasts . . . Like this . . ."

Gently he tugged on the bodice, drawing down the fabric to the neckline of the tight stomacher. Sabrina's breath caught in her throat.

"And if you were truly daring . . . you would rouge your nipples and let them peek over the edge, beckoning your lover . . . like so . . ."

Her breath fled entirely. When he brushed her skin, her nipples instantly grew taut, while her heart began to thud. Yet she made no move to stop him as he exposed the pale swells of her bosom pushed up by stays of whalebone, free-ing her flesh of the confining fabric.

His eyes darkened, his glance making no effort to dis-guise his purpose, a blatant appraisal of her charms.

Instinctively her arms rose to cover her breasts, but Niall drew them away. "No, lass . . . there's no need for shyness between us. Not after the intimacies we've already shared. You are my wife now, Sabrina. You have yet to lose your in-hibitions, but one day soon, you will take great pleasure in showing me every single secret of your lovely body . . ."

Ruthlessly his eyes devoured her, scrutinizing the high, jutting breasts, the rose-hued nipples, still swollen and hotly sensitized from his attentions the previous night. "You are a far greater temptation than you know, pet."

Sabrina felt her heart hammering. There was something warm and exciting and yes, flattering, in the way he was looking at her. But then she dared not trust so renowned a rake. Niall's gaze was full of male appreciation whenever he looked at *any* woman. It was his stock in trade, a talent he had deliberately cultivated—letting his sapphire eyes shimmer with desire while hiding every other emotion brilliantly.

"Aye, I much prefer this charming dishabille," he murmured, his voice husky. Determinedly, he drew a lock of her hair forward, to fall gracefully over her shoulder. "I like your silken hair flowing free like this. I like the way it teases every sweet curve of your breast . . ."

Her nipples quivered beneath his gaze, the peaks distended and hard. Then, with one finger, he touched the tip of her breast, brushing her flesh that was achingly tight and tender, knowing full well the sensuality of it.

Sabrina gasped, even before the long fingers curved, cupping and teasing the furled bud with expert skill.

"My bonny mouse . . ." he whispered.

"I . . . am not bonny. . . ."

Their eyes met, haunted brown to hungry blue.

Niall shook his head at the uncertainty he saw in her features. It was criminal, how little value Sabrina placed on her own feminine attractions. She was convinced that she possessed no beauty, that he could not want her. She had no notion how lovely she could be. She was intriguing with the light of laughter dancing in her dark eyes. She was enchanting in her fury. Her spirited defiance lent a radiance to her skin and a fire to her eyes that was as fascinating as it was alluring. And when passion brightened her face, she was almost incandescent. . . .

Niall smiled faintly to himself. He intended to prove her wrong, to make this lass believe he found her desirable, to understand how very much he wanted her . . . With the right amount of masculine persuasion he could convince her.

"You *are* bonny," he whispered as his hands began their practiced arousal. "You are one of the most intriguing women I've ever met. Lovely and vibrant . . ."

The shimmering-silk words washed over her and made Sabrina's heart ache. He was a scoundrel set on seduction, and she would be powerless to stop him.

"Can you feel how perfectly you fill my hands?"

She gazed down at his bronzed fingers cupping her pale flesh. He had beautiful hands with long strong fingers, aristocratic yet seasoned by battle. He cupped and weighed the soft globes, brushing his thumbs across the aureoles.

"Your slender body is exquisite, Sabrina, made for giving pleasure."

She closed her eyes, feeling a feverish heat throb between her thighs. He was winning. She could feel the reckless hunger rising, slow and insidious.

When his hands covered her breasts completely, she arched her back, thrusting the rigid tips, so deliciously sensitive, against his callus-roughened palms. She wanted to do more, to press her full length against him, until she melted into his hard-muscled form. She felt a need so palpable, it throbbed and pulsed with a life of its own.

"You're a woman of great passion. . . ."

Dazed, she shook her head. "Niall . . ."

Tenderness filled him as he watched a lush sensuality suffuse her face. "I like the sound of my name upon your lips. Perhaps we should see if I can make you cry it aloud again."

Sabrina bit back a whimper, trying to resist the maddening games his touch was playing on her ready flesh.

"Look at me, love."

His eyes were smoldering embers in the candlelight, his voice a velvet whisper. "How bonny you are . . . Your breasts are exquisite, so firm and taut, the nipples pouting like wild rosebuds eager to be kissed."

With light erotic strokes, he caressed each peaking crest

into a rigid, aching hardness, rubbing and teasing the furled buds with expert skill, filling Sabrina with a hot shameless yearning that grew with each heartbeat. Her body felt heavy and tense with wanting, with craving.

Then his dark head dipped, his mouth skimming hot and open against her bosom. A sweet blinding hunger flooded her.

"Do you ache here, sweeting? Shall I ease the pain? Let me taste you . . ."

His tongue was rough and wet on her tender skin as it wrapped around a budding nipple. The arrow of pleasure that shot through Sabrina made her whimper aloud. She would have collapsed against him had he not supported her.

Her fingers clung to his powerful shoulders as his lips captured the pouting crest. Her heart lurched wildly as he suckled the rigid peak. A wave of stunning sensation streaked through her, excruciatingly violent, a fire burning in her blood. Sabrina moaned again raggedly.

The murmur that sounded deep in Niall's throat was one of approval. "Aye . . . let me hear your pleasure . . ."

Slowly, gently, he teased each peaking crest into a rigid aching hardness. Like a lash of dark fire, his tongue flickered and tormented, arousing sweet searing pleasure within her, filling her with a raw, reckless hunger, until she wanted to plead for mercy.

When weakly she tried to pull away from him, though, Niall wrapped her in the sweet prison of his arms. She wanted him, he was certain. He'd known too many women not to recognize need when he saw it, tasted it. Pulling her resisting body across his, he rolled with her, till she lay sprawled among the pillows.

"Lie back," he commanded with a roughened voice. His lips tasting the flare of her pulse at her throat, he pushed up her skirts to her waist.

He was going to take her, Sabrina thought tensely, without even removing her clothes.

But he made no move to cover her with his body. Instead he reached down to stroke the satiny flesh between her thighs. Sabrina gasped as his maddeningly slow fingers made her body flow hot and wanton.

"Please . . . Niall . . ."

"Oh, I shall please you, sweetheart, I promise. I want to do every wicked, delightfully lustful thing we can think of."

Shifting his body to a lower position between her legs, he bent his head. Shock swept through her as she felt his unshaven jaw scraping her bare inner thighs. When she jerked her hips in response, he held them in a gentle grip. "No, lie still. Let me taste your honey. . . ."

She lay there breathless, rigid, as he resumed his masterful attentions. Following the path of his fingers, he found the dewy, throbbing center of her, savored her secret softness with his tongue. He smiled in satisfaction at the slick wetness he found there. Her taut body was hot and explosive with need. One thrust and she'd be twisting beneath him, breathless and ready. But he wanted to show her another side of her passionate nature, one where she cast off all shyness and restraint.

Ignoring her shocked gasp of protest, he held her open to him, his thumbs on either side of her cleft. "You're like a flower, Sabrina . . . delicate, so impossibly sweet. . . ."

Her entire body clenched with anticipation as his caressing lips found her again in a tantalizing act of primitive possession. He kissed her lovingly, as if sipping nectar, suckling gently.

She whimpered at the shameful pleasure and clutched at him, her fingers tightening reflexively in his thick hair. Yet he continued his tender, wicked assault, teasing, exploring the yielding, warm folds of her flesh, finding the aching bud of her femininity . . . Her heart beat wildly, her body pulsed with desire. Then she felt the silken probe of his tongue parting her . . . setting off a firestorm of exquisite sensation.

"Oh, God . . . no . . ." she pleaded, yet trembling with need.

"*Yes,*" her husband insisted. "I want your pulse wild and fast, your breath coming sweet and hot. I want you blind with passion from my tongue, my hands, my heat."

There was no escaping the tender torment, yet she no longer wanted to escape. Each slow, drugging stroke was heaven. He went on suckling her, lapping, drinking from her essence, the erotic assault long and lingering and deliberately drawn out, tantalizing her beyond endurance. When another probing kiss invaded her, he forced a shuddering moan from deep within her throat.

"That's it, love," he urged hoarsely. "Let me hear every sweet gasp. Let me feel every wild leap of your pulse. . . ."

She writhed, her hips straining under the delicate lash of his tongue, the tender plundering of his relentless mouth. A sob built inside her, catching in her throat. Quaking from the unbearable pleasure, Sabrina thrashed her head from side to side, fighting the dark magic he commanded.

"I can't bear it. . . ."

"Aye, you can. . . ."

His triumphant mouth dredged another keening moan from Sabrina as stabbing pleasure flooded her. Madness, she cried silently, mind and body aflame. She arched up to him shamelessly, shaking with silken tremors.

"Better," he breathed. "Tremble for me, sweeting. Moan for me. Give me your passion. . . ."

A blinding wave of pleasure broke over her, cresting again and again. Racked by shuddering, Sabrina dissolved into throbbing, impassioned need.

In the breathless aftermath, she lay dazed and quivering with sensual exhaustion, yet Niall wasn't done with her yet. Stretching his sleek, heavy body over hers, he gently suckled her turgid nipples, intensifying the slow-ebbing pleasure.

It was a long moment before he raised his head. His face was hard, taut, like a man pressed beyond his limits, his voice rough and rasping as he questioned provokingly, "Are you still disappointed, lass?"

No, Sabrina, thought. It had been wicked and wonderful . . . raw pleasure and aching delight. And yet . . . Niall had given nothing of himself, his heart or emotions. "It was . . . adequate, I think," she murmured hoarsely.

He laughed darkly in triumph, mistaking her hesitation for another lie. Bending, he whispered, "Kiss me, sweeting," and took her mouth in an act of sweet possession.

He kissed her as a lover should, tender yet impossibly demanding. He made her forget the ache in her heart by rekindling the ache in her body. As he positioned himself between her thighs, she was agonizingly aware of how hot and hard and huge he was against her swollen sex. His mouth still captivating hers, he fitted his hardness to her softness and pressed home, his thrust slow and careful, as if he remembered how new she still was to such lush carnality.

Sabrina gave a gasp of pleasure as blessedly he filled her. She wanted this man. Nothing else existed beyond the thunder of her heart, the wild hammering in her blood, his magical caresses, his hard body . . .

Instinctively she hugged his sinewed thighs with her own, opening for him, welcoming him with wildness and warmth. Through a haze of desire she heard his harsh whisper in her ear, telling her how hot and tight it felt to be buried deep within her. And as his rhythm increased to urgent need, she could feel the explosive tension build anew. She strained to hold the sleek shaft inside her, but he withdrew to plunge again, stoking the scorching flames ever higher, till she could no longer bear the blinding desire.

As her convulsive shudders began, Niall was gripped by the same fiery talons of sensation, caught in the same fierce tempest. When her climax burst upon her, his restraint shattered. Seizing a rasping breath, he lost control as she did, unprepared for the raw, searing pleasure that ripped through him. With a harsh groan he stiffened, then arched fiercely, surging wildly as he met his own sensual madness. His body shuddered into hers, drenching her with his warmth. His teeth clenched, he shut his eyes as the throbbing, peaking splendor washed over him in heated waves.

Chest heaving, he collapsed upon Sabrina, barely remembering to shield her from the force of his weight.

His breath was a soft mist on her flushed cheeks as they

lay entwined afterward, suffused with warmth and desire. His palm drifted over her bare shoulder, lazily stroking her skin.

"I would hardly call that a disappointment," he murmured with a soft laugh.

Totally pliant, Sabrina exhaled in a sigh. It amazed her that she could find the strength to whisper a hoarse reply. "I confess astonishment . . . I should think it would take a great deal to arouse a jaded man's lusts."

"*Especially* a jaded man's lusts. But you succeeded admirably."

She made a soft, noncommittal sound.

"Have you any notion how such a wanton response inflames a man?" When she gave no answer, Niall's dark lashes lifted languorously, so that he could see her. "When you let yourself surrender to passion, you become quite a woman."

"It was . . . wicked."

"Perhaps, but I prefer the brazen tiger in my bed to the prim and proper mouse."

So did she. She vastly preferred the reckless, foolish, even sinful lass she was with him to the plain, passive spinster. In his arms she was a woman, desired and desiring.

Grasping her chin in his fingers, Niall turned her face up to his. "You look like a lass who's just been pleasured— thoroughly, passionately. You look beautiful."

When she closed her eyes in denial, his fingers tightened on her shoulder. Why did it matter so that she believe him? he wondered. He had never felt it imperative to prove himself to any woman. But then, he had rarely experienced the wild hunger that had seized him a moment ago, or the shattering satisfaction afterward. Sabrina was different from the countless lovers who had come before her, but it was not merely the novelty or her innocence that had captivated him. It was the honesty of her response. The intensity of her desire, wild and unbridled. Her defenselessness just now.

Niall felt an odd jolt in the region of his heart when her searching glance swept his face, uncertain and vulnerable.

He pressed his lips tenderly to her forehead. "It will take time, sweeting, but you will learn to accept your wanting. To accept *my* wanting." His finger forced her chin up. "I want you, lovely Sabrina. I want to see your bonny hair fanning across my pillow. I want to see your face flushed and damp from loving me, your eyes hazed with desire I've just sated. I mean to have you, in every way a man can have a woman."

Desperate to hide the deep ache his gentleness aroused, she buried her face in Niall's shoulder so he couldn't see the turmoil of emotion that was tearing her apart inside. She wanted to weep at the powerful and strange feelings coursing through her . . . tender feelings she would never tell him about.

It would be too easy to love him, she thought wildly. Too easy to expose herself to savage hurt.

And yet the possibility existed that it might already be too late.

Chapter
Ten

Sabrina awoke alone later that same morning, with a
vague recollection of Niall kissing her sweetly at dawn, saying regretfully that the press of duty called him away. For
a moment she lay there in the vast bed, unmoving, lush
memories heating her senses as she relived certain indescribable moments of the night just passed.

She had never before imagined the act of mating could be
so . . . incredible. Yesterday she wouldn't have believed
such shattering pleasure was even possible, or that she
could have responded to a man's touch with such wanton
abandon.

Burying her face in the pillow, she breathed in Niall's
musky male scent. Before last night she would have called
herself a lady, but the demanding intensity of his passion
had stripped away every shred of reserve or shyness, destroyed any lingering will to resist.

Without conscious thought, Sabrina reached up to touch
her breast with her palm, remembering Niall's strong, long-
fingered hands caressing the sensitive bud. She nearly
whimpered at the fire that shivered through her.

Her eyes shut as vivid images assaulted her . . . Niall loving her, his bare, powerfully muscled body moving against
hers . . . his expression feverish, his face dark and strained
with arousal. . . .

His sensuality had astonished her. She had been prepared
for a dispassionate, even painful, bedding, yet he had treated

her with infinite consideration, indeed, as if she were a desirable woman. For a few brief moments, he had made her feel special, cherished, sought after . . .

Rising from the bed, she drew open the window curtains, and caught her breath at the scene that greeted her. Below, the mist-shrouded castle glowed golden in the early morn, while the emerald hills shimmered in the translucent light.

At the scene of enchantment, a feeling of optimism swept her. This was her home, and she would make the best of it. A new life awaited her now, one as Niall McLaren's wife and mistress of his clan. It was a long moment before Sabrina could make herself turn away to begin the mundane tasks of washing and dressing.

She had nearly completed her toilet when a scratch on the door interrupted her thoughts. When she bid entrance, a young woman stepped gingerly into the room. It was the chambermaid, Jean, the same lass Sabrina had discovered with a naked Niall in the herbal just over a se'nnight ago.

Jean kept her eyes downcast as she dipped a curtsy. "Beg pardon, milady . . . but Master Cameron's come to bid ye farewell."

Sabrina brightened at the thought of her stepfather. "Thank you. Would you tell him I will be there directly?"

"Ah . . . milady . . . Perhaps ye should know . . . that day ye came to call . . . there was naught between the laird an' me. I was to minister to his wounds, 'twas all."

"His wounds?"

"Aye. He was injured mending the dam—a nasty gash on his hip and bruises on his side."

Sabrina felt herself frowning as she recalled the scabbed flesh on Niall's body.

"He never bedded me, nor even kissed me," Jean insisted. "Never, I swear it. Not that I would ha' minded kissing him, or ought else . . . but the laird doesna diddle the servants. Never. Ye can ask anyone. We're as safe here as newborn bairns in a kirk. But as ye're the mistress here now,

I wouldna wish to start on the wrong foot, with ye thinking . . . well, I didn't, that's all."

Her confession sounded entirely sincere, not at all like an anxious attempt to placate a jealous mistress.

Relieved that Niall had not been seducing the maids, Sabrina managed a smile. "You have eased my mind, Jean. I too hope we may begin with a fresh slate. If you will forget the incident, I surely will."

Jean bobbed a curtsy and fled the room, leaving Sabrina to her restless thoughts. She was comforted to think she needn't fear her husband's betrayal in her own home at least, but vexed that the confession had to come from a stranger. Niall could have simply explained to her about his wounds and set her mind at ease, but he had purposely let her believe the worst.

Her stepfather awaited her with Rab in the great hall. The dog, who had been banished from the wedding festivities, barked with excitement and fawned around Sabrina's legs joyously.

When she eventually straightened from embracing her pet, it was to find Charles Cameron studying her intently. Her cheeks flushed with warmth as she hugged him as well.

When she would have stepped back, though, he prevented her, his lean hands gentle on her shoulders. "He has treated you well?"

Sabrina had no need to ask who "he" was. "Quite well," she murmured, a bit embarrassed to be discussing so intimate a subject as her wedding night.

Charles shook his head. "I confess I find these Highlanders too savage for my taste, but then I forget you're half Highlander. Well . . . I'm off to Edinburgh, lass, unless you have need of me. I shall miss you more than you know."

An ache knotted her throat. "Never more than I will miss you."

"It goes against the grain, but I intend to release your dowry as soon as I return."

"Thank you, Papa Charles."

His gray eyes concerned, he took her hands in a gentle grip. "Sabrina . . . I've always been of a mind that one who makes his bed must lie in it . . . but I wish you to know, if you find yourself truly unhappy, you may always make your home with me."

"Thank you, Papa," she said huskily through her tears, and embraced him again with all the love in her aching heart.

She greatly regretted her stepfather's departure, and was glad for her dog's companionship. Yet her new position as laird's wife left her little time for melancholy. And happily, she discovered a friend in the McLaren housekeeper, Mrs. Paterson.

Over a breakfast of oatcakes and honey, the elderly woman welcomed Sabrina with genuine warmth.

" 'Twill be good to have a mistress of the house again," Mrs. Paterson admitted with a sigh. "And good for the laird to have a wife, no doubt. Mayhap marriage will settle him down and persuade him to abandon his wild ways."

Sabrina wanted very much to ask about the laird's "wild ways," but did not consider it appropriate.

Immediately after breakfast, Mrs. Paterson gave her a detailed tour of her new home. The three-storied fortified manor had been built two centuries ago to withstand seizes by English armies and warring clans, yet everywhere she turned, Sabrina spied touches of elegance and comfort inspired by the late Lady McLaren.

The walls of the banqueting hall were lined with tapestries and leather hangings to relieve the cold stone, while other chambers had been wainscotted or papered in flocked damask. The most formal rooms boasted molded ceilings, rich wood paneling, brass chandeliers, and intricately carved firescreens, while the family living quarters were decorated with thick carpets, gleaming furniture, and landscapes and portraits done in oils, with the prize possession, the exquisite pianoforte, in the drawing room.

With Mrs. Paterson, Sabrina reviewed the household accounts, yet she was wary of overstepping her bounds, and anxious to discuss her role as mistress with her new husband.

Regrettably Niall remained gone much of the day, returning barely in time for supper. Mrs. Paterson had prepared a special meal to honor the bridal couple, so they ate alone in the blue parlor, in an atmosphere made cozy by candlelight.

As she faced him across the small table, Sabrina found herself dismayingly tongue-tied. After the carnal intimacies she had shared with Niall the previous night, she could scarcely meet his gaze.

"You are too quiet, mouse," he said finally as she toyed with the braised mutton on her plate. "Is something amiss?"

"No. I was . . . simply thinking."

He raised a dark eyebrow.

"I think . . . Do you not agree we should discuss how we are to go on?"

"Go on?"

"As husband and wife. How we are to live our lives." Niall sipped his wine. Of course Sabrina would wonder how she was to fit into his life, his clan. "Aye, that might be prudent. What do you wish to discuss?"

"Well . . . I am a stranger here, and a Lowlander, but I don't care to remain idle. I should like something to occupy my time."

"What do you suggest?"

"I wondered . . . Shall I have the running of your house, for instance?"

Humor lit Niall's blue eyes. "I have no knack for managing a household. You may have the office with my blessing."

Sabrina let out a pent-up breath. She had been prepared for a major battle. "I am good with accounts, as well. I often examined my stepfather's books to verify his clerks' tallies."

"Ah, yes." A smile curved his beautiful mouth. "I recall you claiming that you have a head for figures. I would be glad of the assistance. I'll show you the estate accounts at the first opportunity."

She hesitated. "And I should like to meet your tenants."

Niall nodded, pleased she cared enough to involve herself with his clan. "You are mistress here now. On the morrow, if you wish, we shall tour the McLaren lands together."

Sabrina felt her tension ease measurably. This would not be as difficult as she had expected. Niall was being entirely reasonable. He might not have wanted to wed her, but he seemed prepared to accept her as mistress, at least. "I would like that a great deal."

They conversed about his clan then, with Niall explaining the relations of his kinsmen and describing the people Sabrina might meet on the morrow. Some time later, he asked if she had finished her meal. "We should retire now if we are to get an early start in the morning."

"Retire?" Sabrina repeated, her tension rising abruptly again.

Amusement lit his remarkable blue eyes. "Are you not acquainted with the word, mouse? It means to sleep."

She flushed. "I know what it means. I simply . . . I did not expect us to retire *together*. I assumed we would have separate chambers."

"Are you so eager to leave my bed, then?"

Sabrina lowered her gaze. She wanted to pretend indifference to his magnetic charm, but couldn't manage it. "It is not uncommon for a husband and wife to sleep apart, especially in a marriage of convenience. Indeed, you made it clear you desired us to go our separate ways after the . . . bedding."

Niall grinned. "You must needs grow accustomed to the carnal side of marriage. After a time you may go your own way, if you so wish."

Sabrina felt her heart sink. She would never manage to maintain a safe distance from Niall if they were to continue in such intimate proximity.

Reluctantly Sabrina accompanied him abovestairs to the

master bedchamber. The bed-hangings had been opened and the covers turned down invitingly, she saw, while a fire burned in the grate.

"Do you require assistance undressing, pet?"

Sabrina gave a start, realizing she was staring at the bed. "No. I can manage."

But she tarried as Niall stripped off his clothing and folded it away in the clothespress. When she saw him settle in the bed nude, she was surprised enough to ask, "You do not sleep in a nightshirt?"

He grinned a heart-stopping grin. "What need have I of a nightshirt if I have a willing lass to keep me warm?"

Sabrina felt her mouth go dry at his implication that she would keep him warm.

Niall gave a husky chuckle at her expression. "Cease your dawdling, pet, and come to bed. I shan't bite you." He smiled wickedly. "At least not tonight. You are not yet experienced enough for that."

He reclined leisurely against the pillows, his hands behind his head, while Sabrina found the courage to undress. It unnerved her to have him watch her—which was perhaps absurd, considering the knowledge of her body he had gained the previous night. It unnerved her more that he objected when she reached for her nightsmock.

"No, sweeting. We need no garments between us. I want you naked in my bed."

She hesitated, flushing at his frankness.

Niall understood her shyness, but he refused to indulge it. It wouldn't suit his purpose, for he meant to free Sabrina of her inhibitions. "Pray, contrive to relax, love. You are far too tense."

"I am not accustomed to being on public display," she snapped, "or parading in the altogether for your enjoyment."

"Your inexperience can be easily remedied. Indeed"—he regarded her thoughtfully—"you are sorely in need of instruction."

"Instruction?"

"Aye. I propose to teach you the art of passion, Sabrina."

When she remained mute, he added, "I fancy you would make an apt pupil. You have the right instincts. It remains only to uncover the hidden fire in you."

Sabrina eyed him warily, wondering what new game he was playing. "Why? To what purpose?"

Niall shrugged. "Perhaps because I would gain a proficient bed partner?" His smile softened. "It might prove diverting to discover the kind of woman you can be. I think you could make a magnificent lover, cherie."

Sabrina stared at him in disbelief.

Niall returned her gaze blandly. "You could benefit from lessons in the art of dalliance, as well. You are clever enough to match wits with any man, but it would serve you better to take the sting from your banter . . . But there is no need for haste. We can start your instruction on the morrow. For now, it is time for you to come to bed."

Too distracted to protest, Sabrina blew out the candles and joined Niall in bed, then lay there nervously as he drew up the covers and wrapped her in his arms.

"Go to sleep, sweeting," Niall murmured, pressing her head against his shoulder and closing his eyes.

In only moments, his soft even breathing told her he had fallen asleep.

Staring at the canopy overhead, Sabrina felt an inexplicable wave of disappointment. Niall had made no attempt to make love to her. He hadn't rejected her precisely, but absurdly she felt spurned.

She lay there, absorbing his heat, longing for his hand to ride the aching fullness of her breasts, for his body to cover hers and satisfy the sweet tingling between her thighs.

It was a long, long while before she herself found slumber.

They toured his lands the following day, and called on many of his tenants. Sabrina was gratified yet dismayed by the reception she received. At each home, she was given some small bride's gift as a token of welcome into Clan McLaren.

When she worried that Niall's kinsmen could not afford to be so generous, he dismissed her misgivings. "'Tis our way."

Even so, Sabrina was disturbed by the difficult conditions the Highlanders faced. The simple, sometimes rude crofters' cottages were dark and haze-filled, with floors made of earth and smoke from a peat fire spiraling up through a hole in the roof. More often than not, the dwellings were shared with the family pigs and goats.

When she remarked on the hard life to Niall, however, he shook his head in amusement.

"Save your pity, lass. Life is richer in these hills than could ever be found in a Lowland palace."

It seemed his entire clan shared his view. Highlanders were a dour, practical people, but fiercely proud and highly industrious. The men tilled the fields or watched over herds and flocks, while the women tended their gardens or worked their churns and looms.

As the largest landowner in the district, the McLaren laird received rents paid in money or cattle, yet before the day was through, Sabrina began to realize that the wedding gifts were a mark of affection rather than an obligation. Niall was well liked and respected, by the women in particular. The lasses, young or old, held a special fondness for him, perhaps because he treated each one as if she were infinitely special.

When they visited an aging crone who was nearly blind, her back bowed and bent, Niall bowed over her bony hand like any courtier and teased her about dancing a jig. The old woman cackled with pleasure at his flirtation, and after interrogating Sabrina ruthlessly, sent them on their way with a gift of sweetmeats she had made for her grandson.

As they rode away, Niall offered Sabrina an apologetic,

rueful smile. "You must forgive Dame Morag for her inquisition. She has been like a grandmother to me since before I was breeched."

Sabrina brushed aside his explanation with a shrug. " 'Tis no novelty, seeing you pursued by females of any age. I am growing accustomed to them swooning at the sight of you—though I cannot imagine why they should."

A reckless grin flashed out. "Can you not?"

In truth, she *could* understand. She herself was not impervious to the incredible appeal that made women yearn for Niall. She would swallow hot coals, however, before she admitted her weakness to him.

"You need not worry," Sabrina replied loftily, "that I will play the jealous wife, or that I will suddenly demand fidelity from you. I told you, you are free to take your lusts elsewhere. Although . . . it does seem rather unfair that I cannot enjoy the same freedom you claim."

Niall considered her a moment, his appraisal thoughtful. "I see no reason why you cannot indulge in a discreet affair . . . after you produce an heir, naturally."

"Naturally," she said stiffly, hurt to think she meant no more to him than a broodmare.

The next call, however, disturbed Sabrina, more than she cared to admit. As they rode toward a low-roofed crofter's hut, Niall warned, "This may take more than a moment. The well needs repair and I've not found time to see to it before now."

He had barely finished the sentence before two young, ebony-haired boys came bounding from behind a lean-to shed. They gleefully called to Niall as he dismounted, yet came to an abrupt halt when they spied Rab.

Without waiting for Niall's assistance, Sabrina slid off her horse to place a hand on her dog's head. "Come and greet him. He will not hurt you."

She spent a moment letting the children and dog get acquainted. When she rose, she realized that a woman dressed in traditional Highland garb had joined them in the yard.

She had raven-wing's hair and a delicate, quiet beauty that made Sabrina's heart sink.

Niall's familiarity with the family was evident as he made the introductions. "Sabrina, this is the Widow Fletcher, and these worthless bairns"—he tousled the boys' hair—"are her sons, Simon and Shaw."

"We're no' bairns!" they protested, even as they clung to him like limpets and gazed up at him adoringly.

Studying the children of perhaps eight and six years old, Sabrina could not help but note the resemblance to Niall. With an ache in the vicinity of her heart, she wondered if he had sired them.

"I am Fenella," their mother said in a soft, musical voice. "Please, my lady, will ye join me for refreshment?"

"I should be grateful," Sabrina replied. "But I hope you will call me by my given name."

While Niall went to inspect the crumbling stone of the well, Fenella guided her inside the cottage and offered her tea. Rab remained outside to play with the boys.

The widow had been sitting at her loom, Sabrina saw. "Pray, do not let me interrupt your work."

"Oh, no, I will be glad to rest a wee spell."

Lifting the kettle which had been left boiling over the hearth fire, she made a pot of tea while Sabrina examined the tartan cloth in the McLaren colors.

"How beautiful," she murmured, admiring the exquisite workmanship.

Fenella smiled sweetly. Going to a chest in one corner of the room, she pulled out a long length of the plaid fabric and held it out to Sabrina. "For ye, mistress."

"Oh, no, I didn't mean . . . I could not take it."

"Please. 'Tis a wedding gift. Ye should have yer own plaid, now that ye're a McLaren."

Sabrina smiled, forcing back her dismay at such generosity. "I should be honored to wear it." She stroked the fine wool as she settled on an oaken bench. "Are all the ladies of Clan McLaren so talented with the loom?"

"Aye, most. And we can set a neat stitch as well."

"Cloth as excellent as this should fetch a goodly sum at market in Edinburgh."

Fenella glanced over her shoulder skeptically, as if Sabrina had suggested she fly to the moon.

Just then they heard shrieks of youthful laughter mingled with excited barks coming from outside the cottage. Sabrina glanced out the low window to see Simon wrestling on the ground with Rab, while Shaw attempted to mount the dog like a pony.

"Your boys seem fine children," she said somewhat wistfully.

"Aye, they're the delights of my life. Niall has been like a da' to them since my dear husband Gowin passed on."

"Was that some time ago?"

"Four years." Before Sabrina could say more, Fenella volunteered with quiet sadness, "Niall's elder brother Tom was best friend to my Gowin. They perished together at sea. Niall's grief was nigh as great as my own."

Sabrina was aware of a stab of sorrow deep in her breast. A twinge of envy pricked her as well as she gazed at the rough-and-tumble boys. She wanted children, and wondered if Niall felt similarly. He had treated Simon and Shaw with fond indulgence, but no more so than an uncle might.

The visit ended too swiftly to the boys' mind, with Sabrina promising to call again with Rab soon. As she rode away with Niall, she remarked on the proficient job he had done repairing the well stone.

He grinned. "Confess, cherie, you thought me solely fit for wenching."

Her mouth curved wryly. "The notion had crossed my mind."

"I have a few other talents besides."

"Mistress Fletcher seems to agree," Sabrina said probingly. "She is exceedingly grateful for the care you've given her and her sons."

Surprisingly, Niall answered more soberly than expected.

"I've given her no more than is due the widow of my brother's friend. Despite my dissipated reputation, I'm not a man to take advantage of a vulnerable woman."

Sabrina raised an eyebrow, yet strangely she believed him. "I wonder, then, why you claimed to have no qualms about taking advantage of the serving maids."

When Niall gave her a quizzical glance, she said with sugary sweetness, "You deliberately encouraged me to believe you were seducing Jean that day I discovered you naked with her in the herbal. But she has since told me you had injured yourself and she was tending your wounds."

Niall showed no sign of remorse for misleading her. "Mayhap so, but as I recall, you had tried and convicted me before I could plead my case."

Sabrina shrugged, pretending nonchalance. "It is a matter of supreme indifference to me, whom you dally with," she lied.

"You wound me, sweeting."

"I doubt it."

He gave a warm chuckle. "You truly must learn the knack of flirtation, Sabrina. It isn't politic to display your apathy so baldly to a man. You would do better to try and persuade me to change my licentious ways."

She grimaced wryly. "In the first place, changing you would be nigh impossible. And in the second, I haven't the talent to attempt a flirtation. I've never professed to possess your amorous skills."

"Even so, you can learn. In fact, I mean to teach you."

"Do you, indeed?"

"Aye. In a flirtation, your primary goal should be to pique a man's interest."

"And just how do I go about doing that?"

" 'Tis not so difficult," Niall observed thoughtfully. "You laugh and smile at even the most inane remarks a gentleman makes. You pretend an attraction, hanging on his every word, while lowering your gaze coyly. Now and then you flash him a longing look, as if you cannot help your feelings of desire. In short, you make him feel as if he is the only man in the world."

Much the way you make a woman feel, Sabrina reflected. "It seems such a frivolous exercise."

"But first," Niall insisted, pointedly ignoring her comment, "you begin by sweetening that tart tongue of yours. Honey will gain you more than vinegar."

His eyes danced with the laughter that was so much a part of him. Niall was goading her, she knew, yet it was impossible to take offense, or to resist his notorious charm.

He exercised that lethal charm fully in the days that followed. During her first week at Creagturic, Sabrina even began to hope their uneasy alliance might blossom into a worthwhile union, if not a true marriage.

Her days began to assume a pattern. Niall was away much of the day, seeing to clan affairs, but he usually returned for supper, which he spent conversing with her about his clan and hers or giving her lessons in dalliance. Afterward she often took up her needlework while he read—sometimes aloud to her. The first time he opened a serious volume, Sabrina was startled enough to express surprise.

Niall gave her a long, level look, his eyes laughing at her. "I do enjoy pursuits other than carnal ones. I'll have you know that in my misspent youth, I applied myself to my studies with nearly as much seriousness as I did my amorous endeavors."

At this subtle reminder that he had been educated in the finest universities of Europe, Sabrina felt an unwilling admiration. If she'd once thought him shallow and frivolous, she was having to revise her assessment. Niall McLaren was much more complex than she had ever suspected, showing depths she could only begin to fathom.

"It must have been supremely taxing," she said dryly, "to be forced to labor at such mundane chores as studying."

"Indeed, it was."

"I fear you will get little sympathy from me, sir," Sabrina advised.

"You're a hard lass, mistress."

She shook her head ruefully, surprised to realize how much she was enjoying their exchange. "No, merely truthful."

"I'm not half as debauched as you prefer to believe."

"Well . . . perhaps not *half*."

She was pleased to win a wry chuckle from him. It was exhilarating to be matching wits with such a man, like challenging a swift-moving Highland storm. And Niall encouraged her in their verbal skirmishes with scandalous remarks bordering on the outrageous.

His instruction in the art of dalliance gave her more enjoyment than she anticipated. To her bewilderment and dismay, though, her marital bed proved her greatest disappointment. After the first night, her husband made no attempt to make love to her.

In truth, his disinterest was no more than Sabrina expected. She was not the sort of woman to inspire lust in a man of Niall's legendary passions. Yet she could not claim he had abandoned her entirely. She slept naked in his arms, since he would not allow her to wear her night smock.

Their physical intimacy grew little by little, with nudity becoming more natural between them. Sabrina grew accustomed to seeing the whole of his magnificent body, and grew familiar with his touch as well, for he made it a point to caress her casually and often.

He seemed highly concerned about her arm wound, and each night checked its healing himself. His solicitous regard, however, disturbed her more than neglect would have done. He was infinitely more dangerous than she'd feared, and she was far more vulnerable.

Her relationship with his clan at least proved satisfactory. To Sabrina's surprise and relief, they appeared to accept her willingly. She felt welcomed in her new home, while the magnificent Highlands had captured her soul.

Later that same week Niall took her to explore the mountain valley that had been in possession of Clan McLaren for generations, introducing her to lofty peaks and tranquil lochs and magical glens, and watching with amused indulgence her expression of delight and awe.

With such splendor, she could almost forget that danger and bloodshed ruled the Highlands. Peace had not come with her marriage to Niall, yet she had reason to hope. The terrible feud with the Buchanans continued, but Clan Duncan would be safe, now that Niall had been designated Angus's successor.

The morning immediately after the ceremony, Sabrina had learned, Niall had paid a visit to his archenemy; she heard about it from Geordie when he came to call.

"He warned the Buchanan most harshly," Geordie claimed. "Clan Duncan is to suffer no more raids. 'Twas odd, though. Owen claimed he wasna the one to resume the feud, that he never lifted our cattle. Wheesht, ye canna believe such blethering."

Niall refused to discuss the Buchanans with her, however, and grew testy whenever Sabrina even hinted at the subject.

He did approve of her becoming involved with his clan, at least. Her visit to the Widow Fletcher had given Sabrina an idea, which she broached to Niall one evening at supper.

"The tartan cloth Mistress Fletcher has woven is quite beautiful. I have rarely seen such fine quality, nor have the markets of Edinburgh, I suspect. I would very much like to write my stepfather, asking him to propose an arrangement with the merchants there."

"What did you have in mind?"

"If our kinswomen could be persuaded to produce enough woolen cloth to sell, they could make a small fortune. It would perhaps ease their burdens by providing a steady income."

"I am impressed, sweeting," Niall remarked seriously. "You do indeed have a head for business."

His praise warmed Sabrina more than she cared to admit. She wanted to prove herself worth more than just the wealth her dowry would bring, and aiding her new clan in some small measure was a start.

As for her duties as mistress, she had plenty to occupy her time seeing to the household and clan concerns that were not a male purview. Mrs. Paterson helped greatly, as did the Widow Graham.

Eve paid a visit two days after the wedding, offered her advice on dealing with the tenet crofters and suggesting they make plans for the May Day celebration that would be held the following week.

It was a tradition for the castle to supply food and drink for the populace during the pagan festival of Beltane. When Eve accompanied her to the open market in Callander to shop, Sabrina felt quite domestic choosing giant wheels of cheese and ingredients for meat pasties.

By silent consent, they avoided the subject of Sabrina's husband. Yet he was constantly in her thoughts. Despite her best efforts to ignore him, she was not proof against his bewitching appeal.

Her emotions swung between elation and dismay whenever she considered the future of their relationship. Niall McLaren was the most charming, infuriating, fascinating man alive, and against her will, she was falling under his irresistible, tender spell. It frightened her to realize how very vulnerable she was to him.

It was the fourth day of their union when they had their first argument. To her dismay, she learned at breakfast that Niall had ordered a half dozen gowns made up for her from her stepfather's gifts of fabric and some other bolts he himself had chosen.

Despite the large dowry she would bring to her husband and his clan, Sabrina's sense of frugality rebelled at the unnecessary extravagance.

"The material is already paid for," Niall replied when she objected. "Your stepfather obviously intended it for you."

"But there is no need to hire a seamstress. I can make up my own gowns."

"I prefer to maintain *some* semblance of style and fashion," he said dryly.

When Sabrina protested the expense, Niall looked at her oddly. "Do you ken how few women would refuse a new wardrobe?"

"Perhaps not many. But I hope I am not like the simpering, fashionable ladies of your acquaintance."

He gave her an amused glance. "That you are not, but you are a laird's wife now, with a certain presence to uphold. You require styles and colors that flatter and enhance your features to best advantage. And even if the dull frocks you wear didn't offend my sense of dignity, a comely lass should be gowned in silks and lace."

"If I were comely—"

He pressed his fingers to her lips, silencing her. "Hush, sweeting. Be a douce wife and indulge me in this."

Sabrina bit her tongue and subsided, knowing it was useless to protest. Niall had no more than a stranger's acquaintance with the word *no*. He knew how to bend a woman to his every whim, and would have his way by any means necessary.

It was when the seamstress came to take her measurements, however, that she discovered her husband intended to watch the proceedings. Niall settled himself in a chair before the fire, saying he wished to advise. Short of causing a scene, Sabrina could do little to prevent him from remaining in his own bedchamber.

She tried to ignore him as she stripped down to her shift, yet she was palpably aware of his presence. He wore a leather waistcoat and trews, his hair drawn back in a queue, and though he looked quite at home amidst the rich bolts of fabric, his potent masculine energy was disquieting. As was the spark of interest she saw in his eyes when a swatch of lace was pulled tightly against her breasts.

"The décolletage should be lower," Niall recommended. "To show her bosom to advantage."

"Any lower would be indecent!" Sabrina protested.

"Nay," the seamstress said, agreeing with the laird, " 'tis all the rage, milady. For daytime, ye may wear a modesty piece tucked into the bodice."

"Aye," her husband concurred. "A fichu will provide a softness for your features that will be exceedingly alluring."

When Sabrina muttered again about the cost, Niall brushed aside her opposition. "These simple gowns cannot hope to match the extravagance of the costumes currently being worn in Europe. There the price of a single ball gown would feed a crofter's family for a year, whereas these can be made up for a pittance."

And so it went, with Niall tossing out a suggestion here and there, and ordering accoutrements to go with each gown.

When the seamstress had finished, Niall dismissed her, saying pleasantly, "I shall help my lady dress."

Sabrina tensed at the husky note in his voice. How did he make the prospect of dressing her sound like the most sensual thing in the world?

"So," Niall said when they were alone, "do you deny my expertise?"

"No," she had to admit; his choice of color and style was impeccable. "Your fame is well deserved."

"What is this, love? A compliment from your pretty lips?"

Love. Sabrina bit her lip as she drew on her dressing gown, annoyed with the casual intimacy of the endearment. "Where did you learn about women's fashions?"

"I had a year in France and Italy."

She could easily picture him moving about the lavish courts and glittering salons of Europe, dancing attendance on princesses and duchesses. "I suppose that is where you honed your skills in the art of dalliance. The French are known for amorous talents."

"Indeed." His smile was languid. "The French lasses nearly wore me out with their demands."

"How unfortunate they did not succeed."

Niall ignored her wry gibe. "It is time you had some gowns that don't obscure your best features. You will look quite lovely in these new ones. I predict you will be the envy of every woman in the Highlands."

If they *were* envious, Sabrina reflected, it would solely be because she had wed the legendary Niall McLaren. "You don't have to keep giving me false coin. I have no pretensions to beauty."

"Not in the common way, perhaps." His thoughtful look took the sting from his frank assessment. "Yet the adage is entirely true about beauty and the beholder. Often much of a woman's allure results purely from perception."

She regarded him skeptically.

"Comeliness is much overrated," Niall asserted, crossing his arms over his chest. "A charming vivacity, a clever wit, an intimate glance, a beguiling smile, can compensate for a multitude of physical shortfalls. Many a lass has made excellent use of more meager charms than you possess, cherie."

She made a face, but was unable to keep a hint of wistfulness from her tone when she replied, "I know very well gentlemen prefer beauty to plainness."

"Some do, perhaps. But believe me, classic beauty is not the prime attribute that attracts a man."

"In my experience, it is."

"But then, you have not had a vast deal of experience, have you?"

"I've had enough." She dropped her gaze. "I was betrothed once. He . . . found someone he preferred over me. Someone much more beautiful."

"He sounds like a fool."

"No, never that. He fell in love. He . . . wed my cousin."

Niall's heavy dark brows drew together. "Ah, the cousin

whose betrothal ball I attended last year. Tell me, is this the same man who cannot pleasure a lass in bed?"

Sabrina remembered confiding her cousin's view that only men enjoyed the act of lovemaking—and Niall's swift response that her cousin was to be pitied. "I have no idea what his mating habits might be," she retorted in embarrassment.

"But your cousin has found no enjoyment in her marriage bed." He smiled softly. "At the risk of sounding immodest, it seems that you made the better bargain in your marriage."

Had she made the better bargain? Sabrina wondered, searching his handsome face. Oliver would at least be faithful to her cousin, she was certain. She had no illusions about Niall. He had made very clear the terms of their union. He wanted to be free to continue his dissolute pursuits outside the marriage bed.

Niall returned her regard speculatively, an unbidden tenderness tugging at him. It was lamentable, how little confidence Sabrina had in her own beauty. But he intended to prove her wrong. If he did nothing else in this marriage, he would make his sweet mouse blossom as a woman, with a woman's passions.

Rising slowly from his chair, he went to her. With his hands on her shoulders, Niall turned her slightly, positioning her in front of him so that she could see her image in the cheval glass.

"Every woman has her own special beauty ... her own scent ... her own passion. Yours merely requires a sharper eye to uncover."

Was that his secret? Sabrina wondered dazedly. Was his incredible success with the gentler sex because he knew how to make a woman feel beautiful, desired?

"Look at yourself, sweeting," he murmured softly, "and see what I see."

She stared at her reflection, her breath faltering at her wanton image. The front of her robe had fallen open, and beneath the thin fabric of her shift, her nipples stood out like twin peaks, while her face was flushed with delicate color.

"What . . . do you see?" she asked in a whisper.

"A lovely lass whose charms are myriad. Look at this hair . . . so dark and rich, glimmering with hints of fire . . ."

His fingers pulled the pins from her hair, letting it tumble past her shoulders in a wild, lush riot. "A man dreams of having such silken tresses wrapped around him. And this skin . . ." His hand lovingly cupped her slender throat. "A courtesan would kill for such soft, satin skin."

He eased the robe from her body, leaving her standing only in her linen shift. "And this form . . . Delicate white shoulders . . . sweet, firm breasts crowned with such exquisitely budded nipples . . . pale thighs that offer a man a glimpse of heaven . . ." His palm swept gently over her, arousing a sweetly aching awareness in all the places of her body where he'd touched. "Trust me, pet. I take great pleasure in the female body—and you have a body worth a king's ransom."

Sabrina felt her breath shallow as she studied the muted reflection of the mirror, almost believing.

"You really are utterly enchanting."

"I . . . don't . . ."

His hands on her shoulders, he drew her gently back till their bodies were lightly touching.

"Yes, you are," he repeated emphatically. "You have an allure all your own, sweet Sabrina. One most potent when you're aroused. I relish that flash of fire in your eyes when your passion or fury is inflamed."

His arm slid around her body then, his hands gliding up to cover her breasts, molding her to him. Sabrina suddenly went weak all over.

"If you . . . find me . . . a-appealing"—she stumbled over the word—"then why didn't . . . why haven't you . . ." She flushed, unable to complete the question.

"Why haven't I made love to you since our wedding

night? Because, pet, your body needed time to grow accustomed to my hard usage."

The ache of her breasts within his gentle grip distracted her. "I thought you . . . had no interest in me."

"No, sweet mouse. I have a very keen interest in you. I assure you, abstinence has not been easy." His intimate smile made it the grandest compliment ever received. "But I am about to remedy the situation."

"Now? You . . . cannot be serious."

"I am always serious about seduction."

She started to draw away, but the powerful muscularity of his arms prevented her.

Arrestingly, arousingly, his fingertips made a slow, circular motion around the peaks of her breasts, making her feel the soft friction of the linen fabric.

Her breath checked sharply, while lower in her body, surprised flesh pulsed to life.

"See how well we fit together?" His lips nuzzled the curve of her throat. "Your height makes you an ideal match for me. I have no need to strain when I bend to kiss you. . . ."

His teeth grazed her ear, making her shiver. His breath was a raw whisper. "Shall I tell you what it feels like to kiss you? How sweet you taste . . . Your lips are like wine, your breath like nectar, your skin so soft and silken . . . I want to drink you in."

That bewitching voice vibrated against her skin, while sensations, warm and hot, surged inside her. He was caressing her again, stroking her nipples with his long fingers, making her flush with intense heat.

"Yet there is so much more I want to show you, sweet. To lead you to discover your own lush sensuality . . ."

She already was discovering it, Sabrina thought dazedly. Shameful pleasure flared wherever he touched her. With a soft, breathy sound of capitulation, she shut her eyes against the knowledge of his scandalous caresses.

His mouth moved slowly over her skin, down the side of her slender neck, lower, along the gentle slope of her shoulder. Each caress seemed to define the word sensual. And with every inch he left her more breathless, more confused, until she couldn't seem to frame a complete sentence. "Niall . . ."

"I think it time we hold another lesson in wifely conduct." His hands fell away from her. "Bare your lovely breasts for me, sweeting."

"W-What?" Her dazed eyes fluttered open. "Why?"

"Because I wish to see you. I want to teach you about pleasure, sweet Sabrina. I want to learn each curve and swell and hollow of your body . . . and have you learn mine. I want to show you how to please me . . . Now, do as I say."

She hesitated, her cheeks flushing at his brazen command. In the glass, she could see him smile. "We really must practice with great diligence to conquer your shyness."

With trembling fingers she reached up to free the tiny buttons of her chemise. When she drew down the neckline, liberating the pale globes of her breasts, the rosy peaks were already budded tautly.

"Excellent," he said lazily. "Now touch your nipples."

"I . . . don't . . ."

"Remember your vows, love. Did you not promise to honor and obey your husband?"

Feeling utterly shameless, Sabrina acceded to his demand, her fingers rising to close around her straining nipples. At once she shut her eyes at the tingling shafts of pleasure that arrowed through the sensitive buds.

"Perfect. Now hold that pose. Remain just as you are."

Her eyes flew open as Niall moved away. He did not go far, though. Merely to the clothespress, where he drew off his waistcoat and shirt, exposing his heavily muscled chest.

She was smotheringly aware of his magnificent body, of the throbbing of her hot nipples beneath her fingers. Niall was offering a wild, reckless excitement, an exquisite promise of passion and fulfillment.

A promise she desperately wanted him to keep.

She stood rooted to the floor as casually he settled himself in the chair before the hearth. Then he looked at her, his gaze fired by a smoldering sensuality.

She was becoming more accustomed to his open expression of desire, but it startled her when he proceeded to unfasten the buttons of his close-fitting trews. In an instant his hard flesh sprang free, huge and rigid, from a nest of curling black hair.

The sight, so decadent, so sinful, held her shocked, rapt attention.

"Do you remember how I kissed you between your thighs, pet?" Niall asked, a heated quality in his voice that made her think of dark passion, spent and rekindled. "One day soon you will learn to take me in your mouth, to stroke me eagerly with your lips and tongue. But you are not ready yet for such pleasures. For now we will simply enjoy one another. Come . . . sit on my lap."

He had to repeat the soft command before Sabrina could force her weak limbs to move. A wave of the most potent sense of anticipation she'd ever felt flooded through her as she approached him guardedly.

When she was near enough, he caught her hand and drew her down to sit sideways on his lap. Sabrina found herself captured in the light, protective circle of his arms.

"Don't be afraid to be a woman, sweeting," he murmured huskily.

"I am not afraid," she lied. She felt his maleness rigid and hot against her thigh, felt the rippling sinews as she braced her palms against his chest . . . all warm, taut muscle against her softness.

"Good. Then we shall play a love game. *You* are to seduce *me* this time."

"I . . . don't know how."

"I shall teach you. Hold your breasts for me, sweeting."

"Like . . . this?" Tentatively she cupped the swells in her hands.

"Lift them higher . . . press them together, so I may kiss them."

He made her feel wickedly seductive, yet she felt an instinctive, feminine urge to please him. Brazenly, Sabrina did as she was bid, lifting so that her firm flesh gleamed pale above her fingers, exposing the rigid nipples to his warm breath.

He nipped lightly, dredging a gasp from her throat.

"Your nipples are such hard delicious points . . . they appear very eager for my mouth. Do you wish me to suckle them?"

She nodded in breathless embarrassment.

"Say it, pet."

"I . . . wish you to . . . suckle them."

"Then offer them to me."

With her breasts raised high and mounded in her hands, she leaned forward, arching her back a little so that he could reach. Niall lowered his dark head to taste her. When his tongue flicked over a hot, peaked tip, a shaft of pleasure streaked through her so keen it made her gasp. He paused at the engorged crest to circle and probe, teasing with his tongue, taunting.

Heat and dizziness swept over Sabrina. Her senses swam. His mouth was a searing flame upon her bare, aching breasts. She shivered at the sweet spasms of desire that arrowed down to her belly. Craving the forbidden throbbing pleasure he promised, she almost protested when he drew away.

"How enticing." His voice was warm and lazy. "Your breasts are beautiful, wet and gleaming from my tongue. . . . The ripe buds merely whet my appetite for the rest of you."

He thrust his hips upward gently, pressing his hardness against her thigh, reminding her of the incredible desire he could make her feel.

With a whimper, Sabrina pressed against him, warm and soft to hot and hard, fighting the gnawing restlessness that plagued her. How could he so effortlessly make her want him?

"Slowly, love. Let this be your chief lesson. . . . Anticipation makes the pleasure all the more sweet."

His lips plundered her breast again, the soft sound of his sucking powerfully erotic, caressing till her flesh was tender and swollen and tingling from his kisses. She arched against him, wanting to cry out. When he drew away, the air was cool on her taut, thrusting nipples.

His mouth soothing the hurt he had inflicted, assuaging the terrible ache, he murmured, "Do you wish to pleasure me?"

"Yes . . ."

"Let me hear you say it."

"I wish to pleasure you, my lord."

"And how do you intend to go about it?"

"I . . . you . . . should I make love to you?"

"Exactly. Do you want me, sweet?"

"Yes."

"So tell me how much."

"Niall . . . I want you."

"You want me to fill you?"

"Yes . . ."

The soul-stopping smile stole her breath away. "All in good time," he pronounced in that rich, caressing resonance that recalled warm bodies writhing together in ecstasy. "I'll fill you to bursting, but not yet, sweet Sabrina . . ."

He shifted her body a little, till her shoulder lay against him, her loosened hair spilling down over his supporting arm. Then he raised the hem of her chemise, gathering it around her waist. "Part your thighs for me."

Sabrina obeyed, letting her legs fall open to his heated gaze, till her sex was lushly on display.

"Now touch yourself."

Her eyes closed in mortification, but she complied, moving her hand over her belly, lower, over the dark triangle of curling hair, till her finger just brushed the cleft of her womanhood. Her hips jerked at the fierce, arousing pleasure.

"Are you getting wet?"

To her utter shame, she was. "Yes . . ." she whispered.

"Let me feel."

His caress probed the dusky curls crowning her thighs, his thumb discovering her heated nectar between the pouting folds. Sensation, shocking and primal, flared through her. Languorously he inserted a deft finger inside her, and brought it out, drenched with her juices.

"Just as I suspected, sleek and wet. Like hot velvet."

"Please . . ."

"Please what?" He slowly thrust again. "Please take my fingers out of you, or put them back in?"

Sabrina shuddered convulsively. Her breath was gone, the scent of wanton need warm in her nostrils.

"Do you want to feel me inside you?" he asked.

Unable to answer, she twisted restlessly, helplessly. His fingers stroked her again, teasing a moan from deep within her throat. His touch was magic. Sensuality was a fine art to him, but he was too good at it, too good . . .

"Take me in your hand," he urged.

Blindly Sabrina shifted her weight so that her fingers could close around his jutting shaft. He was huge and hot and throbbing, all rigid male, and she trembled with excitement when the thick length surged in her hand.

"Do you feel how painfully you've made me swell? The thought of all I'm going to do to you is pure torment."

When she would have released him, Niall shook his head and muttered hoarsely. "No . . . hold me tighter. You cannot hurt me. Squeeze me harder. Do you know what it's like to have you touch me? I want your luscious wet heat sheathing me, shivering around my hardness."

A pulsing began deep inside Sabrina at his raw words of lust, a sweet mindless wanting that swept away all reason. She felt faint with the pain of desire.

He kissed her mouth then, his masterful arms holding her tightly, and the blazing heat became a hurting, painful need. She clung to him, every soft silken curve melting into his hard-muscled form. His bold tongue plunged rhythmically into her receptive mouth, showing her exactly what he intended to do with his male weapon.

She felt his hot desire lick at her senses, his erection stiff against her pulsing flesh.

"Now, cherie, I think you are hot enough . . . You may ride me if you so wish . . . Do you desire me, cherie?"

"Yes . . ."

"Then sit astride my lap."

Trembling she tried to turn, but had difficulty shifting her weak limbs when her chemise tangled around her thighs.

"Help me," she pleaded.

A slow devilish smile flooded his handsome features. "Gladly."

His hands on her narrow waist, he lifted her to meet the full hard length of his arousal, positioning his member at the entrance to her hot honeyed crease.

Her heart thrumming a wild, uncontrollable rhythm, Sabrina tried to press closer, driven by urgency.

"Steady, my little tiger," Niall murmured. Expertly guiding her, he slowly impaled her on the rampant blade of taut male flesh.

Sabrina's breath caught in a sigh of rapture as pleasure slammed through her, full and rich and heavy. She fell against him, her face buried in the sweaty silk of his shoulder, wishing she could stay like this always.

But Niall was by no means through with her. Letting his hands slide down to her flaring hips, he penetrated deeper, groaning as the slick heat of her body enveloped him fully. "You're so tight . . . Sweet heaven, how you fire my blood . . ."

Erotically he rocked against her, making slow lazy circles with his lean hips. When Sabrina arched in response, he urged her on. "That's it, my bonny lass, let me feel you move. I want you wanton and reckless for me . . ."

Excitement flared through his senses as his erection swelled upward into her clinging heat. He wanted her beyond reason or logic. He wanted her mad with need for him. With a fierce effort at control, he applied himself to the delightful task of truly making her moan.

Watching the tawny-pink flush that had crept to her cheekbones, he showed her how to move, matching each silken thrust to her half breaths. Not giving her a moment's surcease, his hands kept her hips moving in that maddening rhythm, working her up and down on his impaling shaft till she was flame-hot and trembling.

When Sabrina sank her teeth into his shoulder, Niall laughed in triumph, and surged into her again, deeply, powerfully, forcing her frenzy ever higher.

His movement touched off an explosive wildfire of sensation; suddenly it was too much for her to bear. Sabrina strained madly against him, but Niall held back until he felt her release beginning, the delicious spasming, the convulsive tightening of her loins around him. Each tremor burning through him with an exquisite torture, he held her surging body, feeling her ripple and contract in her ecstasy.

When she sobbed and cried out his name, his restraint slipped; all his senses seemed to crest and shatter. He caught the frenzied woman in his arms and drove into her with hammering wildness.

Sabrina screamed with pleasure, but his hot, hungry mouth smothered the keening sound as he possessed her with a savage tenderness, an endless raw pleasure so intense it seared. His shaking arms crushed her as he found his own hot, sweet insanity.

In the quiet afterward, she clung to him, gasping, her limp body collapsed against him. Niall sat unmoving, his head tilted back as a peaceful wave of exhaustion and pleasure flowed over him.

Sometime later he roused himself enough to ask hoarsely if she was all right.

Sabrina stirred unwillingly at the intrusive thought. Her face nuzzled against her lover's throat, she nodded weakly. Niall had left her barely coherent, but he had not hurt her.

Except for her heart. That vulnerable organ was more endangered than ever, she realized with aching awareness.

She hadn't been mistaken about his terrible secret—the reason for his incredible power over members of her sex. He knew how to make a woman feel utterly desirable. Needed. Wanted. And after so many years of unfulfilled dreams to comfort her, her lonely heart craved such masculine assurance. Her inexperience made her helpless against him.

When she felt his lips brush her temple, Sabrina drew back, wanting to escape, but Niall would not permit it. With a gentle finger under her chin, he forced her to meet his gaze.

"You are an apt pupil, sweeting."

The burning sensuality in his look sent a fresh tremor of desperation coursing through her. He could command her desire at will, while she meant nought to him but another conquest.

With effort she managed a semblance of a smile before turning her face again into his shoulder.

You'll break my heart, she thought despairingly. And there would be nothing in the world she could do to prevent it.

Chapter
Eleven

She wanted him, and nothing seemed strong enough to make her stop wanting. Niall had awakened in her an irresistible hunger, stripping away her defenses and exposing a brazen, primal need.

The remembrance of her own wantonness made Sabrina flush with dismay. She thought of herself naked in his arms, allowing him—no, begging him—to do things to her body that no lady would permit, and she wanted to hide.

And yet she was indebted to him as well. Niall made her feel beautiful, desired, fully a woman. When he looked at her with such erotic tenderness, she could almost believe he wanted her as much as she did him.

It was folly to delude herself so, Sabrina knew. She commanded his attention for the moment. She was a novelty to him, a diversion. He considered it a challenge to transform her into the kind of paramour he fancied. But there were scores of women waiting in the wings should he lose interest in his latest amusement.

She was forcibly reminded of that likelihood when Eve Graham called the day before the Beltane festivities to tell her about some of the superstitious customs Highlanders observed.

"You must wash your face in the morning dew to beautify the skin," Eve explained, "and plant a hawthorn branch before the door of your sweetheart. And when evening falls . . ." Eve smiled. "The bonfires are lit to ensure fertility for the crops, but the surrounding darkness presents an opportunity for much ribaldry. I recall last May Day with great fondness. Couples paired off into the wood, and Niall and I—Ah, forgive me for my wayward tongue. You would not wish to hear of *that*."

Never accomplished at hiding her emotions, Sabrina felt despair claim her features at this reminder of Niall's former intimacy with the beautiful widow.

Eve immediately assumed an expression of sympathy. "I feared this would happen, Sabrina. That rogue of a husband has bewitched you. I warned you to keep your heart safe." She sighed. "'Tis only to be expected, I suppose. Niall is a champion seducer of females. That handsome devil knows the key to a woman's heart."

"And what is that?" Sabrina asked, half in curiosity, half in envy at Eve's wealth of experience.

"Why, fulfillment, my dear. He provides a woman with whatever she craves most. He treats a lady like a tavern wench, and a tavern wench like the finest lady. A lass who covets respectability will swoon for a man who will honor and worship her, while a gentlewoman thrills at the chance to behave scandalously."

Fulfillment, Sabrina reflected. That was indeed what Niall offered. *He can make an ordinary woman feel beautiful and desired.*

"But I have no wish to play the wanton," she murmured, her thoughts distracted.

"There are scores of women who would give a king's ransom to take your place," Eve returned frankly.

Sabrina stiffened. She had to remember that for all the widow's generosity, Eve was still a foe when it came to her husband.

"Beware, my dear," Eve suggested. "Niall never remains satisfied for long. Perhaps you should make an effort to attach him. If I were in your position, I would fight for him with every weapon at my command."

"Attach him? How?"

"Well, certainly not by wearing your heart on your

sleeve! You must never permit a man to know you've been captured."

"I'm not certain I understand."

"The thrill for men is in the chase, Sabrina. If they win too easily, they become bored and lose interest."

"But you just advised me to fight for Niall."

"Yes, but you must be extremely subtle about it. The object is to arouse him, not drive him away. A man like that much prefers to be the predator than the prey. Trust me in this, I *know*. I held him longer than any other of his paramours, and it was *not* by pursuing him overtly. In the game of dalliance, it is deadly to admit your surrender. You must remain elusive, Sabrina. In any event, 'twill be good for Niall to realize he does not have you at his beck and call."

"*That* I can agree with," she murmured wryly.

"It would not hurt, either, to encourage the interest of other gentlemen as well. If you are sought after by others, it piques a man's vanity and encourages him to compete for your favor."

"It seems somehow . . . disloyal to my marriage vows."

"Never! All is fair in the battle of love, and you are vying for a prize of inestimable value."

Sabrina smiled weakly. The prize was Niall McLaren's wayward heart.

Watching her, Eve shook her powdered, bewigged head. "Faith, why am I confiding this to you? You are my chief rival."

It was all too true, Sabrina thought, her heart wincing. The widow very obviously wanted Niall back in her bed.

Nevertheless, the advice plagued her long after her visitor had gone. *Should* she attempt to fight for Niall? Could she win his regard if she dared try? Could she possibly hope to hold him with her own charms?

The following day gave Sabrina reason to hope. Preparations for the holiday kept her busy, but after helping make pies and seeing to last-minute details, she donned the traditional form of women's Highland garb: a simple bodice of blue homespun with a white muslin fichu tucked over the bosom, secured by a brooch, and a skirt made of green and blue tartan cloth, belted at the waist. The cloth was long enough to drape over her shoulders like a plaid.

Her breath caught when her husband's eyes roamed over her with approval. "You are a fetching sight, mouse."

No more fetching than he was, Sabrina thought mutely. Wearing the McLaren kilt and plaid, Niall looked every inch the bold Highlander. "I would have thought the neckline far too modest for your taste."

He responded with a slow, deep curl of the lips. "For my taste, aye, but for the mistress of Clan McLaren, 'tis entirely appropriate."

"I am overwhelmed by your adulation."

"Termagant," he remarked mildly, a teasing light in his eyes.

Offering his arm, Niall escorted Sabrina beyond the outbuildings of Creagturic to a distant meadow where the festivities were beginning.

The late afternoon air was filled with mouth-watering aromas from the oxen and sheep roasting on huge spits, while beer and malt whisky flowed freely among the crowd. At the far end of the field, men played games: tossing the caber—a long, heavy wooden pole cast end-over-end—and the sheaf—a hay-stuffed burlap bag flung with a pitchfork. At the edge of a birchwood copse, bagpipes and fiddles provided music for dancing in the interval before supper.

Sabrina felt her heart sink at the sheer number of Niall's former interests she recognized: Betsy McNab, the dairymaid of Banesk. Jean McLaren, the chambermaid of Creagturic. The beautiful Eve Graham. Fenella Fletcher, although that widow had brought her two young sons.

And yet, to her surprise, Sabrina discovered she had admirers of her own.

Geordie's eyes went wide when he beheld her in full Highland dress. "Ye make a bonny Highlander, mistress," he said, sounding startled.

Sabrina laughed. Niall's efforts to increase her appeal were evidently working. "I would that my grandfather could see me."

John McLaren came forward to greet her then. "Ye do us proud, my lady," he said appreciatively.

Curtsying, Sabrina flashed him a smile. "A high compliment indeed, coming from you, sir. I feared you disapproved of me."

"Nay, ye mistake me. 'Tis glad I am that Niall took ye for his bride. Not since his da passed have I seen the lad so carefree."

Sabrina felt her smile waver. She glanced over her shoulder at her husband, who was occupied greeting others of his clan.

"In truth, our kinsmen are pleased to have ye as mistress," John added.

"I suspect I cannot hope to measure up to Niall's mother. By all reports, Lady McLaren was a saint."

"Aye, but ye'll do."

Sabrina flushed at his unexpected praise.

To her astonishment, she found herself in great demand as a dancing partner. Niall claimed her for the first dance, a Highland reel, but afterward, the men of both their clans sought her out and kept her occupied, leaving her flushed and breathless from the sport.

She was flattered and a bit dazed by so much masculine attention. Geordie hovered beside her with a proprietary air, and she found herself enjoying a light flirtation, testing her newfound skills at dalliance.

As day melted into dusk, Niall returned to her and they partook of a delicious supper. He remained at her side even when night fell and the Beltane fires were lit.

In the chill air, Sabrina relished the warmth. A luminous full moon, huge and misty white, hovered over the dark hills as the merrymakers gathered around the bonfires to celebrate the pagan rituals of May Day.

Tongues of flame licked the night, while the pipes wailed

a haunting melody. Sabrina watched in excitement and awe as a dozen Highland lads vaulted over the blaze, barely escaping the sparks that shot skyward.

As the night wore on, the revelry grew wilder. Within the fire's glow, shadowy figures cavorted in frenzied abandon.

Sabrina fell silent as the heat and magic wove a dark enchantment around her. The whisky she'd imbibed had gone to her head, but it was Niall's nearness that affected her more. To her surprise, he had not left her side.

"Ah, now the true frolic begins," he bent to whisper in her ear.

"Frolic?"

He nodded toward the copse. Sabrina felt her heart beat faster as she watched a couple disappear into the dark wood, knowing their intent.

"Beware, lass, lest some bold rogue carry you off."

Her breath wavered with telltale unevenness at his warning. Yet some devil prompted her next words. "Am I in danger of ravishment, sir?"

"Would you like to be?"

"I . . . believe so."

The smoldering light that flared in Niall's eyes mirrored the blaze of the flames.

Sabrina shivered at the sight, thrilling at the power of her femininity. Tonight she was no mouse. Tonight she was beautiful, the object of this remarkable man's desire. It was a dazzling triumph to know that he wanted her.

And yet it would be unwise to capitulate so easily. She would do better to tease Niall, to pretend to resist his blandishments, though resistance was the last thing on her mind.

"I should think frolicking with your own wife too tame for a rogue like you, though," she remarked lightly.

The sultry grin he gave her was pure seduction. "Let us put it to the test, shall we?"

She returned a coquettish smile. "I have no wish to freeze

to death, my lord. The night is far too cold to be engaging in such depravity."

Watching her, Niall chuckled, the sound rich and amused. "There are times when you are too transparent, lass. The hunger in your eyes betrays you. Confess, you are yearning to indulge in a bit of wicked adventure. Come, mouse," he said when she hesitated. "I will show you how it is done. I promise to keep you warm."

"Very well . . . if you insist."

"How charming to have such a docile wife," he murmured huskily, a hint of laughter edging the words.

He took her hand and led her away from the bonfires, into the chill night. Sabrina could feel her heart hammering as they threaded their way through dark stands of alder and birch. Beyond the wood, plump grazing sheep dotted the meadow, their thick fleeces silver in the moonlight.

She told herself she was only satisfying her curiosity regarding the debauchery of a pagan festival. Yet when he discovered a hidden copse far from the revelry, Sabrina realized she was merely deceiving herself. The anticipation of being in Niall's arms was enough to make her throb and burn, and the thought of the pleasure to come aroused a wonderful, moist, aching weakness in the secret place between her thighs.

Her pulse leapt violently when Niall paused to glance at her quizzically, his chiseled features heartbreakingly beautiful in the silvery shadows. Her gaze fastened on those sensual lips as he bent his head . . .

When his mouth touched hers, her breath fled. He kissed her lightly, but she was helpless against the surge of warmth that washed through her.

She wanted to cry out when he stepped back to spread his plaid on a bed of bracken, but he returned to her at once, his hands reaching for her hair.

His fingers pulled the pins from her bound tresses till the rich cloud tumbled down. "A man likes his woman's hair down, hanging loose and free."

His woman. If only she could believe she meant that much to him. It was folly to think she could ever claim his sole attention—and yet he was here with her now. Tonight she alone could command his passion.

His fingers stroked her hair, tangling in the shining fullness. With a hushed delicacy, his hand dropped to the neckline of her bodice, freeing the fragile skin of her shoulders and breasts to the night's kiss and to his own. Her breasts tumbled forward, begging for the touch of teeth and tongue, her nipples impudent spikes in the chill air.

Niall's jeweled eyes took in her nudity, before his gaze lifted abruptly, midnight fire. "You're trembling," he murmured, his voice husky with intimacy.

When he held out his arms, Sabrina went willingly into his embrace, her body craving his heat and strength, a force as powerful as the moon's spell. He drew her down to the soft bed to lie beside him, breast to breast. His arms around her, Niall wrapped them both in his plaid. The fabric held his body warmth, his alluring scent, mingled with the aroma of woodsmoke and crushed bracken. For a moment he simply held her close, arousing her with his mere nearness.

But when his hands began moving over her skin in a soft murmur, Sabrina took a steadying breath and pressed a palm against his chest. "No . . . 'Tis my turn. I mean to pleasure you this time."

"Indeed?" His tone was smokily sensual.

"Yes."

"Are you certain you can manage it?"

She saw the smile lurking in his eyes and resolved to meet his challenge. Niall was a champion at this game of seduction, and she a mere novice, but she intended to make love to *him* this time. To seduce *him.*

"I was taught by the premier rake of Europe. You yourself said I was an apt pupil."

At the defiance in her tone, Niall acquiesced gracefully, his lips wanting to smile at this sign of his proper bride's growing confidence in her allure. He could have caressed her, charmed her, seduced her into willing submission, but he wanted Sabrina to take the lead.

She was far different from other women he'd pursued. Sabrina understood loyalty and duty and sacrifice, yet she had no notion of the usual feminine arts—cunning or wiles or the carnal games of dalliance. Yet, he'd seen in her eyes the fire of long-hidden desire. He meant to jolt her from her prim notions, to dare her to fulfill the promise of passion he sensed in her, to heed her reckless heart. Despite her unrelenting sense of propriety, he knew she could be as wild as any woman he'd bedded.

When she tentatively brushed her mouth against his, he felt his entire body clench. Her kiss tasted incredibly sweet, but the anticipation of the lovemaking to come was even sweeter. Closing his eyes, Niall lay back, leaving her solely in command.

Her first fledgling steps were uncertain. He felt her fingers trembling as she fumbled with the laces of his shirt, but she refused to allow him to aid her. She bared the strong column of his throat to her lips, but then seemed to falter.

When she hesitated, he murmured helpfully, "My shirt, mouse. Remove it."

Sabrina wanted to demand "How?" Frustratingly her arms were tangled in his plaid, permitting her little access or room to maneuver.

Biting her lower lip, she rose to her knees. The plaid fell away from their bodies, but she scarcely noticed the chill, so intent was she in easing the lower hem of Niall's shirt from his belt and pulling the garment over his head. She felt devilishly alive, throbbing with a sense of adventure and excitement. Never in all her tame existence had she engaged in any escapade so scandalous or daring.

He lay very still, the moonlight outlining the sleek muscle and sinew of his powerful chest, his breathing controlled, faintly rapid.

Sabrina drew a deep breath, remembering his counsel: *Don't be afraid to be a woman . . .*

Placing her palms against his skin, she smoothed her hands up his torso, tantalized by the heat and hardness of him. Never before had she seen such perfection. It made her wild to possess all of him. Tonight she wanted to conquer him as he had conquered her.

"Now, what will you do, sweeting?" he taunted when she hesitated.

"I shall think of something."

His lips curled with that dangerous, sensual smile that had the power to liquefy her limbs. "I trust you will."

Reaching down, her fingers found his strong, sinewed thigh. Briefly she stroked the hair-roughened flesh, pausing at the hem of his kilt.

She heard the light, quick intake of his breath as her fingers crept upward, felt the hot coil of tension in his body. The muscles in his hard stomach quivered.

Relying on instinct, she raised his kilt to his waist, baring his splendid, blatant erection.

The vital depths of his eyes caught like kindling.

Deliberately she closed her fingers gently around him. The thick length surged in her hand, iron-hard yet silken to the touch. She felt his breath heat and quicken.

"Temptress," he murmured.

Perhaps she was indeed a temptress, Sabrina thought triumphantly. In truth, there was a brazen little witch inside her she'd never before perceived.

Emboldened, her fingers curled more tightly around the heated shaft, squeezing gently, exciting her as well as him. She was dazed, heady with the incredible power she felt as he opened himself to her touch . . . the sense of being in control, a realization of her own femininity. He was all hers, to do with what she would.

"I want to please you," she murmured.

"You do please me, lass."

Unconsciously she allowed her instincts to take over,

fondling the soft sacs beneath his rigid member, squeezing, kneading, teasing. . . .

When she saw the intent look of pleasure on his face, Sabrina recalled what Niall had once told her . . . that one day she would willingly kiss and caress him between his thighs, pleasuring him with her mouth the way he had her.

Still holding him in her hand, she boldly bent her head. Shivering with delight, she pressed a kiss on his hard flesh.

"Sabrina . . ." His voice was throaty, rough—and yet he had no desire to protest the swelling sublime anticipation as she ventured further into the realm of wicked passion.

Incredibly she lowered her lips again to his throbbing groin, where his manhood strained in hot, unrelieved arousal. Niall sucked in his breath sharply when her warm mouth lightly caressed him.

"Is . . . this," she asked uncertainly as she drew back a little, "the correct way?"

"Exquisitely correct," he rasped with a husky laugh.

His rough chuckle disintegrated into a strangled moan when, with her tongue, she lightly traced the pulsing length of his erection. It quivered at her touch, growing perceptively.

"And this . . . ?" She licked him tentatively, with a sensual innocence that was maddening.

"Sweet mercy, aye." His hand involuntarily came up to cradle the back of her head, offering guidance as she tongued him. "God . . . what you do to me."

Erotically she roamed with slow thoroughness, instinctively experimenting with her unskilled caresses, tasting Niall as he had done her . . . savoring the feel of his beautiful manhood throbbing, begging for her touch . . . reveling in the power of his body . . . relishing the novelty of having her sensual, carnally sophisticated husband at her mercy.

And then she took him in her mouth.

Niall arched on the plaid as desire shot through his groin, white-hot and explosive. Pleasure poured through his senses as she sucked gently, and he groaned, the sound agonized in the hush of the night. He had taught her too well.

His hand clenched in her hair. "Sweet saints, you're testing my fortitude, love. If we continue this, I'll not vouch for my control."

"Good," Sabrina murmured, intoxicated by her feminine power. Her hunger turned to greed as she feasted on his sweet, marble-hard flesh.

"Bonny witch . . . come here . . ."

Swept away by the fierce thundering of his blood, he reached for her and dragged her into his arms, his body hard with need, taut against her softness. "Ride me . . ."

His gaze plunged deeper into hers as he positioned her above his wild pulsing erection, anticipation screaming through his senses. Niall made a deep raw sound as he felt her glide lusciously around him, his lips parting as they emitted a broken breath. *Agony,* he thought, sheathing himself to the hilt in her welcoming heat. Every sleek velvet inch of her.

His hands splayed possessively over her back as he penetrated deeper, then protectively moved lower, trying to still the sensual movement of her hips. When she rocked gently, he shuddered, seizing a raw breath, savage need held barely in check.

"No . . ." she commanded breathlessly, determined to retain control. "You are to remain still."

"While . . . you . . . torment me?"

"Precisely."

The fierceness of her desire to give him pleasure was part of her need for him. She glided down with exquisite slowness, then lifted herself up, until she found a sensual rhythm, her tight sheath embracing him with an urgent demand. His hands kneaded her buttocks for an instant, then clenched tightly as a violent hunger caught him by surprise. His face contorted with pleasure and pain as desire, savage and blinding, ripped through him. It was her name he groaned when he exploded into bliss.

Sabrina felt the convulsive clench of his body, every

pulsebeat of his hot shuddering release as he poured himself into her.

He was still vibrating with powerful aftershocks when his arms tightened around her, drawing her down. She went willingly, burying her face in the wide protection of his shoulder, her naked breasts pillowed in the warm skin of his chest. She felt powerfully female, deliciously weak, even though her body was still feverish for his touch.

With a sigh, she nestled against his hard, muscled length, cherishing the closeness. She wanted to remain like this forever, treasured in his embrace. Perhaps she might have to, Sabrina thought with a faint wry smile. Certainly she could not return to the celebration like this. She would never be able to explain her dishabille.

"Forgive me, lass," she heard Niall murmur huskily.

"Forgive you?"

She felt the warm pressure of his lips at her temple, his hand scraping the tangled veil of her hair to one side. "For my impatience. You did not reach your pleasure."

"Oh, that. It doesn't signify." In truth, she didn't mind. It was satisfying enough to have aroused her sensual, hedonistic husband to the point where he lost his much-vaunted control.

"Ah, that rankled. Signify, indeed. 'Twas inexcusably remiss of me."

"No, truly . . ."

His hands on her bare shoulders, he lifted her up so he could meet her gaze. "Am I to understand you would not care if I left you unsatisfied?"

She hesitated to confess her need, the wild longing he had aroused so effortlessly in her. A flush suffused her cheeks as she remained silent.

"Are you still hot for me?"

She could answer that truthfully. "Yes . . ."

He smiled that celebrated smile, devastating and suggestive. "Never let it be said that I left a lass unfulfilled."

Amazingly she felt his shaft start to fill and throb again

within her. Giving her no time to protest, he drew her down till his mouth could reach her throbbing breasts. His lips closed over a nipple that was pebble-hard with desire, and instantly the flames in her body fanned to life.

He laved the sensitive swollen tip, pulling at her flesh, nipping softly. When he began to suck hard, Sabrina gasped at the exquisite sensation.

With a husky murmur of triumph, he rolled over her, pinning her beneath him. His hands caressed her hips, then slid under her buttocks to cup and squeeze and lift her tighter against him.

"Say you want me, sweeting."

She shuddered with delight. "Yes . . . Niall . . . I want you."

Pressing her honeyed thighs wide, he thrust deeper. Sabrina went rigid at the unbearable surge of pleasure, the overwhelming sense of being penetrated and filled. But it was his look that made her heart nearly stop beating. His jeweled eyes glimmering in the darkness held a tender sensuality that made her feel cherished, desired. She could almost believe it was love she saw there in his gaze . . .

Sheer madness, she reflected dazedly.

He drove deeper still and she gasped, arching her back at the almost unbearable fullness enveloping and possessing her. Yet Niall gave her no surcease. He made love to her with a slow, lingering power, assuaging and intensifying the terrible sweet ache within her at the same time.

He took her with long, deep, protracted strokes, driving himself unhurriedly, fully, into her, till her slender body twisted against him, writhing helplessly.

"Aye, sweet Sabrina," he urged against her lips. "Be reckless for me . . . be wanton and hungry."

She obeyed, having no choice. As the explosive delight built relentlessly, she said his name in a raw, ragged voice and caught at his shoulders, her nails digging into his sleek skin. When the first convulsive tremors began, he fitted his mouth over hers, deeply, muffling her cries of ecstasy. She clung to him, shaking as he plunged harder, faster . . .

Only when she lunged frantically against him, sobbing, did he relax the rigid control he had maintained over himself. His body contracted like a bow, raking her with violent possession, claiming . . . pitching them both into a wild, heated dimness before the firestorm finally peaked.

Niall sank upon her, grimacing at the tumultuous pleasure flowing through him. The satisfaction was shattering . . . again.

They lay in each other's arms, exchanging heartbeats, sprawled in a tangle of hair, limbs, and pleasure. He could feel Sabrina's body still trembling, feel his *own* trembling.

At the realization, Niall shut his eyes, shocked by the power of the relentless climax he'd just endured. He couldn't remember when a woman's touch had elicited such a wrenching response in him.

It should be impossible. *He* was the seducer. He was the sensualist. With all his vast expertise, he should be able to control his rampant desire with any wench, most definitely with a virginal, unschooled lass who made no claim to beauty or feminine art.

He shook his head, marveling at the incredible hunger his innocent bride had aroused in him. He had planned simply to make love to Sabrina, but his strategy had foundered somewhere between the first sweet kiss and the second. His only intent was making her sexually responsive, awakening all the exquisite, undiscovered passion in that lovely body, yet he had become lost in the explosive ecstasy himself . . . twice.

His powerful response had startled him. Never had he expected to experience such fierce need himself, such feverish craving . . . or this haze of contentment that wrapped around him now. He felt almost intoxicated, as if he'd drunk too much potent *usqueba*.

Mayhap he was losing his touch.

With a sensual sigh, Niall shrugged aside the serious

thought. He would do better to merely savor his bride's wanton surrender, to simply enjoy the pleasure of the moment.

"*That* is how you stay warm on a raw night, mouse," he breathed faintly when he could speak.

Sabrina's low, hesitant reply was just as faint, no more than a whisper, but he heard it. "Would you . . . perhaps . . . mind showing me again?"

Remarkably he felt his male flesh stir. Drawing her close, Niall laughed helplessly against her hair.

"'Twould be my pleasure," he murmured, before resettling her body beneath him once more.

Chapter
Twelve

Thus began a magical time for Sabrina, engendered by Niall's sensual, bewitching spell. They spent nights of heated enchantment together, tangled in each other's arms. She wanted to touch him a thousand times a day, and when he was away, he preyed constantly on her mind and heart.

He taught her the meaning of pleasure. He seemed to worship her body, arousing in her a tremulous passion, a ravenous desire as savage as the wild Highland hills. Under his tutelage, she discovered a hedonistic, uninhibited side of herself she never expected existed.

He made her blossom as a woman. Her fragile self-esteem grew as he continually challenged her modest view of her attractions. She was beginning to believe that she was beautiful in his eyes, that he wanted and desired only her. She could almost hope that their marriage might flourish.

And yet . . . even as she succumbed to his tantalizing touch, she was haunted by the apprehension and uncertainty any woman would feel in the arms of a man she knew would ultimately hurt her.

In truth, Sabrina warned herself sternly and frequently, she had to remember that all this—their marriage, her seduction, Niall's instruction in the sensual art of desire—was merely a game to him. His heart was not engaged, nor would it likely ever be. Their bond was purely physical, and even that might cease to exist the moment his interest was captured by another woman more beautiful and experienced than she.

At least her grandfather seemed pleased by the reports of her marital felicity. When Sabrina paid one of her regular visits to Angus at Banesk, he crowed mercilessly.

"What did I tell ye, lass?" he cackled. "Dinna I say the lad would settle down and make ye a fine husband?"

Sabrina refrained from responding too tartly. The aging chieftain had not left his sickbed, although his health seemed measurably improved.

" 'Tis early yet, Grandfather," she murmured wryly. "We've been wed but a few weeks."

"Aye." His rheumy gaze turned sober. "But ye did well by yer clan, Sabrina. We've had no more trouble with the Buchanans. For that ye have m' gratitude."

Her stepfather, too, seemed relieved that her marriage was proceeding smoothly. She had corresponded frequently with Charles Cameron, primarily to arrange a shipment of woolen cloth from the women of Clans McLaren and Duncan. His return letters had praised the quality of the Highland fabric and renewed his offer of refuge should Sabrina require it. She had written back, assuring him that she was quite content with her lot.

She was indeed surprised to realize she was not so very homesick. She missed Papa Charles deeply, but not her dull existence in Edinburgh. Her moments were rarely dull here in the Highlands. Her duties kept her fully occupied.

As spring ripened and June kissed the land with warmth, the Highlands bloomed in all their magnificence; the hills dusted lavender with wild bell-heather, the glens with shimmering greenness.

The untamed beauty beguiled Sabrina, though no more than did her charming rogue of a husband. She felt enraptured by his seductive spell.

She couldn't ask for a more devoted lover or bridegroom, yet she was continually discovering depths to Niall that she never expected. Beneath the elegant charm and wicked wit, Sabrina found, he possessed a sober side to his nature that she could respect and admire.

One afternoon, after she had dryly wondered aloud if he enjoyed other sports than frivolous carnal pursuits, he took her trout fishing. He chose a stunningly beautiful place, where the burn rushed through a wild glen, emerald with rowan trees and mountain ferns and bracken.

Niall spread his plaid in a patch of sunlight, and they shared a luncheon of bread and cheese, boiled eggs, and a jug of hard cider, while Rab bounded along the banks ecstatically, intent on scaring any fish away.

"My father often brought me here as a lad," Niall murmured after a time.

Sabrina heard the note of sorrow in his voice. "You miss him deeply, don't you?"

His look grew wistful. "Aye. There was no finer man . . . nor laird."

"You seem to be filling his shoes admirably."

Niall smiled humorlessly and shook his head. "Not so very well. I might do better had I been properly prepared for the chieftainship. But there was no reason. I never thought to become laird. A younger son cannot inherit and must shift for himself. Instead of remaining home, I struck out for the continent to seek my fortune, making use of what gifts I had."

"Gifts?"

"Aye"—a tinge of self-mockery invaded his tone—"my charming address and braw countenance. Such attributes gained me entry into the wealthiest circles, where I kept myself in funds, winning games of chance from moneyed nobles."

She watched Niall restlessly lie back on the plaid, one arm draped across his forehead. He was wrong to think himself unworthy to lead his clan. Even though he hadn't expected the responsibility of leadership, he cared deeply about his kinsmen and was deadly serious about protecting and caring for them. She knew he would make any sacrifice to ensure their prosperity.

"My brother Jamie should have been laird," he said

softly, gazing up at the sky. "Jamie should be here now, in my place. But he died with my father at the hands of the bloody Buchanans." His eyes squeezed closed. "I was spared their death because I was away attending a *ball*."

Sabrina felt a sudden ache in her throat, comprehending the guilt Niall felt because he had survived when his father and brother had not.

"It would have served no one," she murmured, wanting to offer comfort, "had you perished with them."

"Aye, but I might have saved them. Or died in their place."

Sabrina looked away. Perhaps she was being selfish, but she was glad Niall had not perished. She could not imagine the world without this vital, beautiful man in it.

"The culprits were punished, were they not?"

His jaw clenched. "Aye, the murdering bastards paid for their treachery. I saw to that."

"Geordie told me once . . . that Owen Buchanan was not directly responsible for the ambush."

"Mayhap he didn't give the order, but they were his clansmen all the same. A laird is accountable for the actions of his kin."

Turning, Sabrina gazed down at Niall. Sorrow and tenderness pulled at her. "You still seek revenge against him, don't you."

"If so, what of it?" The question was venom-sharp, the tone bitter.

Sabrina winced. She had just been trying to understand Niall's savage intolerance. "Geordie said that at one time . . . before the tragedy . . . Owen desired an end to the feud, that he sought a truce."

Niall made a scoffing sound. "Geordie Duncan talks too much. And the Buchanans are liars as well as cowardly curs. A truce? 'Tis folly to expect them to bargain in good faith. Owen betrayed you when you attempted it. I should think you would have learned your lesson."

Sabrina had no answer for that. "I know ... It just seems—"

"No, lass, leave it! I'll not have you championing my blood enemy."

When Niall rose abruptly to his feet, Sabrina lapsed into an uneasy silence. Time stretched between them, echoing the tension and resentment of their earliest relationship.

Niall felt the strain as well. Fetching his rod, he strode to the bank to fish, vexed at her and at himself. He had said too much to her, divulged more of himself than was wise ... going on about his father and brother so ... letting Sabrina prod him into arguing about the feud. He did not have to justify his hatred of Owen Buchanan, to her or anyone else.

Faith, but his mouse of a bride had a way of slipping beneath his guard—

Except that Sabrina was no longer so much of a mouse, Niall reflected grudgingly as he baited his hook. As his pupil, she was progressing admirably, frequently showing glimpses of the sensual, alluring woman he'd thought her capable of becoming. In his bed she was as wild and passionate as any man could wish. And he felt his heart softening with warmth at the oddest moments ...

Tightening his jaw, Niall cast out his line.

In truth, their marriage hadn't proven the hardship he'd envisioned. To his surprise, he was actually developing a fondness for his wife. He *liked* Sabrina. He liked her intelligence and her courage. He liked her refreshing frankness and the wry laughter lurking in her dark eyes. He found even her tartness refreshing as she endeavored to match wits with him.

And she was fitting into his clan far better than he'd hoped. His kinswomen in particular regarded her as a benefactor, lauding her efforts to augment their meager incomes by selling cloth at the Edinburgh markets.

But Sabrina was stubbornly determined to meddle in affairs that were not her ken. He could not reproach her earnestness, but she was naive to think she could change the conflicts of a lifetime.

And on this issue in particular, he would not brook her interference.

The incident left Sabrina feeling vaguely discontented. Although Niall continued to play the charming lover in the ensuing days, he was never again as forthcoming as he'd been those few sunlit moments by the burn.

She was dismayed, however, when their tenuous affinity was threatened in a manner she never expected: by the promise of peace with the Buchanans.

It began some five weeks after the Beltane festival, when Eve Graham held a musical evening for the surrounding gentry. That night the McLaren and his bride engaged in their first significant argument, one which developed into a battle royal.

Sabrina grudgingly admitted she was partly to blame. Perhaps she should never have become caught up in the puzzling intrigue that presented itself that night.

She had donned one of her new garments for the occasion—a striking sack-back gown of rose silk with an ivory under-petticoat supported by small hoops.

She was finishing her toilet in front of the cheval glass when Niall returned to their bedchamber, carrying a small casket, and dismissed the maidservants who had helped her.

"Beautiful," he murmured as he came up behind her.

She did look pleasing, Sabrina thought, viewing herself in the glass. Her unpowdered hair was dressed in a softer, more natural style, with curling tendrils that formed a halo around her face. She had eschewed paint, merely allowing a touch of rouge at cheekbones and lips to enhance her complexion, as Niall had shown her how to apply. The exquisite gown was flattering to her slender figure, the boned bodice pushed against her breasts, accentuating the ripe swell of her bosom above the square neck.

Shyly, Sabrina met his gaze in the glass. "You . . . truly think I am beautiful?"

"Aye . . . beautiful and vibrant . . . Magnificent in every way."

Niall watched her eyes brighten with a flash of pleasure, and felt a sense of deep satisfaction. He had been right about the rose color for her; it brought out the richness of her hair and eyes, the luminous warmth of her skin. But it was Sabrina herself he needed to convince. He was determined to make her see what a marvelous woman she could be, to believe in her own feminine power.

"Look at yourself . . ." he ordered softly. One hand lifted to her bare, silken shoulder. "How could any flesh-and-blood man resist? Look at this lustrous hair . . . so dark and rich and shot with the red and gold of a Highland sunrise. These remarkable eyes that can flash with fury or passion. This delicate face, with the fine cheekbones and full, kissable mouth . . . This long, slender throat. This skin, so soft and glowing . . . You bring me to my knees, cherie. As you will every other gentleman present tonight."

Sabrina felt herself flushing. Niall's praise warmed her immeasurably. She had tried hard to please him during the past weeks, striving to become the sensual woman he wanted her to be. In truth, she felt like a different person entirely from the staid spinster who had traveled here to the Highlands to pay a visit to her dying grandfather. Tonight, however, she was overwrought with nerves. This would be the first true test of her new identity, attending a function with guests other than their clansmen.

"Faith, you're tempting, mouse," Niall breathed in a husky intimate tone, his thumb caressing the bare curve of her throat.

He was tempting, as well. Having chosen more formal attire than a Highland kilt, he wore a long flaring coat and matching waistcoat of pale blue brocade, with white satin breeches and silver-buckled shoes, and a froth of lace at throat and wrists. The effect was bold, rugged, elegant. His sun-bronzed complexion and unpowdered raven hair, drawn back by a ribbon, would make the other painted, be-wigged lords and gentlemen appear ghostly and effeminate.

Sabrina was gazing at him in admiration when Niall casually presented her with the jewel casket. Opening it, he drew out a pendant encrusted with delicate rubies.

Sabrina gasped at the costly gems as he fastened it around her throat.

"Perfect," Niall observed appreciatively.

Her fingers rose to touch the pendant. "Niall . . . I wish to thank you."

"There is no need, sweeting. The jewels belong to the McLaren's lady. As my wife you are entitled to wear them."

"Not just for the jewels, although they are splendid. I mean . . . for your excellent tutoring these past weeks."

He smiled briefly and pressed a light kiss in the curve of her neck. " 'Twas entirely my pleasure. You have succeeded beyond my wildest expectations."

His touch was casual, but all Sabrina could think of was Niall's soft, demanding mouth, his hard fingers, arousing her to heights of passion she'd never dreamed of.

It came as a disappointment when he merely offered his hand to escort her below to the waiting carriage.

By the time they arrived, however, Sabrina was beginning to feel a reckless sense of daring. For the first time in her life, she felt beautiful, indeed almost powerful, and confident enough of her feminine charms to fulfill Niall's prophecy.

The Widow Graham's home was a stately dwelling built within the last decade, without the aged charm or enduring strength of the McLarens' Creagturic. Scores of expensive candles lit the immense drawing room, which was crowded with guests clad in a blaze of silks, satins, and costly brocades.

Eve met them at the entrance, resplendent in a ravishing gown of pale yellow silk damask heavily embroidered with ribbons and lace.

"How delighted I am you could come," the widow said to Sabrina, though her gaze lingered on Niall. "I trust you will be pleased by the music, my dear. I have arranged for a singer with the most divine voice, as well as performances on the pianoforte and harp. I mean to show that we Highlanders are not such savages as one might think. Pray, let me make you known to my other guests. . . ."

As the introductions were made, Sabrina was grateful for Niall's insistence upon gowning her in a manner befitting a laird's wife. The company included not only the local gentry and clan chiefs, but noblemen and military officers from distant districts, and several prominent Englishmen as well.

It gave her a moment's pause to realize Owen Buchanan had attended along with two of his sons. Beside her, she felt Niall go rigid as he spied the Buchanan. The sheer animosity bristling between the two men was apparent, though they remained in opposite corners of the room.

"If you wonder," Eve murmured to Sabrina, "why the Buchanans received an invitation, 'twas unavoidable. Do you see the lady there in the plum gown? She is a cousin of my late husband's and is wed to Owen's eldest son. But I have every hope the Highlanders will restrain their animosity. They will not wish to let the Englishmen present suspect any dissension among the local clans. Now pray, Sabrina, let me introduce you. . . ."

Sabrina took a deep breath and adopted the hint of an alluring smile, just as Niall had taught her.

She was startled by how easy it was. Not only did the gentlemen respond eagerly to her tentative attempts at flirtation, but to her surprise and amusement, she soon found herself the center of male attention.

Her husband was not at all surprised by her success.

Long familiar with being conspicuous and sought after himself, Niall at first was pleased to see his bride claim the admiration she was due. Ordinarily not an overt beauty, Sabrina seemed one tonight, with the burnished highlights of her hair richly shimmering in the glow of candlelight, her dark eyes bright with eager pleasure, her ivory complexion delicately hued with excitement. He left her side only for a moment to fetch her a cup of punch before the musical program began, and when he returned, it was to find her holding court before a bevy of admirers.

Indeed, Sabrina was in danger of being overwhelmed, most particularly from a lusty Scottish aristocrat casting lecherous eyes on her, and a dashing English colonel determined to win her smile.

Niall could understand the appeal. Discriminating gentlemen appreciated a woman of intelligence and wit, and Sabrina, with her rapier tongue and quick understanding, presented the most fascinating of challenges. She had the added cachet of having captured a notorious rake's hand in marriage, but it was the woman herself who commanded attention. She had changed in some indefinable way, had gained an immeasurable quality that lured male eyes and hinted at beguiling secrets; an enticing suggestion that hidden beneath that serene, unprepossessing facade lay a woman of fire and passion.

It made a man wild to discover if it were true.

Even *he* was not invulnerable, Niall realized in surprise. Incredibly he was attracted to his own wife. When Sabrina lifted her gaze and caught sight of him through the crowd, her face lit in a way that made his loins throb.

His response was so swift, so unexpected, that he could not check it. Frowning, Niall forced himself to look away.

He was still pondering his reaction when his former mistress joined him.

"Your bride seems to be greatly enjoying her conquests," Eve remarked. "I commend you, darling. You have worked wonders with the lass."

Unwillingly, Niall's glance returned to Sabrina. He should feel triumphant. He had accomplished precisely what he'd intended. He had set out to transform his mouse of a bride into a tiger and had succeeded far beyond his expectations. Sabrina was proving to be a magnificent woman.

And yet . . . he wasn't certain he liked her this way. She was flirting and laughing for the admiration of other men, much like the shallow, simpering beauties he'd spent his leisure pursuing in the game of love. The sight of Sabrina engaging in the same amusements left him feeling an inexplicable dissatisfaction.

Faith, perhaps he'd unleashed more of a tiger than was wise, Niall acknowledged. As he watched her parry a wicked remark with a barbed retort of her own, he had to repress the urge to intervene.

Sweet saints, one could almost call the sentiment *jealousy*.

With a stab of annoyance, Niall shook his head. The notion that he would become enamored of his own wife was absurd.

He forced a sanguine smile and answered Eve with a languid question about the program.

It was some consolation, Niall reflected restlessly as he sat through the first musical interval, that he need not worry about Sabrina's interest being attached by some profligate cavalier. She was too enamored of her husband.

It came as an unpleasant shock when at the second intermission he discovered his bride was not the loyal innocent he judged her.

Flushed with success and the warmth of the crowded drawing room, Sabrina had slipped out onto the terrace for a breath of air, hoping that her husband would pursue her there. She wanted to laugh with Niall at her success and quiz him about how to discourage overzealous admirers—a position she'd never thought to find herself in.

Yet when she heard footsteps behind her and glanced over her shoulder, she was taken aback to find the gentleman was none other than Keith Buchanan, the fourth and youngest son to the bloody Buchanan laird, the only one yet unwed. He resembled his father, with the same powerful build and swarthy complexion, though he lacked the beard.

"Pray do not go, milady," Keith urged quietly.

Sabrina hesitated, her fingers clenched on the marble balustrade. This man was a mortal enemy of her clan and of her husband. It was dangerous to be in such close proximity, yet she refused to flee in fear.

Her blood still boiled to remember the Buchanans' perfidy last month. Their laird had pledged his word to become allies, agreeing to a feu duty in exchange for a truce, and then struck without warning, raiding Duncan cattle while professing peace.

Keith Buchanan moved to stand beside her, eyeing her intently. "So this is the lass who threatened to cut out my da's heart and fought hand to hand against my kinsmen." His tone suggested bitterness and something more: admiration. "Ye must be glad of yer success. Ye offered to become allies, only to lure us into yer trap. Ye snagged us as sure as a salmon trout."

"*I?*" Sabrina asked, startled by his vehemence. "I was not the one to deal in treachery."

"Were ye not? We didna start the reiving. Ye thieving Duncans did. We bargained in good faith, yet the moment we lowered our guard, ye dealt us a blow."

"We did no such thing, sirrah!"

He took a menacing step closer, his hulking frame looming over her. "Do ye call me a liar?"

Sabrina took a deep breath. "I have no earthly idea if you are lying, but I assure you, you are gravely mistaken as to the sequence of events. We would never have raided your cattle had you not stolen ours first!"

Keith reached up to grasp her chin with hard fingers, forcing her face up to his. Sabrina held her ground, despite her sudden trembling.

"We dinna start the feud, I tell ye!"

"Nor did we!"

He muttered an oath at her fierce denial, his rough hands gripping her upper arms, crushing the fine silk of her gown.

"Unhand me, sirrah," she demanded breathlessly, "before I cry for aid. My husband would not be best pleased to find you mauling me."

He made no response as he stared at her, his angry eyes searching hers stonily. He must, however, have been surprised by what he saw, for over the span of a dozen heartbeats, his withering scorn took on a measure of doubt, almost of puzzlement.

" 'Tis a rotten fish I smell," he said slowly. "If ye dinna start it . . ."

Never one to be slow-witted, Sabrina grasped what he was intimating. If neither of them was lying about initiating the raid, perhaps they had both been deceived.

Her own brows drew together in a frown. "*Yet someone* had to have resumed the feud. Someone bent on mischief . . ."

"Or treachery."

"But *who*?"

"What of yer husband?"

"Niall? He would never attempt anything so underhanded. He's made no secret of his dislike of your clan."

"Perhaps he wouldna tell ye."

The murmur of voices startled them both from their quarrel. A young couple had strolled out onto the terrace and were eyeing them curiously.

Sabrina tried to pull away, but Keith Buchanan's grip tightened, frustration ripe on his expression. "This discussion isna over, milady. Can ye meet with me on the morrow?"

"Meet with you?"

"Aye. Do ye know Loch Voil?"

"Yes, but—"

"At the northern end, a burn spills into the loch. Ye'll find me there when the sun is highest—"

"Ah, there you are, my dear," a drawling masculine

voice interjected, a voice which held the cutting edge of a claymore.

Sabrina froze. Niall stood at the open French doors, looking ruggedly elegant in his formal attire. Beyond him, Eve Graham hovered, her eyes wide with curiosity and dismay.

Sabrina gave a guilty start. She had not meant for her husband to see her associating with his foe. Yet Niall gave her no opportunity to explain, before saying in a dangerously silken tone, "You will no doubt desire to return to the drawing room, my sweet. You would not wish to miss the remainder of the excellent performance."

Sabrina hesitated. She had no desire to cause a scene, yet perhaps it was wiser to wait till she could speak to Niall privately, when his fury had diminished a bit.

"Sabrina." He said nothing further, his eyes merely impaling her.

"Yes . . . of course," she stammered. With an apologetic glance at Keith Buchanan, she picked up her skirts and fled inside—only to come face to face with the Widow Graham.

"I know," Eve murmured, her eyes troubled, "that I advised you to engage in a flirtation with other gentlemen, but really, Sabrina, was it wise to choose Niall's blood rival?"

"I assure you, I was *not* flirting."

"It certainly appeared that way. He looked about to kiss you."

"You cannot believe I would have permitted such a thing."

"What *I* believe is not the issue, I fear."

Sabrina glanced over her shoulder, wishing she could divine what was going forth on the terrace.

It would have surprised her to know Niall was battling feelings of fury and betrayal—just as it surprised *him*. He wasn't at all prepared for the jealous wrath he'd felt upon seeing Sabrina in the arms of another man . . . especially this man. That she would tarry here with the blood kin of

Owen Buchanan, her head bent close, whispering as she made an assignation to meet with him on the morrow, filled Niall with a rage befitting his savage Highland ancestors.

It required a herculean effort to keep his voice level as he addressed Keith Buchanan. "You will not make your rendezvous tomorrow with my wife, I think."

Buchanan clenched a defiant fist, his reply taunting. "Will I not, now?"

Niall smiled chillingly. "Not if you care to see another dawn."

For a long moment the two men stared at each other.

"By god, mon," Keith said finally, his tone scornful, "I never took ye for a fool. But that plucky lass doesna deserve ye."

He stalked passed Niall then, bristling with ire.

It was a short while later before Niall joined his wife in the drawing room. His blue eyes glittered like ice as he resumed his seat beside her. Sabrina breathed a sigh of relief when the interminable performance at last ended.

The air was brittle with tension, however, as Niall escorted her to their waiting carriage. When they were underway, he sat smoldering in silence for several moments.

In the dim interior, she couldn't clearly make out his features, but his voice, when he finally spoke, held an edge of steel. "I warn you, mouse, I will not tolerate being gifted with a pair of horns."

"Horns?"

"I will not countenance being cuckolded."

Her jaw dropped. Sabrina stared at him blankly, wishing she could see him in the darkness. Had it been any other man, she might have thought him jealous!

"I cannot imagine what put that absurd notion in your head," she finally said.

"Mayhap because I found my wife embracing the son of my greatest foe."

"I was *not* embracing him! We were holding a private conversation, merely that."

"Well, in future I forbid you to speak to him, privately or otherwise."

Sabrina stiffened, her anger roused to be treated like a disobedient child. "Simply because *you* hold such vast expertise in cuckolding indifferent husbands is no justification to accuse *me* of immorality. I am no adulteress."

"Not yet, perhaps."

His reply struck her like a blow, driving her breath away. How could he possibly believe her guilty of infidelity? She had never done anything to warrant such a vile accusation.

When she remained silent, Niall caught her elbow, drawing her close ... so close she could see his features. His mouth hovered just above hers, its beautiful lines stark and sensual, as if etched from stone. "I will brook no impropriety in my bride, do you ken me?"

"Yes, I ken you," she retorted, her voice shaking. "It is clear that your standards of conduct make no pretense of evenhandedness. It is perfectly acceptable for you to behave like a randy stallion, while I must remain altogether virtuous."

"Exactly."

She wrenched her arm away. "You need not fear, my lord. I have every intention of honoring my marriage vows— even though I'm certain you cannot make the same pledge. I doubt there is a female in the district you have not seduced."

"It is different for a man."

"Is it?" Her voice dripped scorn.

"Indeed. As a male, I cannot spawn another man's by-blow."

"So that gives you license to rut with anything in skirts?"

She could feel Niall's narrowed gaze piercing her. "I need no license to seek other companionship. I made no promise of fidelity when I agreed to this damnable union."

Flinching, Sabrina dropped her own gaze, her lowered lashes masking the pain.

"I will not warn you again, madam. Keep away from the Buchanans," Niall commanded tersely, before lapsing into silence once more.

They spoke not a word for the remainder of the short journey. When they reached Creagturic, Sabrina went directly upstairs to their bedchamber.

Niall did not join her—not then, nor anytime during the long night. For the first time since their marriage, Sabrina found herself forsaken. She lay alone in the vast bed, missing her husband's warmth, his hardness, his magnetic presence. Finding sleep impossible, she tossed and turned and punched her pillow a dozen times, brooding in anger. To think he believed her capable of adultery . . . She would never behave so dishonorably.

His double standard infuriated her as well. 'Twas not fair! She was constrained by her vows of fidelity to be faithful, while he suffered no such constraints.

Far worse, she loved the wretched man!

Damn him, damn him, triple damn him . . . If he wanted fidelity and loyalty from her, he should be willing to give it himself.

Sabrina rose blurry-eyed the following morning—long after Niall had already left the house. She was too mortified to ask where her husband had spent the night, though she was certain the servants knew.

When noon approached, she informed Mrs. Paterson that she meant to call on her grandfather. Then, drawing on a cloak and collecting her dog for protection, she had a horse saddled and defiantly rode out to meet Owen Buchanan's son.

It was a dangerous course, Sabrina knew. Yet she refused to allow Niall to dictate her every action, refused to lie down like a doormat while he heartlessly trod over her. And in truth, more than defiance drove her. She had hopes of ultimately getting to the bottom of the mystery regarding the cattle raids.

Keith Buchanan was right. Something smelled rotten. The Buchanans believed that she had started the conflict, that she'd duped them by pretending to arrange a truce. Owen's fury at her on her wedding day had been entirely genuine, Sabrina remembered. He'd accused her of tricking him into leaving his herds unguarded. Of course she had not. Indeed, she'd blamed them for the betrayal. But what if they were no more guilty than she was? If the Buchanans had not struck the first blow, it was understandable they would feel wronged after Niall's midnight raid and his wounding of two Buchanan kinsmen.

Sabrina clenched her teeth in frustration. Clearly she couldn't discuss the situation with Niall. He was too blinded by hatred to ever see the Buchanans as anything but thieves and murderers. But if there truly were a chance to promote peace, she couldn't miss it because she was too timid to stand up to her infuriating, domineering husband. Most certainly if his best interests would be served.

Niall was absurdly misguided to accuse her of seeking to put horns on him. Keith Buchanan had shown no amorous intentions toward her. Indeed, just the opposite; he seemed more inclined to wrap his fingers around her throat and throttle her. There would be no impropriety in their meeting in broad daylight. And such a gray, damp day was scarcely conducive to romance. A heavy mist hung low over the rugged hills, obscuring the highest peaks.

Her thoughts occupied, Sabrina scarcely noticed her surroundings, yet as she and Rab passed verdant forests and valleys, the majesty eventually worked to soothe her temper. When she came to a rushing burn, she followed its path to a lush, pine- and bracken-covered glen. In the distance, the tranquil waters of a loch gleamed silver, its banks heavily treed.

The shrill cry of a curlew pierced the quiet as she drew her mount to a halt. Near the shore stood a typical crofter's cottage, whitewashed stone with thatched roof. From the chimney, lazy wisps of smoke swirled upward toward the rain-laden skies, tingeing the air with the scent of peat fire. Beyond the croft, a saddled horse grazed peacefully.

The raven-haired man leaning negligently against the trunk of a rowan tree had his back to her, but he turned when he heard the soft thud of her horse's hooves.

Keith stared at her a moment, one hand on the hilt of his sword, as she came to a halt before him. "Welcome, milady."

Sabrina managed a smile. "Do you mean to run me through, sir?" she asked lightly.

The corners of his mouth turned up in a reluctant grin. "'Twould be a mistake to attempt it, if what I hear about ye is true. Ye would acquit yerself well enough to threaten my manhood. Nay, 'tis yer animal I seek to defend myself against." With his head he gestured at the giant dog, who was standing at attention, ready to attack if need be.

"Oh, forgive me . . ." Sabrina called to her dog and told him to be easy.

Keith's guard relaxed. "I thank ye for coming, milady."

"There is no need to thank me. I would like to solve this mystery as much as you would."

"I gather the McLaren denies dealing in treachery."

"I did not ask him about it. Niall . . . was rather angry last night. He doesn't know I've come—"

No sooner had the words left her mouth when she heard the rhythmic sound of hoofbeats behind her.

Glancing over her shoulder, Sabrina drew a sharp breath when she recognized the black horse emerging from beyond the crofter's hut, moving toward her at an easy canter. While the horseman possessed raven hair like Keith Buchanan's, the powerful shoulders were draped in a McLaren plaid.

Keith's hand immediately went to his sword again, while Sabrina's fingers tightened on her reins. Evidently Niall had trusted her so little that he had to follow her.

Slowing to a walk, he urged his mount forward, till he was abreast of her. With a whimper of welcome, Rab fawned at his feet, but Niall appeared not to notice. His jaw was clenched savagely, while his eyes burned a fury like blue fire as he stared down at Keith Buchanan. "You have a death wish, I see. You should have heeded my warning."

"And what warning was that?" Keith returned, his scornful tone taunting.

"I told you to keep away from my wife. Clearly I shall have to teach you a lesson in prudence."

"Ye may try," he spat, drawing his sword from its scabbard.

"No!" Sabrina cried as Niall swung down from his horse. "Stop it! Please!"

When neither man paid her any mind, she drove her mount forward, positioning herself between them. "Please . . . this is absurd. There is no justification for bloodshed."

"Sabrina, move away!" Niall demanded.

"Aye, milady," Keith agreed. "This isna yer battle."

"Of course it is!" She gazed down at Keith imploringly, knowing he would be easier to reason with than her husband. "Mr. Buchanan, please . . . this meeting was obviously a mistake. I should never have come. Please will you not go?"

His narrowed gaze shifted from Niall to her.

"Please," she pleaded. "It would be better if you left."

"I dinna like to leave ye alone with him."

"I'll be all right. Please . . . just go."

His jaw clenching, Keith went to his horse. Sheathing his sword, he swung himself up into the saddle and rode stiffly away, only once glancing back.

When he was gone, the resultant silence was deafening. It was so quiet Sabrina could hear the gentle lap of water on the shore of the loch.

Niall glanced darkly up at her. "A pity your craven admirer lacks the courage to stay and fight."

"It isn't craven to refuse to argue with a madman," Sabrina replied through gritted teeth. "What do you mean, following me here like a wretched spy?"

Niall sheathed his blade. "I thought to interrupt a lover's tryst."

"A *lover's* tryst!"

His blue eyes hardened. "I warned you to keep away from our foes. Apparently you cannot be trusted."

Sabrina's temper rose again precipitously. It was the outside of enough that he should accuse her of infidelity without the slightest justification. "Apparently your frequent sojourns in the stews of debauchery have rendered you incapable of objective judgment. Well, you can take your base suspicions and . . . and swallow them!"

She drew back on the reins, intending to turn her horse and ride away, but Niall moved sharply to her side and reached up for her. Pulling Sabrina from her horse, he set her on her feet none too gently. "Listen hard, lass. I'll not have my commands thwarted."

"You do not rule me, sirrah!"

"I do indeed rule you, madam, as your husband and chief! 'Tis high time you accepted that."

"Go to the devil!"

He swore an expletive, his brogue deepening as he retorted, "You'll no' take one of our enemies as lover, do you ken me?"

Sabrina clenched her teeth. "Perfectly, my lord! Should I decide to take a lover, I shall be certain to choose one from among our *allies*."

His irises grew black as he stared down at her, dark emotion streaking through them like lightning in a stormy sky. Sabrina had never seen him so angry. It was recklessness itself to defy him when he was in such a mood, and yet her own mood matched his for explosiveness.

"You suffer from the most colossal case of presumption I have ever witnessed! You are not the only man in existence. If I wish to take a lover, I will! If I wish a *dozen* lovers, I will do so! Do *you* ken *me*?"

It was an idle threat, but she was too incensed for circumspection. She met his fierce gaze measure for measure.

His eyes hard with fury, he closed his fingers painfully on her arms.

"Don't you dare think to raise a hand to me!" she warned.

His jaw set rigidly, Niall visibly gritted his teeth. "I have never touched a lass in anger before, but I vow in this instance I could make an exception."

"'Tis no more than I would expect from a dissolute libertine!"

"Do you ken how to swim?" he demanded suddenly.

"What?"

"Can you swim?"

"No! Why—"

She was abruptly silenced as Niall bent and scooped her up in his arms. Sabrina gasped and clutched his neck as he carried her to the edge of the loch.

Rab growled once, but a sharp command from Niall made him cease. With a whine of confusion, the huge animal dropped to his belly, resting his head on his paws. It infuriated Sabrina to realize she could not even look to her dog for protection.

To her startlement, though, Niall waded directly into the water.

"Mayhap this will cool your lusts!" he declared, before letting her drop with a splash.

The loch was only waist-deep there, but Sabrina gasped as the icy water closed over her head. She flailed in panic for an instant, then came up choking and coughing and sputtering with fury.

"You—w-wretched—b-beast! You—loutish—j-jackanapes!" Half blinded by chilling streams of water, she struggled to her feet, cursing Niall with words she wasn't even aware she knew. On the rocky shore, Rab leapt wildly, punctuating her tirade with excited barks.

"Take care, lass," Niall warned, turning to retreat to dry land. "You'll make me think a dousing wasn't discipline enough."

"Damn your eyes . . . !"

He had thrown her in the loch, and now he had the gall to taunt her! His arrogance made her blood boil.

Shoving her wet hair from her eyes, Sabrina stalked after him—or rather, she *tried* to stalk after him. Regrettably she had great difficulty following him with her sodden cloak and skirts weighing her down. "Come back here, you cowardly brute!"

Niall turned abruptly, one black eyebrow slashing upward in mockery. "Brute?"

"Aye, *brute!*" She reached the shore just then, but stumbled over the hem of her cloak. In frustration, Sabrina tore off the water-logged garment and threw it to the ground.

To her dismay, she realized her muslin scarf had come free, while her breasts had slipped from the confining imprisonment of her boned bodice. All that covered her bosom was a thin, wet chemise.

Niall's gaze skimmed her pale curves, locking on her exposed breasts, where the water-taunted nipples strained darkly against the dampened cloth. A mocking smile curved his lips. "You'll not appease me with feminine lures, sweet. Though I admit the notion is tempting. You make an appealing sight, your face flushed with temper, your eyes flashing fire . . ."

A wild tirade of verbal abuse danced behind Sabrina's clenched teeth. She had always prided herself on her self-control, but now she marveled at the strength of the rage that shook her as she sloshed toward him.

He stood his ground, his hands on his narrow hips. "'Tis such a fascinating change, from prim lady to spitting tiger—albeit a soggy one—"

She hit him. Drawing back her arm wildly, Sabrina swung with all her might. Her fist struck the hard slab of his chest before Niall caught her wrist in a fierce grip.

Danger jumped and pulsed around him like lightning, his blue eyes brilliant with fire.

"Vixen," he breathed as he pulled her brutally against his body. "Apparently a lesson in wifely obedience is in order."

"Obedience!" Sabrina fairly hissed the word. "I shall never obey you . . . you arrogant knave!"

"We shall see about that, wife!"

His hand tangled in her hair in a fist of hard control as Niall brought his mouth fiercely down to cover hers.

Chapter
Thirteen

He was all angry fire and hard, dominating male. He kissed her savagely, ravishing her with his tongue.

Sabrina strained against him, struggling to no avail. When Niall at last raised his head, she was panting from exertion.

"Damn you . . . release me before I . . . I box your ears!"

" 'Tis unwise to threaten a man when you're in his power," he warned, his voice as tight as his imprisoning arms.

She should have heeded his advice, but her blood was up now. When he lowered his mouth to kiss her again, she sank her teeth into his lower lip.

Niall cursed savagely and jerked back. Yet Sabrina hadn't won. She gave a startled cry as he bent and heaved her over his shoulder like a sack of oats.

"Let . . . go . . . of me . . . you swine!" she exclaimed between breathless gasps.

"Nay, lass, not till we have this settled!"

Rab, to her further fury, remained neutral in their battle, barking playfully as with swift, sure strides, Niall carried Sabrina to the crofter's hut.

Shoving open the door with his booted foot, he stepped inside, then kicked it shut behind them.

Inside, the dim interior was hazy with smoke. The peat fire burning in the hearth gave off a welcoming warmth to Sabrina's wet, chilled body, but she scarcely needed the heat, so scalding was her anger. The instant Niall set her on her feet on the hard earthen floor, she swung at him.

Capturing her wrists, Niall ignored her resistance and glanced around the small cottage. The blackened rafters were hung with herbs and weapons, while in one corner of the room stood a rope bed with a heather-stuffed mattress.

"Fergus is away, I see. He'll not mind if we make use of his bed."

Sabrina glared at him. "You must be daft if you think I'll allow you to make love to me!"

"Take off those sodden skirts, madam, or I shall do it for you."

"Devil take you, you'll not lay a hand on me!"

Niall clenched his jaw. Their argument had gone beyond anger or desire. He felt a wild need to mark Sabrina indelibly as his, to brand her with his scent, his touch, his taste, to drive the thought of any other man from her mind. She would never *think* of taking another lover when he was through.

His eyes returned the fire of her gaze. "Do not think to deny me, wife."

His hard-looking mouth hovering over hers, he curled his fingers over the edge of her chemise, drawing down the fabric. When his palm covered her damp breast, her body responded with humiliating swiftness, the nipple tightening to a rigid, aching peak.

"Do you truly think any other lover can please you as I can?"

"Yes!" she retorted scathingly. "Any man would please me better!"

She twisted in his grasp, struggling fiercely. When she brought her knee up between his thighs, Niall barely prevented the blow from doing him an injury. He laughed at the sheer pluck of the wench and tightened his hold.

Lifting her up, he tossed Sabrina on her back on the heather tick. She scrambled to her knees, panting with such passionate fury that she would have scratched his face could she have reached it.

She was unutterably wild and glorious, Niall thought as

fire ripped through his groin: her dark eyes flashing, her cheeks tinged with angry roses, her luscious breasts heaving, begging to be caressed. The jutting nipples drew his admiring gaze.

"You want me," he observed. "I can see your aroused nipples, your flushed skin . . ."

She hastened to cover her nakedness with her arm. "I don't want you, you arrogant cur!"

He laughed again insolently and took a step toward her.

"Keep away from me! I don't want you touching me."

"I'll touch you and more, sweeting. I intend to make you beg for me."

"You will not!"

It was a challenge he could not ignore. Niall tossed aside his plaid. "You really should refrain from saying things you don't mean, pet. You're a hot-blooded wench in need of a man."

"A *man*, yes! Not a ruthless barbarian."

"I can be gentle, as you well know." He shed his leather waistcoat and then his shirt, revealing the wide swath of his broad, bronzed chest. Unfastening his trews to free his erection, he stood half nude before her, all harsh masculinity and bold magnificence. "I'll lay wager that I'll soon have you beneath me, panting and mindless with need."

His blazing arrogance fueled her fury. "You fiend, you can't make me want you! You'll get no response from me."

"We shall see."

Their eyes locked in a silent, fiery battle of wills. In the small cottage, tension vibrated between them, feral and primitive. He intended to demand her surrender, Sabrina knew.

Helplessly, she licked her dry lips as he moved toward her. "I'll . . . I'll scream."

"Aye, you will . . . with passion when you sheathe me in your hot silk."

"I'll scratch you, I'll bite!"

His mouth curled with grim amusement. "I trust you

will, I want you scratching and clawing at me. An angry spitfire makes good bedsport."

"*Bedsport!*" Her fingers clenched into angry fists.

Resting one knee on the bed, Niall stood over her challengingly, his eyes burning into hers. Trapped by his powerful body, Sabrina dropped her incensed gaze to his splendid arousal, huge and thrusting.

She could feel her heart pounding. Niall would win if she let him touch her.

Turning abruptly, she lunged for the foot of the bed, trying to escape, but Niall flung himself after her. Covering her with his body, he pinned her down with his weight, pressing her chest into the mattress. Her cry of outrage was muffled by the covers.

"Aye, play the spitfire for me, Sabrina . . . Let me feel your fury. You're hotter and tighter when you're angry, just how I want you."

Ignoring her wild struggles, Niall drove his straining manhood against her skirts, probing the soft buttocks beneath. "That's it, fight me, sweet tiger. I want you writhing and breathless when I drive deep inside you. I want you moaning my name, pleading with me to love you . . ."

"I *won't* . . ."

Her nipples already hurt, their hard points chafed by the wet linen, but when his hands reached around to cup and fondle her, they contracted into tight aching buds, shooting arrows of excited painfulness deep between her thighs. Roughly he kneaded the peaks, deliberately arousing her.

"Let us see how ardently you protest when I bury myself inside you." He pushed up her wet skirts, exposing her bare thighs. She could feel the cool air on her chilled buttocks, feel his warm fingers between her legs . . .

"Niall . . . plague take you, *no!*"

"*Yes,* sweeting." His voice was dark velvet. "I'll not relent until you burn for me, till I feel the pleasure rip through you . . ."

His promise made her pulse leap wildly. She could feel the heated length of his sex brand her naked thighs like searing steel, feel the pulsing urgency of his lithe, magnificent body.

His teeth grazed her ear, his breath coming harsh and hot against her skin as he said, "Even now the fire in your blood burns for release."

"Curse you . . . get . . . off me!"

In partial compliance, he arched his body over hers, but instead of freeing her, he lifted her on her hands and knees, rendering her completely vulnerable. Kneeling behind her, he stroked the velvet-sheathed hardness of his arousal against her yielding bottom, making her weak with longing.

Sabrina fought to hold back a ragged sob of desire. She tensed rigidly as his hand slid between her legs and brushed the tight nest of curls. He found her cleft hot and slick with her own juices, the feminine bud of pleasure throbbing with heat.

Not allowing her to escape, he thrust two fingers up inside her. Sabrina bit her lip to keep from screaming in excitement.

"You clench so tightly around my fingers," he murmured, his voice as dark and seductive as black velvet. "I can't wait to feel you sheathe my cock."

His bold fingers thrust deeper and she moaned, a pleading sound of need, a shameless yearning to be filled and stretched by this man . . . dominated and possessed . . . She wanted him, hot and deep and male, inside her.

She could feel him poised behind her . . . his fingers parting her honeyed thighs for his taking . . . the swollen head of his shaft potently probing the silky folds of flesh. When she made one last desperate attempt to pull away, he gripped her buttocks in his strong grasp and in a single rough stroke, plunged to the hilt inside her.

It was a stunning act of possession, one that almost made her faint with sensation. Sabrina cried aloud at the incredible feel of his fiery spear piercing her, forcing her wide open, a curse spilling from her lips. Yet when he made to withdraw, she braced her palms against the mattress and thrust wildly back against him, impaling herself on his magnificent flesh.

He laughed, the husky sound raw with triumph and excitement, and swiftly drew back, only to plunge within her again.

She was panting by the time he'd thrust twice, and groaning by the fifth powerful stroke. He drove fierce and full inside her, ramming himself hard within her, his swollen sacs slapping against her mons. Her senses reeled with the feel of him, while brilliant flames leapt against the blackness of her mind.

"Oh . . . God . . ."

"Aye, that's the way of it . . . Moan for me, tiger . . ."

"Sweet mercy . . . Niall . . . please . . ."

She was dimly aware she was begging, yet she didn't care. She writhed wantonly at his savage plundering, the wild frenzy building within her as he ravished her so exquisitely. She shook as the brutal, grinding pleasure surged relentlessly, sobbing aloud with sweet, mindless wanting.

Feeling her shudders, groaning as she trembled tightly around his engorged shaft, Niall drove her ever higher. He was beyond anger, beyond thought, driven by a fierce nameless hunger. He felt her convulsions of ecstasy begin an instant before searing talons of sensation ripped through him. He heard her scream as she shattered, heard his own hoarse shout as his body exploded in an endless, piercing rapture.

Her flesh continued to pulse sweetly long after the moment of orgasm. Niall felt the faint rippling as he collapsed weakly upon her, felt his heart beating in a frenzied echo of her own.

When the last faint, delicious spasm was spent, when the madness had receded a little, he withdrew from her and shifted his body, relieving Sabrina of his weight. He was still breathing harshly, his skin still sheened with sweat from the frantic, almost savage urgency of their lovemaking.

Her silence disturbed him, though.

Forcing open his eyes, he gave her a searching look. He had marked her as his; her face was dewy from the heat and violence of his possession.

"Did I hurt you?" he asked thickly.

"Mortally," she muttered, her withering tone suggesting that her pride had suffered more than her flesh.

Her scathing retort relieved him, yet her body was doubtless wet and chilled from his dousing in the loch. Easing himself from the bed, Niall determinedly stripped off her sodden garments and wrapped her in his plaid.

"I have no intention of remaining abed with you," Sabrina grumbled in protest as he sat beside her and began combing her wet hair through his fingers.

"You cannot return home looking like a bedraggled mouse."

"You might have considered that before throwing me in the loch to drown."

"You deserved it," Niall retorted, remembering just what had brought them to this point. His jaw clenched.

"I did not deserve to be ravished!"

"Come now, admit it." He bent to nuzzle her bare shoulder with his lips. "You enjoyed every moment."

"I shall only admit that you are a bold, arrogant devil!"

"And you were magnificent in all your fury, dripping like a fish and clawing like a tiger."

She turned and struck him, punching his shoulder. The iron-hard muscle didn't budge.

With a grim smile, Niall grasped her arms and pinned Sabrina down on her back. When her bare breasts spilled free of the plaid, he nipped a budded peak.

"Punishment," he said tauntingly.

Sabrina arched against the fiery sensation that streaked through her. "Don't . . ."

"Such an obedient, accommodating wife," he observed mockingly. "So compliant and submissive . . ."

She glared up at him. "You have a positive genius for rousing my ire."

"And you, my sweet, have a decided knack for rousing *me*."

Releasing her abruptly, Niall rose and began hanging her wet garments before the fire to dry.

Sabrina watched warily as he removed the rest of his own clothing, then returned to the bed. Despite her obvious reluctance, he joined her beneath his plaid, wrapping them both in the thick wool.

As he held her naked against him, Sabrina could feel his heat seeping into her frozen limbs. She lay cupped into his body, her throat hurting with the need to cry. Niall had demonstrated very aptly how weak she was where he was concerned. He had taken her in anger, and she had submitted with humiliating eagerness. Perhaps he had been swept away momentarily by lust, as she had, but his heart had remained untouched, while she allowed hers to be trampled on like so much dust.

I don't want to love him, she thought in despair. Loving him was both reckless and foolish. It left her so terribly vulnerable.

She raised her fingers to her mouth, still swollen and tender from the violence of his lovemaking. The conflict had not been settled between them, she knew. The tension still remained, dark and palpable.

She wasn't mistaken. When Niall at last spoke at her back, his voice held a silken edge of warning. "You are my wife, mouse. I'll thank you not to forget it."

Sabrina stiffened. "I have not forgotten."

"Then know this." His low voice reverberated against the sensitive nape of her neck, making her shiver. "I will never permit you to take Keith Buchanan as your lover."

"I don't *want* him as my lover. And I've given you no grounds to think otherwise! I did not come here for a liaison with him."

"Indeed." His tone was acerbic.

"I did not! Had you given me the least chance to explain, I would have told you why I came. I wished to discuss peace with him."

"Peace?"

"Yes, *peace.*" Sabrina held fast to her temper as she raised herself up on one elbow. "There is something peculiar about the accounts we've been given of the recent cattle raids—their order, I mean. Keith Buchanan claims his clan did not initiate the first attack, that they would not break a truce after giving their word."

Niall made a sound in his throat that was pure scorn.

"I know . . . I admit I did not want to believe him at first, either. But Keith swears they did not start the raiding."

He gave her a fierce glance. "How can you vindicate the bastards so readily?"

"I am not vindicating them. I am just trying to discover the truth."

Restlessly Niall rolled over on his back, drawing the plaid with him. "The bloody Buchanans are thieves and murderers. You should ken that. They're to blame for the death of your own father as well as mine."

"Indirectly perhaps, but that was an accident. And it was a long time ago."

"A Highlander has an excellent memory," Niall muttered darkly.

Sabrina bit her lip in frustration. Yet she could not let this opportunity pass without attempting to make Niall view the situation with some degree of objectiveness. He had been enemies with Clan Buchanan for so long that he knew no other way.

"I can understand why you bear them such hatred," she said carefully, "but we will never have peace as long as the feud continues."

"Then we will never have peace."

"I cannot accept that." Earnestly Sabrina gazed down at him. "Will you not at least *talk* to them?"

"No."

His stubbornness stung her to fresh anger. "It seems to me that any fool can wield a sword. But it takes a strong leader to resolve differences without bloodshed."

Niall scowled up at the smoke-darkened rafters. "You are meddling in affairs you know nothing about."

"Well, I am trying to learn." She ground her teeth in vexation. "I agreed to wed you to save my clan, but 'twill have been for naught if you insist on maintaining your blind hatred. It is madness to continue fighting. As chieftain, Niall, you are the key to settling the feud. The men of Clan Duncan answer to you now. They will follow your lead." She hesitated. "You'll think me a stubborn gomeril, I know, but Keith Buchanan seemed sincere."

Niall grunted. "I think you are uncommonly gullible. You've allowed yourself to be used as a dupe. Meeting him here was the height of folly. The bloody Buchanans would like nothing more than to put horns on me."

"Keith Buchanan harbors no feelings of desire for me, I tell you."

"I dispute that, lass, but 'tis beside the point. Did it never occur to you that Owen's kin would gleefully seduce the wife of his foe simply to even the tally with me?"

It was Sabrina's turn to scoff. "What would it matter to you if he did cuckold you? Only your pride would suffer."

Niall's eyes narrowed at her. "You'll not take him for a lover, do you ken me?"

Realizing the futility of arguing, Sabrina lay back down with a flounce. Her anger smoldering anew, she stared up at the ceiling. "I thought ours was to be a modern marriage, that we would go our separate ways. You shouldn't care if I took a lover. You never wished for *this damnable union*, you told me so last night."

He frowned. "I said I would consider allowing you a discreet affair once you presented me with heirs—after an appropriate interval. But I'll not countenance you with a bloody Buchanan."

"Very well, then. I promise you, I will choose someone other than a Buchanan when the time comes."

Rolling on his side, Niall stared down at Sabrina, his gaze boring into hers. Her foolish insistence on peace annoyed him less than her threat to take other lovers.

After a moment of strained silence, he reached his hand up to close possessively around her throat, where her pulse beat sure and warm. Inexplicably he was filled with the fierce urge to prove she wanted no lover but him.

Slowly he trailed his fingers down to cover her bare breast. He felt her nipple tighten, felt the sensual shiver that ran through her body. The same shiver surged through him in a savage stroke of need.

"Don't . . ." she whispered, shutting her eyes.

"I thought we had settled this," Niall replied, his jaw hardening. "You'll not deny me, wife. You'll not deny yourself . . ."

Bending, he covered her lips with his own, pressing his swelling flesh into her soft belly, feeling a grim satisfaction at the helpless moan of surrender Sabrina gave as she twisted against him.

He made love to her slowly this time, demanding everything she had to give and more, wringing cry after cry of ecstasy from her, refusing to relent until she lay gasping and shuddering and pleading with him for surcease.

In the heated aftermath, Sabrina sank into an exhausted slumber, but Niall found sleep elusive. He held her in the protection of his embrace, frowning at some vague point in the distance.

What the devil was happening to him? Sabrina's interference in clan affairs had sorely vexed him, but that wasn't what had set his blood to boiling or aroused such intense feelings of fury and betrayal within him.

Remembering their tempestuous confrontation by the loch, Niall grimaced. He'd been angry enough to strike Sabrina—he who had never touched a lass in anger in his life. In truth, his own conduct dismayed him even more than the rash actions of his gullible young wife. He had behaved like a grasping, jealous husband.

It had to be jealousy. Mere male pride could not account for his rage when he'd spied Sabrina in Keith Buchanan's arms. Nor could bitter hatred for an enemy clan explain his covetousness. He would have reacted that way with any man.

Niall shook his head, wondering how he'd become so obsessed with his own bride. He'd thought his fascination with Sabrina would fade to indifference in time, yet his passions had only grown stronger. The more determined he was to deny his desire, the more fierce his need grew to possess her. Even now he was stunned by the driving urgency he'd felt to brand Sabrina as his alone.

Absently he fingered a damp tendril of her hair as he contemplated his remarkable madness.

Jealousy was an alien notion to him. He'd never been so enamored of a woman that he cared if she took other lovers. He'd never felt such primitive possessiveness toward any lass . . . until Sabrina.

There was no explanation for the ravenous need she incited in him. Beautiful women had been a constant in his life since adolescence, and he'd managed to elude being snared by any of them. Sabrina was no raging beauty certainly, and yet . . . she *was* beautiful when her lustrous eyes flashed with fury, more beautiful still when he had her naked and hungry beneath him, her skin flushed with desire, her eyes flaming with passion.

He wanted her beyond reason. She could stir up a maelstrom of need and hunger in him that defied logic. Her body fired his blood in a way no lass's ever had.

He hadn't foreseen that. Sabrina could make the fire in him blaze up till it raged out of control.

A fierce stab of desire pierced Niall at the memory of their violent coupling a short while ago. They'd mated like animals, and yet she had craved it as much as he, responding to him measure for measure.

Her passion had shaken him to the core. He'd experienced an explosion of desire he hadn't felt in years, perhaps not ever.

Niall's frown deepened as he raised himself up on one elbow. It was not, however, merely the carnal gratification he found with Sabrina that attracted him. She had insinuated herself into his life against his will. He found himself craving her company. He cherished the closeness and companionship he'd discovered with her. He admired the way she'd stubbornly championed her clan and pressed for peace. Jealousy pricked at Niall again, because all that fire was for her clan, and not for him.

His eyes darkened as he watched her sleep. How had his plan gone so awry? In turning a prickly mouse into a woman he desired, he had given Sabrina too much power over him. She was like a fever in his blood. Fascination had turned to obsession—and something even more primal. The nameless emotion knotted in his gut, as intense and dangerous as a double-edged sword.

He pushed it away, scowling.

Bloody saints, he didn't like feeling this way . . . so threatened, so vulnerable. He didn't like this desperate feeling of need. He was no callow youth to be carried away by passion, letting lust rule his head.

Faith, but he needed to rid himself of this dangerous madness before he made an even greater fool of himself.

What he needed was another woman. Another lover. He needed to sate himself with physical pleasure in someone else's arms, to make him forget his craving for Sabrina, to get her out of his blood.

He needed to purge himself of his incomprehensible feelings for her, to prove to himself that she had no consuming hold over him.

Eve Graham came to mind. His former mistress would cure him of this strange malady, Niall was certain. She would cool his fever and help him conquer the obsessive feelings of jealousy and possessiveness that had begun to haunt him of late.

Perhaps then he would be able to control the insatiable hunger his own wife roused in him.

Chapter

Fourteen

They didn't speak of their fierce quarrel beside the loch or of Sabrina's interrupted liaison with Keith Buchanan, yet a dark tension remained between them, as did the perplexing question regarding the cattle raids.

Too incensed to let the matter drop simply because her domineering husband commanded it, Sabrina pondered discussing the puzzle with her grandfather. However, when she paid an unexpected visit to Banesk the following morning, she received a greater shock than she bargained for.

A storm had blustered through the Highlands during the night, leaving a gray mist hanging low over the heathered hills. Rab bounded happily beside his mistress's horse . . . until they neared Clan Duncan's family seat, when his ears pricked forward nervously. It was several moments more before Sabrina recognized the clash of steel—swordplay, she had no doubt.

Fearing an assault on her grandfather's castle, she set her spurs to her mount and raced forward, her heart lurching. She slowed only when she came to a clearing. Through the swirling gray mist she could detect two combatants. One of them she recognized as Liam Duncan.

The other, to her vast startlement, was her elderly grandfather.

"Aha!" Angus exclaimed heartily as he parried a wicked thrust with a heavy blow of his own broadsword. "Ye'll no' harm me w' that wee jab. A bairn could do better."

It took her a moment to realize they weren't trying to

murder each other, but were honing their battle skills on the practice field. Even so, it was sheer madness for an invalid to attempt such exertion.

"Merciful heaven, Grandfather!" Urging her horse forward, Sabrina drew up behind him. "What are you doing out of bed?"

He spun around to face her with the agility of a man half his age, though he was panting slightly. "Sabrina, lass . . . I wasna expecting ye."

"Evidently not. You'll kill yourself with such folly."

"Nay, I'm as hale as may be—" He broke off suddenly, looking somewhat guarded. "I'm well enough, lass. Dinna fash yerself."

"You're well?" She stared blankly in confusion. "A month ago you were on your deathbed."

His bushy white brows drew together warily. "Ah . . ." He cleared his throat. "In truth, I was ill for a time. The ague in ma chest gave me fits. But I've recovered."

Her breath checked sharply. "That was what ailed you? An *ague*? You said your heart was failing you."

Angus had the grace to look self-conscious. "Aye, ma heart was a bit weak, too. 'Twas a bad bout, but I'm well enough now."

Sabrina felt herself grow white about the mouth. He was not at death's door—and apparently never had been. "Your illness was all pretense?" she asked faintly.

"Not *all*. I was ill, in truth. Just no' so ill as ye believed."

Dazed, she shook her head, a turmoil of emotion assaulting her: hurt, confusion, betrayal. His desperate infirmity had been feigned. "You deliberately deceived me," she whispered.

"Aweel . . ."

"You said I was the last hope for the future, that it was vital I wed the McLaren to save our clan."

" 'Twas for a good cause, lass."

"A *good cause*?" Her voice trembled. "Is that all you have to say? You lied to me, tricked me into agreeing to your plans . . . I *wed* Niall only because I thought you were dying. Because Clan Duncan needed a leader to protect them from the Buchanans after you were gone."

"Aye, but I feared ye would refuse the marriage unless the need was dire. Come, lass, admit it. Ye wouldna even have come to the Highlands had ye not thought me dying."

No, she would never have come. She would never have wed a legendary rogue who resented having her as his bride . . . or fallen so desperately, hopelessly, in love.

Sabrina squeezed her eyes shut. Angus had played on her sympathies and her clan loyalty in order to win her compliance. She felt a stark hollowness in the pit of her stomach.

She glanced at Liam Duncan, who lowered his eyes. "Were you an accomplice to his plan?" she asked.

"Nay," Angus interrupted his reply. "Liam knew naught of this till after the nuptials."

Sabrina shifted her gaze back to her grandfather, who was starting to scowl.

"Come now, lass, would ye rather I'd died in truth?"

"No, of course not. I'm glad you're well. What distresses me is your deception—" She recoiled as another thought struck her like a blow. What had he told Niall in order to compel him to wed her?

"What hold did you have over Niall to force his hand?" she asked slowly.

"Why do ye think I had to force him?"

"Because he clearly never wanted a marriage between us."

"'Twas a debt of honor his da owed. I saved Hugh McLaren's life once."

Her heart twisted painfully. "So it wasn't simply his wish to wed an heiress, as you claimed. I wondered. He was too anxious to avoid the betrothal, and too relieved when I broke it off. That would have been the end of it, except that I was wounded in the raid—"

Her eyes narrowed in dismay as another notion occurred to her. "Did you deceive me about that as well? About the Buchanans stealing our cattle?"

"Now, lass—"

"You said Owen Buchanan himself led the raid."

"Aweel . . . perhaps he wasna the one."

"Perhaps it never happened at all! That would explain why they deny initiating the thieving, why they accused us of breaking the truce. Did you steal their cattle first?"

"Nay, 'twas not the way of it. But I may have been mistaken about their thievery . . ."

Sabrina raised a hand to her temple, a sick sensation of disbelief gnawing at her insides. It was all beginning to make sense. "You said the bloody Buchanans would ravage our clan if we had no laird strong enough to prevent it. But Clan Duncan never needed saving from the Buchanans, did they? You orchestrated the entire threat."

Her grandfather's ruddy features took on a pleading expression. "Ye dinna ken, lass. I acted for the good of the clan."

"Oh, I think I ken well enough," Sabrina replied raggedly. "We could have had *peace*. Dear God, Owen Buchanan had already agreed to a truce! We could have settled the feud for good, or at least enjoyed a momentary calm. Instead you deliberately rekindled the conflict. Merciful heaven, Grandfather . . . People could have died! Niall was almost killed during that raid—and two of the Buchanans were wounded. So was I, for that matter."

His heavy brows drew together mutinously. "Even so, I had to act. Ye had broken off the betrothal and wouldna listen to reason. I had to show ye the danger. Ye needed to see what would happen if Clan Duncan didna unite under a strong leader."

"So you risked a bloody war to force my hand."

"Mayhap I did, but I had no choice. I'm growing old, lass. Our clan needed a laird, and the McLaren was the right mon to succeed me. Ye were the only one who could provide him."

Angus took a step toward her, but she held up her hand to ward him off. "Don't, Grandfather!" Anguish seized her features. "Nothing you could say can justify the risks you've taken with other people's lives. You thought to play God—" She shook her head. "I had best leave before I say something I would forever regret. Rab, come!"

Without waiting, she whirled her horse and rode blindly toward home, anger and hurt and humiliation warring within her breast. She had been used as a pawn in her grandfather's machinations, played for a fool, while he had imperiled hundreds of lives.

Worse, Niall had been given no choice but to wed her. She'd been forced on him through subterfuge and guile. He'd submitted to the marriage only because he thought her clan endangered. *But there'd been no reason for them to wed.*

Shame flooded Sabrina at the thought. How could she ever face him now? Did he even know about Angus's sham illness?

Her heartbeat faltered. When Niall learned he'd been tricked, would he want to end their union? It was too late to petition for a grant of annulment, but he might wish to be free of the alliance he had never wanted.

Dismay swept through her with the power to make her tremble.

There was another issue to resolve as well. The feud with Clan Buchanan. Perhaps it was not too late for peace. Owen had wanted a truce all along. And once Niall learned the truth about the cattle raid, it might temper his hatred for his foes, enough for him to reconsider an end to the hostilities. In any event, the matter of the cattle thefts must be set right with the Buchanans.

But first, Sabrina thought with a bleakness she couldn't shake, she had to speak to her husband and discover if he still wanted her for his bride.

As she neared Creagturic, Sabrina steeled herself to face Niall, but when she rode in, she discovered that her crucial conversation would have to wait.

Eve Graham had come to call.

Sabrina left her horse with a groom and her dog happily sniffing for rodents, and entered the house. Rigid with nerves, she went upstairs.

Her guest was not in the drawing room, she discovered to her surprise, nor was she in any of the other chambers on that floor. The serving maid, Jean, thought Lady Graham might have ventured to the orchard behind the castle, for she'd glanced out a window earlier and had seen the laird strolling with the lady there.

Niall and Eve in the orchard? An inexplicable misgiving gripped Sabrina.

She considered waiting for them to return, but chided herself for acting the coward. Making her way from the manor, she followed the stone path up a hill, to the walled orchard where apple and cherry and quince trees grew in gnarled profusion.

She faltered when she heard hushed voices emanating from beyond the stone wall, yet she took a deep breath and forced herself to peer over the top edge. The intimate scene that greeted her barely a stone's throw away made her blood turn cold.

The beautiful Widow Graham and the handsome Laird McLaren were lying on his plaid in the grass, embracing.

Sabrina clasped a hand over her mouth to stifle a cry. She knew she should go, yet she remained riveted where she stood, paralyzed by the sight.

Niall lay on his back with Eve straddling his hips, kissing him fervently. The skirts of her elegant gown were hitched up, while her bodice was loosened nearly to her waist, baring her ripe, heavy breasts.

Pushing herself up then, Eve grasped both of Niall's hands and guided them to cover the swollen mounds.

His expression was strangely grim as he gazed up at the beautiful woman above him. "You're a randy tart, sweetheart."

"As I recall, you used to consider that one of my charms."

Provocatively, Eve arched her back so that her peaked nipples jutted forward into his palms. "You still enjoy my charms, do you not, Niall?"

His fingers closed over her nipples, squeezing lightly. Eve released a whimpering moan, shutting her eyes and letting her head fall back.

Sabrina stared, riveted with anguish, the air trapped in her lungs. The erotic image of those strong bronzed fingers cupping pale voluptuous breasts would be forever branded in her memory, as would Niall's face, taut with sensuality as he pleasured another lover.

She took a stumbling step backward, a sick fury cramping her heart. When Eve gave another moan of delight, Sabrina choked back a sob and forced her feet to move. Turning, she fled before they could see her.

She ran, tears blinding her eyes.

Somehow she made her way back to the house and found herself in her bedchamber, *their* bedchamber ... the one where Niall had stripped away her innocence and initiated her into lovemaking. Where he'd shown her so many hours of indescribable pleasure. Where they'd begun to build a bond of tenderness and trust between them. ...

Desperately Sabrina clutched at the bedpost, bracing herself against the wild trembling that had invaded her limbs. Betrayal burned like acid inside her, while a savage pain raked her heart.

She felt cold, sick inside, beset by tumultuous emotions, one bleeding into the other. She hadn't expected this awful pain in her heart, this heaviness in her chest that threatened to strangle her very breath.

"Niall ..." she whispered in agony.

How close she'd come to confessing her love for him, to baring all the secret longings of her soul. The remembrance made her ill with craven self-knowledge. She had only been deluding herself to think her libertine husband would ever come to care for her. That he might be faithful to his vows.

Sabrina raised a hand to her eyes, fighting the tears, the

raw ache in her throat. In truth, she shouldn't be so devastated. She'd always known she was wed to a notorious rake. Niall had been entirely honest with her from the first. He'd told her—indeed, on more than one occasion—that he would never be faithful to her. She couldn't complain if he sought his pleasures outside the marriage bed.

She dashed a hand roughly across her eyes. She would not die, no matter how searing the pain was at just this moment. She was strong enough to endure it. Indeed, she would have to develop thick calluses around her heart if she was to survive this mockery of a marriage.

Her head came up. She would not be relegated to so pitiful a role as the spurned wife. She would never let Niall know how deeply he had wounded her.

Yet she couldn't wait for him to return. She couldn't face him just now. Not until she had regained some measure of composure and gathered the remnants of her shattered pride.

Her spine stiffening, Sabrina returned to the barn, where she called for her horse. As she rode away, she drew her cloak around her, almost grateful for the coldness that had crept through her body. Lead lay where her heart belonged, numbing the pain.

She was unsure at first where she was headed, but she found herself riding in the direction of the Buchanans' land. Remembering her earlier confrontation with her grandfather, then, she set her jaw and spurred her horse onward.

To her relief she came across Keith Buchanan on his way home. She had no desire to face his father alone.

When she explained her purpose, Keith willingly escorted her back to the castle. They found Owen about to sit down to dinner in the great hall.

The moment he saw her, he leapt to his feet, bristling with indignation that she would dare show her face to him. Before she could say a word edgewise, he launched into a verbal attack.

"I dinna ken what deep game yer playing, lass, but I'll no' abide any more of yer Duncan treachery."

" 'Tis no treachery," Sabrina said, forcing a smile. "I've come to offer apologies for my clan. I can explain about the raids, if you will allow me. And perhaps afterward . . . you might listen to my proposal."

The pleasure was missing, Niall thought, frowning as he returned the beautiful widow's fervent kiss. His loins were aroused, yet he felt strangely . . . dispassionate.

He knew that physically Eve could satisfy the needs of his body. Her voluptuous, perfumed flesh was no different now than the scores of other occasions when he'd taken her to their mutual delight. Yet somehow he no longer found his former mistress quite as desirable as in the past.

Worse, he found it difficult to summon even a semblance of enthusiasm for his task. To his dismay, while he was kissing Eve's lush lips, stroking her splendid breasts, his thoughts kept straying to another woman, another lover, this one a slender, defiant lass with lustrous dark eyes that could spark with fire or soften with passion.

His own wife.

Niall's jaw hardened in annoyance.

Faith, he'd intended to purge himself of his craving for Sabrina, to vanquish his ridiculous obsession by losing himself in some other female's silken flesh, but it wasn't working the way he'd intended. The pleasure he normally experienced with lovemaking was dismayingly absent.

Inexplicably he felt *dis*satisfied.

Eve was too perceptive not to sense his lack of ardor. Her eager caresses tempered, then ceased altogether. When she lifted her head to study him, her lips were still wet and red from their kisses.

"Never tell me I have lost my touch," she said lightly.

Solicitously Niall reached up to run his thumb across her cheekbone, delicately tinted with paint and rouge. "Never, sweeting. You're as delectable as ever."

"Now why do I find that difficult to credit?" She managed an arch smile. "You would not, perhaps, be experiencing a twinge of guilt due to your recent married state, would you now?"

Niall frowned and refrained from replying. Incomprehensibly he did feel guilt—and anger because of it.

Eve gave a musical laugh as she stared at him. "How droll. I never would have suspected it of you, the Darling of Edinburgh. You must have indulged in countless affairs with married ladies. I confess astonishment that you should balk now that the shoe is on the other foot, so to speak."

Niall's gaze narrowed. "Don't presume too far, witch. My temper is not the sweetest at the moment."

Smiling archly, she shook her head. "Truly you should not let a minor breach of your vows concern you, Niall. After our long acquaintance, it cannot be said that you and I are *strangers*. And you know I can be discreet. Sabrina never need know."

"Sabrina's a canny lass."

Eve's sigh was heavy with despair. "I suppose this means you intend to cast me aside."

His mouth curved in dry amusement. "Melodrama does not become you, sweeting."

Her hazel eyes grew serious. "But you mean to end it for good between us." It was not a question.

"The notion had occurred to me," Niall replied truthfully.

"I know you want me." Reaching down, Eve pressed her palm against his trews, caressing the bulge at his groin. "I can feel how huge and hard you are."

Niall winced at the ache in his erection. "I am human, after all, cherie. And as I said, your charms are quite delectable."

"But not enough to make you change your mind."

Self-mockery laced his low laugh. "Lamentably, no, although it pains me greatly to say so."

He returned home, feeling vexed and restless. Sabrina was nowhere in evidence, a fact which annoyingly relieved him as he washed Eve's scent from his skin.

It was Liam Duncan who first made Niall realize his wife

was missing. Late that afternoon, Liam rode to Creagturic to seek an audience with Sabrina, and seemed unduly concerned when she was not to be found.

"Where could the lass be?" he asked Niall gravely. "I made cert she would have come home."

"She is not at Banesk? She meant to visit her grandfather."

"Aye, that she did, but I fear the lass was muckle fashed."

Niall's gaze narrowed. "Mayhap you had best explain."

In a minimum of words, Liam disclosed what Angus had done—the old man's duplicity in gaining protection for Clan Duncan by wedding his granddaughter to the McLaren—while Niall heard him out grimly.

"I didna ken Angus's cheatry, my lord," Liam vowed, "till after the deed was done. He's hale now as any lad in his prime."

A muscle in Niall's jaw hardened. "I suspected as much, but in all honor I could not challenge his word."

"But 'twasna fair you should pay the price."

"It was my decision to wed Sabrina in the end. And I must allow, I—"

It was just at that moment that Geordie Duncan came rushing into the great hall.

"There's word of Mistress McLaren!" he exclaimed without preliminaries. "The bloody Buchanan has her."

Niall felt his breath stop as cold fear smote him. "How do you ken?"

"He sent Angus a demand for ransom for Mistress McLaren's safe return—three hundred head of cattle."

Niall clenched his jaw so hard his teeth grated. "Should that bloody bastard harm a hair on her head . . ."

He left the sentence unfinished as Geordie added, "Angus has summoned our clan together to effect her rescue. He desires ye to come at once."

"Aye, I'll come. Liam, find John and raise the cry," Niall commanded as he turned to bound up the stairs in search of his claymore and targe. "We're for Buchanan's lair!"

The fighting men of Clan McLaren were swiftly mustered, while Geordie rode to Banesk to intercept Angus. An army of mounted Highland warriors was soon galloping toward Buchanan's castle.

They slowed as they approached the massive fortress, surprised to find the gate open and the portcullis raised.

Niall held up his hand, signaling his men to halt. For a moment the only sound was that of snorting steeds and chomping bits.

"Think you 'tis a trap?" Angus asked Niall warily.

"Mayhap. You'll bide here till I can discover what goes."

Angus looked as if he might protest, but one glance at Niall's savage expression silenced him.

His claymore drawn, Niall urged his mount forward and rode alone across the drawbridge, into the bailey. Not a soul was in sight, nor any hint that the Buchanans expected a visit of retribution.

It made no sense.

The massive wooden door to the tower swung wide just then, and Keith Buchanan stepped onto the upper landing of the stone entrance stairs. He wore a leather frock coat but no sword. Apparently he was unarmed. "Greetings, Laird McLaren," he called down to the yard. "We expected Angus, but you are welcome as well."

"Where is she?" Niall demanded, his tone explosive with rage.

"Safe and sound—and 'tis not what ye're thinking."

"My thinking be damned! Tell me where my wife is, or God rot you, I'll slice your gullet open and feed your vitals to the corbies!"

"I'll gladly spill what I know, if ye allow me the chance. Your lady is here of her own accord."

Niall made a visible effort at control, though his eyes remained narrowed in mistrust.

"She came here to seek peace."

Niall's jaw clenched as he stared. "The de'il she did," was his muttered curse, but the knife-edged tone was blunted with the briefest hint of uncertainty.

"Pray, come and see for yourself."

Keith stepped back, gesturing within the tower.

Dismounting, Niall held his claymore at the ready and swiftly climbed the entrance stairs. He followed the son of his fiercest foe through a great hall and up a winding flight of stone steps, to a chamber that was apparently used as a salon. Even before he reached it, he heard the sound of Sabrina's laughter.

"Check, sir! I warned you not to risk that move."

His hand clenched on his sword hilt, Niall stood in the doorway, staring grimly.

Before a crackling hearth fire, Sabrina sat facing Owen Buchanan across a chessboard, obviously at ease, while the Highland chieftain scowled down at the knight she had just captured.

"See you, milord," Keith said smugly at Niall's shoulder. "'Tis no abduction. Your lady is clearly enjoying our Buchanan hospitality."

Chapter
Fifteen

As if sensing Niall's presence, both Sabrina and the elder Buchanan looked up.

Owen grimaced, his good humor disappearing instantly. "I've won our wager, lass. I told ye he would come."

"So you did." She offered the Buchanan laird a charming smile. "It seems I owe you half a crown. But I shall have to redeem it by trouncing you soundly in our match."

Niall moved into the room, his face set like flint, anger hooding his gaze.

"He doesna look pleased to find ye here," Owen said.

Sabrina's smile cooled. "I think you may be right. But he's doubtless concerned that I've set up a flirtation with you. You must forgive him. His suspicious nature, I fear, results from lurking behind too many bedchamber doors, avoiding jealous husbands."

Owen threw back his head and let out a roar. "By God, lass, ye're a treat for an old man!"

"I trust you mean to explain the meaning of this, wife," Niall said through gritted teeth.

Turning, Sabrina eyed him calmly. "If you wish. I have had an exceedingly pleasant visit with Lord Buchanan. I came to apologize for our clans' breaking the truce, and for my grandfather's deception. You might be surprised to know Angus was never as ill as he led us to believe."

"So Liam informed me."

"Did he also tell you that Grandfather orchestrated the

entire tale of cattle thievery by the Buchanans? He duped us into retaliating for a raid that never happened."

Niall disciplined his expression into unreadability. "I am not concerned with what Angus might have done. I've come to escort you home."

She folded her hands serenely in her lap. "But I am not inclined to leave, my lord."

"Sabrina," Niall said warningly, fury flaring through him at finding his wife in league with his enemies. He had expressly forbidden her to go near the Buchanans, and here she sat defying him to his face.

"I intend to speak to my grandfather," she insisted. "I anticipate his arrival any moment."

Niall gathered his control, willing himself to patience. "Angus is here, awaiting my word."

"Then he should join us. He owes the Buchanans three hundred head of cattle, and I intend to see that he pays it."

"That is the price demanded for your ransom?"

"It is not a ransom precisely. Those cattle actually belong to the Buchanans. Angus would merely be returning those we took, with interest. I think it fair payment for the grief he caused."

"And if he chooses not to pay?"

"Then I will remain here for some time." When Niall simply stared, Sabrina explained. "I will consider returning home with you only under one condition, sir. When you've held a civilized discussion with the Buchanans to address ending the feud. Until then I intend to remain here as Lord Owen's guest."

He regarded her as if she had suddenly sported horns. "You are interfering in matters beyond your purview."

"I don't think so. Faith, it astounds me how men only think of fighting. You should leave the negotiating to women. We at least rely on reason."

His eyes blazed with warning, but she refused to back down. "I intend for Grandfather to accept a truce with the Buchanans. And I expect you to help persuade him."

"Indeed? Why the bloody hell should I?"

"I think," Sabrina replied with sugary sweetness, "you might find it difficult to explain why your wife chooses to remain with your blood enemy. And why you cannot fetch her home."

"It would be the work of a moment to carry you from here."

"You could take me by force, perhaps, but I shall simply return at the first opportunity—unless you are prepared to keep me under lock and key for the rest of my days."

Somehow she kept from flinching as Niall's gaze warred with hers.

After a moment, his jaw clenched. "Do you ken what you're asking of me?"

"I believe so." Her expression softened. "But Owen swears he did not order the ambush of your father and brother, and I believe him."

"Aye, lad," Owen said quietly. "I had naught to do with such a foul deed, and I would hae stopped it had I kenned of it. Hugh was a good mon, and a worthy foe. Despite our differences, he dinna deserve such a dishonorable end. I grieved at his death, 'tis God's holy truth."

Niall stared at him for the space of several heartbeats. It was a long, long moment before he sheathed his claymore. "I seem to have little choice," he said grimly. "I'll fetch Angus."

"Niall," Sabrina said imploringly as he turned to go, "please understand this is for the best."

His gaze found hers, pinning her. "What I understand, madam, is that you've turned on your own kinsmen."

Sabrina lowered her gaze to hide her pain. "No," she said quietly, "I have not. I've tried to make sense out of madness. I did not ask to come here, my lord, or to become involved in this senseless feud. I did not ask to wed you. I was duped into it, just as you were. But now that it's done, I intend to do my utmost to settle our differences so that we can live in peace."

*   *   *

It was long into the night when a truce of sorts was hammered out between the warring clans. The tentative peace, however, was only the beginning of the war between the McLaren and his lady. Their journey home to Creagturic was accomplished in smoldering silence.

Sabrina thought she understood Niall's fury; she had made him look the fool by joining his enemies against him, and had forced him to end the feud. But she would not allow herself to regret what she'd done. Someone had needed to intervene in the madness, and she was the only one objective enough to attempt it.

Her defiance, Sabrina told herself resolutely, had naught to do with retaliation for Niall's betrayal of her, yet in some secret corner of her heart, she wanted him to hurt as she was hurting.

When they arrived home, she retired directly to their bedchamber, yet to her surprise and dismay, Niall followed her.

They undressed in grim silence. Sabrina wished he would simply go away. His coldness made her ache. He was a stranger to her, nothing like the tender lover she'd known during the past few short weeks of wedded bliss. She fought down the urge to cry, her wounded heart aching at her loss.

She was starting to pull on her nightdress when Niall's low command stopped her.

"Leave it off."

Sabrina froze, unwilling to obey his orders like a trained lapdog. "Why? I have no desire to share your bed."

"Your desires matter little to me, madam."

He came up behind her, placing his hands on her bare shoulders. "I told you, mouse, you'll not defy me."

She stood stiffly as his hands skimmed over her skin, knowing he only intended to prove his mastery over her. It hurt to have him touch her after what he'd done. Hurt to endure his caresses when all she could think of was Niall caressing another woman, making passionate love to another woman. She wanted to fight him, to rail at him for his betrayal and pound his chest with her fists.

Yet it was a battle of wills which she lost. The instant Niall drew her into his arms, she melted.

During the following fortnight, their relationship grew ever more volatile. By day they argued frequently, over the most inconsequential matters. By night they tried to conquer each other with passion, their coupling ruthless and primal, their hunger fraught with anger and wounded pride.

Sabrina had never felt such turmoil of the heart. The explosive tension was almost unbearable.

Her clansmen felt it as well. The household servants tread lightly, while the number of visitors to Creagturic dwindled to a trickle. Niall remained in a savage mood, snapping heads off at the least offense. Few dared to confront him or even to attract his attention for fear of earning his displeasure.

Sabrina found her own temper raw as fresh-killed meat, her usual serene disposition nowhere in evidence. The dissension with Niall had dismayingly brought out the dark side of her nature, and she did not like the woman she was becoming.

The conflict had the additional unexpected effect among the clans of setting husband against wife—or so Mrs. Paterson told her. In cottages and crofts, the McLaren's lady was branded a saint or an interfering witch. The women applauded her efforts to bring peace to the Highlands, but the men were less forgiving. Some even considered Sabrina a traitor. John McLaren in particular could not regard her without breaking into a scowl.

Of all the Duncans, Geordie seemed the most tolerant, but Angus refused to hear her name spoken.

It was a letter from Sabrina's stepfather which finally brought matters to the boiling point—or rather a letter from Charles Cameron's clerk. Sabrina had not heard from Charles for several weeks, and even with her troubles, had begun to grow worried, though she told herself letters were often misdirected, particularly in the wild Highlands.

It was with relief when the missive arrived from Edinburgh, relief that swiftly turned to alarm. She recognized his clerk's hand in the neat, even strokes, but the signature was her stepfather's, weak and nearly illegible.

My dearest daughter:

I have not written of late as I have been bedridden for a time. Pray do not worry, a slight inflammation of the lungs, merely . . .

He went on to say that the shipments of tartan cloth her clanswomen had delivered to market had thus earned forty-three pounds, ten shillings, and sixpence, a fortune by Highland standards. Sabrina's gratification at such welcome news, though, was entirely overshadowed by her concern for her stepfather.

She went directly upstairs and packed a valise, and then paced the floor of the great hall, anxiously awaiting Niall's return home. She confronted him the moment he entered the hall.

"My stepfather is ill. I intend to go to him in Edinburgh—at once."

Niall frowned. "Is such haste necessary? I cannot permit you to set out with dusk nearly upon us."

She stiffened. "I am not asking your permission, sir. I am going, whether or not you forbid it."

He shot her a sharp glance. "I have no intention of forbidding you. I only wished to understand the seriousness of his illness and to ensure that you have a safe journey."

Sabrina bit her lip. "I don't know how serious it is. But he is truly ill—unlike my grandfather," she couldn't help adding with a trace of bitterness.

"Very well. I shall need a moment to set my affairs in order before we can leave."

"No, please . . . there is no need for you to accompany me. You are needed here."

He hesitated, his eyes focusing on her face with searing intensity. "Then I'll send an armed escort with you."

"I don't need—"

"You'll have one, nevertheless."

"I wish to leave without delay," Sabrina said anxiously.

He nodded brusquely. "I shall find John."

"No, not John. . . . It would be too awkward. We are not exactly on speaking terms at the moment."

"Colm will do, then."

Niall turned on his heel and quit the hall, while Sabrina went upstairs to their bedchamber to fetch her cloak. She was arranging the hood over her hair when Niall entered.

"Colm is prepared to ride at once, along with four of my men. He's gone to ready the horses."

"Thank you," she murmured in a low voice.

"How long do you expect to be away?" The question was casual, but Sabrina thought she heard an edge to his tone.

"I am not certain." She took a deep breath and met his gaze in the cheval glass. "I have been thinking . . ."

"A dangerous exercise," Niall remarked with a trace of his former teasing charm.

"I thought," Sabrina repeated, refusing to let him divert her, "that I might remain in Edinburgh for a time. Perhaps it would be better if . . . if we lived apart."

She glanced over her shoulder at him, but couldn't read his reaction; his features remained shuttered, enigmatic. Doggedly she plunged ahead. It would be a relief to escape the bitterness and anger that had marked their tense relationship the past weeks. They had only hurt each other, and would continue to do so if she stayed.

"I cannot imagine that you would object if I didn't return at once. It is not as if we have a true marriage. We were both deceived into agreeing to this 'damnable union,' as you termed it."

Niall's jaw hardened. "Perhaps, but we are wed now, and there's no escaping it."

She winced at the grimness of his tone, unsure whether to be relieved or dismayed that he had accepted the finality of their union. "Even so, we need not endure each other any longer."

When he remained silent, regarding her stonily, Sabrina's chin lifted. "My leaving should prove a relief to you. You cannot claim that you want me as your wife. I am merely an encumbrance to you."

"You gravely underestimate yourself, mouse."

"Do I?" Her glance was less challenging than despairing. "Were I a woman you desired, you would not be so eager to seek feminine companionship elsewhere."

"Elsewhere?"

"I saw you in the orchard with the Widow Graham. Don't think to deny it."

He stared at her a long moment while a dull flush crept over his cheekbones. "I regret you saw that."

Sabrina looked away, cursing her rash tongue. She had not intended to confront Niall with his transgression, yet his response wounded her anew. She had wanted— desperately hoped—for Niall to deny his liaison with Eve Graham meant anything to him, but he had not. The shimmer of guilt she'd seen in his eyes was little consolation.

"No doubt my sensibilities are too tender," she forced herself to say dispassionately.

"I think you are making too much of what you saw."

"Am I?" Her angry gaze fixed on him again. "How tiresome of me to want my husband to remain faithful to his marriage vows."

His brows snapped together. "What of you and Keith Buchanan? How different is that from my dalliance with Eve?"

"I never made love to him! I never even *thought* of kissing him!"

When Niall merely glowered darkly at her, Sabrina swallowed miserably, her throat achingly tight. "I should not be dismayed. I know very well what a libertine you are."

"Have I ever pretended otherwise?"

Sabrina flinched. "No. And I have never pretended to care. I've told you often enough, you are free to indulge your illicit pursuits elsewhere."

He leaned casually against the doorjamb, his arms crossed over his powerful chest, his countenance stark and unyielding once more. "I do not recall requiring your permission, mouse."

"Indeed, you do not. I doubt you will miss me, in any case. I'm certain the Widow Graham will be glad to offer you solace in my absence."

"I suspect she will."

"She is welcome to you," Sabrina retorted, ashamed at how her voice quavered. "Of course, you need not limit yourself to her. With me away, you can take the opportunity to bed every wench in sight."

"Mayhap I will."

She would not cry. His callousness rammed into her like a fist, but she would not let him see her pain. She would not give him the satisfaction.

Summoning every shred of dignity she possessed, Sabrina turned on shaken limbs to fully face him. "Well then, there is nothing more to be said, is there?"

Niall regarded her narrowly, knowing he was to blame for the bruised look in her eyes, for the suspiciously bright moisture that gleamed like tears. Beneath his savage anger, guilt knifed at him.

Mrs. Paterson rapped on the door just then, to say Colm was ready to escort Sabrina to the waiting horses.

Her spine rigid, Sabrina brushed past Niall without a word.

He did not accompany her below. Nor did he watch as she reached the yard and collected her dog and then mounted her horse.

Instead, he stood with his back to the wall, his jaw clenched, as she rode away, out of his life.

His foul temper did not improve with Sabrina's absence. Colm returned to Creagturic, reporting her safe arrival in Edinburgh, but although Niall vowed to resume his life without her, he couldn't quite manage it.

He couldn't stop thinking of her, remembering the taste of her. He missed Sabrina, and not simply for the carnal pleasure she brought him. He missed arguing with her, missed her stubborn defiance. He missed her gentleness, her courage, her wry humor, her scathing wit.

The slightest things reminded him of her. He could find nowhere in the Highlands to hide from her memory. No refuge where he could forget.

More damning, his savage humor was taking a toll on his clansmen, and proving a danger as well. Several days after Sabrina's departure, Niall was engaged in a practice fencing match with John in the yard, when he parried a thrust and struck a return blow too fiercely.

With a grunt of pain, John dropped his rapier and gripped his arm, blood dripping from beneath his fingers.

Niall swore darkly at himself and took a step forward, intending to inspect the wound, but John waved him away, scowling.

"Ye'd best find yerself a willing lass to soothe yer temper, lad. Ye're like a wildcat with a burr under yer arse. Till then, I'll thank ye to keep away from me. 'Tis for cert, I'll no longer act yer whipping post."

Turning, John stalked off, leaving Niall to run a hand raggedly down his face as he cursed himself roundly. He had no right to punish his kinsman for his own misery.

Venting another oath, he retreated inside the house, upstairs to the drawing room, where he poured himself a generous tumblerful of Scotch whisky and flung himself into a chair.

Fiend seize it, he did need a lass. The trouble was, he

wanted a certain lass he couldn't have, one who wished him to perdition.

Niall stared morosely at the cold hearth as Sabrina's damning words from their last bitter argument echoed in his mind.

I did not ask to wed you. I was duped into it . . .

We need not endure each other any longer . . .

You cannot claim that you want me as your wife. I am merely an encumbrance to you . . .

Niall squeezed his eyes shut. Sabrina was utterly wrong on that score. She might wish to be free of him, but she meant far more to him than any encumbrance. He was reconciled to their marriage now. Perhaps he'd been compelled by honor to wed her, but he was no longer interested in gaining his freedom. For reasons he couldn't comprehend, she had become increasingly precious to him.

Niall took a long swallow of the potent liquor, welcoming its fierce burn down his throat. He didn't know how many women he had made love to in his lifetime, but he knew Sabrina was different from them all. With her he'd felt an intimacy, a connection, that he'd never felt with any other woman. She filled a loneliness he'd never even realized existed.

Curse her.

He'd been captured by her spirit, her strength, the incredible softness of her, her sweet excitement when she was in the throes of passion. He had taught her about pleasure—and inexplicably experienced a soul-deep pleasure in return. Even her defiance and sharp tongue aroused him.

She was his match in every way.

She made a splendid chieftain's bride. Though he had fought her every effort, she had forced him to look beyond his blind hatred to bring peace to the Highlands. She would doubtless make an admirable mother of his bairns. She would give him strong sons and passionate daughters. . . .

Niall shut his eyes at the startling thought, yet his mind persisted in seeing Sabrina cradling a child at her breast, a tender smile on her lips. *His* child. The vision had a powerful charm to it.

A bairn of his loins would bind Sabrina to him in a way that merely uniting their clans never could. It required a vast leap of imagination, however, to picture them enjoying such domestic happiness together.

Emotion came in an uncomfortable flood as Niall remembered Sabrina's wounded look at their bitter leavetaking, when he'd refused to deny the meaninglessness of his dalliance with Eve Graham.

Were I a woman you desired, you would not be so eager to seek feminine companionship elsewhere.

Niall drained his glass, trying to dismiss the memory, but the sight of Sabrina's pale face couldn't be banished. There had been a harsh vulnerability in her eyes, a torment that *he* had put there.

Standing to refill his glass, he cursed himself for his folly. Admittedly, when he'd realized how obsessed he was becoming with his rebellious wife, he had panicked and tried to drive her out of his mind, his heart. He'd been a fool, though, to think he could forget Sabrina in some other woman's arms.

He infinitely regretted his idiocy now. It had been nothing short of criminal, and not solely because he had nearly broken his marriage vows. He couldn't shake the feeling that he'd destroyed something fragile and precious: Sabrina's trust.

And then he'd pretended not to care.

His callous insistence that he had every right to commit adultery had been cruel. His only excuse was that he'd felt inexplicably wounded himself. Sabrina had declared her intention of leaving him, and he'd wanted to strike back at her. He had intentionally hurt her—brave, proud Sabrina.

A sharp longing knotted Niall's insides. He didn't want to hurt her in any way. He wanted to hold her, make love to her, cherish her . . . He wanted more than a carnal union with her. He wanted to know her thoughts, what she felt.

He wanted her honor and trust. He wanted her respect and loyalty.

He wanted fidelity from her.

And yet he'd done little to earn any of those things. She thought him a worthless libertine, a wicked adulterer. In truth, he'd given her scant reason to believe him otherwise. More damning, he'd given her no reason to want him for her husband.

A scowl darkened Niall's brow as he stared down at the liquor in his glass. He would not, could not, allow himself to believe he'd lost Sabrina. She belonged to *him*. And he had never failed to win a woman when he put his mind to it.

Determinedly he raised his glass to his lips and tilted his head back.

It was hours later when Eve found him there in the drawing room, brooding in the dark. When she lit a lamp, Niall grimaced and tried to focus his unsteady gaze.

"I had hoped," she said doubtfully, "you might be desirous of company, since Lady McLaren is away. But I never expected to find you in such a state. You are not ill, are you?"

"Aye," Niall admitted truthfully, his words slightly slurred. "A fever for a wench."

Eve knelt at his feet, placing one delicate hand on his chest. "I can cure your affliction, you know. I can make you forget her."

Niall shook his head. He couldn't forget. Didn't wish to forget.

Eve raised a delicate eyebrow as she studied him. "I cannot credit it," she said slowly. "You're enamored of your own wife. You, the greatest lover in Europe, ensnared."

He laughed harshly. "A supreme irony, is it not?"

She lifted her hand to his mouth, her fingertips tracing its shape. "Perhaps you only need a taste of the pleasure we once shared. Come, darling, let me ease your pain."

Niall drew his head back. Whatever desire he had once felt

for Eve Graham paled in comparison to what he now felt for Sabrina. "It wouldn't be enough."

"No?"

"No. You aren't Sabrina," he said simply.

When Eve rose, making a visible effort to control her frustration, Niall stood unsteadily and made for the door.

Giving a start, Eve took a step after him. "Niall . . . where do you go?"

"To Edinburgh," he said grimly. "To fetch my bride." He intended to find Sabrina and demand her surrender—and put an end to this torment once and for all.

Chapter
Sixteen

Dawn broke over the city of Edinburgh, but neither the clatter of horses's hooves nor the rumble of cart wheels on the cobblestone streets below penetrated Sabrina's awareness as she stared blindly out her bedchamber window.

Her eyes burned with unshed tears and lack of sleep. She'd had little rest in the four days since she'd left the Highlands, her heart shattered and bleeding.

Curse him, curse him, curse him! Why had she allowed herself to love him?

Squeezing her eyes shut, Sabrina rubbed her throbbing temples. Niall was not to blame for her misery. From the first he'd made it manifest he didn't want her love. Yet that reminder didn't help to dull the relentless ache within her, or quiet her tumultuous reflections. No matter how determinedly she refused to think about him, the memories persisted, stabbing through her mind in harsh rebellion.

What an utter fool she'd been! She had vowed never to let herself succumb to Niall, but she'd failed wretchedly. She should never have journeyed to the Highlands. She was more desolate now than she'd ever been as a spurned spinster, before Niall had opened up the fissure in her heart.

She could only pray that someday the pain would diminish. Until then she would try to bear up grimly.

She intended to remain in Edinburgh with her stepfather. Though still weak, Charles had nominally recovered from his recent illness, yet she would care for his household as she'd done in the years before her marriage. She could make a life for herself here, a life that was dull but safe from the beguiling rake who had devastated her heart.

Now that peace with the Buchanans was at hand, her clan no longer needed her. Nor did her husband, Sabrina thought with a bitter ache. Without her presence to inconvenience him, Niall could resume his former relationship with his beautiful mistress.

Turning away from the window, Sabrina forced herself to begin the chore of tidying her bedchamber, though she had no heart for it.

A short while later, her pulse lurched as she caught the low murmur of a familiar masculine voice from somewhere within the house, the velvet tones edged with impatience. *Niall!* What in God's name was he doing here? Faith, she wasn't prepared to confront him. Yet there was no time to hide . . .

She heard footsteps—the sound of booted feet taking the stairs two at a time. When Niall appeared in the open doorway, his powerful body seemed to fill the small chamber.

He wore the McLaren plaid and a deadly broadsword, while his jaw was unshaven and his hair clubbed back carelessly with a plain ribbon. With his sapphire eyes narrowed, he looked every inch the Highland warrior. He must have ridden through the night, Sabrina realized, and somehow managed to discover the location of her stepfather's town house.

"Is something amiss?" she managed to ask, torn between alarm at facing Niall so unexpectedly again and worry at the urgency of his mission.

He stood gazing at her, his eyes drinking her in. "Aye, very much amiss."

"My grandfather?"

"Angus is well."

"Then . . . what . . . why have you come?" Her voice was a breathless whisper.

"I've come to fetch my bride."

Bewildered, Sabrina stared at him, trying to judge the expression on his beautiful features. She could read fatigue there, and grim determination. "I . . . I don't understand."

"I've missed you, Sabrina. I want you to come home."

"Home?"

"Aye, to the Highlands where you belong."

She shook her head in disbelief, remembering the harsh words she'd exchanged with this man at their bitter parting. "I don't belong there. And I don't wish to return. My stepfather has need of me here."

"The servant said Cameron had recovered his health. That he had left early for his offices."

"He is still weak, however, and I mean to care for him. I shall make my home here, Niall. You've endured a long journey for naught."

His gaze cool, Niall propped a shoulder against the doorjamb, looking prepared to stay forever. "You have some objection to remaining as my wife?"

Sabrina hunched her shoulders protectively. Yes, she wanted to cry. She never wanted to be so deeply hurt again as she'd been these past weeks. She couldn't bear to live with Niall as his wife. She couldn't bear to watch his infidelities day after day. Her heart would shrivel a little more each time, till it crumbled to dust. No, she could only pretend indifference and hide the savage pain as she shielded them both from this mockery of a marriage.

Her chin rose. "I should think you would be pleased to be rid of me. Surely you can pursue your amorous affairs more freely without a wife's presence to inconvenience you."

"I have no desire to pursue any affairs, amorous or otherwise."

"I expect your mistress might have something to say on that score."

Niall's mouth tightened with impatience. "Eve is not my mistress, Sabrina, and has not been for a long while."

"What is she then?" Her sarcasm was cutting. "What do you call your frolic with her in the orchard—an afternoon tea?"

His gaze never wavered. "A momentary act of lunacy. One I profoundly regret." His intense eyes held hers. "I swear to you, it never went beyond a few caresses. I admit I intended to. I thought Eve could make me forget you . . . my obsession with you. But being with her had precisely the opposite effect. It made me realize what a treasure I had in you. How much I wanted you and only you."

Sabrina stared at him, unable to speak.

" 'Tis true." Niall smiled humorlessly. "The entire time I was thinking of you . . . wishing you were the one in my arms. I felt no real desire for her."

"Indeed?" Sabrina retorted, finding her tongue. "You looked as if you were enjoying yourself mightily."

He shrugged. "Carnal pleasure is but an indulgence of the flesh. It means little if one feels nothing for one's partner." His voice softened. "You taught me that."

"I . . . don't believe you."

"Believe it, Sabrina. Eve means nothing to me. She is merely a memory, one in my past."

"And you think that should make any difference to me? How could I ever trust you again after what I witnessed, Niall? Even if you stopped short of rutting with her, it was still a flagrant betrayal. You couldn't possibly understand how much it hurt me."

"I'm sorry, Sabrina. More than I can ever say."

Sabrina shook her head. She couldn't accept Niall's professions of regret. The wound was too raw.

Nor could she yet comprehend why he had pursued her here. Unless perhaps his stalwart Highland pride had been affronted because his wife chose to live apart from him. Or he feared losing the dowry his heiress bride had brought him. . . .

Her eyes stark with unhappiness, Sabrina stiffened her spine. "You can keep my dowry. My stepfather's holdings are immense enough that he won't miss it."

Niall's gaze narrowed. "The dowry be damned. I never wedded you for your wealth."

"Oh, yes, I recall now, it was a debt of honor. Well, I absolve you of any obligation to me."

"Confound it . . . I don't want to be absolved."

"You cannot possibly wish to remain tied to me."

"Aye, I can."

"But *why*?"

"Mayhap because I love you."

Sabrina's eyes widened in shock, while Niall went still.

He lowered his own gaze, his features shuttered, enigmatic, as he comprehended the strange words that had issued from his mouth. Yet his admission of love had come so naturally, so instinctively, he knew it for the truth.

Sweet saints, when had it happened? He loved Sabrina. The realization was frightening, exhilarating, unreal. His heart had been captured by her spirit.

He laughed raggedly. "I . . . love you . . . Sabrina." He said the words slowly, as if testing the concept.

"Surely you jest."

His dark-lashed eyes lifted. "No. 'Tis no jest. You've bewitched me, mouse. I think I've loved you since the moment you threw yourself into the fray against the Buchanans to save my skin."

Stunned and disbelieving, Sabrina shook her head. *Niall loved her?* She had never dared hope he would come to that. Never.

No, she couldn't credit it. Her mind reeling, she pressed a hand to her temple, trying to comprehend his intent. Why would he make such a patently false claim?

Perhaps he was simply vexed because she had defied him. Perhaps his vanity couldn't bear to have any woman resist him, and he considered this the swiftest means of gaining her surrender. He was a practiced rake, accustomed to winning feminine devotion with blandishments and bold persuasions, so what was one more lie to him?

She stood staring at him, her arms bound tightly across her middle. "I can only guess what you're about. You think me so besotted that I'll fall at your feet in gratitude if you only throw me a crumb of your affection. So you lie and profess to love me."

" 'Tis no lie, Sabrina. I swear it." Niall spread his hands in supplication. "Why do you suppose I was so infuriated when I thought you were dallying with Keith Buchanan?"

"Because you hate all Buchanans."

"Aye, but not enough to have behaved like such a bloody fool. I was insanely jealous."

"Is it any wonder I cannot believe you?" she whispered in a voice raw with bitterness. "You're a wicked rogue who would say anything to suit your purpose."

Muttering a curse, Niall regarded her narrowly. "By the saints, I vow to you, no lass has ever claimed my heart before."

"Perhaps because you have none."

"Sabrina . . ."

When he took a step toward her, alarm welled within her. She held up a hand to ward him off. She couldn't permit him to touch her. She knew herself well enough to realize that if she allowed it, she would be lost.

"Sabrina, love—"

"Don't call me that! I am not your love. You can't even comprehend the *meaning* of the word." Her voice trembled as she pointed to the door behind him. "You think you have only to snap your fingers and I will leap to do your bidding. Well, I won't! And I won't return to the Highlands with you, either. So go *away*. I bid you good day."

"I am not leaving, Sabrina."

"You are!"

When he wouldn't move, she pressed her fist into his chest, thrusting Niall backward to drive him from the chamber.

"Sabrina . . . you're distraught—"

"Aye, and you're the one who made me so! Damn you, leave me be!"

With a final shove, she pushed him over the threshold and slammed the door in his face.

Shaking with anger and pain then, Sabrina turned and buried her face in her hands, releasing a sob that came from the deep grieving hollow of her heart.

Niall stared at the carved wooden panel with incomprehension, wanting to pound down the door. He had never failed so wretchedly with a lass.

He could insist that Sabrina return home with him. He had the right, since she was bound to him by marriage. But he wanted her to come with him freely. If he stormed back into her chamber, their conflict might elevate to violence, for he had every intention of making her see reason. He would do better to let his temper cool first.

Indeed, he needed to marshal his dazed senses and attempt to fathom what had happened to him. For weeks he had denied his own heart, but he could escape the truth no longer. He loved Sabrina.

The realization stunned him.

Turning, Niall made his way down the steep stairway and quit the house, his thoughts in turmoil. He needed time to grow accustomed to the notion.

As he wandered the narrow streets haphazardly, losing himself in the maze of closes and wynds of the old city, he tried to recall precisely when the incredulous change had come over him. From the first he had been attracted to Sabrina beyond reason, but what had begun as a rake's game to free her of her prim inhibitions had ended in a devastating complication. He had fallen in love.

Niall's mouth twisted. *Love. Use the word, man. It won't burn your tongue off.*

He had never believed in love, never been stricken by the disease that made helpless victims of mighty men. But there was no other word for the sorcery that enthralled him now. The emotion storming his body was strong enough to bring him to his knees. He was awed by the possessive feelings Sabrina engendered—tenderness, joy, hunger . . . the most powerful turmoil he had ever experienced.

It was a revelation to know his heart was not invincible. *I love her. I love Sabrina.*

Niall shook his head with mingled humor and disgust. The Darling of Edinburgh had been felled by a tart-tongued spinster heiress. His own wife, no less.

Oh, he'd claimed undying devotion before this. He'd said the beguiling words to countless women; it was what they wished to hear, and one of the cardinal rules of dalliance. But he hadn't truly loved any of the soft, willing beauties in his bed. Love for him had always been a sumptuous sport. No lass had ever touched the deepest part of him, that hidden core Sabrina had discovered without even trying.

Niall's eyes grew soft and distant with remembrance— Sabrina challenging him, Sabrina laughing with him, Sabrina shyly offering her body to him in willing surrender, Sabrina matching him in passion . . . Each memory provoked a fresh swelling of awareness and wonder within him. How could he have been so blind?

All his previous dalliances now seemed nothing but meaningless games, a restless search to satisfy an unnamed hunger. He wanted more than games in his future. He wanted more than a beautiful feminine body sharing his bed, his life. There had been women past counting, but none so rare as Sabrina, with her wit and spirit and warmth and courage.

She had possessed him. She made him feel oddly complete. With her he'd found a fulfillment that he treasured beyond measure. Only with her had he ever known this fever, this desperate hunger.

His heart had been well and truly caught. He was powerless to stop needing her. He might as well deprive himself of a limb.

He lusted after the lovely woman she had become, yet it was no longer just pleasure he wanted, or even conquest. He would not be satisfied until he had all of her. He wanted to protect her from everything and everyone but himself.

He wanted whatever would give her happiness. He wanted a future with her, wanted to give her children. . . .

Yet . . . what did *she* want?

Niall came to an abrupt halt. Sabrina desired him, he was certain, but did she love him? *Could* she love him? Had she lashed out at him just now because he had inexcusably hurt her, or because she truly wanted nothing more to do with him?

He'd done little in the past weeks to secure her affection or respect. He'd seen the bleak pain in her eyes moments ago when he'd confessed his love for her. She hadn't believed him.

But then, was not he to blame for her doubts?

He had never wooed Sabrina as she deserved. On the contrary, in the beginning at least, he'd deliberately endeavored to make her feel unwanted. And then he'd violated her trust in an insane attempt to deny his own feelings.

Upon his honor, he intended to be completely faithful to Sabrina in future. Yet given his licentious past, it would be difficult to convince her of his change of heart. Harder still to win her love. But he *would* win it.

He was a changed man, but he had to show her. He understood what true love was now, but he had to prove to her how deep and steadfast his feelings were. Most of all, he had to prove that he was worthy of her trust.

Perhaps though . . . he needed an ally in his fight.

Finding himself in a narrow alleyway, Niall turned and strode swiftly toward the busy docks of Edinburgh. Sabrina's stepfather had offices there. Perhaps a wiser head would stand him in good stead.

Even the worst pain eventually lessened, Sabrina told herself as she oversaw the preparations for supper that evening. She had soaked her eyes with a cool compress after her confrontation with Niall, but they were still red from a foolish bout of weeping, and she was unable to hide her emotional turmoil from the housekeeper or scullery maid.

She hoped to do better with her stepfather. Charles Cameron was expected home at any moment.

When she heard a disturbance at the front entrance, she wiped her hands on a dishtowel and hurried upstairs from the kitchens. The sight that greeted her made her halt abruptly. The gentleman with her stepfather was the same intruder she had ordered from the house barely hours ago. The same bold, enchanting rogue who had savaged her heart so recklessly with his betrayal.

Her husband.

He had shaved the stubble from his jaw, Sabrina noted with despair. His clean chiseled features were more beautiful than ever—and made him nearly impossible to resist.

"We have a guest, lass," Charles said pleasantly.

"Guest?" she repeated witlessly, her gaze locked unwillingly with intense blue eyes.

"Aye, Laird McLaren is to sup with us."

Niall bowed politely, appearing not to notice her appalled expression. "I am obliged for the invitation. Fortunately, Charles agrees with me—that a wife's place is with her husband. And since you will not come to me, my love, I must do the honors."

Sabrina's despairing gaze turned to her stepfather. How could he have betrayed her this way? Charles had not questioned her when she'd fled the Highlands and taken refuge here, nor had she expected him to. She'd thought—mistakenly, it seemed now—he would be disinclined to interfere in a feud between husband and wife. This, however, was no simple misunderstanding. This was a rift of irreparable magnitude.

"Have you no proper greeting for your husband?" Niall queried lightly.

Sabrina stiffened. How could he behave as if nothing was wrong between them? "Papa Charles, might I have a word with you in private?"

"Can it not wait till after our meal, my dear? I trow I am famished."

When he met her gaze, the gray eyes in his gaunt face were kind but resolute. He meant for her to welcome her husband, and she would not sway him.

She bit back an oath, accepting defeat for the moment. In any event, this was his home. She had no right to turn away his invited guest. "Very well. Supper is nearly ready."

Just then Rab came bounding down the stairs from her rooms. Whining joyously, he rubbed his great body against Niall's legs with enough force to fell a less powerful man.

"Traitor," Sabrina muttered under her breath.

Niall looked up from stroking the dog, the brilliance of his smile taking her breath away. "What can I say? Animals find me appealing."

Her heart turned over at that wickedly beguiling smile, and it was all she could do to keep from throwing herself at Niall the way her misguided dog had done.

Charles turned to lead the way to the dining room then, but when Sabrina would have followed, Niall caught her arm, staying her a moment.

"I am not leaving Edinburgh without you, mouse," he said in a quiet undervoice. "If you will not accompany me home, I shall have to remain here—even though my clan needs me, and yours needs you."

She pulled away, unable to bear his tender touch. He would not make her feel guilty for abandoning her clan. She had more than fulfilled any obligations toward them.

Sabrina scarcely knew what she ate at supper; the herring-broth soup tasted much like the second course of spit-roasted pigeons and stuffed breast of veal, which tasted like the dessert of pear tarts wrapped in marzipan. She was torn between the need to weep and the need to satisfy the rise of desire she felt just looking at Niall.

The congenial conversation ebbed and flowed around her, but she took no part in it. Instead, she sat stiffly across the table from him, wishing fervently that he would go. It would prove impossible to shield her wounded heart if she couldn't even avoid his company.

It startled her when, at the close of supper, Charles stood.

"I shall take my port in my study, my dear, and leave the two of you to settle your differences in private."

"Papa Charles—" Sabrina murmured, but he shook his head and withdrew before she could finish her plea.

In the resulting silence, she kept her gaze trained on her wineglass, refusing to look at her husband. The tension drew out unbearably, until she was at last moved to speak. "I desire you to go."

"I know, sweeting," Niall returned gently, "but I wish to stay. Charles has invited me to remain the night."

She was certain she would find him grinning smugly, but when she raised her gaze, the tenderness in his eyes startled her.

"How did you coerce him to agree?"

"The truth? I humbled myself and threw myself on his mercy. I told him I do not deserve a lass as remarkable as you, but that I would do my best to prove myself worthy of you."

"In fact, you used that golden charm of yours to deceive him."

Niall held her gaze intently. "It was no deception. I told him I was in love with my wife."

Her lips parting, Sabrina stared at him in frustration. "He could not possibly believe you."

Niall smiled. "That has always been your trouble, mouse. You gravely underestimate yourself. Just as you underestimate me if you expect me to give you up without a fight." He leaned back in his chair. "Besides, how would it look, with both of us in town yet not living together as man and wife? I would be accused of abandoning my bride."

"It will only be expected of you," she replied. "Society will assume you are up to your usual pursuits, seducing anything in skirts."

"Society would be wrong. My days of seduction are over forever." He saw her doubt and all mirth vanished from his expression. "Sabrina . . . I know I've done nothing what-ever to deserve your trust, but I mean to change that."

She looked away, unable to put much faith in his vow of faithfulness. Perhaps for now he intended to cleave only unto her, but her lusty husband would doubtlessly yield to temptation sooner or later. And she couldn't bear to see it.

"I ask you to let us begin anew, Sabrina. I ask for the chance to earn your trust."

Her throat suddenly aching, she shook her head. She would never desire any man but Niall. Never love any man but him. But she could not act as if his betrayal had never happened. Someday she might possibly be able to trust his avowals, but for now the pain in her heart was like an open wound.

Sabrina stood abruptly. "I intend to retire for the eve-ning. Since you refuse to leave, perhaps you would care to join my stepfather in his study."

She started to turn away, but Niall's quiet voice prevented her. "Of course, there is the matter of marital rights."

"What . . . do you mean?"

"You are my wife, Sabrina, bound to me before man and God." He toyed with his wineglass, his finger moving slowly along the rim, reminding her vividly of the sensual power of his touch. How many countless times had Niall stroked her delicately like that, arousing her with the light-est of caresses? "I could seize you from this house now, and no law would gainsay me."

"M-My stepfather would stop you."

"Would he?" Niall smiled, his head bent, his jeweled eyes hidden by a fall of thick dark lashes. Softly, he said, "I give you fair warning, mouse. This is a battle I intend to win."

His brilliant gaze lifted and locked with hers.

She stood transfixed, paralyzed by the bold intent in his eyes, by the seductive promise in his magical voice. Even when Niall rose with easy grace, she remained helplessly immobile—until he moved around the table to her side.

Sabrina stepped back in alarm, but Niall caught her hand

and raised her fingers to his lips, pressing with exquisite sensuality. Desire spread with downy softness through her body at his erotic touch. It was all she could do to utter a breathless plea: "Do not . . ."

"As you wish," he said in that dark velvet voice that never failed to arouse her and set all her nerve endings trembling.

He released her hand, which incredibly filled her with disappointment. Her vanity felt slightly bruised that he had abandoned his pursuit so easily—an undeniably absurd response. She most certainly didn't wish him to pursue her.

She took the opportunity, nonetheless, to flee to her bedchamber.

Her heart pounding erratically, Sabrina carefully locked the door behind her and spent the next quarter hour glancing over her shoulder as she made her toilet and drew on her nightshift.

In bed, she attempted to read, but her restless mind refused to concentrate. Her thoughts kept wandering to the Highland devil on the floor below. When finally she blew out the candle, she lay there in the darkness, staring at the canopy overhead, tense and unsettled.

It was perhaps an hour later when she heard a key turn in the lock. Wide awake, Sabrina sat up abruptly. The door swung open, letting in a golden flood of light from an oil lamp.

At her gasp, Niall stepped into the room and shut the door softly behind him.

"How did you . . . ?"

"Your stepfather gave me a key," he answered congenially.

"Get out!" Sabrina exclaimed.

Ignoring her demand, Niall let his interested gaze roam around the chamber, coming to rest on the narrow bed with its blue damask curtains. "So this is where you sleep."

"Are you simpleminded? Or merely thick-witted? You are not welcome here!"

"I am only claiming my rights as your husband."

Sabrina took a deep breath, forcing herself to calm. "I tell you, sir," she enunciated as though he could not understand the King's English, "I will not share my bed with you."

Niall's gaze surveyed her white night smock, sweeping over her dark, rich hair, which hung loose and unbound. "Do you ken how sweetly virginal you look?" His mouth softened in a smile. "Yet I know better. I've seen the fire you hide from the rest of the world."

Depositing the lamp on the dressing table, Niall strode across the chamber and, despite her look of outraged alarm, settled beside Sabrina on the narrow bed. His eyes lingered on her nightshift, where her nipples strained darkly against the white linen. She felt them grow taut beneath his probing gaze.

When he leaned closer, Sabrina pushed futilely at his chest. "Don't! You can indulge your lust elsewhere. Doubtless there are countless women who would swoon with ecstasy at the chance to welcome the renowned Niall McLaren into their beds."

Niall contemplated his defiant bride calmly. He wanted no other woman. He only wanted the flashing-eyed lass who aroused such a fierce passion in him.

His hands moved lightly over her hair, rearranging it so that her tresses fell in deep, rich ripples over her shoulders.

"I want no other woman, Sabrina. I want a wife, not countless lovers. I want you." Niall's smile faded, leaving only the hungry look in his eyes. "I can't remember ever wanting like this."

It was true, he thought, gazing into the dark, liquid depths of her eyes. He had never felt this craving to possess, to protect, this all-consuming fire in his blood that he felt with Sabrina.

His voice lowered to a murmur. "I want your love, sweet mouse. I want to be the man you need, the one you carry deep inside of you, here."

When he touched her breast tenderly, she felt as if he had

reached into her heart, and she couldn't stand it. She tried to draw away, but he wouldn't permit her escape.

His fingertips sculpted the high planes of her face . . . stroked the fullness of her hair. "You cannot deny the bond between us, love. I know you feel it . . . when I bury myself inside you, when I drive deep and take you with me to paradise. When you sheathe me in sweetness and welcome me home." He bent to press his lips against hers, and every familiar gesture brought Sabrina fresh agonies of tenderness and need.

"I intend to convince you, Sabrina," he whispered against her softness. "I mean to love you until dreams of me haunt your nights and torment your every waking hour. I will fire your blood as you do mine. I won't relent until you wear my scent on your skin, my teeth marks on your silken thighs. Until my memory is branded on your heart and mind."

You are already branded on my heart, she thought helplessly. She closed her eyes, shaking with love and pain that mingled into a tangled knot.

"Don't . . ." she whispered as he bent and trailed velvet kisses along her throat. When he paused at the fragile hollow, tonguing the delicate pulse point, she tried to twist away. "Damn you . . . must you always resort to seduction to gain your ends?"

Niall suddenly went still, his caresses halting.

He drew a deep, shaky breath.

"No, you are right." He pulled back, his eyes bright and burning. "I won't use seduction to win you."

Sabrina stared at him in startlement.

She watched warily as he bent to pull off his boots, then stood to remove his coat.

"What . . . are you doing?" she asked uneasily.

"Undressing. Don't be alarmed, sweeting. I shan't force my attentions on you. I simply mean to ease my weariness in sleep." His mouth curled in a wry smile. "I've had little enough of it the past few days, owing to you."

He shed his clothing but for his linen undershirt and put

out the lamp, then joined Sabrina beneath the covers in the narrow bed. When he tried to gather her into his arms, though, she went rigid with resistance.

"I only want to hold you," he murmured in the darkness.

"No," she said unevenly.

When she turned away, giving him her back, Niall made no move to stop her. He'd made that mistake before. He had tried to bind Sabrina to him sexually, to conquer her with passion, but he needed to do it with love.

He could feel her tension as she lay there, waiting for him to resume his sensual assault on her defenses, but he crushed the temptation. He wanted to make love to her, urgently, but an enchantment of the flesh would no longer suffice for him. He wanted more than her body. He wanted her heart, freely given.

Niall shut his eyes, bedeviled by unaccustomed sensations of helplessness and inadequacy. He'd proven countless times that he could seduce a woman's body, but her heart? He might find it impossible.

He didn't know how to love a lass. He could *make* love in countless ways, but this heartrending, breathtaking, *relentless* emotion was completely foreign to him.

One thing was certain, however. He was determined to woo and win her. As his wife, Sabrina belonged to him by law, but he vowed to make her his own, in love as well as in name.

He wanted, needed, her heart. And he was willing to settle for nothing less.

Chapter
Seventeen

He woke to an empty bed. In the chill of dawn, Niall reached out to draw Sabrina to him—and encountered only rumpled sheets.

In moments he had risen and dressed and was startling sleepy-eyed maids and footmen as he searched the house from bottom to top.

He found her in the attic, in a small cubbyhole that served as a maid's quarters, curled up on a pallet, fast asleep. A wealth of tenderness engulfed him as he gazed down at Sabrina's pale face. There were shadows beneath her eyes, shadows he suspected he had put there.

Just then she stirred awake and caught sight of him. With a groan, she buried her face in the pillow. "Sweet heaven, can I have no peace?"

Niall sank down to sit beside her on the plank floor, which only made her stiffen.

"Would you care to explain why I find you in the servants' quarters, love?"

"You are clever enough to venture a guess. I am attempting to avoid you. I pray you, go *away*."

He shook his head, unwilling to leave her like this. Smoothing her tresses from her neck, he massaged the satin skin of her nape. "Not until we reach an understanding."

"Devil take you," Sabrina muttered. "There is nothing more to be said."

His voice dropped to a quiet murmur. "Do you truly want me out of your life, mouse?"

The sudden ache in her throat prevented her from replying. She could feel the warmth of his hand on her nape, gentle yet infinitely compelling.

"I've missed you, Sabrina. I've missed your fire, your courage, your passion, your clever tongue. Have you not missed me as well?"

Of course she had missed him, damn his eyes. Since leaving the Highlands, she'd done nothing but struggle against tormenting memories of Niall. " 'Tis only a temporary obsession. It will pass, I'm certain."

"No. There is obsession as well, but I think I've enough experience to recognize the uniqueness of my feelings. I've never felt this yearning of the heart, this need to fill the loneliness. I'm empty inside without you, Sabrina. You're in my blood. I'll never be free of you . . . I don't want to be free."

She lifted her head to gaze at him searchingly.

"I love you, Sabrina. Can you not feel it every time I take you in my arms?"

Sabrina squeezed her eyes shut, haunted by the memory of his male body saying so openly and truthfully that he wanted her. But lust was not love. "Whatever you feel for me, it isn't love."

"If so, then how do you explain this appalling misery I feel when you spurn me?"

" 'Tis simple. You're like a spoiled bairn denied sweetmeats for the first time in his life."

Niall shook his head. "I've never loved any woman before, Sabrina. It's the most bewildering, joyous feeling I've ever known. Look at me, sweeting."

She didn't *want* to look at him, yet she couldn't stop herself. She obeyed, and her heart ached to see those astonishingly warm eyes gazing so tenderly at her.

"You're the only lass who has ever captured my heart."

Sabrina swallowed hard, her face showing too much of the hope that fluttered in her heart. She wanted to believe him so badly that the depth of it terrified her.

"I intend to remain constant to you," Niall replied quietly. "Upon my honor, Sabrina, I swear it."

A shadow passed over her eyes. "It is not your honor I doubt. It is your making pledges you cannot keep."

A breathtaking, whimsical smile tugged at the corners of his lips. "Oh, I most assuredly will keep this one. Never again will I endure such torment as I have of late. My life has been a misery without you."

"Your life was a misery *with* me, as I recall. We did nothing but fight."

"And make love."

"It isn't enough, Niall. Marriage is more than lovemaking or physical pleasure. More than games or dalliance or flirtation. What we had was no true marriage."

"No," he said gravely, "it was not. But it will be."

Gazing into his eyes, Sabrina felt a most disastrous weakening of the heart she was trying to steel against him. But it was foolish to succumb to his blandishments. "What I want from a union is not what you want."

"And what do you want?"

"Love and loyalty and honesty . . . sharing thoughts and dreams, working together, building a future, a family."

"You are wrong, Sabrina. I want those things as well. With you."

When he reached for her, she was too dazed to resist.

His eyes darkening to a midnight shade, he framed her face in the gentle vise of his palms. "You are my wife, Sabrina. My only love. You belong to me. But I know I must convince you."

My love. She shivered. The golden-throated words seemed so natural somehow, and they warmed her as little else ever had.

To her utter dismay then, Niall bent and kissed her, a soft, mind-numbing, devastating kiss that reached inside her and tore at her heart.

When Sabrina made a despairing sound of protest, he drew back, exhaling a shuddering breath. "I swore I would not take unfair advantage of you . . . Very well, sweeting. You win. You may have your bed back. I shall stay out of it till you issue me a personal invitation to return." He straightened his shoulders, as if girding his resolve. "If you wish me to make love to you, you must ask."

"You will have a long wait."

"Then it shall be a bleak season for me, alas." He gave a sigh. "If you won't have me, then I shall have no one. You see, I intend to take a vow of celibacy."

"A vow of *what*?"

Teasingly, Niall touched a gentle finger to her mouth, which was gaping open. "Never say I've rendered you speechless, mouse. Celibacy. Have you not heard of the term?"

"Certainly *I* have. But I doubt you have more than a passing acquaintance with it."

"Fortuitously, no. But I can suffer great hardships if I must. I'm a Highlander, after all."

Her bewilderment turned to suspicion. "I cannot credit you would give up so easily."

"Oh, I am not giving up. I'll not abandon the war, merely alter tactics."

He rose and turned toward the door. "Sweet dreams, my own. Mine will be unquestionably desolate. I have sworn off all carnal pursuits until you can return my love."

She had not seen the last of him, Sabrina knew. Niall was not a man to concede failure. And he had recruited allies.

Dismayingly, her stepfather earnestly championed his cause.

"I ken the lad's sincere," Charles said to her at breakfast that morning. "Can you not bring yourself to return home with him where you belong?"

"I don't belong with Niall."

"I'm not so certain. I've watched you, lass. You've changed since you wedded him. For the better. There's a light in your eyes that was missing before . . . a flush on your cheeks. You come alive when he's near. And now that you've had a taste of adventure, I'll warrant you'll find your existence here much too tame."

That much was true. She missed the enchantment of the Highlands, the raw beauty, the stunning vibrancy. She missed the sense of newness and adventure she'd awakened to each day as Niall's wife and mistress of Clan McLaren. She didn't miss the pain.

Sabrina looked down at her plate. "I never expected to find a grand passion. I only desired a quiet union, based on mutual affection and respect. A husband who could care for me . . . children. Niall has no desire for those things."

"He claims to love you."

She nodded unwillingly, torn by conflicting emotions of hope and doubt. She wanted desperately to believe Niall meant his professions of love.

"Do you love him, lass?"

She couldn't deny it, not without lying. She did love Niall, deeply and irrevocably. She hadn't realized how much sheer joy he added to her previously humdrum existence. When he was away, she felt empty, abandoned, bereft of his spirit. When he was near, she wanted to burrow into his embrace and become part of him, the rest of the world be damned.

What had made her think she could walk out of his life?

"Well," Charles said solemnly as he rose from the table, "one thing is clear. He seems determined to have you. And I, for one, would not care to stand in his way."

Her stepfather quit the room, leaving Sabrina alone with her troubled thoughts. Her stepfather was right. Niall was a dangerous, ruthless rogue determined to pursue her. He knew how to bend a woman to his every whim, and he intended to give no quarter.

But she would prove herself a match for him.

Sabrina's chin rose stubbornly. She refused to surrender so fecklessly. Niall thought he had only to waltz back into her life and she would fall at his feet. But he was taking a great deal for granted. She was no longer the passive mouse he had wed.

He would have to earn the right to her hand.

If he sincerely wanted to resume his place as her husband, if he truly meant to give her his love and loyalty, then he would have to prove it.

Only later that morning did Sabrina begin to comprehend precisely what her renowned rake of a husband meant when he vowed to change tactics. She had been relieved when Niall left the house before breakfast, but to her dismay, he awaited her when she stepped outside accompanied by a maidservant.

"May I be of service, milady?" he queried, sweeping her the exquisite bow of a cavalier.

Sabrina shook her head, resolved to be patient. "I require no assistance, thank you, sir."

"Where are you bound?"

"To market, if you must know."

To her surprise, Niall dismissed the maid. The meek lass was so awestruck by the handsome Highland laird, she could only bob a curtsy and, with a pleading look at her mistress, flee back inside the house.

"I shall carry your parcels, pet," Niall asserted innocently, anticipating Sabrina's disapproval.

"You cannot possibly be interested in shopping for dinner."

"In truth, my soul shrivels at the prospect, but I have a keen interest in sharing your delightful company. If this is my only avenue, then I accept with magnanimity and grace."

Determined to repress her amusement and resist his charm, Sabrina turned and started down the narrow street. Following, Niall captured her arm, tucking her hand within the crook of his elbow. "Can you fault me for desiring a liaison with my own wife?"

She smiled sweetly. "I fault you for making a wretched nuisance of yourself."

" 'Tis not my intention, pet."

"No? Then what *is* your intention?"

"To show you how greatly I've reformed. That I've come to my senses."

"On the contrary, your senses have gone begging."

"I can fully understand your skepticism. But I've changed my wicked ways. It remains for me to convince you of my devotion."

"It will require an extraordinary degree of convincing."

"I am up to the task. If you wish to be wooed, so be it."

Sabrina halted in her tracks, gazing up at him. "I don't wish to be wooed."

"You deserve it, nonetheless. I made a grave mistake neglecting to shower you with the proper attention before our union. A mistake I intend to rectify forthwith."

Sabrina took a deep breath, realizing he would insist on escorting her, whether she wished it or not. Niall McLaren was a bold, daring devil accustomed to gaining his way in all things.

"There is absolutely no need for this charade," she replied as she resumed her pace toward the market square of old Edinburgh.

" 'Tis no charade. I want the world to see how enamored I am of my wife."

Sabrina's only reply was a shrug.

The market was crowded and noisy, filled with the cries of fishmongers and butchers, bakers and flower merchants, all vociferously urging customers to sample their wares.

It came as no surprise to Sabrina when Niall appeared as much at ease here as he would in the most lavish ballroom or bedchamber. What took her aback was his deliberate display of affection. He was obviously intent on courting her, staking a public claim—and calling attention to his devotion in a highly visible manner.

His solicitation proved highly embarrassing when they came to a puddle of mud on a street corner. Before she knew what he was about, Niall had swept her up in his arms and carried her safely across. And then he had the audacity to chuckle at her flushed cheeks and snapping eyes.

She had scarcely recovered from that incident when they stopped at a butcher's booth. When Niall held up a leg of lamb for her inspection, Sabrina couldn't repress a laugh.

His eyebrow rose in mock query. "Something amuses you, sweeting?"

"I confess it diverting to see the greatest lover of all Europe stooping to forage for mutton."

Niall grinned in response, an effect that was dazzling. "Indeed. How my friends would howl to see me dancing attendance on my wife. But there is no limit to what a man may do once struck by cupid's arrow."

Her smile fading, she forced herself to turn away.

Moments later, Sabrina wanted to refuse his gift when he presented her with a rose.

"For the loveliest lass of my acquaintance," Niall murmured in a lilting tone that was pure seduction.

Breathless, Sabrina drew back. "Enough of your blethering. As mistress of my stepfather's household, I have duties to attend to. Unlike *some* persons, pleasure is not my consummate goal in life."

He ignored her pointed look and bent to whisper in her ear. " 'Tis a pity. If there's anything you were made for, 'tis pleasure. Your lovely body was made for arousing a man."

Sabrina felt herself tremble at being subjected to the full force of Niall's golden charm. The effect was devastating and oh, so successful. His sublime sensuality was potent enough to weaken her knees.

"I'll thank you to remember your promise," she returned unevenly.

Undaunted, Niall leaned closer and pressed a featherlight kiss on her lips. "I promised I wouldn't try to bed you, not to abandon my suit."

Stunned, wanting, Sabrina could only stare helplessly at him.

A cackle of laughter penetrated her dazed senses, and she glanced around to find an old crone watching them with avid delight. With a flush of embarrassment, Sabrina spun on her heel and fled, leaving Niall to follow if he would.

To her surprise and unwilling dismay, when she concluded her purchases, Niall deposited her safely at her stepfather's doorstep and declined an invitation to enter. He made no appearance that afternoon, nor did he come to supper that evening.

That night Sabrina tossed and turned alone in her bed, cursing him for making her life such a misery.

Niall, however, spent a solitary night in a nearby inn, more concerned than he cared to admit by his wife's spirited defiance. Women had always come so easily for him, it was rare for one to withstand a concerted assault. But if he'd thought overcoming Sabrina's resistance would be a simple matter, he swiftly relinquished his delusions.

He called at the Cameron residence the next morning, with renewed resolve to lay siege to her woman's stubborn heart. When he requested Lady McLaren and was shown into the study, he discovered Sabrina pouring over ledgers. Regrettably she was not alone; her stepfather was present.

Charles greeted him cheerfully, but Sabrina's demeanor was coolly indifferent. Niall regarded it as a challenge.

Before he could kiss her hand, however, she drew it back safely.

"I cannot imagine what brings you here," she murmured archly.

" 'Twas I who invited Laird McLaren this morn," Charles explained. "I asked him to escort you to the shops. The lad has convinced me your wardrobe is lacking."

"Lacking?" Sabrina repeated. "But he has already spent a fortune on new gowns for me."

"Gowns appropriate for the country," Niall interjected. "The city is another matter. The Highlands have much to recommend them, but I fear fashion is not one. And you require proper accoutrements as well."

Sabrina eyed him warily, not nearly so unaffected by Niall's arrival as she pretended. His raven hair was pulled back carelessly into a queue and tied with a black ribbon, while his well-tailored frock coat was fashioned of plain black broadcloth. Yet even modestly attired, Niall managed to eclipse every other gentleman of her acquaintance. His physical presence engulfed her senses, and the breathtaking smile he offered her made her pulse race.

"Regretfully, I am occupied at the moment. The account books suffered sorely in my absence—"

"I wish you to indulge me in this, lass," Charles said solemnly. "The accounts will wait."

Sabrina reluctantly admitted defeat. Her stepfather asked so little of her. If he desired her to walk over hot coals, she would do so. Another public shopping expedition in Niall's company could not be so difficult . . . But it irked her that her stepfather seemed to be in league with her devious, infuriating husband.

Niall was obviously in a jovial mood; she could see his eyes were full of laughter.

"If you don't care to visit the shops," he murmured with a bland tone of benevolence, "we could always return to my rooms at the Bull and Bear Inn and spend the morning exploring mutual delights."

At his suggestive remark, the uncertainty in her expression was replaced by exasperation. "There is nothing I would enjoy less."

Niall clucked his tongue. "I gather you mean to act the shrew this morning. 'Tis a pity you've refused me admittance to your bedchamber. You are far more agreeable when you've been bedded."

Her jaw dropped in outrage at his audacity. "I would be more agreeable still if I needn't set eyes on you."

The laughter in his eyes spilled over to his mouth as he took her arm. "Sheath your claws, tiger. 'Tis merely a shopping expedition, nothing more. I shan't seduce you unless you are willing."

Sabrina did not trust his assurances one whit. Niall was

wooing her, the way he'd never done before their marriage, but she didn't care for it in the least. Although he seemed to be making a concerted effort to please her, he was plotting her downfall, playing a game of cat-and-mouse where she was the prey.

She knew how to play his game of seduction, though. She'd been taught by an expert, after all.

Sabrina eyed Niall thoughtfully as he strolled beside her. Since resistance did not appear to be working, she would try using what feminine weapons she had at her disposal—flirtation and charm and teasing banter—to make Niall fawn over her. She would give him a taste of his own medicine. And in the end she would demand nothing less than his complete surrender.

They toured the finer shops of Edinburgh, milliners, modistes, furriers, jewelers . . . It did not take long for Sabrina to realize she was the object of great curiosity among the females they encountered. Ladies and serving maids alike obviously envied her being escorted by such a handsome rogue as the McLaren. The compelling Highlander possessed an indescribable appeal that lured and dazzled.

Sabrina was not immune, in truth. A secret part of her was thrilled to be wanted so fiercely by this magnificent man.

What truly gratified her, though, was discovering that she had her own admirers. Any number of gentlemen they met cast appreciative glances her way, and the feminine side of her could not help but be pleased. More satisfying still was Niall's frown each time she managed a flirtatious smile at a stranger.

To her dismay, Niall purchased countless items for her, lace fripperies, ribbons, fans, gloves . . . a cloak of rich bronzed brocade trimmed with marten.

"To complement your sparkling eyes," he suggested provocatively in a voice she could not trust.

Sabrina forced herself to thank him for his generosity. She even held her tongue when he fingered a bolt of emerald satin. But when he ordered it made up into a ball gown studded with crystal beads, she forgot her plan and protested his extravagance.

"This is too much, Niall! Such largess is not only unnecessary but decadent. Your silver would be better spent on your clan."

"That is one of the things I admire about you, mouse; your frugality. But I have the wherewithal to gown my lady in finery. And the Duke of Kintail is holding a ball a sennight hence."

"I shan't attend. Purchase the gown, if you will, but I mean to remain at home with my stepfather."

He flashed that teasing, wayward smile that always constricted her throat. "I shall take great delight in persuading you to change your mind."

Taking a deep breath, Sabrina made herself smile sweetly in return. "And I," she murmured under her breath, "shall take great delight in making you plead."

It was when they entered a millinery shop in search of bonnets that she had to hold her tongue for a different reason. There they encountered a noblewoman and her two lively daughters who positively gushed over the McLaren laird, but evidently mistook Sabrina for his latest inamorata. The ladies' frost turned to shock when Niall presented Sabrina as his wife.

"As you see," Niall said with a male grin when they were alone once more, "you should be honored to have captured me. Matchmaking mamas have been throwing their daughters at my head for years, yet I have never succumbed until I met you."

She sent him an arch look. "I am not yet convinced you have truly succumbed."

"Use your wits, sweeting. Would I make a laughingstock of myself pursuing my wife in so public a manner if I meant to continue my licentious career as a libertine?"

"I hardly consider escorting me shopping as making a laughingstock of yourself."

"You mean to make me grovel, is that it?"

She gave Niall a considering glance. "That might prove amusing, I admit."

"I will, if that will convince you. I will prostrate myself at your feet."

Smiling serenely, Sabrina gathered her skirts, raised the hem a few inches, and proffered her slippered foot.

Niall laughed out loud, his devilish eyes full of mischief and affection. "Ah, what a treasure you are, mouse! How I cherish you."

It was when they entered a jeweler's shop that Sabrina encountered a gentleman of her acquaintance. He was engaged in examining a pearl brooch at the counter.

Sabrina's heart turned over. "Oliver!" she exclaimed breathlessly before she could prevent herself.

Turning, he froze an instant before his expression brightened. "Sabrina, my dear . . . what do you here?" His eyes narrowed admiringly as he peered at her through his quizzing glass. "Is this truly you? You appear . . . different, somehow."

She understood his surprise. Her full-skirted gown of yellow sprigged muslin attractively flattered her tall figure, while her pale complexion held a heightened color that had naught to do with cosmetics. She did not need her mirror to tell her that her looks had improved since Oliver had last seen her—and not merely due to her stylish gown. Under Niall's tutelage she had bloomed like a flower beneath a nurturing sun.

Oliver, on the other hand, appeared much as she recalled, except perhaps for his more ornate attire. Yet with his powdered wig, voluminous satin frock coat, and fashionable red heels, her former suitor seemed overly effeminate compared to the powerful, sinewed, totally male Highlander she had wed. She could not imagine Oliver wielding the rapier at his waist the way Niall did a broadsword, or leading a midnight cattle raid, or riding furiously to her rescue to avenge her supposed abduction by an enemy clan.

"What do you here?" Oliver repeated curiously.

"She is enjoying the company of her husband," a sardonic voice drawled at her shoulder.

Sabrina gave a start. She had forgotten Niall was so near.

"Will you make me known to your friend, my love?" he queried in a silken tone.

"This is Mr. Oliver Irvine," she managed to reply. "Husband to my cousin Frances."

She could see the speculation in Niall's blue eyes and immediately regretted ever telling him about her failed courtship. "Mr. Irvine, may I present Niall McLaren, Lord Strathearn. My . . . husband."

"Ah, yes. I admit I was surprised to hear you had wed so suddenly." Oliver bowed stiffly. "Your servant, milord."

"What is the surprise?" Niall asked in a dangerous tone Sabrina mistrusted. "I was smitten the moment I laid eyes on so lovely a lass, and I could not wait to make her mine."

She winced at that falsehood. "Is my cousin not with you, Mr. Irvine?" she asked to change the subject.

The faintest flush suffused Oliver's painted cheeks. "I fear Frances is indisposed at the moment. She is . . . er . . . *enceinte*."

"Oh . . . how . . . delightful," Sabrina murmured, even as a pang of envy pierced her at the news her cousin was to bear a child. It was a bittersweet reflection to consider what might have been. Had Oliver not fallen in love with her cousin, *she* might be the lady in an interesting condition. "You must be pleased."

"Er . . . quite," Oliver replied, looking strangely ill at ease. "Ah . . . forgive me. I have just recalled an errand I neglected." He returned the brooch to the jeweler. "By your leave, my lady . . . my lord." Oliver bowed over Sabrina's hand and touched his hat to Niall, then made a swift exit from the shop.

Sabrina glanced up to find Niall observing her closely.

"A jealous lover, pet?"

She considered returning a coy riposte, but couldn't bring

herself to make light of such a subject. "I have no lovers, jealous or otherwise."

"You are mistaken. You have me. I am discovering what a possessive bore I can be." Niall's gaze slanted to the door. "He is a fool to have jilted you."

Discomfited, she could not fashion a reply.

"I confess, I find it difficult to see the fellow's appeal—or comprehend how you could have fancied yourself in love with him."

Sabrina bit her lip in vexation, yet, disloyally, she agreed. She couldn't help but wonder what she'd ever seen in Oliver. Niall had cured her of her girlish infatuation for her former suitor; that love had been a pale imitation of her present feelings for her husband. "Oliver makes no claim to expertise in carnal affairs. His amorous talents certainly do not match yours."

"I am gratified, but I was speaking of deeper emotions of the heart."

"Surely you do not profess to be an expert on such matters?" Sabrina asked archly.

She expected a blithe retort, but Niall's mien was entirely sober as he searched her face. "You must regret losing your love."

"Oliver is not my love. We were once betrothed, that is all."

"Good," he murmured with satisfaction. "I intend to make you forget he ever even existed."

You already have, she reflected silently.

"If he was purchasing that bauble for his wife," Niall mused, glancing at the jeweler, "I would be much surprised."

Her eyebrow rose at the implied accusation. "Simply because you are incapable of fidelity does not mean you must impugn others."

His gaze narrowed on her sharply. "I am not incapable of fidelity. I've simply never had good enough reason to exercise it before you."

"I imagine the first beauty who comes along will divert you."

"No." Niall reached up to stroke her cheek. "How can I look at another lass when you're my only love?"

Realizing the jeweler was regarding them curiously then, he grasped Sabrina by the elbow and drew her into a darkened corner of the shop.

His voice turned quiet, deep. "I love you, Sabrina. So much that I ache with it. I only wish I could make you understand how much . . ."

He bent his head then and kissed her. With beguiling tenderness, his mouth settled on hers, soft flesh to soft flesh.

Sabrina felt her heart pounding at his warmth, felt the heavy rise of his desire even through her layers of skirts and petticoats. Alarmed, she pressed her palms against his chest and made a soft sound of distress.

Yet she wanted to cry out when he obeyed.

He broke off his kiss but stood rigid, his forehead pressed against hers, his breath uneven. He seemed to be waging some internal battle with himself.

His better instincts must have won, for he finally exhaled a soft gust of mirthless laughter. When he lifted his head, his smile was forced and held a hint of pain. "I suppose this is my punishment for past sins. For years I searched for a woman I could love, one with courage and honor, who could make me shake with fury or passion. Yet when I find her at last, she refuses me."

Releasing her unwillingly then, Niall turned away.

Bereft, Sabrina watched as he returned to the counter, her fingers moving to her tingling mouth. How could he walk away and leave her like that, aching, empty, starving for his touch?

How could she continue to resist him when resistance hurt her more than it did him?

Chapter
Eighteen

It was a dance of seduction, one that neither of them seemed able to win.

After a sennight, Niall's deliberate and highly public campaign was taking a severe toll on Sabrina's heart. It required every ounce of fortitude she possessed to continue withstanding his calculated, sensual assault.

He was quick to take advantage of every opportunity to bedevil her. Though Niall kept his promise not to charm his way into her bed, he relied upon subtler methods to remind her of what she was missing . . . a tender glance, a beguiling caress, a devastating smile.

She in turn employed all the feminine weapons at her disposal, personifying a female version of *him*. She charmed Niall just as he charmed her. She laughed and flirted just as intensely, making teasing promises and leading him on an elusive chase.

It was only fitting punishment, Sabrina told herself. In the course of his licentious career, Niall had made countless women fall in love with him. Now, for the first time in his life, the legendary rogue was experiencing the same turmoil he'd engendered in all those unfortunate women: the despair of loving someone who professed not to love him in return. The pain of wondering if she would remain faithful.

And yet, Sabrina knew, they could not go on like this much longer. They were at an impasse, an impasse she desperately wanted to end.

The opportunity came at the Duke of Kintail's ball, although in a manner she never expected.

Sabrina had not truly wished to attend the event, but her stepfather swept aside her objections. All of Edinburgh society would be there, Charles claimed, and though he did not feel well enough to accompany her, he wanted his daughter to enjoy the admiration she so richly deserved.

Niall insisted on helping her dress for the ball, against Sabrina's will.

"Dear heart," he murmured, his sapphire eyes full of amusement and affection, "you may as well give in with good grace. You know in the end I will have my wicked way with you."

"That is precisely what concerns me," she retorted wryly.

He turned the simple art of dressing into an exercise in pleasure. Sabrina refused to allow him into her bedchamber until she was bathed and perfumed and safely garbed in a lounging robe, but when her persistent husband rapped on her door for the second time, she could delay no longer.

He was already partially attired for the ball, looking impossibly handsome in a fine lawn shirt and satin breeches and silver-buckled shoes. Niall immediately lit a dozen more candles for the task ahead, and went to work supervising her transformation.

From the first Sabrina realized his goal was not simply to gown her for the ball, but to create a masterpiece. When she was settled at her dressing table, he directed the maids in the application of cosmetics, insisting on a light hand—a hint of blush at the cheekbones, a touch of kohl to darken the eyes, a deeper red for the lips, and absolutely no face paint. Her hair was permitted no powder, but piled high upon her head, with a shining sweep of curls falling elegantly over one shoulder.

It required three servants to help her don the fabulous crystal-studded ball gown which the modiste had created, and to arrange the wide, stiff panniers of the skirts. Sabrina worried that the hue of the fashionable gown was too bold and the décolletage too daring; the emerald satin contrasted vividly with the pastels worn by most ladies, while the swell of her breasts revealed by the swooping décolletage would draw every eye.

Yet the gasps of awe and admiration from the women reassured her.

"Ah, mum, ye look like a fairy princess."

"Nay, a queen."

Niall, however, said not a word while refusing to allow her to look in the mirror. After dismissing the maids, he added the finishing touches himself . . . an emerald necklace and ear bobs for which he'd sent home to the Highlands . . . a delicate black beauty patch which he seemed to relish placing on her right breast . . . and an ebony lace fan for her to carry.

He gave her a final inspection, his fingers sensuously dragging unwilling curls to feather dance on her cheeks. Then he whispered, "Perfect," and turned her slowly to face the cheval glass.

Sabrina started in shock, wondering if the sensual creature in the mirror was truly her own image. Somehow Niall's sorcery had transformed her into a breathtaking enchantress.

The skirt of soft rich satin—flattened in front and held out to the sides by hoops—was covered with crystal beads that shimmered in the pale candlelight like diamonds. The long, pointed bodice accentuated her narrow waist while making her breasts swell alluringly above the square neckline.

The effect was stunning, but it was Niall's expression reflected in the mirror that made her feel beautiful beyond words.

"Niall . . . the gown is breathtaking."

His smile was indulgent. "No. The lass wearing it is breathtaking . . . Magnificent."

Bending, he nuzzled her naked shoulder. "I've told you before, a woman's beauty is not determined by her outward appearance, but her inner fire . . . And you have enough fire, cherie, to keep me constantly aflame." His husky voice was thick and slow, like honey flowing through her veins, sweeping down the walls that had protected Sabrina's heart.

When he slipped his arms around her from behind, she drew a determined breath with every ounce of willpower she possessed. "Niall . . . the ball . . ."

He groaned softly and buried his face in her shoulder, not wanting to release her. She was the cause of his greatest joy, his greatest torment. He spent his nights craving her, tortured by his aching loins, the constriction in his chest, not sleeping. He spent his days endeavoring to prove she'd stolen his heart.

Sabrina was the only one who failed to see it, Niall reflected despairingly. All of Edinburgh was watching his pursuit of his wife in fascination and awe. From his friends he'd endured much ribald laughter regarding how hard the mighty fall, while the rest of society was desirous of meeting the remarkable woman who had managed the impossible. It was a nine-day wonder, his vanquishment on the battlefield of love.

Yet he'd faced Sabrina each day with a growing disquiet. With all the scores of women in his past, he'd never met with such overwhelming resistance.

When she tried to draw away, Niall closed his eyes in an agony of need. He wanted Sabrina. Desperately. He wanted her writhing and hungry. Wanted her crying out with love for him. Yet . . . he wanted her to come to him. He heaved a jagged sigh. "Ah, yes, the ball."

He did not release her entirely, however. Instead, he turned her slowly to face him and bent his head.

He kissed her so softly, so deeply, she felt a silky fire flow between them.

"Sabrina . . ." he whispered against her lips, "my sweet bright flame of a woman. How you make me burn . . ."

He stepped back then, letting his hands fall away. Sabrina stared, shivering with desire and need.

Niall left her standing there, trembling and aroused, while he retired to another chamber to finish dressing.

She had still not fully recovered when he rejoined her moments later. He wore a full-skirted satin coat of ivory, with lace ruffles of purest white at throat and wrists. The pale hues presented a stark contrast to his dark good looks and a striking foil to the deeper colors of her own attire.

But it was the rich, ardent glow in Niall's sapphire eyes that stole her breath away. When he looked at her like that, she could have absolutely no doubt that he cherished her as he claimed.

The Cameron carriage transported them to the ball, but Sabrina felt as if she were floating. The summer sky shimmered a deep star-dusted black as she descended before the Duke of Kintail's magnificent mansion.

When they entered the glittering ballroom and were announced to the illustrious guests, an excited murmur rushed through the crowd. Niall was well known among the throng of courtiers, macaronis, dukes and duchesses, lords and ladies, but it was the vibrant beauty beside him who drew all eyes.

"Your reputation precedes you, my love," Niall murmured with satisfaction.

"Mine?" She noted the swiveling, powdered heads of the onlookers and felt a rush of feminine power. She was grateful Niall had gowned her like his queen. The vast room was filled with a dazzling array of gentility resplendent in silks and brocades and jewels, but she could hold her head high among them. She was a chieftain's bride, with the blood of Highland warriors in her veins.

"Aye, you, Sabrina. You are the talk of Edinburgh. And if I am not mistaken, here is one of your admirers now."

The elderly Duke of Kintail himself came forward and begged to be presented to the beauty on the McLaren's arm. "You did not tell me she was such a ravishing creature, milord."

"I thought I would permit you to see for yourself, your

grace. May I present the love of my life, my wife, Sabrina, Lady McLaren."

The duke bowed elegantly over her hand. "Charmed, milady. So this is the lass who's caused you to wear your heart on your sleeve. Where have you been hiding her?"

Niall appraised Sabrina, his glance caressing her in an affectionate way. "Oh, I am not the culprit, your grace. She has been hiding herself. I fear she is rather shy."

Sabrina nearly choked at such a blatant falsehood.

"It required," Niall continued smoothly, "a herculean effort to persuade her even to attend this evening."

"Well," the duke replied, beaming, "I trust we will make it worth your while, milady. Pray allow me to partner you in a dance later."

He took his leave then, while Sabrina gazed after him quizzically.

"Do not look so startled by his attentions, sweeting," her husband admonished. "Kintail has a discerning eye to seek out the most alluring woman present. In truth, I was of two minds whether to permit him your hand. I would far rather keep you all to myself."

His smile was lavish and heart-familiar. Sabrina found herself staring at that blatant, sensual mouth that could make her go wild with a grin or a caress.

"You cannot," she observed archly, "dance solely with me. What will the company think?"

"They will think me captivated by my beautiful wife, which is no less than the truth."

She might have replied, but the duke's departure seemed to be the signal for the crowd to converge upon her. Dozens of guests came forward to be presented to the remarkable woman who had captured the elusive Highland laird who was the bane of every feminine heart.

Niall watched in satisfaction as she was fawned over by the company, relishing the stir she'd caused with her uncommon beauty. Tonight Sabrina positively glowed. Among the ladies armored in wide, panniered skirts, wielding gaily painted fans, she stood out like an exotic hothouse flower, her unadorned tresses shining in the gleam of a thousand candles. Yet she responded to the attention as he had taught her, accepting their accolades as her due, with a lively grace that charmed and titillated.

For the next quarter hour as she was made known to the assembly, Sabrina was scarcely permitted a chance to catch her breath, but when the crowd finally parted, she felt her heart catch in her throat. Across an open space stood an extraordinarily beautiful woman with her own court of admirers. It was the English noblewoman, Sabrina realized. The colonel's wife whom Niall had been seducing when they'd first met at her cousin Frances's betrothal ball. Lady Chivington wore a rose velvet gown adorned with gold lace and distended by an enormous hooped petticoat, and she was giving Niall a sultry glance from a distance, her perfect, bow-shaped mouth turned down in a pout.

Sabrina's fingers clenched around her fan, before she looked up to find Niall watching her. Their gazes locked, and she knew he too was remembering that first encounter.

"Ah, no, sweeting, that is not the way to show displeasure. Here, permit me." Gently grasping her fingers, he snapped open the fragile sticks and made three short, brisk passes with the fan beneath her chin. "There, 'tis an art, you see."

Vexed, Sabrina gazed up into his laughing eyes. "An art you seem to have perfected," she returned waspishly.

He smiled. "I am gratified that you're jealous. It gives me hope that you care more deeply for me than you're willing to admit."

She arched an eyebrow. "You think me jealous?"

"Aye. Come now, love, confess. You are as smitten by me as I am by you."

" 'Tis a wonder anyone else can fit in this vast ballroom alongside you, my lord, considering the inflated proportions of your self-esteem."

He laughed, amusement spilling out of his eyes. "Sabrina, sweet Sabrina, how I ache with wanting you."

Just then the musicians struck up the stately strains of a minuet.

"May I have the honor?" Niall murmured.

Allowing her no opportunity to protest, he took her arm and led her in the genteel steps of a minuet. As he did all else, Niall executed the intricate turns of the dance with flawless grace. Sabrina felt dazed by his nearness, and by the way he was gazing at her. His attention was fixed solely on her, his eyes caressing, as if she were the only woman in the world. When the set concluded, he gave her up with obvious reluctance.

Afterward Sabrina found herself in great demand as a dance partner; she was not allowed a moment's rest. It was a heady feeling, in truth—and yet she found herself yearning for the simple honesty of the Highlands. This company seemed too civilized, too pretentious, too frivolous, with its preoccupation with banal chatter and physical beauty.

And then her triumph was nearly spoiled by her cousin Frances. When the music paused and Sabrina's partner left to fetch her a glass of punch, Frances approached her, swathed in a gown of stiff pink brocade.

"Brina, there you are. I could not get near you, what with the crowd fawning around you. I would never have credited it, you making a byword of yourself, wearing a gown that calls such provocative attention to yourself. Mama is shocked, let me tell you."

"You need not tell me," Sabrina murmured wryly. "I am well aware of my aunt's subservience to fashion. How is my aunt, by the bye?" she asked to change the subject.

"Well enough, not that you care. I hear you have been in town more than a sennight, yet you have never called on us." Her cousin frowned petulantly. "I cannot think why not. It is not like you to be so self-centered."

"Oliver said you were unwell."

Frances's gaze narrowed sharply. "You have seen Oliver?"

Sabrina stared, surprised to think her beautiful younger cousin might be jealous of her. She had never provided Frances the least competition, but blended in harmlessly with the rest of the wallflowers. Even with Oliver, who had professed to love her, there'd been no contest once he'd spied Frances. The girl had the petite delicacy of a porcelain doll, with an animated charm that was warm and real—a charm that seemed to be entirely missing tonight.

"We met by chance on the street," Sabrina replied lightly, "when my husband was escorting me to the shops. Oliver told me the happy news then. You are pleased by the coming child, are you not?"

"Yes . . . I suppose so."

"I did not think to see you here tonight if you are feeling poorly."

"We are not so high in society that we can refuse an invitation by the Duke of Kintail. I cannot attach the title of milady to my name. I am only plain Mistress Irvine."

Sabrina raised her eyebrows in astonishment. She had never seen Frances in such a mood. Usually her cousin displayed the sweetest of dispositions, even if she was perhaps a trifle spoiled. But it seemed Frances somehow blamed her for wedding a Highland laird. Perhaps she'd forgotten the true course of events; if Frances had not vanquished Oliver with a smile, Sabrina would have wed him herself.

"But then," Sabrina murmured consolingly, "you were fortunate enough to marry for love."

To her astonishment, Frances's lower lip trembled. "Oh, Brina, I do not mean to act the witch. It is just that I am so unhappy." Her pretty features turned bleak. "There . . . are other women."

"Surely you are mistaken."

"No. Oliver has a . . . a mistress. I've seen her. She is uncommonly beautiful. And he spends a fortune on gifts for her." When Sabrina's expression remained slightly doubtful, Frances said insistently, "How else do you explain how Oliver has managed to run through so much of my dowry in so short a time?"

"His wardrobe is a bit more spectacular than I recall."

"He buys the latest fashions in order to impress that *woman*. At least she dares not show her face in polite company. She is an *actress*, Brina." Her lower lip quivering, she raised a hand to her brow.

"Frances?" Sabrina asked, concerned.

"No, I will be better presently." Fumbling in the pocket of her skirt, Frances withdrew a vile of sal volatile and breathed deeply, wincing at the pungent odor.

"I do not know how you manage to remain so unaffected, Brina. But then I imagine you are accustomed to such betrayal, wed as you are to a celebrated libertine. How I envy your fortitude. How do you bear it?"

"Bear what?"

"Your husband's infidelities."

She was fortunately spared a reply when a gentleman approached. Frances stiffened, while Sabrina found it difficult not to stare.

She scarcely recognized Oliver. Resplendent in a coat of yellow satin, he sported a full white wig, gold-buttoned cuffs, and high-heeled, gold-buckled shoes. The gentle suitor she'd known had been scholarly, serious, personally ambitious. This man was a stranger to her.

He bowed deeply before them, though he appeared to ignore his wife. "I am enraptured to greet the bonniest ladies at the ball."

His gaze drifted down Sabrina's bosom, making her overly aware of her exposed flesh. Frances apparently noticed his wandering eyes as well, for she sent her husband a withering look that was at once murderous and verging on tears.

When she stalked away without a word, Oliver leaned close to whisper gravely in Sabrina's ear. "I must speak to you in private. Will you join me in the library in a few moments' time? 'Tis along the main corridor to the right."

He gave her no time to reply, but bowed again and turned away.

Puzzled, Sabrina waited for a moment and then followed. She found the library with little difficulty, but entered warily when she saw that only a single lamp had been lit. Oliver startled a gasp from her when he appeared from the shadows.

He closed the door behind her and took both her hands in a warm grasp.

"You came," he murmured, gazing at her intently.

Sabrina felt ill at ease with his inexplicable fervor. Yet Oliver seemed not to notice as he launched into what was evidently a prepared speech.

"I can scarcely credit how greatly you've changed, Sabrina."

"I might say the same about you."

"*You* cannot claim to have acted the fool. Seeing you again has made me realize what a terrible error I made."

"Error?"

"In forsaking you for Frances."

"Oliver, you shouldn't . . ."

"No, I must say this. I should never have left you. Oh, my dearest, my life has been empty without you."

"Surely . . . you mistake your feelings."

"No, indeed not. My feelings for you have never been stronger."

Highly discomfited, Sabrina managed to withdraw her hands and move away, to a safer distance. She had never seen him behave this way. "Oliver, you have a wife."

"Frances does not understand me the way you do."

"I am not certain I understand you."

"Then I must speak plainly. I miss you, Sabrina. I want you. And I cannot see why we must endure the misery of being apart. Say you will be with me, cherie."

She stiffened. "What are you proposing? That we commit adultery?"

"Do not look at me that way, my dear. You are a woman of the world now. How could you be less—wed to a libertine whose affairs are legion?"

He moved toward her purposefully, startling her with his aggression. Was this the same Oliver who had always been gentle, solicitous, respectful in his behavior with her? His glittering eyes just now made her wonder if he was foxed.

Slipping an arm around her waist, he bent his head to kiss her. Stunned, Sabrina could only stand there as his lips pressed hotly against hers.

At her silence, Oliver tightened his embrace, but it was another instant before Sabrina marshaled her shocked senses. She struggled in his arms for a moment, but he was stronger than he appeared, and he refused to release her, only becoming more passionate.

When finally she managed to pull free with a jerk, she drew back her hand and delivered a resounding slap.

Oliver stared at her, rubbing the offended cheek. His gaze held astonishment and admiration.

Sabrina was surprised to find herself trembling. "I will forget this incident ever occurred, Oliver. Now I strongly suggest you return to your wife, while I return to my husband."

Oliver's mouth curled scornfully. "Your husband is otherwise engaged at present. Only moments ago I spied him with his English mistress, making an assignation to meet. Why else would I suppose I could find you alone?"

"His mistress?" Sabrina asked, her voice fainter than she would have liked.

"Yes, Lady Chivington."

She shook her head, unwilling to credit his claim. After all Niall's protestations of love, he would not openly pursue another woman . . . Would he? Perhaps she simply did not wish to believe.

Whatever the troubled state of her marriage, though, she

realized how fortunate she was to have escaped a union with her former suitor.

"I pity my poor cousin," Sabrina said, her disdain for Oliver apparent in her expression. "She does not deserve you. Now I bid you good evening."

Escaping the library, she paused in the corridor to smooth her disheveled skirts and to allow her flushed cheeks to cool. Shortly she found herself in the ballroom, searching the crowd for her husband.

After a moment she spied Niall's tall figure across the floor, near the French doors, which had been left open against the heat of the myriad candles and press of perfumed bodies. Beside him stood Lady Chivington, smiling like a cream-filled cat.

Sabrina felt her heart wrench.

When Niall bent to whisper something in the lady's ear, eliciting a gay laugh, Sabrina's hands curled into fists. She watched in dismay as Lady Chivington turned and slipped through the doors to the garden terrace.

Niall did not immediately follow, but seemed to be searching the crowd. It would not be the first time he had made an assignation to meet his paramour in a garden, however. If so, he would doubtless wish to avoid being seen by the lady's husband, or by his own wife.

Fury, sharp and piercing, assaulted Sabrina. Never had she felt such a vicious urge to do violence, to Niall most of all, but to the English witch as well. She would have raked the lady's beautiful face with her nails if she could have managed two minutes alone with her.

She was not alone, however, Sabrina realized regretfully; she was in a crowded ballroom, with several hundred onlookers who would be highly titillated were she to cause such a scene. Whatever action she took would best be effected in private.

Clenching her jaw, Sabrina made her way through the crowd toward the terrace doors. The last time she'd discovered her philandering husband in a compromising position, she had fled in wounded mortification.

But she had no intention of abandoning the battlefield now. This time she would fight for Niall, to prevent him from pursuing his favorite sport in some other woman's arms.

Chapter
Nineteen

He was conversing with a footman when Sabrina reached him. When the servant nodded and moved away, Niall turned to her, his eyes lighting with quick warmth.

The smile Sabrina sent him was brilliantly lethal as she stepped close enough to slip her fingers beneath his elegant frock coat. He had not worn a rapier to the ball, but had belted a dirk at his waist as usual.

When she drew the blade from its sheath and stepped back, his eyebrows shot up quizzically.

"Pray excuse me," she murmured, the sweetness of her tone belied by her sparking eyes. "I have need of this for a moment."

Spinning on her heel, she marched through the open doors and out onto the terrace.

She was trembling with rage when she came to a halt. Allowing her gaze to adjust to the dim light, Sabrina spied the English noblewoman near the balustrade overlooking the garden.

"Lady Chivington."

Arabella turned, her expression one of eager anticipation. "Ni—"

Her welcoming smile fractured when she recognized Sabrina. Then her eyes grew huge as she saw the gleaming blade in Sabrina's grasp. "W-What . . . do you here?"

"I came to offer you a warning, my lady. Niall McLaren is my husband. I strongly suggest that you keep away from him."

The lady eyed the dirk with alarm. "Are you *mad*?"

"Perhaps," Sabrina replied tightly. "I doubt you would wish to put it to the test."

Behind her she heard Niall's incredulous chuckle.

Sabrina spun around, her features fierce as she brandished the dirk. "I'll not share you with her. Do you ken me?"

He raised a hand to his brow, but his shoulders were shaking. "Thank God . . ." he murmured. "I feared you would never relent . . ." He shook his head, unable to contain his relief, a relief so profound he knew it as joy.

"I am entirely serious, sir!" she exclaimed, furious at his apparent amusement. "I'll not abide your affairs any longer, with this lady or anyone else."

Niall took a deep breath. "I am all gratitude, my bonny Highland warrior, but an affair with this lady was the last thing I intended."

"You arranged an assignation with her—"

"No, sweeting," he replied, all seriousness, all laughter. "For once you greatly mistake the matter."

Just then a stalwart, ruddy-cheeked gentleman garbed in a scarlet military coat stepped out onto the terrace.

"My dear, what—" Colonel Lord Chivington faltered when he saw the McLaren and his lady. "Beg pardon, milord, I understood my wife was here."

"She is," Niall interjected smoothly. "She has been anxiously awaiting you."

"Richard!" Arabella said breathlessly. "How glad I am that you are come." She edged around Sabrina carefully, keeping her gaze trained on the dirk. "I am feeling faint, and I beg that you will take me home."

When she reached the colonel, she clung weakly to his arm. He looked a bit puzzled but replied easily, "As you wish, my dear. Your servant, milord, milady."

With a bow to Niall and Sabrina, he escorted his wife within the ballroom, leaving them alone.

Sabrina's fingers clutched the hilt of the dirk as she faced her husband.

"You never fail to amaze me, mouse," he said softly. "I am honored that you chose to do battle for me."

She felt her cheeks flushing as she comprehended her error. "You never made an assignation with her?"

"No. In truth, I only thought to elude her pursuit. The lady suffers from boredom and neglect, so I arranged for her to enjoy a liaison with her husband."

"I thought . . ."

"I know what you thought, my love. And in the past I've given you little reason to presume otherwise. But that is all in my past, sweeting. I've told you so countless times, though you choose not to believe me."

Sabrina stared at him. Niall took the dirk from her slack fingers and returned it to his belt. Then grasping her hand, he drew her to the far side of the terrace, away from the glow of candlelight and music that spilled through the open French doors.

His expression suddenly grave and intent in the shadows, Niall looked at her searchingly. "Sabrina . . . I cannot endure this misery any longer. It's draining me of my soul." Holding her gaze captive, he said quietly, "You are my heart, Sabrina, and will always be so. I'll want you till I die."

Her breath lodged in her throat. Never before had Niall looked at her with such raw emotion in his eyes, so desperate and haunted.

"I want you, Sabrina. I want you as my lover, the mother of my children, the mistress of my clan. I want to grow old with you. I want to spend the rest of our lives convincing you how remarkable you are."

"How can you be sure?" she whispered.

His gaze softened. " 'Tis simple. I'm in love. And I think you love me, too. Do you, Sabrina?" His voice had gone beyond strained and sat on the cutting edge of pain as he waited in an agony of uncertainty.

She could not continue the pretense any longer. "Yes . . . I love you. How could I not?" she said simply.

The release of his breath was shaky and powerful; the

emotion that went through him left him weak. Niall grasped her arms in a grip that was painful, his gaze riveted on her face, his eyes gleaming with uncertainty and hope and a thousand fervent prayers.

"Say it again," he demanded hoarsely. "The truth, Sabrina."

"I love you."

Drawing her to him, Niall wrapped his arms around her, holding on with a kind of tight, quiet desperation, his heart beating painfully. It seemed as though he had wanted her all his life. Sabrina roused and angered and entranced and tempted him as no other woman in his life ever had. And he wanted desperately for her to believe it.

He drew back, needing to see her face. "Can you ever forgive me for the pain I caused you?"

She nodded, an ache of love for him swelling within her. "Yes . . . but . . ."

"But what?"

"I cannot continue as we have, Niall. I need honesty between us. I need an end to the games." She gazed at him uncertainly. "I am not a mouse or a tiger or a *femme fatale*. I am simply a woman. I cannot continue to play this false role you've devised for me. I can't abide this constant struggle to keep your attention."

"Aye, no more games. We've wasted far too much time battling each other, and ourselves."

Sabrina searched his face. "I only need to know that I can trust you, that you will be true to me."

He returned her gaze intently, the fire in his heart reflected in his eyes. "I vow with every breath I take, with every beat of my heart, there will be no other lovers between us. I cannot change my wicked past, Sabrina. I can only promise you the future. I pledge you my oath, I am yours and yours alone."

Fraught as she had been with doubts, his declaration was a healing balm to her heart. Willingly, she moved into his arms, resting her head on his shoulder.

"Does this mean," Niall murmured into her hair some quiet moments later, "that you will return with me to the Highlands as my beloved bride?"

"Yes. If you truly wish it."

He made a sound of disbelief. "Sabrina . . ." he said warningly.

Tightening his embrace, he found her mouth and kissed her with fierce passion and matchless tenderness. Sabrina moaned deep in her throat, a cry of helpless surrender and need.

"Niall," she whispered when at last he raised his head, "I want you . . ."

He shuddered, resting his forehead on hers. "I made a vow, you'll recall."

She nodded, remembering his pledge not to return to her bed until she invited him. "Please . . . will you make love to me?"

When he drew back, his smile was tender, magical, impossible to resist. "I am your willing servant, my sweet."

Grasping her hand, he led Sabrina across the terrace and into the ballroom, startling the nearby guests. Purposefully he pulled her after him, forging a path through the dancers and curious onlookers.

"Niall . . ." Sabrina murmured breathlessly as he headed for the stairs, "you will cause a scandal with such haste."

"Does it matter, mouse?"

"Well . . . no . . . I suppose not."

When he reached the front entrance, he called for their carriage and her cloak.

"Where are you taking me?" Sabrina asked.

"To your stepfather's home, where we may be private."

After a few moments of waiting, Niall handed her inside the carriage and directed the coachman to return to Cameron House. Joining her inside then, he immediately gathered Sabrina in his arms.

"This is scandalous," she murmured in the darkness. "Everyone will know what we are about."

She felt Niall smile against her hair. " 'Tis no more than is expected of the darling of Edinburgh. The world admires a bold lover. And with so alluring a lass as my companion, I'll be the envy of every male in the company."

No, *she* was the one to be envied, Sabrina thought. She shook her head. She still found it hard to believe that such a splendid man could be in love with her. What had she done to deserve her good fortune? Against all odds she had discovered a passion as savage as the wild Highland hills.

As if he could read her heart, Niall tightened his embrace. "Sweet, priceless, Sabrina . . . How could you doubt what I feel for you? My pursuit of you this past week has been nothing short of remarkable." He laughed in genuine amusement. "The entire multitude of Edinburgh is aware of my devotion. You were the only one blind to it."

Suddenly shy, she buried her face in his shoulder. "How could I trust your methods? For all I knew, you were set on making me a byword so that I would capitulate to avoid a scandal."

"The scandal will die down once we return to the Highlands."

Sabrina found herself smiling wryly. "Until the next incident. You attract notoriety naturally." She sighed. "Just as you attract women. I expect I will have to accustom myself to dealing with all your former love interests."

"You have nothing to fear from them, sweeting."

"There will always be countless beauties pursuing you."

"Since I want only your lovely self, it makes no matter. I mean to save all my carnal attentions for you and only you. In truth, I intend to spend the rest of our lives persuading you that you're the only woman I want. The only one I will ever love. 'Tis you who command my heart. We were born for each other, Sabrina."

He put a finger beneath her chin, searching her face in the shadows. "Thank God for your grandfather's machinations," he whispered before his lips found hers.

"Oh, Niall . . ." she murmured—the last coherent words she spoke for a long while.

By the time the carriage drew up before Cameron House and Niall handed her down, Sabrina was trembling with need and love and a hundred other powerful emotions. Using the lamp which had been left burning in the foyer for her, she led him upstairs to the bedchamber that had been hers since childhood.

When Niall shut the door softly behind them, he gave her a smile no less dazzling than the sun.

Her hands unsteady, Sabrina set down the lamp and moved to stand before him. She could feel her heartbeat quicken as she reached for the lapels of his satin coat. "You do not need this, do you?"

Niall studied her quizzically. "I suppose it depends on what you plan."

"I mean to undress you."

"Then by all means, proceed."

She kept her touch light as, without a word, she began removing his clothing: first his coat and waistcoat, then his lace cravat. For a moment she stroked the fine linen of his shirt, feeling the hard outline of chest muscles beneath. Then that garment went as well.

Niall aided her by removing his shoes and stockings. He paused with his hands on the waistband of his breeches, a soft light of anticipation in his sapphire eyes. Then he stepped out of his breeches and he was naked, his rippling, sinewed skin bronzed and luminous in the lamplight. His heavy arousal rose thick and full from his groin, iron-hard with lust, the sight so raw and virile it made Sabrina's stomach quiver.

Yet the desire between them was far more profound than physical intimacy. She drew a sharp breath as she stared at the powerful man before her, so beautifully, heartrendingly masculine. This man was her husband. Her lover. Her love.

Tonight they were not conqueror and conquered, seducer and seduced. They were equals . . . husband and wife.

She was certain Niall shared the same sentiment as he drew her into his arms and held her close.

"I would that you could see inside my heart," he whispered against her hair. "I feel joy just being with you. I feel pleasure at the sound of your voice. I feel desire, the like of which I've never known before you." He drew back to gaze at her. "I need you, Sabrina. I've never needed like this before."

He looked at her with all the tight, helpless longing in his soul. She stared back at him, hearing the pounding pulse of her own heart. His vulnerability touched her.

"Nor have I," she whispered, "ever needed . . . this way."

His eyes flared with something powerful and helpless. He bent then and kissed her with a deep, greedy hunger, fiercely, possessively, knowing that she felt the consuming fire between them that defied all reason. When he raised his head, his heart leapt. He could see in her lustrous eyes a hunger and need that matched his own.

His hands reached for the hooks at the back of her gown. Making short work of the fastenings, Niall eased away her bodice, freeing her breasts. The soft lamplight bathed the milky paleness of her skin, highlighting the twin peaks that stood proudly gleaming before him.

He took a long breath to draw air into his tight, aching chest. "Lovely mouse . . ."

His gaze arrested as he caught sight of the gash she'd received defending his life. The flesh had nearly healed but would forever leave a scar.

Sabrina saw his beautiful mouth tighten. When mutely he bent and pressed his lips to the puckered skin, she felt her heart wrench.

"Niall . . ."

"Hush, sweeting." He raised his hand to brush her mouth with a sensual finger. "Let me show you how deeply I feel for you. Let me love you, Sabrina."

"Yes . . ."

Her lips ruby with desire, her eyes hazed with longing, she swayed against him.

Impatiently Niall undressed her, destroying all his careful handiwork in moments, dropping the exquisite gown heedlessly upon the floor, scattering her jewels and undergarments upon the carpet.

Then lifting her in his arms, he laid Sabrina on the velvet coverlet, among the pillows. His heart thrumming, he gazed down at the exquisite perfection of her lush rosy-tipped breasts, slender waist, gently rounded hips, long shapely legs . . .

She trembled for him, waiting in an agony of anticipation for his touch, her nipples so erect they hurt, the hollow between her thighs throbbing for his possession.

"Niall, please . . ."

It was all the invitation he needed. Emotion flared in his eyes as he settled beside her on the bed.

She was so lovely, Niall thought achingly. He felt himself drowning in the dark luster of her eyes.

His face taut with emotions held fiercely in check, he ran his fingers over her skin, her slim body sleek and supple under his hands, making her stir restlessly. When he brushed the dusky curls crowning her thighs, she moaned.

"Sabrina . . . So beautiful, so wild and ready for me . . . Slowly, love . . ." he urged when she strained against his hand. "I don't wish to hurt you."

"You would never hurt me."

"Not intentionally." A pained smile pulled at Niall's mouth. "But I am so hungry for you, I cannot guarantee finesse."

"I don't care . . ."

Urgently Sabrina drew him down to her, shuddering with hunger, sighing when his nude body eased over hers. Any doubts shattered when she was in his arms. He made her believe in dreams. He made her feel beautiful, desirable . . . wholly a woman. He made her feel loved.

"My heart," he whispered against her lips, "I love you so much that I ache with it."

Sabrina heard the endearment through a mist of desire; joy shimmered through her with the urgency of pain as he showered her with hot, deep, soul-stirring kisses. She reveled in the possessiveness of his embrace, in the magnificence of his aroused body.

When he heard the sob of need that ripped through her, Niall raised his head. "Sabrina? You are trembling . . . Do I frighten you?"

"No . . . I frighten myself, I want you so much."

Niall felt his heart swell. He knew the same trembling, the same wonder. He'd never imagined lovemaking could be like this. He shook with the need to have her wrapped around him, to become part of her.

"Show me, my bonny mouse," he whispered as he fitted his body to hers, covering her with his naked heat.

He spread her thighs, intimately knowing the cradle of her femininity. "Look at me, Sabrina," he ordered hoarsely. "I want to see your eyes when I take you. I want to see you all stunned and wanting . . ."

She obeyed, her eyes dazed with sensuality, her face flushed with longing.

"I want to feel every shudder, every sigh." Bending, he lowered his mouth to hers again.

He felt as though he were a hot-blooded lad on the brink of losing his innocence. Except that this desire, this yearning, was far more profound.

He wanted Sabrina.

He wanted to love her until all the shadows in her eyes were gone. He wanted to show her every pleasure ever felt between a man and a woman. He wanted to lose himself in the sleek, welcoming heat of her luscious body . . . to lose and find himself.

He tasted deeply of her, drinking of her essence, yet a kiss was not nearly enough. He pressed closer, desperately wanting more of her. He could not fathom this fierce want, this need to bury himself so deeply he could never pull free, yet it was there, pulsing and rich and immutable.

Shaking with urgency, he mounted her with powerful thighs. Hard and virile and throbbing, he slid upward into her hot silky sweetness ... groaning at the sleek, heated rapture he found as he entered her.

Agony and bliss. He wanted to go slowly, savoring the moment, yet he couldn't hold back. Passion, hungry need, erupted at the first thrusting stroke.

He said her name in a raw, shaking voice, and with a hunger too long denied, sank deeper into her, trying to absorb her body into his so that nothing could ever separate them.

Sabrina welcomed him inside her, giving a soft cry of pleasure, of surrender and victory. Her fingers clutched mindlessly at him as she wound her legs more tightly around him.

Niall shuddered at the forceful primitive glory of it, as desire and love flamed out of control. Unable to restrain himself, he surged into her, driving deeper, desperately trying to sate himself with the beautiful fiery woman writhing beneath him.

He loved her. He told her so unforgettably, with an honesty more profound than words. He swore it with each fierce stroke, a promise made not just by his body, but his heart and mind as well.

And Sabrina believed.

She strained against him with shameless joy as uncertainty was swept from her mind forever.

She clung to him as he pounded into her, yet Niall was oblivious to her fingernails clawing down his naked back as they strained together in frenzied passion.

It was the most intense joy he had ever felt, all heat and hunger, all madness and desire. His body clenched as savage, unrestrained pleasure ripped through him, the convulsions wild and endlessly ravenous. A primitive, jubilant cry burst from his throat as he furiously pumped his seed into her in a bonding fierce beyond anything he had ever known.

He lacked the strength to roll away from her afterward. Instead he lay collapsed upon Sabrina, reveling in the richness of her passionate abandon, her skin dewy with erotic warmth, her hair, silken wild, tangled around them both. He had forgotten such raw, soul-wrenching pleasure was possible.

The pleasure lingered long after the last shudders died away; the embers of passion still smoldered.

When she stirred beneath him, he shifted his body gingerly and lifted his head.

"My heart," he whispered, his eyes indescribably tender and pleasure-hazed.

Sabrina buried her face against his shoulder, too torn with rioting emotions to reply. He had reached inside of her and touched the essence of her being. Passion had bred more passion, and culminated in their deepest bonding.

Niall felt the same sweet bond as an incredible contentment filled him. Rolling onto his back, he pulled Sabrina into his arms and drew the cover over their nakedness. He wondered if they had made a life that night. He devoutly hoped so. His lips moved sensually over her hair as she nestled against him, cherished in his embrace.

It was long, long moments later before Sabrina gave a replete sigh and rubbed her cheek tenderly against his shoulder. "I still cannot comprehend how you ever came to fall in love with me."

Niall's languid expression turned thoughtful as he gazed up at the canopy overhead. "I suppose at first you were a challenge. You were the only lass I'd ever met who dared match wits with me. And no woman breathing had ever denied me. There you were, declaring you wanted nothing to do with me or my lascivious ways. The more you resisted, the more it whetted my desire. You are utterly magnificent when you're raging with fury, did you know that?"

Sabrina gave an arch laugh. "Most gentlemen regard defiance or a sharp tongue as unappealing qualities in a lass."

"Yet I find myself enamored of it. I have no desire for you

to govern your saucy tongue. Subduing it is only that much more delightful."

"Still, a mouse is no proper match for a hedonist."

Reaching for her hand, Niall entwined their fingers. "You are no mouse, sweeting. That prim demeanor you exhibit to the world hides a vibrant, magnificent woman who can reduce me to a panting schoolboy. One who can match me in passion and rival a Highland warrior in courage." His voice dropped to a husky resonance. "You're absolutely perfect for me, Sabrina. You're everything I've ever wanted in a woman . . . a mistress to warm my bed and excite me . . . a virago to keep my wits sharp . . . a loyal lady of compassion and wisdom to help me lead our clans . . ."

"Niall . . . I am not—"

Rolling over her, he pinned Sabrina beneath him. "Hush, sweeting, cannot you see I am intent on baring my soul? I didn't believe in love, Sabrina, but you taught me the meaning of it. You forged in me a passion that blazed all others to ashes. And your courage shamed me. I realized if you could make such sacrifices for your clan, I could do no less. I love you, Sabrina. If you believe nothing else in this life, believe that."

"I do believe you, but—"

"No . . . no buts. No more doubts. All I want to see in those lovely dark eyes, my sweet enchantress, is wildness and lust and love . . . Say you love me, Sabrina."

She gazed deeply into the laughing, devilish eyes that were so dear to her. Her own eyes brimming with bold honesty, brilliant with joy, she nodded. "I love you, Niall."

"I shall not let you renege, wife, do you ken me? On the morrow, I expect you to shout it from the rooftops."

"Do you, indeed?"

"Aye. For once you'll do as your lord husband commands."

That disarming smile she loved so well hovered around his lips, yet he was giving her a deliberate challenge, Sabrina knew—and it roused her blood. Her eyes flashed defiantly. "You are willfully trying to provoke me again."

He smiled. "Aye, that I am." Affection pierced his passion-rich voice. "I like you spitting fire. I like you any way you are."

His heart twisting into knots of desire, he pressed his hard body against her, warm flesh to warm flesh. Gazing down at her exquisite, flushed face, he knew he would never tire of watching the many faces of her passion.

"I love you," he said, suddenly fierce.

With a taunting smile of her own, Sabrina reached up to wrap her arms around his neck. "Professions of love come cheaply, my lord. 'Tis actions that prove sincerity. I think you should show me again what you feel for me."

Niall laughed and tightened his hold. His heart had been well and truly conquered. Sabrina had taught him what he had never known in the arms of the most dazzling courtesans and captivating noblewomen of Europe. Love.

Their marriage would doubtless always be a turbulent dance of clashing wills and tender reconciliations. She would defy him, infuriate him, challenge him to open his reckless heart, yet they would remain irrevocably bound— fighting, sharing, loving, rapt with this rare, fierce splendor they'd found.

"As you wish, mouse."

His eyes smiling into hers with the rapture of love, he bent his head to prove his sincerity.

Read on for a sneak peek at
Nicole Jordan's

Lord of Desire

Kent, England
1840

The rawboned stallion looked out of place standing before the Duke of Moreland's family estate. The august mansion, golden-hued and boasting magnificent proportions, was the epitome of grace and elegance, while the sweeping lawns and topiary yews had been clipped and manicured and cultivated within an inch of their civilized existence.

In contrast, the fiery Barb with its sinewed haunches and overlong mane seemed almost savage. Indeed, it bore scant resemblance to the sleek thoroughbreds in the fabulous ducal stables. This animal had been bred for endurance and speed in the harsh desert climate of the , and trained for war. Held by a wary, liveried groom, the bay stallion snorted defiance and pawed the ground while awaiting its master.

The horseman who at last came bounding down the wide stone steps of the ducal mansion also contrasted with his noble surroundings—despite his tailored frock coat and starched cravat of black silk, despite even his claim to noble birth. The young gentleman was the duke's grandson, but his bronzed skin and hawklike gaze lent him a hard, ruthless air that the refined British gentleman of his class would never attain. There was nothing refined, either, about the way he leapt on the stallion's back or wheeled his mount as if he'd been born in the saddle.

Muscles quivering in response to its rider's innate restlessness, the horse strained eagerly at the bit, in anticipation of freedom.

Yet Nicholas kept the Barb tightly reined as they traversed the smooth graveled drive between two rows of stately oaks; for once he checked his impatience to be away. He could afford this last mark of obeisance, this final show of respect for his grandfather. His interview with the duke successfully concluded, he was at last free to pursue his own life. Ten years. Ten long years in this foreign land, enduring what had felt like captivity. But at last he could shed the trappings of his civilized English upbringing, as well as the English name that had been thrust upon him.

The taste of freedom was sharp on his tongue, as sweet as the spice of fall in the air, as vivid as the oaks turning the colors of autumn. The stallion seemed to sense his mood, for the animal began a spirited dance, nostrils flaring, ears pricked forward, as they passed beneath the canopy of the giant oaks.

The horse never flinched as an acorn whistled over its head and fell to earth, a credit to the stallion's training. Nicholas absently murmured a word of praise, his thoughts occupied by his impending departure from .

The next instant he heard another faint whistling... then a small, dull thud as his silk top hat went flying off his head to land in the drive. Scattering gravel as he spun the stallion around, Nicholas reached for the curved dagger at his waist—a habit learned in youth—before remembering he had no reason to carry a weapon in this tame country. He had not expected danger to be lurking in a British tree.

Or a female, either.

But that was precisely what met his astounded gaze as he stared overhead. She was hard to see. If not for the acorns he would have passed her by; her black gown was nearly hidden in the dappled shadows. Even as he peered up at her through branches and leaves, she defiantly flung another acorn at his fallen chapeau, missing it by mere inches.

The bay stallion, taking exception to this aggression, thrust its forehooves squarely on the ground, tossing its proud head and snorting in challenge. Soothingly Nicholas laid a gloved hand on his mount's neck, but his mouth tightened in anger.

"The first acorn," he said softly, "I mistook as an act of nature. Even the second, when you targeted my hat, I excused as an accident. But not the third. Would you care to know the consequences of a fourth?"

When she didn't reply, Nicholas's gaze narrowed. By now his vision had grown accustomed to the shadows, and he could see that the perpetrator perched on the limb overhead was a young girl of perhaps thirteen, with chestnut hair, several shades darker than his own dark gold, styled in ringlets. The hem of her gown was a scant four feet from his head, giving him a glimpse of lace-edged pantalettes. The quality of the material was unmistakable, bespeaking wealth if not current fashion.

Even as he fixed her with a hard stare, the girl tossed her head defiantly, much like his stallion had just done.

"Tuppence for your consequences! You don't frighten me in the least."

The novelty of her reply gave him pause. He was not accustomed to being challenged by a female, certainly not by a child. Staring at her, Nicholas was torn between amusement and the urge to turn her over his knee. Not that he had ever raised his hand to a woman. But he didn't intend to divulge that particular fact just now. Repressing amusement, he schooled his features into suitable fierceness.

"If you decide to throw another acorn," he warned, "I shall be persuaded to give you the thrashing such willful misbehavior deserves."

In response, the girl raised her chin another notch. "You will have to catch me first."

"Oh, I shall. And I guarantee you won't like it if you put me to the trouble of climbing after you." His tone was pleasant, yet carried a hint of something soft and deadly. "Now, do I disarm you, or will you surrender your weapons without a fight?"

She must have believed his threat. After a moment's hesitation, she let the fistful of acorns drop harmlessly to the ground.

Nicholas was satisfied that she wouldn't again dare hurl one of her missiles at him, but he couldn't leave her to pelt other unsuspecting travelers with acorns. "You should have considered what might have happened," he added more casually. "Had my horse been any less well-trained, he might have bolted, perhaps even sustained an injury or delivered one to me."

"I wasn't aiming at your horse, only your hat. I would never hit an animal. Besides, he didn't bolt. You didn't have any trouble holding him, for all that he looks so savage."

"You presume to be a judge of horseflesh? I assure you, this beast is far more valuable to me than any of the pampered animals in the duke's possession."

"Will you sell him to me?"

The sudden question, delivered in such a hopeful tone, took him aback.

"I can afford his price," she said quickly when he hesitated. "My papa was exceedingly wealthy."

Several answers immediately came to mind. That his horse was not for sale. That a stallion was not a suitable mount for a young lady. But his curiosity was aroused. "What would you want with him?" Nicholas asked instead.

"I shall need a horse when I run away."

He raised an eyebrow at her. The rebellion was back in her tone, echoing a sentiment that was familiar to him. "Where do you intend to go?"

"India, of course."

A smile tugged at the corner of his mouth. "I'm afraid you cannot ride a horse to ."

"I know that! But if I am to find a ship to take me, I must first travel to a seaport. And I cannot *steal* a horse, you see."

"Ah… no, I fear I don't see."

"I am not a thief!" She sounded indignant. "And if I were to steal one, they would discover it missing and come after me sooner. Well," she demanded as he silently pondered her logic, "will you sell him to me or not?"

"This particular horse is not for sale," Nicholas said, managing to keep the laughter from his voice. "And in any case, I expect your parents would be rather concerned if you were to run away."

He expected her to be disappointed, but to his surprise, the girl suddenly swung down from the tree limb with a flurry of skirts to land on the low stone wall beside the drive. There she stood for an instant, staring back at him.

She was an intriguing child, with huge storm-gray eyes that seemed too big for the rest of her plain features. Eyes that were angry, defiant... anguished. He caught the reflection of tears in those haunted eyes, before her defiance crumbled. "I don't have any parents," she whispered in a grief-stricken voice.

The next moment, she leapt down from the wall and fled across the manicured lawn, to the shelter of a copse of willows.

So strong was the impression of a wild young creature in pain that Nicholas had to follow. Reining back his mount, he urged the stallion over the low wall, then cantered across the lawn and skirted the willows. He found her lying facedown on the grass beside an ornamental lake, sobbing as if her world had shattered. Unexpectedly, he felt guilt. Had he caused her tears?

Dismounting, Nicholas sank down beside her and waited. Not moving, not touching her, merely letting her feel his nearness, the way he would one of his horses. She didn't acknowledge his presence in words, yet he knew by the stiffness of her shaking young body that she was aware of him. And after a while, her sobs lessened enough for her to speak.

She didn't want to answer his probing questions, though. Her first reply, when he asked her what was troubling her, was a husky "Go 'way."

"What kind of gentleman would I be if I left a young lady in distress?"

"I am n-not in distress!"

"Then why are you filling the lake with your tears?"

She didn't reply; she only curled her knees up more tightly and buried her face in her arms, in an effort to shut him out.

"Tell me what the trouble is and I will go away." Again no answer. "I can be very patient," Nicholas warned quietly as he settled back for a long wait. "Why do you not have any parents?"

He heard a watery sniffle. "They… they died."

"I'm sorry. Was it recent?"

After a moment the girl gave a faint nod.

"And you miss then?"

Her nod was a bit more vigorous this time, but still she didn't volunteer any answers.

"Why don't you tell me about it?" Nicholas prodded. "I would like to hear what happened. Was it an accident?"

It took some time, but by gentle persuasion, he learned the cause of her grief: her parents had died from cholera in , and she had just been sent back home to to attend boarding school. That was why she was dressed in mourning. That was why she was sobbing so bitterly.

Nicholas remained silent, understanding now. He had once felt the same anguish, a grief so deep it seemed fathomless. Grief and a fierce hatred. He knew what it was like to be orphaned without warning. To have childhood abruptly ended in one brutal, mind-branding moment.

"I should have died, too!" she cried in a voice muffled by her arms. "Why was I spared? It should have been me. God should have taken me."

Her desolate plea brought the memories crowding in on him. Her death wish was something Nicholas also understood. Guilt for having lived, for having cheated death when loved ones had not escaped. He had seen his father struck down by a French bayonet, his mother brutalized and murdered by soldiers who were no better than ravening jackals.

"I hate !" the girl exclaimed suddenly, fervently. "I despise everything about it! It's so cold here…"

Cold and wet and alien, he thought. The constant chill had bothered him, too, when, against his wishes, he had been sent to live among his mother's people ten years ago. was so very different from his native country—the vast deserts and rugged mountains of . Watching the girl shiver, he wanted to console her. He fished in his pocket and found a mono-grammed handkerchief, which he pressed into her hand.

"You will grow accustomed to the cold," he said with quiet assurance. "You've only been here… what did you say? Two days?"

Ignoring his handkerchief, she sniffed. "I like hot better." Lifting her head then, she turned those huge, gray, glistening eyes on him. "I *shall* run away. They shan't keep me here."

Seeing her mutinous expression, he was struck again by the passionate nature of her defiance. She was a strong-willed, rebellious child… Not so much a child, really. Rather a young girl on the brink of womanhood, a bud beginning to unfold. And just as intriguing as he had first thought. Hers was a plain little face, true. Plain and piquant and rather incongruous. Nothing matched, and yet it was arresting on the whole. Given a few years she might be fascinating. Her heavy, straight brows gave an exotic, almost sultry look to those haunted eyes, while her sharp little chin indicated a stubbornness that boded ill for anyone who tried to control her.

He felt a strange kinship with her, this young English girl who wanted to return to where she had been raised. He understood her compelling need to defy authority, to lash out at even those who had her best interests at heart.

He knew; he had been there. Leaning back on his hands, Nicholas recalled the half-wild boy that he'd been. He had run away twice before he'd agreed to his grandfather's bargain: he would remain in to be educated, until he reached his majority. Then if he was still of a mind to return to , the duke would fund his passage.

Had the bargain been worth it? For ten years he had chafed to return to his homeland, while his grandfather had nearly despaired of turning "a savage little Arab" into a civilized English gentleman.

The transformation, though ultimately successful, had been painful. He was only half English, born to a woman enslaved by a Berber warlord after her ship had been captured by pirates. He couldn't deny his warlike Berber blood—though his noble English grandfather would have preferred to ignore it altogether. He was considered by some to be a dangerous rebel, by others an infidel. Even though his parents had eventually married, his father had been of a different faith.

But he had mastered to perfection the fine art of acting the aristocrat: boredom, cynicism, hypocrisy, seduction. Not only was he accepted by the fashionable world, he was sought after by the opposite sex with fascination. Despite his mixed blood and questionable legitimacy. Or perhaps because of it. The ladies of his grandfather's class who were first to profess themselves shocked at his background were willing, even eager to invite him to their beds, curious to find out if he was the dangerous savage they conjured up in their ignorant imaginations.

Nicholas's gaze shifted to the young girl beside him. His term in was ending, while hers was just beginning. She would have to endure the lonely existence, just as he had endured.

His probing gaze surveyed her damp face. Though the flood of warm tears had abated, she was still grieving; her trembling lower lip lent her a vulnerability that was heartrending. Nicholas longed to comfort her.

"Have you any family here?" he asked gently. "Did your parents have relatives?"

Her young face clouded with pain before she looked away, her fingers clutching the handkerchief he had given her. "I have two uncles... three if you count the one in . But they don't want me. I would just be a burden to them."

At the mention of , Nicholas felt his stomach muscles tighten, yet he forced himself to reply lightly. "Then I suggest you convince them differently. Perhaps you should contrive to become indispensable to your uncles—give them good reason to want you."

When she turned to stare at him, the thoughtful expression that crept into her eyes almost made him smile. "Wipe your face," he said gently. "You have tearstains on your cheeks."

She obeyed him almost absently. When she was done applying his handkerchief to her damp face, she held it out to him. "I should give this back... thank you."

The handkerchief bore the initials of his English name. "You may keep it," Nicholas replied. "I won't be needing it any longer where I am going."

She eyed him quizzically. "Where are you going?"

"Away. To another country."

Sudden hope lit her face as she scrambled to her knees. "Will you take me with you? Please? *Please?* I won't be any trouble to you. I can be a model of decorum if I truly put my mind to it. Truly I can."

The impropriety of asking a perfect stranger to escort her to a foreign land obviously hadn't occurred to her. Yet Nicholas hesitated to correct her. The plea in her voice, in those huge gray eyes, made him suddenly wish he could do what she asked.

Slowly he lifted his hand to her face. Tenderly, with his thumb, he wiped away a tear she had missed. "I'm afraid I can't," he said softly.

Just then the bay stallion which had been standing obediently lifted its head to sniff the wind. Nicholas turned to watch as a small, dark-skinned man appeared from behind the willows. He wore the native dress of , a white cotton tunic and loose trousers, and a plain turban wrapped around his head.

Seeing him, the girl sat down abruptly, smoothing her rumpled skirts and wiping at her red eyes again with the handkerchief.

The small man approached with a soft tread and bowed low before the girl, his dark forehead nearly touching his knees. "You gave me great fright, missy-sahib. You should not have strayed so far in this strange place. The Erwin Sahib will say I do not take care of you. He will beat me and cast me out—may Allah protect me."

Nicholas expected the girl to take exception to the servant's scolding, but instead her tone was one of fond exasperation, not defiance.

"Uncle Oliver will *not* beat you, Chand. He never blames you when I misbehave."

"You have been hiding yourself from me again." The Indian raised his eyes heavenward. "What have I done to deserve such ingratitude?"

She actually looked contrite. "I am sorry. But you needn't have worried, Chand. I've come to no harm. This gentleman—" She gave Nicholas a quick glance that carried a hint of shyness. "—has been kind enough to lend me his handkerchief."

Protectively, the servant scrutinized Nicholas and his manner of dress, but the dark little man must have been reassured, for he tendered another bow before addressing the girl again. "The Erwin Sahib has requested your presence. May I say you will come, yes?"

She sighed. "Yes, Chand, tell my uncle I shall be there in a moment."

The servant did not appear pleased with her response, but he bowed again and withdrew, muttering under his breath. Nicholas was left alone with the girl.

"My Uncle Oliver," she said by way of explanation. "He is paying a call on the duke. Uncle Oliver brought me here to because he feels responsible for me, but I know he will be happy to wash his hands of me."

Nicholas smiled, gently. "Then you had best begin at once to change his mind."

The faint smile she gave in return was tentative, shy, but a smile nonetheless. "Thank you for not telling Chand... about the acorns. He would have been ashamed of me." She hesitated, twisting the handkerchief in her fingers. "I owe him my life, you see. In , when I was a child, he pushed me from the path of a rogue elephant and saved me from being trampled. That was why my papa engaged him—to watch over me and keep me out of mischief."

"Is he ever successful?"

Her eyes widening, she stared at Nicholas a moment before apparently realizing he was teasing her. The rueful smile she gave him this time was genuine. "I suppose I am a sore trial to him sometimes."

Nicholas could well believe it. "Just promise me you won't throw any more acorns. You are dangerous with those things."

"Well... all right, I promise."

He rose then, dusting off his buff trousers. Looking down at the girl, he felt strangely lighthearted; she had quit weeping, and the grief had faded from her eyes.

Without another word, he mounted the Barb. But as he rode away, he gave a final glance over his shoulder. The girl was sitting with her arms wrapped around her knees as she stared at the lake—contemplating her future, he guessed.

Satisfied, Nicholas turned his attention to his own future, to the bitter score that needed settling. Today he had turned twenty-one. He was celebrating not his birthday, but his freedom; today he had received the duke's reluctant blessing to return to his country, the land the French had named .

Freedom! For himself and his father's people. He would return, with but two purposes filling his heart: to drive the French from his homeland, and to seek vengeance against the man who so brutally had claimed the lives of his beloved parents.

Freedom! How sweet it would feel to set foot once more in his native land. To gallop across the hot desert plains, to slake his thirst at a well, to find refuge from the heat in the rugged mountains. How glad he would be to give his back to this cold, damp country with its hypocritical morals and twisted notions of civilization.

A moment later, when he passed his silk hat where it had fallen, he left it lying in the dust. No longer would he have need for that or any other English thing. Not his fashionable clothing, not his name of Nicholas Sterling.

Henceforth he would resume the noble Berber name he had been given at birth. Henceforth he would be known as Jafar el-Saleh.

Available digitally from *Rouge Romance*:

WHEN WICKED CRAVES

J K Beck

Petra Lang is cursed never to love

One touch of her skin unleashes demons of the vilest
nature. Afraid of her unfortunate powers,
the Shadow authorities sentence her to death....

He knows he can never give in

Vampire advocate Nicholas Montegue risked his own life
to save Petra, but their explosive attraction could prove
the death of them. Together, they must find a way to lift
the curse, for only a love this strong has the power to
overcome such monstrous evil.

Red-hot romance...
www.rougeromance.co.uk

FIERCE COMPETITION
Michelle M Pillow

With a dream job, great roommates and a wonderful boyfriend, Jane Williams has everything her heart desires – that is until her vicious social rival, Vanessa, finds out her most humiliating secret and sets about bringing her social world crashing down. When her boyfriend's senator father hears of the scandalous secret, Jane is likely to lose not only the gorgeous Dean but also her hard-earned social credibility.

There's only one way for her to avenge herself: by playing Vanessa at her own game. Vanessa once stole Jane's man, so she is going to do exactly that. But Jane is still in love with Dean. With no social integrity intact, just how far is she willing to go to exact retribution and how much is she willing to risk before she loses it all?